PLOT TWIST

Carmen Sereno

Translated by BETH FOWLER

PLOT TWIST

A Novel

Previously published as *Dos formas de escribir una novela en Manhattan* by Principal de los Libros in Spain in 2022. Translated from Spanish by Beth Fowler. First published in English by Amazon Crossing in 2024.

Published by Amazon Crossing, Seattle

www.apub.com

ISBN-13: 9781662516597 (paperback)
ISBN-13: 9781662516603 (digital)

Cover illustration and design by Philip Pascuzzo
Cover image: ©Dedy Setyawan / Getty; © KVASVECTOR / Shutterstock

Printed in the United States of America

To my brother Pablo, who never gave up on following his dream.

Prologue

It was the second time in a week that she'd missed her subway stop and then had to walk four blocks in the unforgiving East Coast cold. It was apparently becoming something of a habit. Four blocks! So much for the express line. Jeez. As a true New Yorker, Siobhan Harris knew the importance of always having a pair of comfy sneakers tucked in her purse; she also knew that the worn-out soles of her pink Chucks couldn't withstand the fierce bite of winter for much longer. Her state of distraction had been caused by the last forty pages of *Kiss an Angel*, a book so compelling that her worries had faded into the background. And she certainly had plenty of those. She loved the escapism of romance novels. She'd discovered Amanda Quick's *Ravished* at her aunt Harriet's house at the age of fourteen and had been devouring them ever since. It was no surprise that an incurable romance addict like her would lose all sense of time and space whenever she became engrossed in a new story. With *Flowers from the Storm*, she had actually broken her own record: thirteen hours straight reading and terrible raccoon eyes the next day.

It had been worth it though.

Because in romance novels, dreams come true, broken hearts get mended, and the endings are always happy.

Love conquers all. Always.

Real life, on the other hand, STINKS.

Sighing, she had tied the laces of her sneakers and left the subway via the Fulton Street exit, woolen hat pulled down over her ears and fists buried deep in her coat pockets. It was late. The city rose dark and hostile amid the sound of sirens, bursts of music muffled by car windows, the *bee-bee-bee* of a reversing truck, and a barking dog that some heartless person had left tied to a streetlight. A homeless man was slumped against a building, jingling the coins in his paper cup without managing to attract anyone's attention. In New York, you need luck. Everyone's in a hurry, everyone's looking for something, everyone wants something. Nothing is free. Even the air has a price. Brooklyn's ascent to the latest hot spot of yupster culture had a lot more to do with the exorbitant rents in Manhattan than with the supposed intention of humanizing that gray borough. Siobhan quickened her pace, shivering, her toes numb in her shabby sneakers. The wind lashed against her face and brought tears to her eyes. In front of the typical brownstone houses of BoCoCa, the filthy remnants of the last snowfall had been shoveled to one side. The steel ventilation grates in the sidewalk rumbled beneath her urgent steps. A superstitious or overly cautious person would take pains to avoid walking across those steaming metal grates, given the multitude of urban legends about a friend of a friend of a friend who had absentmindedly stumbled into an open shaft and ended up like melted butter in the horrific heat of the subsoil. Although on this bitterly cold night, perhaps it was a risk worth taking.

Turning onto Lafayette Avenue, she went into her local deli, grabbed a Dr Pepper and a pastrami sandwich, and placed them on the counter. It wasn't the most appetizing dinner, but it was cheaper than a hamburger, and at least she didn't have to stand in line.

"Eleven dollars fifty-five," the store clerk announced, with a strong South Asian accent.

Siobhan blushed as she realized her wallet was empty. She silently cursed herself for having spent a small fortune on a double caramel latte that morning. Perhaps the time had come to switch to herbal teas.

"Damn it"—she smiled nervously—"I . . . I don't seem to have any cash on me." The reptilian part of her brain was pushing her toward a timely and dignified retreat, but the knowledge that there was nothing but a few ketchup packets in her refrigerator at home dissuaded her from leaving. She set her pride aside and asked: "Could I add it to my account?"

The man arched his dark bushy eyebrows and regarded her seriously.

"To your account? What do you mean? You think this is the Hilton or something? This is a grocery store, young lady. We don't give credit here. Pay by card and job done. But not American Express, we don't take that."

Well, I would pay, she thought. *If I hadn't spent my last dime paying off Buckley's debts.*

"See . . . I lost my card. On the subway," she ad-libbed. "My head's in the clouds these days, you know? Anyway, I live right here, at number 123. You know me, I come in here all the time. I always buy the organic hummus with Kalamata olives. You must have noticed." She paused and summoned a beseeching expression. "Please?"

The storekeeper sighed condescendingly and raised his hands in defeat.

"Fine, fine, I'll make an exception for you. But just this once," he warned. "Oh, and report your card as lost, or they'll clear you out."

She could barely contain her laughter. She was *already* cleared out. And desperate.

She was officially someone who would be referred to in banking circles as a "B" citizen; that is, someone on a low income and with a level of debt that meant buying a microwave in installments could lead to bankruptcy. Or even worse, to sleeping on cardboard boxes in a corner of the Battery; what the banks would call a "C" citizen.

Welcome to America, the land of opportunity.

"Thank you so much. And don't worry, I'll pay back the eleven dollars as soon as I can."

"And fifty-five cents," he added.

As she opened her front door, she tripped over one of the annoying paint cans from Home Depot that were stacked up on the floor next to several piles of boxes. *Home sweet home.* The apartment was so small that you could take in the whole thing from the entrance: living room with integrated kitchen, bathroom not much bigger than a closet, and a bedroom just slightly too narrow for two people. Although the thermostat was kept high enough to stop the pipes from freezing, it nonetheless felt arctic.

It also needed quite a bit of work: the ceiling had a leak, the walls were peeling, and there was a stain from something that bore a disturbing resemblance to blood on the bathroom floor. But it was the most reasonable one she had found, bearing in mind that, in New York, there's a fine line between what you can afford and what you're willing to live with. Siobhan nudged the paint cans with her foot and promised herself she would sort those out this weekend, no excuses. She had been living here for three months; it was time to stop procrastinating.

After a much-needed shower, she glanced in the mirror.

"Heavens . . . not even Instagram's Clarendon filter could fix this." She sighed.

Her coppery hair was in dire need of a cut, and her eyes, blue as the Hudson in June, were dulled by the dark circles around them. Without the attractive freckles that broke out along with the sunshine, she looked no better than a corpse bride. Although Siobhan was undeniably attractive, her face lacked the glow it should have had at the age of twenty-nine. She had lost so much weight in the last few weeks that even her size-*XS* jeans were feeling loose. And that wasn't the only thing she had lost. Where the hell were her breasts? And her hips? She had always been on the slim side, but this was too much.

"Well, I suppose this is what happens when your boyfriend leaves you only days after signing a lease agreement on an apartment, and the only treats you can allow yourself are Starbucks coffees and a crappy pastrami sandwich you didn't even pay for," she muttered, patting her ribs.

Was anything worse than being the girl who had been dumped?

Yes, actually. Being the girl who had been dumped with a bunch of outstanding bills.

On the cusp of thirty, no less.

She threw on some sweats and forced herself to silence her negative thoughts. She settled onto the sofa with her laptop. As she waited for it to fire up, she savored what might well be her last solid meal until February. Eating was less important than renewing her MetroCard so she could get to work. She hadn't been able to access her WriteUp profile all day, and she was dying to know what her readers thought of the latest chapter of *Only You* she had posted. They could be very . . . intense. There would almost certainly be a whole string of recriminatory messages. Messages like these:

Angry Reader: WHAT THE HELL IS GOING ON HERE?

Or:

Sensitive Reader: WHAT KIND OF SICK AND TWISTED WRITER WOULD PLAY WITH OUR FEELINGS LIKE THIS?

Or even:

Impatient Reader: WHEN WILL YOU PUBLISH THE NEXT CHAPTER? WHEN? WHEN? WHEN? I CAN'T WAIT!

Siobhan smiled mischievously. She couldn't deny she had thrown in an unexpected twist. Who would have thought Damon would leave a note stuck to the refrigerator door with an Atlantic City magnet, and then up and leave, given how much he loved Jessica? A cloud of despondency descended on her. Posting on WriteUp was one of the few things that had cheered her up since Buckley had left. What had started as a kind of therapy had become a necessity. *Only You* might be a modest story with no literary value, but it was important to her. Because it was *her* story. And because somewhere out there, somebody needed to know what happened next.

The doorbell jolted her from her thoughts. She figured it must be her landlady, Jolene. Siobhan knew what Jolene wanted and for that reason considered pretending she wasn't home. But she knew that was pointless, given that Jolene lived in the apartment above; she had probably heard her arrive. She thought about making a speedy getaway down the fire escape, but rejected that idea outright because:

Number one, if she were to fall and crack her head open, her medical insurance wouldn't cover it;

And number two, that hypothetical mishap could cause her to lose her job as "errand girl" in the digital marketing company where she had worked for the last couple of years.

Being errand girl involved doing tasks ranging from looking after the corporate social media and email accounts and making telephone calls to taking her boss's suits to the dry cleaner and ensuring that first thing on Monday mornings, at the account executives' meeting, the conference table would be replete with a box of Magnolia Bakery cupcakes—vastly overrated thanks to Carrie Bradshaw, in her opinion. It wasn't the job she had dreamed of when she graduated in Communications from NYU, but given her current situation, it was worth holding on to.

She took a deep breath, put on her best smile, and opened the door.

"Hey, Jolene! What can I do for you? I don't have any wine, but I've just opened a can of Dr Pepper."

Jolene stared at her impassively as she chewed her gum.

"Girl, what Jolene needs is a pack of Xanax and a tenant who pays rent. You owe me two g's. Do you have any idea what it costs to look after a teenage daughter in this day and age? Nuh-uh," she said. She wore the most dazzling fake nails Siobhan had ever seen. They were red, glistening like pomegranate seeds, and so pointed they could have burst a balloon with a single swipe.

"Actually, I owe you eighteen hundred," Siobhan said, correcting her.

"The rent's gone up two hundred bucks since New Year's. Check the lease agreement. Anyway, the deal is you pay me on the first of the month and guess what: today's January 12."

Siobhan swallowed.

"I need a bit more time. See, I'm going through some complicated personal stuff right now and . . ."

"Nuh-uh. Not my problem. Jolene ain't no nonprofit. She's a businesswoman. And if Jolene don't receive a bank transfer in the next seven days, you'll have to look for somewhere else to live. My house, my rules."

While the ultimatum was reasonable, she had no idea how she'd come up with the money. Asking her parents for help was out of the question, because that would mean telling them about the breakup, and she wasn't ready to do that yet. They loved Buckley; it would break their hearts. It had been hard enough making up a convincing excuse to explain her boyfriend's absence when she turned up alone in Mount Vernon for Christmas.

Ex-boyfriend.

"He came down with measles," she had told them.

Robin, her older brother, didn't buy it. "I know you, Shiv. I know things aren't going well. You get that twitch in your eyebrow. So you may as well tell me the truth right now, or I'll dangle you from the apple tree like when you were four." So Siobhan had told him everything. But how could she admit to him—or to any of her supportive family, who had always believed in her—that she had failed in every aspect of her life? She had always assumed that by the time she turned thirty, she would be successful and happily married.

She just couldn't do it.

Asking for an advance on her next paycheck wasn't an option either. Her boss was a busybody, and the last thing she wanted was for her problems to become office gossip. And her friends Paige and Lena deserved a break. *Okay. Let's see. Think. Summon your guardian angel, come on. You have a natural talent for survival.* She could always apply for a bank loan. And be crippled by interest charges? No chance. Or maybe sell off some of her belongings to a pawn shop. But that would require that she had anything of value, which she didn't, other than her laptop and her HBO subscription. Or find a weekend job on Craigslist. Preferably not as a stripper though. She needed a plan. And she needed one fast. But what?

She didn't know.

Her guardian angel had turned its back and was lighting a cigarette.

"My boyfriend left a few days after we moved in here," she confessed, suddenly inspired. "He left a note and disappeared. Just like that." She snapped her fingers. "I just had the worst Christmas ever, I've got twelve dollars left in my account, and to top it all off, I have to paint the walls of this crappy apartment all by myself."

She said the last part mostly to herself. She hadn't meant to sound so emotional.

"What a bastard. What did the note say, if you don't mind my asking?"

"He said he needed space."

Jolene's expression hardened.

"Space, huh? Well, that means one of two things: either that dickwad dipped his sausage in the wrong can of gravy"—Siobhan regarded her with horror—"or he's one of those flaky immature types with a Peter Pan complex."

"He didn't . . . There are no third parties involved."

"Okay. That's what Peter Pan says. The question is whether you believe him."

Did she believe him? Sure she did. They'd been together since college. Buckley might be a lot of things, but he wasn't unfaithful. Maybe this was just a fleeting crisis. Maybe he just needed some time to find himself before coming back to her. It did happen. If he'd at least been honest with her before leaving her in the lurch, she might not have found herself in such a sorry situation. And she didn't understand why he had blocked her on all his socials. Couldn't they like each other's posts every now and then like two civilized adults?

Jolene's eyes suddenly widened, as if she had solved some kind of universal mystery.

"Wait, wait, wait. Tell me you didn't base Damon's character on that shithead?"

What on earth?

Siobhan raised her eyebrows.

"How did you know . . . ?"

"That you're a writer?"

Writer. That's a stretch.

"Maya, my daughter, she told me. She dabbles in WriteUp too. Nothing serious—school gossip, hypersexualized zombies, that kind of thing. She saw your profile by chance and recognized you. It's her fault I got hooked on *Only You.* Christ! I almost had a heart attack with the last chapter. Girl, what were you thinking, splitting them up like that?"

Siobhan felt a kind of aura of power enveloping her like a cloak and gave a slight smile. She had discovered that she loved keeping people in suspense. And that her landlady embodied the angry, the sensitive, and the impatient reader all rolled into one.

"You need to sort that mess out pronto, because Jolene is not happy," she continued. "You'd better hope that Damon sorts his shit out, gets his chakras in line, and goes back to Jessica." She paused, briefly but theatrically, and fixed her visibly offended gaze on Siobhan. "Except that you've gone and based him on that jerk, your ex. In which case, the only acceptable ending is that Jessica gives him the finger and slams the door in his face." Another pause. "Anyway, I can see you've got a gift for writing. You should think about writing a book," she concluded.

She had thought about it. Many times. It was her dream. Always had been. She'd imagined herself sitting at a beautiful desk next to a window with views of Manhattan, writing the kind of love story that would make her readers sigh with pleasure. She wanted with all her heart to be guilty of making someone miss their subway stop. But Siobhan didn't think she had what it took. Yes, the readers of *Only You* were growing in number, and inexplicably rapidly, but telling a story chapter by chapter on a fan site didn't make her a real writer. She sang in the shower too, and that didn't make her Lady Gaga.

Her weak smile faded, and she felt pinned to the ground by the full weight of reality.

"It's just a hobby." A half-truth. "Anyway, I wouldn't know where to begin. Sadly, I don't know any editors."

She knew that talent, confidence, and contacts were the triumvirate of publishing success.

"But maybe you know someone who knows someone, and that someone knows someone and . . . Have you never heard of six degrees of separation? This is New York; there's always someone who knows someone. You just need a bit of luck."

Luck. She hadn't had much of that recently.

"So . . . is Damon your ex or not?"

Silence. Jolene drummed her long fake nails on the doorframe, and Siobhan realized she was waiting for an answer.

"If I tell you, will you let me pay at the end of the month?"

She thought Jolene would find it funny. People feel more relaxed after laughing, it's a fact.

"Hell no." Her bubblegum burst with a resounding pop.

Okay, yes. Damon was Buckley. And she was Jessica. Except that, working in installments as she did, Siobhan had planned for them to have an ending worthy of a romance novel. It was a kind of readjustment of destiny. In the end, Damon-Buckley would come back repentant, asking Jessica-Siobhan to forgive him for having gotten cold feet, they would each pay their half of the bills and paint the walls together (that small detail hadn't changed), and they would turn that newly rented Brooklyn apartment into a home.

A place where they could be happy forever.

The end.

Of course, she wasn't going to tell her landlady all that.

"Damon is just a fictional character. Any similarities to real life are pure coincidence."

Jolene didn't look convinced.

"Whatever . . . Anyway, don't take too long writing the next chapter. And don't forget what we spoke about."

"You mean about publishing a book?"

Jolene pursed her lips and relaxed them, swift as an arrow.

"No, girl. I mean the money you owe me. Seven days, no more." Then she turned on her heel and headed up the stairs to her apartment.

As Siobhan closed the door, an unbearable feeling of impotence lodged in her chest.

She decided to take refuge in fiction. She had lost her appetite, so she wrapped the remains of the pastrami sandwich and put them in the refrigerator. She took a swig of Dr Pepper and tossed the can in the trash. Then she stretched out on the sofa, pulled a fleece blanket over herself, balanced the computer on her lap, and logged in to her WriteUp profile. She had seventy-six messages. Not bad. She scrolled through them without stopping until one caught her attention. It had been sent by a Bella Watson a couple of hours earlier. The subject said, "Proposal to represent Siobhan Harris."

She had to read it twice.

"Oh my god, oh my god, oh my god."

The same day, a few hours earlier

The eggs Benedict at Café Boulud were the quintessence of the Upper East Side. The texture of the yolk bordered on perfection, the bacon was always crispy, and the organic rye sourdough hit just the right note of acidity. It was one of the few places where you could still read a print edition of the *New York Times* and inhale its papery aroma, which was why Marcel Dupont ate breakfast there every morning. Well, that and also because he was a man of unalterable habits who was fanatical about his routine and hated change. On fair days, without exception, he woke early and ran precisely six miles around Central Park. In bad weather, he worked out in the gym of his midcentury penthouse with dizzying views over the sharp silhouette of Manhattan. His apartment consisted of nineteen hundred square feet of pale, neutral furnishings, high ceilings, underfloor heating, and walk-in closets with wall-to-wall mirrors. The neighborhood was full of bistros, designer boutiques, and wealthy housewives stiffened with hairspray and Botox. After his workout, he took a shower and dressed in one of his dark suits, which matched both the color of his skin and his somber nature. He went out to eat and returned around an hour later. He did not usually bump into any of his neighbors, exchanging only a few words with Gonzales, the building's concierge, out of courtesy. "You have a good day, Mr. Dupont." "Thanks, you too." Small talk wasn't his forte. Upon his return to the penthouse, he shut himself away in his study until dark.

Maximum efficiency, that was the key to everything.

Before starting work, he would:

1) Turn off his cell phone. Nothing was more irritating than one of those ill-timed sales calls where an operator with a ridiculously optimistic name like Faith or Hope tried to convince him to switch phone companies. "Sir, you're losing money with AT&T. What if I told you that with Verizon, you could save up to 15 percent on your next bill? Hello? Are you still there? Please, don't hang u—"

2) Put on his Malcolm X–style browline glasses. Although they did lend him a sophisticated air, he wore them out of necessity. At thirty-five, he knew that eagle eyes were a thing of the past. Particularly if you spent half your life with your eyes glued to a screen.

3) Sit on his ergonomic chair with genuine leather upholstery that reclined into three different positions. It had cost him twenty-seven

hundred dollars at Roche Bobois, but this was no impulse buy. In his line of work, comfort was paramount.

4) Give the corkboard on the wall the once-over: photos, maps, notes organized by color; all connected tidily by a red string. This quick appraisal reassured him that he hadn't forgotten a single detail. He hated improvising.

5) Fire up the computer.

6) Open the document called draft_V1.pages.

7) Stretch his neck before placing his hands on the keyboard.

At that moment, Marcel Dupont became Marcel Black, one of the most successful crime writers in the United States and the most intriguing author of the decade, according to *Library Journal.*

Fourteen-time bestseller in the *New York Times Book Review.*

More than thirty million copies sold.

Translated into twenty-five languages, including Russian and Japanese.

Short-listed for the National Book Award (Colson Whitehead won it, as it happened).

A major Netflix production underway and a small fortune of twenty-two million dollars in the bank. Not as much as Stephen King, admittedly, but enough that he could allow himself the luxury of a Lamborghini in the garage—who the hell has a Lamborghini in New York?—and a Gatsby-style mansion in the Hamptons. The kind of guy banks would call an "A" citizen. Marcel, however, had more constructive ways to invest his money, so he hadn't splurged on the Lamborghini or the mansion.

And the most surprising thing of all: his secret identity.

The only people who knew he was the elusive author of the William J. Knox series—about a sharp-eyed detective and frequenter of speakeasies in the days of gangsters and prohibition—were his agent, Alex Shapiro; Bob Gunton, his editor at Baxter Books; Charmaine, his older sister, and, of course, his lawyer. How could someone have fourteen bestselling novels when he didn't grant interviews, never turned up at public events, wouldn't sign copies, and had no online presence?

A man without a face at a time when image was everything.

There were two reasons:

First, the quality of his work. Marcel Black was known for his unpredictable plot twists and his ability to throw even the most experienced reader off course. The critics called his style brilliant and claimed his dialogue was the most intelligent in the genre since Raymond Chandler.

Second, an astute neuromarketing campaign based on the magic of mystery and anonymity. It's the Streisand effect: the more you try to hide something, the more you draw attention to it.

But why would a successful writer like Marcel Black want to linger in the shadows instead of basking in recognition?

It was a mystery that gave rise to all manner of rumors and speculation in literary circles. It was hard to know which of these stories were true and which were made up.

At 9:27 on that icy January morning, a young server in Café Boulud carefully set down the breakfast and the newspaper on Marcel's table.

"Can I get you anything else, sir?" he asked.

Marcel gave a slight shake of the head. Though he was talented as a writer, his literary skills did not extend into the social realm. Indeed, were it not for his unmistakable Louisiana drawl, anyone would have thought Dupont a typical upper-class New Yorker convinced the world belonged to him by right. Anyone except Alex Shapiro, of course. This was partly because people tend to minimize the defects of those they admire. But, above all, because his agent understood him better than anyone. A few months earlier, when his sudden decision to bring the William J. Knox series to an end had triggered the wrath of Bob Gunton, Alex had not only defended him tooth and nail, but also threatened to take his star author away from Baxter Books and seek out the competition.

"You're bluffing, Shapiro. There's not a single publishing house in America that could improve on our contract terms. Not even HarperCollins," Gunton had argued.

Maybe he was right.

Or maybe not.

The fact was that Marcel was tired of it. He didn't like change, true, but he had spent so long living in the skin of William J. Knox—his whole career—that he was starting to get bored. A bad sign. While he was writing novel number fifteen, he felt as though the character had run out of steam; he had become a stereotype incapable of surprising anyone. After a few glasses of bourbon, he made the second-most important decision of his life: he would kill Knox—and the series along with him. He rewrote the manuscript in a matter of weeks and sent it to Alex. The first thing his agent said when he read it was:

"Gunton's gonna rip my balls off and make a book out of them."

He sounded shaken.

"Pocket edition, I presume," Marcel joked.

"Hilarious. Your New Orleans roots are showing through. Is it too much to ask that you consult me before making such drastic decisions?"

"You know me. I'd rather ask for forgiveness than permission."

Alex gave a long, heavy sigh. He had good reason to be worried about how the publisher would react. His client had a contract for three more installments in the series, and yet he had just slit the throat of the golden goose.

"You can't just do whatever you like. You know perfectly well they could sue if they wanted."

"Exactly: if they wanted. But the thing is Baxter Books has made millions of dollars off of me. You think they want to get involved in a lawsuit at this stage? Listen, I'm tired of always writing the same old stuff. I need to do something different."

"Why the hell didn't you tell me sooner?"

"To spare myself the sermon. Sometimes I'm not sure if you're my agent or my legal guardian."

"You could at least have given Knox a more dignified send-off than an overdose in a clandestine opium den."

"What's wrong with that? I think it's kind of poetic."

"If you say so."

"Am I to understand you didn't like the novel?" asked Marcel with a hurt expression.

"Sure I did. I like every word you write."

Marcel knew he wasn't just saying that. Alex Shapiro wasn't the kind of literary agent who massaged his authors' egos with meaningless and superficial praise. If he wasn't convinced by something, he would say so. They had known each other too long to mince words. That's why, when Marcel told him what he was planning to write next, he wrinkled his nose.

"Racially motivated murders in the Deep South? I don't think this is the time to go there. Black Lives Matter might take exception."

"You do know I'm Black too, right?"

Alex sighed again.

"And you know the majority of your readers are most likely Caucasian?"

"But don't you always tell me that race is a social construct and that Barack Obama is the best demonstration of that?"

"And I stand by it. Half the country thinks Obama's not Black enough to be the first Black president of the United States, and the other half thinks the opposite, which gives us an idea of the sociological dimension of the issue. All I'm saying is books on very controversial subjects can become rather problematic."

"Or bestsellers. Shall I write you a list? *The Satanic Verses*, *Lolita*, *Animal Farm*, *The Catcher in the Rye* . . . Should I go on?"

"This isn't the nineties anymore. People have a very different sensibility these days. It's pretty much impossible to have an opinion on anything now without offending some group or other. Remember all the fuss in Mississippi over *To Kill a Mockingbird* because it contains the N-word? It's crazy."

Marcel burst out laughing.

"You don't have to call it the N-word with me. I think I can deal with it. Lil Wayne says it in his songs."

"Hell no. I prefer the term African American. It's more . . ."

"Condescending?"

"I was going to say politically correct. Listen, why don't you write something simple? A domestic noir, perhaps. They're becoming really popular these days. Lots of blood and a female protagonist with difficult relationships, you know, a bit of an outsider. I'm sure Gunton would be all over it."

But Marcel didn't want to write something simple or submit to the brutal rules of a literary market in crisis. Nor did he want to have to self-censor because of some kind of totalitarian trend that seemed to dictate that fiction must have a moralizing purpose. What he wanted was to get out of his comfort zone and create a new world; only then would he know for sure that he hadn't sunk into mediocrity as an author. The very idea of that tormented him, made him feel like he was on a tightrope.

Of course, no one needed to know that even a bestselling author had his own insecurities.

Not even his best friend.

"I'm not planning to sell myself, Alex. And I don't give a shit whether my editor likes it or not. So do your goddamn job and let me do mine," he declared.

"Fine, fine, don't get defensive. I'll take care of Gunton. In return, you have to promise me this novel will be the bomb."

"It will be; have some faith."

Several months had passed since that conversation. As expected, Bob Gunton had no alternative but to accept this twist in Marcel Black's career. You don't just let a moneymaker like that slip through your fingers. The last installment of William J. Knox would go on sale in forty-eight hours with the prophetic title *The End of Days.* Although many readers had expressed their dissatisfaction on social media at the unexpected conclusion of the series, the publishing house was predicting it would be a hit. Marcel had the skeleton of his next story ready. He had done extensive research, mapped out a plot in painstaking detail, taken notes, and profiled the characters. Enthusiasm was tripping through his veins like a jazz number.

He was ready to embark on his new adventure.

Or so he thought.

His breakfast steamed invitingly on the plate. He cut a generous forkful of eggs Benedict and lifted it to his mouth. As he savored the first bite, he opened the *New York Times* and flicked through it until he reached the Books section. He started to read, but the couple canoodling at the next table distracted him.

For the love of god, get a room, he thought, sending a severe look their way.

This kind of thing made him sick. Once, dining on the sixty-fifth story of 30 Rockefeller Plaza—a restaurant with one of the best views of Manhattan; from the terrace you could see both the Chrysler and the Empire State Buildings in all their glory—a man got down on one knee to propose to the woman he was with. "Mary Josephine Caroline Smith, would you do me the honor of becoming my wife?" Marcel almost threw up right there. The man took a Tiffany box out of his blazer pocket and showed her an engagement ring with a rock the size of Liberty Island; it must have cost him a fortune. The woman turned on her tears like a sprinkler, as a general *awwww* broke out around the restaurant. Someone shouted, *Come on, Mary Jo! Say yes!* And suddenly it turned into some kind of Broadway show. Obviously Mary Jo said yes. Marcel rolled his eyes and left the restaurant, his storyteller's instinct unconsciously imagining a very short future for Mary Jo and Mr. Diamond Ring. He was a practical man. He liked to enjoy himself every now and then, but the words *relationship*, *commitment*, and *marriage* caused him to break out in hives. He didn't believe in love. How could you believe in something that didn't exist? Love was nothing more than an invention by Bloomingdale's to sell perfume and expensive purses. That's why, never, under any circumstances, did he date the same woman more than once. A few drinks in a bar in SoHo or the Village to warm things up followed by good sex was all he was prepared to offer. No exchanging of numbers or promising to see each other again; that way he avoided any tiresome emotional involvement. Being a very attractive man, he didn't lack for good candidates. He was tall and broad shouldered, with strong arms, dark, piercing eyes that observed everything from a regal distance, a shapely nose, and full lips. He wore his hair very short with a few days' worth of carefully groomed stubble on his jaw. He smelled of expensive aftershave, had a deep, seductive voice, and conveyed the indifferent elegance of a man at his peak.

Disgusted, he averted his eyes and focused on the paper, trying to block out the insultingly happy pair of lovers. He took another bite, then he froze midchew.

He had just caught sight of a headline that read: "Is this the *End of Days* for Marcel Black?"

He dropped his fork with a clatter and started to read. Mira Yamashita, the *Times*' star critic and the most feared woman in the world of publishing, according to *Vanity Fair*, had destroyed his book forty-eight hours before its launch. "Black tries to pass off his work as high-end literature. This hastily sketched finale, however, reveals itself to be no more than another vapid and superficial detective story." Marcel ground his teeth. A sudden uncontrollable rage made him rip the page from the paper and tear it to shreds. The lovers gaped as they watched the scene unfold.

"What the hell are you looking at?" he roared, without giving them a chance to reply.

Seconds later, he took out his American Express card and summoned the server; there was no time to lose.

PART ONE

Setup

Chapter 1

Siobhan

As winter faded into a distant memory, the fresh air represented a sign of freedom to New Yorkers. People forgot about the discomforts of snow and ice; they stowed their coats in their closets and took to the streets again. Spring settles gently upon New York, beckoning like an invitation to live. It was one of those glorious early June evenings. The mercury was showing a balmy 68 degrees. The last rays of sun reflected in the skyscrapers, and the whole city seemed to shimmer like a poem. If she hadn't already been late to meet Paige and Lena, she would have stopped to take a photo for her Twitter account.

> **Siobhan Harris** @siobhan_harris 1m
> I love #NewYork. The people, the traffic, the noise; that constant buzz, like there's always something going on just around the corner.

She had been on Twitter a lot recently. Bella Watson, her literary agent, had stressed the importance of staying active on social media, especially in the early days. "Baxter Books is making a big investment in you. In return, you'll have to do your part for this to work. An author's image is crucial these days," she had said at the contract signing some months earlier.

A few things had changed as a result of that meeting on the eleventh story of the colossus that housed the publisher's headquarters in the heart of Manhattan.

First: the title of her novel. *Only You* was now *With Fate on Our Side*; much more appealing, so Bella said.

Second: the format. Since Baxter Books had bought the publication rights, the novel was no longer available on WriteUp.

Third: Siobhan's debts, or a substantial portion of them. Thanks to the publisher's generous advance, she could live for a while without fear of eviction. And no more living off pastrami sandwiches! Yes, she still needed her job, but she hoped to soon have the great pleasure of writing a resignation letter, tossing it on her boss's desk, and walking away with her head held high.

> *Dear (ironic mode activated) boss:*
> *Fuck you. You and your shitty company. I'm a writer now, so DASVIDANIYA (or however the hell you say it).*

And last, although certainly not least as far as she was concerned: her popularity. Siobhan had gone from 174 to 10,439 followers on Twitter since the publisher had revealed her to the world as "the next big thing in romance novels, coming this spring to steal readers' hearts."

Well, spring was here.

In every sense of the word.

As usual at that time of day, the Sky Room was packed. As soon as the sun came out, the rooftop terraces of Manhattan's most imposing buildings turned into trendy happy-hour hot spots. The Weeknd's latest hit was playing, low enough not to hinder conversation. Siobhan scanned the crowd for her friends and caught sight of them sitting in the lounge area overlooking Times Square.

"Sorry I'm late, girls," she apologized, as she settled into a modern white armchair. "The Uber guy took ages to show up. Is this for me?" she asked, referring to the only untouched glass on the table, next to a scented candle.

"Yup. We ordered three flutes of champagne while we were waiting," Paige explained. "And since we have a lot to celebrate tonight, we told the waitress to bring another round in twenty minutes."

Paige D'Alessandro. Thirty years old. Wasp waist and hair like Jessica Chastain's. She had an air of sprezzatura and would have looked elegant even with spinach in her teeth. She worked in public relations for a Wall Street bank whose reputation had gone down the tubes thanks to WikiLeaks, and, like many New Yorkers, she planned to become a millionaire by the age of fifty. She didn't eat carbs—except for her grandmother's *bucatini all'amatriciana* and Junior's cheesecake when she had PMS—and did cardio four days a week to compensate for the calorific temptations that abounded in New York. She followed the latest trends and was up to date on all the celebrity gossip. Her motto was "Men are like shoes: you have to try on a lot of pairs before you find the right ones. And even then, you have to make sure you don't wear them too long, or else they'll start to aggravate you."

"I'd better get a move on, then," Siobhan said, before downing almost half her glass in one go.

Lena pushed her enormous black-rimmed glasses up her nose with her fingertip and adopted her usual expression: permanently at odds with the world.

"Have you written a negative review on the Consumer Affairs website? About the Uber guy," she clarified. "Do it. Last week, Noor and I complained about a homophobic driver. If the two neurons in your heteronormative brain short-circuit just because a couple of girls kiss in the back seat of your car, maybe you need help."

Lena Midlarsky. Twenty-nine. Five feet two inches of activism and ninety-nine pounds of *don't lay a finger on me if you know what's good for you.* At fourteen, she was expelled from school for a week for accusing the history teacher of antisemitism (most of her classmates didn't even know what *antisemitism* meant; some thought it had something to do with porn). At sixteen, she announced that she wanted to be like Natalie Portman in *V for Vendetta* and shaved her head. At eighteen, she came out of the closet at her sister's bat mitzvah. At twenty-two, she had a feminist tattoo inked on her arm. At twenty-four, she was arrested for disturbing the peace at an LGBTIQ+ demonstration. And at twenty-six, she announced she was moving in with Noor, a blogger of Palestinian descent who designed hijabs for empowered Muslim women and sold them on Etsy. None of this stopped her parents from believing she was a good Jewish girl and the best public interest lawyer in Greenpoint, Brooklyn.

"Amen, sister," agreed Paige. "Hey, Shiv, there's a guy at twelve o'clock who keeps looking at you. Don't turn round."

"At me?"

"No, at Hillary Clinton," replied her friend.

"Well, that would make sense, because Hillary's more interesting than I am."

"I disagree," said Lena. "What's so interesting about a woman tolerating her husband ejaculating on another woman's dress?" Paige grimaced in disgust. "And the thing with Monica Lewinsky wasn't even the first time. What's the point in committing to another person if that person has no intention of respecting it? Hillary should have filed for divorce as soon as she suspected it. I know I would have."

"Me too," agreed Paige. "I would have grabbed Chelsea and all those wonderful Ann Taylor Loft pantsuits from my First Lady closet, and I would have gotten the hell out of the White House before that cynic dared to say, 'I'm sorry. It was a mistake.' And then I would have gone on *Oprah* to tell my story, because revenge is a dish best served on prime time."

"Better going on *Oprah* than becoming a puppet of the system. To be honest, I don't get why she allowed herself to be humiliated like that. The same woman who said on *60 Minutes* that she didn't plan to stay home and bake cookies. For god's sake, she's not Betty Draper!"

"And Bill Clinton isn't exactly Don Draper."

"Maybe she still loved her husband and that's why she forgave him. That isn't so ridiculous," ventured Siobhan.

"But love is based on trust. How can you trust the person you share your life with after something like that?"

"Come on, girls, don't get all deep and meaningful on me," Paige said. "Anyway, in the extremely hypothetical case of Hillary Clinton being in this bar right now and being the epitome of the empowered twenty-first-century woman, that guy would still be looking at you, Shiv. And I'm not surprised because you look . . . radiant. Are you having a fling, or have you been watching contouring tutorials on YouTube?"

Siobhan snorted.

"I'm not having a fling, Paige."

"Hey, the occasional screw is not a bad thing. Did you know you can burn up to six hundred calories in just one session? I read it in *Esquire*."

Lena raised a quizzical eyebrow.

"Six hundred calories. Uh-huh. I bet the author of that article is the one who wrote"—she made air quotes with her fingers—"'Come ten times in a row without getting soft, tough guy. All you need is willpower.'"

"And Viagra," added Paige. "Returning to Shiv's sex life, I bet you ten bucks the only man who's been down there recently is her gynecologist."

"I'll raise you twenty."

Siobhan looked at her friends, feigning outrage, but then she dropped the act.

"I have a female gyno, so you owe me forty dollars. Don't worry, I take payments on Venmo," she said. "And you know me. I'm not into one-night stands. Sex is an emotional thing for me. If I slept with someone without being in love, I'd feel guilty."

"That's a very patriarchal way of thinking, Shiv."

"You're not one to talk, given that you and your girlfriend took forever to get to third base," said Paige.

"Noor was still exploring her sexuality when we met. I didn't want to pressure her."

"Anyway," Paige continued, turning back to Siobhan, "if you want to meet someone special, get married, and have children, a golden retriever, and a little house with a backyard in Rhode Island, you'd better get ready to be alone. I hate to be the bearer of bad news, but this is New York; people don't fall in love here. Much less after thirty. Everyone's too busy for that."

Thirty. What was the deal with that number? It seemed like the clocks started ticking faster after that.

The mere idea of taking Paige seriously made Siobhan want to fill her pockets with stones and walk into the river like Virginia Woolf. It wasn't true that people didn't fall in love anymore. It couldn't be. Love deserved a victory once in a while, a happy ending.

A real one.

Not just in fiction.

Like Lena and Noor.

Or her parents.

"Anyhow, you're on the market. You've only laid eyes on one penis in the last few years; seeing another should be your absolute priority from now on."

"Why do I need a penis? I have a vibrator."

"In the shape of a dolphin. It's not the same."

She was about to contradict Paige when Lena interrupted her.

"Okay, I'm tired of this phallocentric conversation. I don't want to hear another word about penises. Do you realize we've all been here for ten minutes and we haven't even brought up the really important thing yet?"

And with that, her friends pulled from their respective purses copies of *With Fate on Our Side*.

"Happy publication day, Siobhan Harris!" they shouted in unison.

Siobhan pressed her hands to her chest and thanked them.

"Oh my god! You didn't have to buy it. I was going to give you each a copy."

"And forgo the opportunity to tell the cashier in Barnes & Noble that our names appear on the acknowledgments page of the book of the year? No chance!"

"About that, thanks for the photos from the bookstore, girls. I forwarded them to my family. My mom told me Robin has told the whole of Mount Vernon that if they don't buy my book, he'll make their lives impossible."

"Your jerk of a boss should be sued for not giving you the day off," said Lena. "So, tell us, how does it feel?"

"I . . . I don't know, it's a strange feeling," she said, running her fingertips over her name printed on the cover. "It's like this isn't me at all, like I'm living someone else's life. It's been a crazy day: I had to put my cell phone on silent."

"Have you heard from Buckley? I mean, did he call?"

Lena cleared her throat and shook her head several times.

"Paige . . . ," she muttered. "Don't mention the unmentionable, remember?"

"It's okay, Lena," Siobhan said. "Buckley is water under the bridge. And no, I haven't heard from him, so I have no idea whether he's aware of . . . my new situation."

"Does that mean you've finally stopped checking to see if he's unblocked you on Facebook?"

Paige pressed her palms together imploringly.

"Come on, who's still using Facebook?"

Siobhan took a sip of her drink before replying to Lena's question.

"Technically."

Her friendship with these two girls, whom she had met back in her college days, was priceless to her, but to admit to them that a small part of her still thought about her ex-boyfriend was a weakness she couldn't, or wouldn't, allow herself.

Lena was kind enough to redirect the conversation.

"Well, I hope you brought a pen."

Ten minutes later, Siobhan had signed her first two books, taken a selfie with her friends to immortalize the moment, gone to the bathroom, bumped into a very tall man who smelled very nice, and returned. By then, the second round of drinks was on the table.

"If you had told me six months ago that a publisher like Baxter Books would take an interest in me, I wouldn't have believed you. I got so lucky."

"Lucky? Bullshit," protested Lena. "Baxter Books is a company, and companies don't like to lose money. They would never have taken a risk publishing an unknown author if they hadn't been certain of your potential."

"Lena's right, Shiv. I have a vision of your future in the literary world and guess what: you're a highly successful writer. In fact," she added, in a confessional tone, "I tried to get someone in Barnes & Noble to tell me how many copies they had sold so far, and, although he said he couldn't give me the exact number, he admitted it was selling well," she said and then winked exaggeratedly.

"We're really proud of you. Let's toast to the start of a dazzling career. May you keep writing until you're ninety and the arthritis in your fingers won't let you type."

"That's the spirit!"

They raised their glasses and clinked them noisily. In that moment, Siobhan felt so grateful for her friends and the possibilities of this new life that she forgot about everything else.

Chapter 2

Marcel

"Couldn't we have met somewhere a tad more discreet?" protested Marcel when he returned from the bathroom. "There are more people on this damn rooftop than on the set of *Game of Thrones.* Some of whom are very rude, I might add. Some girl bumped right into me and didn't even bother to apologize."

Or perhaps he was the one who had bumped into her. He hadn't seen her face, but she smelled very nice.

"Argh! Where will it end!" exclaimed Alex ironically.

"That's what I want to know. And don't get me started on the music."

"What's wrong with Taylor Swift?"

"She's for fifteen-year-olds?"

Alex shrugged.

"I like it."

"Well, you have terrible taste, then."

"Okay, why don't you stop complaining and just enjoy the moment, Mr. Scrooge? They make the best dry martini in all of Midtown here. I took the liberty of ordering you one while you were powdering your nose, so you'll see for yourself. And just look at the views, my god!" he exclaimed, gesturing toward the iconic One Times Square lit up by billboards for Apple,

Walgreens, and Forever 21, at the intersection of Broadway and Forty-Second. "Don't you feel privileged? Winter's miserable, but Manhattan in June is beautiful. There's no humidity, the air is balmy, Shakespeare in the Park gets going soon, and the girls start baring their midriffs."

"Have you started smoking weed, or is it the midlife crisis that's causing this stream of garbage?"

"I haven't smoked since my college days. And no crisis. I might have lost a bit of hair recently," he admitted, running his hand over his very short blond cut, "but I'm still in decent shape. In fact, there's a really hot girl over there who can't take her eyes off me," he claimed, jerking his chin in her direction.

"The one with the glasses and the feminist tattoo?" asked Marcel, who had turned around to look.

"No, the redhead. And try to be a bit more subtle. Looking at a woman like that is kind of frowned upon nowadays; it could be seen as harassment."

"Isn't she the one who's supposedly looking at you?"

"Well, you never know. Things can get tense in the era of MeToo. That's why I'm on Tinder. Things are far less complicated in the virtual world, I can assure you. Hiding behind a screen means you can be yourself; the great paradox of the times in which we live."

Marcel looked at him skeptically.

"So, you use a dating app because you're afraid of not being as politically correct as a white, hetero, paid-up member of the Democratic Party with a college education and a social conscience ought to be."

"You say it as though I'm an oddity, when in actual fact 48 percent of Americans use dating apps. And for your information, I'm not affiliated with the Democrats."

"But you vote for them."

"Don't you?"

"I don't vote. And when I like a woman, I go and tell her; I don't mess around."

That had sounded arrogant. Of course, for Marcel, relationships with the opposite sex did nothing more than obey a biological imperative, and as long as all parties involved were in agreement on the what, the how, and the when, he saw no need to be so formal about it.

"It is what it is. We don't all have that exotic Southern accent that drives New York women wild."

"Oh, I can assure you it's not my accent that drives them wild," replied Marcel, a mischievous smile flitting across his lips.

Alex mimed shooting himself in the temple, as if to say, *Lord, give me patience.*

"You're an arrogant bastard," he said reproachfully.

"I know. You tell me about two hundred times a day. So, why did you want to see me?"

"Ah, yes. That." Alex rolled up his sleeves and interlaced his fingers on the table. "How's the novel coming along?"

Marcel didn't answer, not immediately anyway. A muscle twitched in his jaw, and a sudden panic churned his insides. He tried to calm himself down. He feigned an imperious tone and eventually said:

"Is that why you brought me here? I understand you can't live without your wonder boy, but you could have found a better excuse. You know perfectly well I don't like talking about my work until it's finished. I mean . . . asking an author about the book they're writing is like asking someone with a terminal illness how they're feeling."

"Come on, there's no need to get all passive-aggressive with me. Give me an approximate date when you'll be done, and I'll be happy."

Marcel's face contorted in barely concealed anguish. He took a sip of his drink and let the liquid slosh from one side of his mouth to the other before swallowing, in a vain attempt to soothe his anxiety.

Or to gain time.

"There's a chance I might need a few extra weeks."

"How many? Two? Three? A month?"

"How the hell should I know!" he exclaimed dramatically. "Why the hurry? We're not talking about the final installment of a Patrick Rothfuss trilogy. This is an independent work."

"I refuse to believe that you don't know how this industry works yet, Marcel. Gunton is a real pain in the ass, that's why the hurry. I won't lie to you: *The End of Days* hasn't sold as well as we hoped, and as far as I know, you don't have a safe full of unpublished manuscripts like J. D. Salinger. So I need something to placate your editor and get him off my back at the same time. Why the hell do you think I'm losing my hair? Listen, here's what we'll do. You let me read a few pages of the manuscript, and I'll take care of him. Fifty or sixty should do it."

Silence.

"The first chapter?" Alex countered.

Marcel averted his gaze.

The truth was that he hadn't written a single word. His mind had been blank for months, and he hadn't dared admit it to his agent. He had tried. God knows he had tried. Every day he shut himself away in his study for hours and forced himself to type. Something, anything. He would write a sentence, then go back and delete it. He would stare at the computer screen for a while, cursor flashing, the glow of the white page blinding. He would try again. And again, he went back and deleted it. Nothing was up to the standard he expected of Marcel Black. Expectations. He wanted to crush them to bits. His mind was like a tangled ball of yarn: the threads were there, but he couldn't unravel them. It was the first time anything like this had ever happened to him, and he felt lost. The discovery that having written fifteen novels didn't mean he knew how to write number sixteen was a cause of terrible distress. Perhaps the moment had come to face up to reality and accept the consequences.

He silently counted to three and turned to face his companion.

"There is no novel, Alex," he said. "I'm really sorry for not telling you sooner."

His agent stared at him, his face suddenly pale.

"What do you mean there's no novel? Writer's block?"

Marcel's lips tightened.

"I suppose Mira Yamashita was right: I'm finished," he muttered. "Do you know how many emails from angry readers your assistant has forwarded to me since *The End of Days* came out? That bastard William J. Knox is still plaguing me even after I got rid of him."

Alex shook out his hands energetically.

"Okay, number one: you're not finished. Number two: since when have you cared what people think? Don't you always say you don't owe anyone shit? And number three," he added, noticing their glasses were almost empty, "we need more alcohol."

"Since I haven't been able to string together a single miserable sentence."

He was referring to point two, of course.

"In that case, we need to take urgent corrective action."

"Okay. And by that, you mean what, exactly?"

A veil of suspense fell between the two men. Alex took a deep breath before verbalizing what he was thinking. He sensed it would be no easy task to convince the man in front of him.

"Twitter." Marcel's thin brows shot upward. He opened his mouth to reply, but his friend put his hand up to stop him. "Before you get mad, hear me out. Everyone is on Twitter." He counted them off on his fingers: "Politicians, journalists, Hollywood actors, NFL players, writers, and—the cherry on top—readers; a whole bunch of readers who want the authors of their favorite books to interact with them. You know why? Because it makes them feel important, which is good for the industry as a whole. Getting to know a writer you admire helps you understand their work better. You follow?" Marcel nodded. "Good. There are two types of reader we're interested in: those who still haven't read anything of yours and those who have but are disappointed in you for having eliminated Knox and who aren't planning to read anything else. Your job is to show up where they are and get them eating out of your hand. You know, make them feel important. I don't mean revealing your identity—just let them get to know a little bit about you, that's all."

Marcel folded his arms and pinned Alex with the gaze of a hardened criminal.

"Let me get this straight. You want me to open a Twitter account and turn on the charm for everyone? To talk about my writing process and answer questions about my political preferences and my private life. Wow." He shook his head and applauded sarcastically. "A brilliant and flawless plan. What a shame you've forgotten one tiny detail. I. HATE. PEOPLE. Wanting to get to know a writer because you like their books is like wanting to get to know a chicken because you like nuggets; it makes no sense. The only valid relationship between a reader and an author lies in the act of reading. Period. For god's sake, Alex, are you sure you're not smoking weed? You know perfectly well this won't work; we've known each other long enough."

"Okay, you aren't exactly the sociable type, I know, but that's what PR consultants are for. You have to adapt to change, Marcel. The publishing industry isn't what it used to be. There's nothing less profitable than a book nowadays. People are more interested in the artist than the art. Their life, their face, their past, their romantic relationships, which party they vote for, and whatever bullshit they publish on the socials. That's why editors look for authors who know how to connect with their audience. Being likeable is important for sales. Why do you think Jimmy Fallon is so successful?"

"Well, that's a dumb example. A writer isn't the same as a *Tonight Show* host on NBC; the only thing you can demand of them is literary quality. Whether they're handsome, friendly, witty, or able to achieve the requisite level of social outrage is irrelevant. Or at least it should be." Marcel exhaled and rubbed his eyes vigorously. "I don't want to be part of the show or the center of attention. My job is to write books, not to sell them. I could give you a thousand reasons, but I don't think I need to. That's why I chose to live anonymously."

"And I respect that, you know I do. Even so, the world is changing fast these days. Are you willing to keep up with it, or would you rather fall into the void? Think about it."

"There's nothing to think about," he replied. "Now, if you'll excuse me, I'm going to Blue Note to listen to some real music." And with that, he got to his feet.

Chapter 3

Siobhan

She had been picking out and discarding clothes for fifteen minutes. Ripped jeans and sneakers? Too informal. Short dress and heels? Too provocative. Nothing was quite right. *I should have borrowed something from Paige,* she thought. She sighed in defeat and flopped backward onto the bed. In less than five hours, she was scheduled to appear at McNally Jackson, the legendary Nolita bookstore, to celebrate the publication of *With Fate on Our Side*. She was more nervous than she had ever been in her life; even the night of her prom, when she almost lost her virginity to Jimmy Steelballs, the most popular player on the school team, on the back seat of his pickup truck.

Bella, her agent, had tried to calm her down over the phone. "It's perfectly normal to get stage fright, but you'll be great."

"What if no one comes?" Siobhan had asked her brother the night before.

Of all the disastrous scenarios she had contemplated, this was the one that terrified her most.

"That won't happen, Cheerios," replied her brother.

"How many people in Mount Vernon have you bribed to be so sure?"

"Oh, I didn't have to go that far. Believe me: talent and free food can be very persuasive. Let me give you a bit of brotherly advice: go to that bookstore tomorrow and have a bit of faith in yourself. It'll be a walk in the park, you'll see."

"Okay. And how do I do that?"

"Pretend you're the one in charge. That's what being an adult is all about, Shiv. Constantly pretending. Until one day you wake up and realize you don't need to pretend anymore because you've become the person you wanted to be."

"Are you speaking from experience?"

"Hardly. I got that from a fortune cookie in some joint in Chinatown."

Wise words. It was just a pity that she tended toward self-sabotage. Imposter syndrome had set in as soon as people started referring to her as "the writer of the moment." Everyone was calling her that now, even her boss—albeit with a hint of sarcasm. Was she? Wasn't she just another girl with a bit of luck and a certain talent for storytelling? The week since the release of her novel had been dizzying. Reviews, comments, and mentions circulated daily on social media and literary blogs, and a fan group had even created the hashtag #Passiobhan. It wasn't the greatest play on words, but how many brand-new authors could claim to have their own hashtag?

Lesson one: the best kind of marketing campaign for a book is word of mouth.

Siobhan received so many messages from readers excited about the story that she felt happy and overwhelmed at the same time. All this recognition implied a great responsibility unlike anything she had experienced before. She was playing in another league now, and she had to live up to it. She didn't want to disappoint anyone.

And it's easy to feel deflated when imposter syndrome strikes.

Lesson two: a moment of glory can simultaneously become an internal ordeal because the line separating the two is finer than we think.

And lesson three: doing all this thinking makes you ravenous.

Her growling stomach brought her back to reality. She decided to leave her fretting for another time, jumped off the bed, and went to the kitchen to make a peanut butter sandwich. As she carefully cut off the crusts, an alert lit up the screen of her cell phone. She wiped the traces of peanut butter from her fingers and swiped to check her notifications.

What she saw left her speechless.

Or nearly.

Letitia Wright has just tagged me in a photo? It can't be true. I must be hallucinating.

Letitia Wright was not just known for being the charming wife of Rufus Wright, the Democratic senator from Washington, but also because any book she liked automatically became a hit. In fact, a recent HBO series starring Nicole Kidman was the adaptation of a drama that Letitia had found profoundly moving. She was a literary influencer of the highest order, with millions of Twitter followers. Not as many as Bill Gates, but more than J.Lo or even NASA.

AND SHE HAD TAGGED SIOBHAN.

Letitia Wright @letitia_wright 2m
Deciding what to read next. Which of these two should I start with? Suggestions welcome. #CrimeOrRomance

The tweet was accompanied by an image showing Letitia herself, stunning as ever—how did she manage to keep her skin so smooth after fifty?—in the garden of her house in Bellevue, Washington, with a book in each hand. In the right, she held *The End of Days*, by Marcel Black; in the left, *With Fate on Our Side*, by Siobhan Harris.

"What? Letitia Wright wants to read my novel? Oh my god! Oh my god! Oh my god!" she exclaimed. And possessed by a sudden euphoria, she started dancing and skipping around the kitchen as though she had just won forty million dollars in the Powerball.

It didn't take long for doubts to start creeping in and then kill her festive mood. What if Letitia didn't like the book? What if she found the story superficial? Or if she hated her writing style? How could a debut author like Siobhan stand a chance against an author of the stature of

Marcel Black? For god's sake, Marcel Black himself! The most famous writer without a face in America.

Easy: she couldn't.

Letitia Wright's tweet was starting to go viral; she had to reply. She thought about calling Bella to ask for advice, but she had already abused her agent's patience enough that day. And what the hell. Wasn't she an adult woman capable of writing her own tweets? She took a deep breath to calm herself and pondered her words.

"Pretend you're the one in the driver's seat," she told herself.

> **Siobhan Harris** @siobhan_harris 1s
> What a wonderful surprise, Mrs. Wright! I'm so honored that you would take an interest in my book. And since you're open to suggestions, I would say start with Marcel Black. Sweets are best saved for last. 😉
> #CrimeAndRomance

She searched for the least tasteless GIF of thanks she could find and inserted it. "Sweets are best saved for last," she reread. Didn't it sound a bit presumptuous, bearing in mind who Marcel Black was? Possibly. Even so, she wasn't about to beat herself up in public just because she was a debut writer. She deserved a chance too. And, anyway, Black had no social media profiles, so he wouldn't even see it. She clicked "Tweet." Thankfully, she didn't have to wait for long.

> **Letitia Wright** @letitia_wright 1m
> I like your philosophy. And call me Letitia. Good luck with the launch this evening! <3 #CrimeAndRomance

Five seconds later, another notification popped up:

> **Letitia Wright** has just followed you.

Chapter 4

Marcel

He had done it. He had finally allowed his arm to be twisted and created a Twitter account. On two conditions. One: that, at the slightest sign of conflict, he would close it down. And two: that he would manage it himself; no communications managers paid for by the agency. He would publish whatever he pleased, when he wanted, and at whatever frequency he chose. Alex was not entirely in agreement, sensing that his client's brusque demeanor would give him no shortage of headaches, and he told him as much.

"You push me to the edge of the cliff, and now you don't want me to jump?" Marcel complained.

"You have to be diplomatic on social media and you . . . Don't take this the wrong way, but you're about as subtle as a brick. Perhaps you could let a PR professional guide you a bit?"

"Who do you think I am? Audrey Hepburn in *My Fair Lady*? No way, Alex. Either we do it my way or not at all. That's my final offer."

End of discussion.

◆ ◆ ◆

The next day, Marcel created an account on Twitter with the username @InvisibleBlack. For his profile picture, he used a black-and-white photograph of his treasured Underwood Number 5 collector's edition, purchased from Gramercy Typewriter Co., Paul Schweitzer's iconic store. Things got slightly more complicated when it came to filling out his biography, which only allowed one hundred and sixty characters. *Crime author with Baxter Books. Creator of William J. Knox. Fourteen-time* New York Times *bestseller. Translated into twenty-five languages.* Library Journal*'s Man of the Decade. Shortlisted for the National Book Award* sounded as pretentious as the resume of a recent Ivy League graduate. And it was too long to fit. Instead, he selected his favorite William Faulkner quote.

Since no one had any business knowing his birthday was in August and that he lived in New York, he omitted that information. He clicked "Create account" and . . . voilà.

> Welcome to Twitter, @InvisibleBlack!
> This is the best place to see what's happening in your world.
> Let's go!

The first thing he did was follow the main progressive American newspapers—he was tempted to add the *Times-Picayune* to the list, but that would give too many clues as to his place of birth—before adding Shapiro Literary Agency, Baxter Books, *The New York Review of Books*, and *Publishers Weekly*, and finally, a select group of writers who were active on the network, including Stephen King, Bret Easton Ellis, Don Winslow, Patricia Cornwell, and Chuck Palahniuk. None of the accounts followed him back immediately. He looked at his new timeline but found nothing of interest.

So, he decided to publish his first tweet.

> **Marcel Black** @InvisibleBlack 1s

I've succumbed to the unfathomable attraction of this social network. In my defense, I'll say I was forced to.

He waited the requisite minute. When he checked and nothing had happened, he got out of his chair and left his study with wounded pride.

He spent the next few hours in his designer chaise longue, immersed in reading *Galveston*, by Nic Pizzolatto, pencil in hand. The bad—or perhaps good—thing about being a writer is that you stop reading purely for enjoyment. He didn't put the book down until he had finished it. It was no masterpiece; on the contrary, it was sensationalist and riddled with clichés. Even so, it had kept him hooked until the final page, which was one point in its favor. He removed his glasses, placed them on the rosewood coffee table, and rubbed his eyes vigorously. It was past nine when he stood up. As he stretched, he contemplated the cityscape through the large windows. From that height, Manhattan seemed enveloped in a kind of ethereal calm. Beyond Central Park, the buildings rose from dusky shadows that suggested intimacy. Sometimes he missed New Orleans. The omnipresent jazz, Cajun food, Mardi Gras, the Saints games, the democratic joyfulness of his native city, and even the stench of putrefaction, like decomposing matter, that characterized it. And of course, his sister, Charmaine. The nostalgia was short-lived though. Because in New York he could be somebody (Marcel Black) and nobody (Marcel Dupont) at the same time. Life moves so fast in the city that never sleeps—an undeniable fact—that the urban chaos somehow guarantees privacy. The Big Apple was the perfect place to stand out and hide away at the same time. His rumbling stomach reminded him he hadn't eaten for several hours. This tended to happen whenever he got caught up in a book. Perhaps that was the great power of books: making people feel like they weren't completely alone. He was in no mood to cook, so he decided to order in. When he picked up his phone, he saw a message from Alex.

Alex
You're the fucking best, man ✌️

It took a moment to register what he was seeing.

"What the . . ."

Marcel Black was trending on Twitter.

Not only had he gained thousands of followers in a matter of hours, but celebrities from the world of literature and entertainment had been talking about his unexpected appearance on social media.

Marcel couldn't help but laugh. All this commotion over a stupid tweet that wasn't even that clever? He called Alex.

"What does the manual say about replying to all these people?"

"Hmmm . . . in an ideal world, you would reply. Leave it for now though. Although you really should say something to Letitia Wright. Something nice," he emphasized.

"Who?"

"Letitia Wright." Silence. "Don't tell me you don't know who she is."

"Should I?"

"Well, yes. Letitia Wright is the wife of the Democratic senator Rufus Wright and one of the most important literary influencers of the moment."

"Impressive," said Marcel, not remotely impressed. "And why exactly should I waste my precious time on a politician's wife?"

"You really ought to call her a literary influencer. Referring to her as *the wife of* sounds terribly chauvinistic." Marcel rolled his eyes. His agent's obsession with political correctness was trying his patience. "Just take a look at her profile, and it will all make sense."

He ended the call and did as Alex had suggested. Apparently, Letitia Wright had asked which of two books she should read next. One was his and the other . . . by a @siobhan_harris. And it seemed Mrs. Wright's interest wasn't the only thing he and this Siobhan had in common; they also shared a publisher.

With Fate on Our Side, he read on the cover. He snorted and shook his head. "I can't believe Baxter Books is publishing this kind of garbage."

Siobhan Harris's biography was most revealing.

New Yorker. Dreamer. Reader and emerging writer of romance novels. Formerly on WriteUp.

"Oh, a rookie."

He clicked on her profile picture and studied it closely. Long coppery hair, blue eyes, delicate features, a television-commercial smile. He had to admit she was attractive, a classic American beauty, although physical appearance wasn't something that impressed Marcel. Scrolling through her timeline, he learned that she had just published *With Fate on Our Side* and that the launch had taken place that very evening at McNally Jackson. A resounding success, by all accounts.

Siobhan Harris @siobhan_harris 27m
Thanks to everyone who came today. I don't know how to express my gratitude. It was incredible, a dream come true! ❤❤❤

Marcel stuck his fingers in his mouth, pretending to vomit. He returned to Letitia Wright's tweet and saw that the newbie had replied.

Siobhan Harris @siobhan_harris 9h
What a wonderful surprise, Mrs. Wright! I'm so honored that you would take an interest in my book. And since you're open to suggestions, I would say start with Marcel Black. Sweets are best saved for last. 😉
#CrimeAndRomance

That really pissed him off, though he didn't know why. Okay, he did know why. First, he hated people who used those ridiculous emoticons to communicate. Second, the fact that a work by him—Marcel

Black, no less, critically acclaimed fourteen-time bestseller, translated into twenty-five languages—should appear next to a third-rate romance novel made him sick. Mrs. Wright might be highly influential, but she didn't have a goddamn clue about literature. How could anyone compare his work to that of a rookie? And what the hell was the deal with this novice princess? *Sweets ah bey-uhst saved fuh lay-uhst nah nah nah . . .* He would bet his right arm that she couldn't string a sentence together. She must have gotten lucky for some agent with a keen sense of smell to take an interest in her, exploiting the commercial gold mine of that corny, superficial trash for bored women; one of those mawkish pieces of junk about the redemptive power of love and that kind of horseshit. "Romance novel, my ass." He didn't need to have read any of them to discern their literary quality.

Which was precisely zero.

Offended as he was, he decided to counterattack. To hell with Alex's tips about courtesy. He wrote:

> **Marcel Black** @InvisibleBlack 1m
> Too many sweets are bad for your health.
> #CrimeNOTRomance

Sent.

He had been gentle.

Although he hoped that changing the hashtag would cause the impact he wanted.

"Let's see if you get the irony, princess."

Harris responded immediately, of course. She must be a slave to hyperconnectivity who spent all day glued to her smartphone, exposing before the murky spotlights of social media the vacuousness of her millennial New York life—what she ate, how she dressed, which trendy bar in the Village she had gone to the previous night, or which must-see series she had watched on Netflix, as if any of those banalities were of the slightest interest.

Frickin' Generation Y.

Siobhan Harris @siobhan_harris 6s
I'm not sure blood is much better.
#NOTCrimeBUTRomance

Crime no, romance yes? Well, well, well. Perhaps he had underestimated this young romance novelist.

"You like to play, huh? Very well, let's play."

Marcel Black @InvisibleBlack 9s
Blood is for adults. Go play with your dolls and come back when you've grown up. #CrimeNOTRomance

Siobhan Harris @siobhan_harris 30s
I'm not sure I understood that one. 😅

Marcel's lips curved into a contemptuous smile.

Marcel Black @InvisibleBlack 10s
Reading comprehension is a basic requisite. Didn't the article mention that?

Siobhan Harris @siobhan_harris 6s
Sorry, which article do you mean?

Marcel Black @InvisibleBlack 10s
The one called "Top 10 tips on how to become a writer overnight (number 8 will surprise you)"

His reply had been crude, but he was damned if he wasn't going to enjoy this war of words. As he waited for the newbie to answer, he went to the living room and poured himself a bourbon from the bar. Back in his study, he noticed that his cell phone was lighting up with an incoming call from Alex. He rejected it. He wasn't interested in hearing what he had to say right then; and anyway, he already knew.

The reply came at last.

Siobhan Harris @siobhan_harris 1m
I think you're a troll.

Marcel snorted.

"Is that the best you can do?"

Marcel Black @InvisibleBlack 3s
I'm no troll, I'm Marcel Black.

Siobhan Harris @siobhan_harris 5s
Well, that's a pity. I never would have imagined the mysterious Marcel Black would turn out to be some obnoxious guy with a superiority complex who's cruel to his colleagues.

Marcel Black @InvisibleBlack 15s
Colleagues?

Siobhan Harris @siobhan_harris 10s
Is this gratuitous attack because I'm a woman?

Second call from Alex. Once again, Marcel ignored it. A moment later he received a text message:

Alex
You have to stop. NOW.

He turned off his phone. He would deal with the consequences of this little game some other time.

Marcel Black @InvisibleBlack 1m
It has nothing to do with you being a woman. I simply believe we do things very differently. Mine is literature and yours is . . . entertainment?

Siobhan Harris @siobhan_harris 1m
Who are you to decide? Seems very presumptuous to me. Anyway, what's so bad about entertaining people?

Marcel Black @InvisibleBlack 3s
Nothing. As long as you realize you're not going to change the world.

Siobhan Harris @siobhan_harris 0s
And of course, you are. 😂

Marcel Black @InvisibleBlack 3s
I don't write to give people escapism but to make them reflect on human nature.

"Christ. Even I found that painful."

Siobhan Harris @siobhan_harris 1m
You must think I'm stupid just because I write romance novels.

Marcel Black @InvisibleBlack 10s
I don't know you. I don't know whether you're stupid or not. What I do know is that we're not on the same level. My novels are noir; yours are pink and fluffy. The difference is clear even if you're color blind.

Siobhan Harris @siobhan_harris 6s
Your joke is ridiculous and offensive to people with color blindness. And it's "romance novel," if you don't mind, "pink fluff" is not a flattering term.

Marcel Black @InvisibleBlack 1s
I wonder why that is.

Siobhan Harris @siobhan_harris 10s
You haven't read much romance, have you?

Marcel Black @InvisibleBlack 2s
I assume that's a rhetorical question. OF. COURSE. I. HAVEN'T.

Siobhan Harris @siobhan_harris 5s
Then what the HELL is your basis for suggesting it's a lesser genre?

Marcel Black @InvisibleBlack 1m
Do you need to touch boiling water to know that it scalds?

Siobhan Harris @siobhan_harris 30s
Oh, please. That's such a disingenuous argument . . . Make a bit of an effort here. Given how much you know about human nature and all that.

Marcel laughed and shook his head. *Touché,* he thought.

Siobhan Harris @siobhan_harris 1m
What's up, Mr. Black? Words failing you? It's clear you don't know what you're talking about. It just so happens I grew up reading romance novels so at least I DO KNOW.

"Calm down, princess. Don't get ahead of yourself."

He took a swig of bourbon and cracked his knuckles as though preparing to go into battle.

Marcel Black @InvisibleBlack 1m
Very interesting. And have you ever read a REAL BOOK, or is your ample literary knowledge based on Barbara Cartland trash?

Siobhan Harris @siobhan_harris 1m
A bit of respect for Barbara, please. She published more than seven hundred novels over the course of her long life. And if by "real book" you mean noir, I confess that crime isn't my thing, either real or fictitious.

Marcel Black @InvisibleBlack 45s
And sugar isn't mine.

Siobhan Harris @siobhan_harris 3s
That's certainly clear. Perhaps you should try some.

Marcel Black @InvisibleBlack 10s
No thanks, I'd rather die.

Siobhan Harris @siobhan_harris 1m
Since when has evil been more appealing than love?

Marcel Black @InvisibleBlack 1m
Since the dawn of time. The world and its customs are still governed by ancestral rules that can't be changed. Love as a sentiment doesn't exist. It was invented in twelfth-century lyrical poetry to keep the nobles entertained.

Siobhan Harris @siobhan_harris 9s
Not only do you have no face, you have no heart.

Marcel Black @InvisibleBlack 15s
Of course I have a heart. And it beats like clockwork, precisely because I steer clear of sugar.

Siobhan Harris @siobhan_harris 6s
Better to die from stabbing than from diabetes, I suppose.

Marcel Black @InvisibleBlack 1m
Naturally.

Siobhan Harris @siobhan_harris 1m
Your prejudices won't make me ashamed of who I am, however many books you've sold. I like romance novels because I believe in love. Don't you watch the news? People need hope.

Marcel Black @InvisibleBlack 45s
What a load of bullshit. What people need is good stories. Hope is for the sick.

Siobhan Harris @siobhan_harris 10s
Define "good."

Marcel Black @InvisibleBlack 2s
Anything not classified as romance.

Siobhan Harris @siobhan_harris 25s
It's pointless trying to talk to you. It's like all the dark and twisted stuff you write has poisoned the way you see the world.

Marcel Black @InvisibleBlack 1m
Things aren't black or white. We live in a scale of grays that are so indistinct from each other that even the best among us can be susceptible to committing the worst offenses.

Siobhan Harris @siobhan_harris 1m
For my part, I prefer to focus on the brighter side of life. My novel might not change anything, nor do I expect it to. I'm happy just to know that someone out there will go to bed with a smile on their face. #NOTCrimeBUTRomance

"My god! How corny!"

Marcel Black @InvisibleBlack 1m
I'm glad your aspirations are so low. It's more realistic, given the circumstances. Literary quality aside, crime novels will always be superior to romance. Evil is an intrinsic part of the human soul. That's what makes the world go round. GROW UP, Miss Harris. #CrimeNOTRomance

At this point, Marcel felt the conversation was over. To carry on would be a waste of time. Perhaps he had gone a little too far, but he had to put this insolent child in her place. He drained his bourbon and stretched his neck. His Twitter notifications were starting to go crazy, but he ignored them; he had had enough for one day, more than he could bear, in fact. Then, just as he was about to sign off, something caught his eye, like a typo in a billboard ad.

The influential Letitia Wright had reappeared on the scene.

Letitia Wright @letitia_wright 15s
This is what I call a good show.

Letitia Wright @letitia_wright 11m
I understand that everyone defends their favorite genre to the hilt, BUT neither is better than the other, they're just different. In fact, they could live happily side by side in the same story. #CrimeANDRomance

Letitia Wright @letitia_wright 10m
And to show I'm right, I want to propose a challenge: Why don't you write a novel together that's noir and romance rolled into one? I'm one hundred percent sure it would be a hit 🙌 #CrimePLUSRomance

Chapter 5

Marcel

"No way. Absolutely not. And the very fact that you've made me come in on a Sunday morning to discuss it is offensive."

Marcel folded his arms over his chest and lifted his chin defiantly. Across the table in the luxurious office at Baxter Books, Bob Gunton regarded him with wide eyes as he drummed his fingers on the wooden surface.

"You should have thought about that before the little number you pulled last night, don't you think?"

"It wasn't that bad."

"What do you mean, it wasn't that bad? For the love of god, Marcel! You insulted that girl in front of the world! One of our authors no less!"

"I didn't insult her. I just gave my opinion on the chick lit she churns out, that's all."

"Romance novels," said Alex, who was sitting next to Marcel.

"No one asked for your opinion. Have you been on Twitter today?" asked Gunton, unbuttoning his polo shirt.

"No," lied Marcel.

He had, of course, but he wasn't about to admit in front of his editor and his agent that he had read the—not insignificant—series of tweets branding him as chauvinistic, misogynistic, arrogant, ignorant, a snob, an opportunist, and even a failed author following his heated "debate" with the shiny new Siobhan Harris. He had lost followers, and most people seemed to have taken her side, not that any of that mattered to him. What really annoyed him was that the little princess had had the gall to accept Wright's proposal without a moment's hesitation. Had she no dignity? Not even a smidgen of self-respect? Was she so convinced of her own worth that she would presume to write in collaboration with an author with years of experience under his belt and commit herself to writing in a genre she wasn't even familiar with?

> **Siobhan Harris** @siobhan_harris 13h
> That's a FABULOUS idea, @letitia_wright! I'd love to write that novel. As long as @InvisibleBlack has what it takes to accept the challenge, of course 😉
> #CrimePLUSRomance

Marcel hadn't replied, nor did he need to. He sensed that getting involved with these two women would send him tumbling into a nosedive that would see him writing about some multimillionaire and his eccentric sexual proclivities. So, thanks but no thanks. Much as this Miss Harris's insinuation that he was a coward rankled—and it rankled more than he cared to admit—he had no intention of giving in. Did nobody realize how ridiculous it sounded? A romantic crime novel. Had the world suddenly gone mad? Twitter users had congregated into two groups, #TeamCrime and #TeamRomance, according to their preferred genre. The results were fairly even, to be honest. Until #TeamCrimePlusRomance came on the scene, championed by that busybody Letitia Wright, and things started to spiral out of control.

Now even Reese Witherspoon was clamoring for this lousy novel.

"Well, you should take a look," Gunton snapped. "And while you're at it, apologize to Siobhan and anyone else you've offended. The Comms department has forwarded me a complaint from the Delaware Color

Blindness Association." Marcel furrowed his brow. "You'd better hope they don't sue," he moaned, raising his hands helplessly. "I should be playing golf in Chelsea with my brother-in-law right now, you know that? Jeez!"

"I'm not planning to apologize to anyone, Bob. Forget it," countered Marcel.

Gunton shook his head and met Alex's gaze.

"What do you think?"

"I . . ." He turned to face Marcel. "I think you should do it. You should accept Letitia Wright's challenge."

"What the fuck, Alex? Siobhan's a rookie! A rookie who writes romance novels!"

"Marcel, you aren't looking at this the right way. Listen, this morning I exchanged a few emails with Bella Watson, Siobhan's agent. I don't know her personally, but I get the feeling she has a sharp nose. Just a few weeks after she discovered Siobhan on WriteUp, she had managed to get Baxter Books interested in a complete unknown and secured her a tasty offer; let's at least concede that Watson knows her stuff." Gunton nodded his agreement. "See, I've done a bit of research. I gather her novel is selling well. Isn't that so, Bob?"

"Very well indeed. I spoke to her editor just a few minutes ago. They think the next reprint might have to be three times the initial run."

"Really? So, Siobhan 'One-Hit Wonder' Harris is going to single-handedly save the American publishing industry from its current mess, huh? Wow! I'm impressed. Anyone can write these days," Marcel retorted.

Alex narrowed his eyes.

"Be as sarcastic as you like, but she has a lot of what it takes to become a mass sensation. How many debut authors do you know who can pack the room in a bookstore like McNally Jackson?" Silence. "Exactly, none. In fact, Watson told me there were so many people who couldn't get in that they're having to organize another two events next week. And her Twitter numbers are impressive, you must have noticed. So however new she might be, it's in your best interest to associate yourself with her."

An ironic smile flitted across Marcel's lips.

"It would be rather more in my interest to associate myself with Beyoncé. Can you get me her number?"

"I doubt Jay-Z would be amused. Anyway, I've been following the hashtags," Alex continued. "Almost everyone who commented was in favor of you two writing a novel together. In fact, the vast majority want her name to come before yours on the cover, although that doesn't matter right now. You know what this means, Marcel?"

"That readers are idiots and are happy to let Letitia Wright decide what they should read?"

Gunton snorted.

"Readers are anything but idiots. And Letitia Wright is a visionary, so we're going to listen to her. If she thinks this would be a success, then so do I. You're doing it, Marcel. Period."

"I don't give a damn what Letitia Wright thinks!" exclaimed Marcel. At that moment, the fury that had settled in his stomach started climbing to his throat. "I've been writing crime novels for fifteen years. I'm one of the most respected authors in this country. And most importantly, I work alone. Far from the spotlights. In anonymity. Are you really asking me to do this? It's humiliating, for fuck's sake."

"Marcel," said Alex. "*The End of Days* didn't go as well as expected, you have one hell of a creative block, and your reputation . . . Well, let's just say you didn't come out of last night's exchange very well. Getting into a Twitter spat with Siobhan Harris was a terrible idea, but what's done is done. Hey," he added in a conciliatory tone, after a brief pause, "maybe this will turn out to be a good thing. Every cloud has a silver lining, as they say."

"Don't tell me you've been at the self-help books again."

"Working with her could help you improve your image." He swept his hand sideways as though visualizing the hypothetical headline that accompanied this highly promising future. "Marcel Black: from the depravity of crime to the redemption of love."

The editor whistled.

"I like it. The marketing is all yours, Shapiro."

"Thanks."

"Please. Don't make me laugh."

"Think about it, Marcel. An experienced crime novelist writing under a pseudonym, an author of romance novels who's new on the scene but very popular, and a commission for a romantic thriller. It's out of this world! It's . . . metaliterature!"

"Metaliterature. Huh. You're fucking with me, right?"

"Nothing like this has ever been done. It could be hot shit."

"I said no."

"I'm afraid you're in no position to negotiate," said Gunton. "Might I remind you that you haven't fulfilled your contract. You still owe me three novels, and it would appear that your ideas have dried up since you killed off Knox. So you'll have to let yourself be guided by others for a bit."

Marcel clenched his jaw. The thing that hurt most wasn't the certainty that his prestige would plummet if he took part in this ridiculous experiment. The fact was that his editor was right.

He had hit a rough patch. There was no denying it.

"When you light a fire, it's up to you to put it out. You're going to apologize, and you're going to write that novel. Or I could sue you for breach of contract. Or accidentally reveal your identity."

Something inside Marcel quivered like barely-set Jell-O. He turned in his chair and faced his editor.

That old bastard was a cunning fox.

Alex flapped his hands dissuasively.

"Bob, I don't think we need to go that—"

"Are you threatening me?" Marcel asked.

The editor held his gaze for a few moments. Then he composed a disingenuous smile and said:

"Of course not, my friend! As they say in detective novels, I'm just applying a bit of reasonable pressure."

Chapter 6

SIOBHAN

Leaving the subway on Seventh Avenue, she was met by a brilliant blue sky. The buildings glittered in the sun as though vying to capture the attention of passersby: Top of the Rock, or the Chrysler, the most iconic building in the city, with that extraordinary Art Deco crown and spire and its eagle gargoyles. Having arrived a half hour early, she decided to engage in a bit of window-shopping. The usual Sunday inertia doesn't affect New York, not ever. The same weekday tide of people who stride along briskly with their gym bags and king-size coffees can be found heading at a more leisurely pace toward MoMA or the High Line. The traffic moves just as slowly, the ventilation grates still spit out steam, the air buzzes with phone conversations, and restaurants are packed at brunch. As she approached the imposing tower of Baxter Books, her heart was pounding so hard it felt like she might burst. Before entering the building, she took a deep breath. She had to stay calm, at all costs.

Or appear calm, at any rate.

The night before, Bella had called to wish her luck.

"Text me when the meeting ends, and we'll get together."

"Aren't you coming?"

"I wish I could, but I can't. Marcel Black's identity is a state secret known only by his editor, who is now your editor too, and his agent;

that's why they called you in on a Sunday, because it's the only day when there's no one in the office." Bella paused dramatically. "Don't worry, okay? Bob Gunton has a very good reputation as an editor. You'll get on fine with him, you'll see. And anyway, you have me."

"I know, I know. And I'm grateful to you. It's just sometimes I think all this is too much for me. It's going to be hard to meet these crazy expectations and even harder to bring them back down to earth. Hasn't this all moved too quickly?"

"Have faith in yourself."

Ding! The elevator door opened on the eleventh floor. As she had been instructed by the weekend security guard, she turned left, then right, and then continued down a long, carpeted hall to the room where they were waiting for her. She gave two light knocks on the door and focused on projecting confidence. After a few seconds, a middle-aged man opened the door. His face was nondescript; he had salt-and-pepper hair, skin the texture of leather, and the deep furrow of a worry line down the center of his forehead. She recognized him as Bob Gunton. They had held an informal video conference a few days earlier. Marcel Black had finally accepted the idea of writing a novel together; before meeting him in person, however, she had to sign a confidentiality and nondisclosure agreement. Siobhan received a rather draconian document in which she agreed not to reveal any details about Black's identity or about the project they would be working on together over the next few months. Breaking this agreement would have serious legal and financial ramifications for her. She couldn't help but wonder about the reason for all this secrecy. Who was Marcel Black? Was he someone important? Perhaps his decision to remain anonymous was simply in line with the philosophy of other artists like Banksy, Daft Punk, or Elena Ferrante, who prioritized the work over the creator. Gunton had also sent her a draft contract for the novel, which set out her share of the advance—$75,000. Woweeee. Nowhere did it state how much Marcel Black would pocket—although she had guessed that it would be at least double. "Check over the draft before we sign the contract. If you have any concerns, we'll sort them out in advance," the editor had instructed her. The only doubt Siobhan had was whether they had made a mistake with the figures. Seventy-five thousand dollars was more than she earned in a year.

"Thanks for coming in on a Sunday," Gunton said as he opened the door fully. "I know it's rather unusual. But then, it's fair to say this isn't exactly a usual situation."

"No problem. Sunday is as good as any other day to talk about books."

"Well said," he agreed. "Now then, before we venture into the lion's den, I need to be sure you don't have any recording devices on you. I know, it's surreal," he added, "but no precaution is too small for him; he's got an unhealthy obsession with it. Please don't take it personally."

"Don't worry. I left my purse at the security desk in the lobby, and there's nothing in my pockets." To confirm this, Siobhan patted her hips, sheathed in a pair of tight jeans. "I trust I don't have to show you inside my blouse too."

"Oh, that won't be necessary. Okay, ready?"

"I was born ready."

What a liar.

The room was vast. In the center was a huge table with several chairs on each side and four bottles of San Pellegrino with the corresponding number of glasses arranged on a tray. One wall was floor-to-ceiling glass. The gaps in the typical aluminum office blinds offered a tempting glimpse of the breathtaking views beyond. A second man approached her. He was younger than Bob Gunton, around forty. He wasn't exactly good-looking, but he had a pleasant face.

"Alex Shapiro, literary agent," he said. Then he handed Siobhan his card. *Do people still use cards? Wasn't that, like, twenty years ago?* she thought. "Congratulations on your first novel."

"Thanks, that's very kind of you."

She heard a sarcastic laugh issuing from the opposite corner of the room, with a dry timbre of authority that caused Siobhan's heart to freeze.

"And this is my client, the famous Marcel Black."

Siobhan directed her gaze toward the only window with the blind raised. A ray of sunlight refracted off the glass and dazzled her, although perhaps it was something else. The silhouette, facing away from her, was cut out against the light in a way that prevented her from seeing clearly. She squinted and approached slowly.

"Siobhan Harris," she said, extending her hand. "Pleased to . . ."

When he turned around, the atmosphere in the room became so unbearably hot that Siobhan felt like lava was flowing through her veins. "My god . . . ," murmured Siobhan. "You're . . ."

She couldn't take her eyes off him. He seemed to be lit up from within by some unknown energy source. Naturally, the fact that he was taller than the Empire State Building also helped.

"Black?" he asked.

"Sexy," she replied without thinking. And immediately clapped her hand over her mouth.

Shit, shit, shit.

A sensation of overwhelming shame spread through her like acid on metal. Marcel Black raised an eyebrow. The man's intensely dark eyes fixed so firmly on hers that she couldn't bear the pressure.

"Are you always this direct?" he inquired. His voice was gravelly and had a melodic Southern lilt.

Siobhan swallowed before replying.

"No. I'm sorry. I don't know why I said that. I suppose my subconscious betrayed me."

"The subconscious doesn't 'betray,' it just gets rid of our inhibitions to express our innermost thoughts. In other words, if you said I'm sexy it's because that's what you think."

She snorted.

"Do you care what I think?"

"Not in the slightest. In fact, it was you who focused on my physical appearance to begin with," he replied with an odiously triumphant air.

So, in addition to being handsome, you're arrogant, a smart-ass, and a full-blown jerkoff; great.

Alex cleared his throat.

"Now that we've all been introduced, why don't we take a seat and get down to business? I'm sure we all have a lot to talk about."

"Good idea," agreed Bob. "Some water, Siobhan?"

She gulped down her water. Was it just her, or was it infernally hot in this room? A river of sweat flowed incessantly from the nape of her neck down her back, but she had to tolerate it, because Marcel Black had sat down opposite her and was watching her without blinking, as though analyzing her every movement. She felt helplessly exposed.

"How old are you?"

"Thirty."

"You look younger," he said. "Are you sure you know what you're getting yourself into?"

He asked the question with a chilly haughtiness that she was starting to get used to. But Siobhan wasn't about to let him unsettle her.

"To begin with, it would help if you told me what I should call you."

"You can call me Marcel."

"I'd prefer to call you by your real name if you don't mind. It's not much to ask, given that we're going to be working together. Don't you agree? Besides, I've signed a confidentiality agreement that's longer than *War and Peace*, so your secret is safe with me."

Despite the visible pulse in her temple, she was proud of her steady tone of voice. Surely her Tolstoy reference must have won her some brownie points with this asshole.

He shrugged.

"That's my name."

"Oh. Well. I wasn't expecting such astounding originality. Marcel what?"

"Dupont," he answered, not without a certain reticence. "And don't even think about repeating it, even in your sleep."

"Ha. I wouldn't dream about you if I was under hypnosis."

Marcel shaped his lips into a regal smile. The kind of smile that would be attractive if its owner wasn't such a prick.

"I wouldn't be so sure if I were you."

Siobhan rolled her eyes.

"My god, you've got a big one, you know that?"

"Pardon?" he asked, blinking exaggeratedly.

A fresh wave of embarrassment flooded over her from top to toe.

"Your ego! I mean your ego," she clarified. "Anyhow . . . I think we got off on the wrong foot. Siobhan Harris." She extended her hand for the second time that morning. "I'd be lying if I said, *Delighted to meet you.*"

They studied each other for a second, the longest second in history, before shaking hands with notable discomfort. Siobhan was all too aware of the warmth of his skin when they touched and immediately released his hand, as though a spark of electricity had jolted her. The warmth was still there, coursing through her, even after they had separated.

"You seemed more mature on Twitter," he said with a note of superiority that made Siobhan dig her nails into her palms.

"No one asked you, Doctor Phil."

Alex, sitting in the chair next to his client, exhaled loudly.

"Oh my lord . . . I need a whiskey, and it's only eleven in the morning," he murmured, massaging his temples in exasperation. "Can we talk about the contract?"

"For once, and without wishing to set a precedent, I agree with you," said Gunton, who was seated at the head of the table. He took some papers from a file and passed them around. "Here's your copy," he said to Siobhan. "Since I've already sent you both the terms, let's focus on the delivery date."

"Before that . . ." Siobhan became aware of three pairs of eyes turning to her. She concentrated on Marcel's and continued: "I want you to apologize for the other night."

Marcel interlaced his fingers behind his neck and leaned back. The posture highlighted the muscles beneath his elegant black shirt. Broad shoulders, strong arms, firm torso. He definitely didn't look like the kind of man who spent hours at the computer. His features—those piercing eyes, the cute dimple on his chin, the defined jawline covered by two days' worth of soft stubble, the naturally expressive eyebrows, and that small depression between a nose as shapely as it was haughty and his insultingly sensual lips—were just too beautiful. But there was something about this man that went beyond his appearance, a kind of power that enveloped him like an invisible cloak. A magnetic aura that eclipsed everything else. And he smelled so good . . . in a way that struck her as familiar, strange as that might seem.

If he wasn't such a self-important jerk, he would be perfect, she reflected. And immediately hated herself.

"You want me to apologize? Very well, I will." He raised his hands in a gesture of surrender, suggesting that he admitted his mistake. Far from it. "I'm very sorry that crossing paths with you on a stupid social network will have disastrous consequences for my career. Happy?"

"If you find this so distasteful, why did you accept Letitia Wright's challenge?"

"Why did you accept it?"

"I asked first."

Something sparked in Marcel's gaze, a tiny reflection in the depths of his pupils. Then he half laughed. The permanent sneer on his face made it hard for her to tell when he was being ironic and when he was being serious. Although Siobhan suspected that sarcasm was part of his DNA.

"Maybe I'm just a bit of a thrill seeker."

She nodded as she clenched her fists under the table.

"Heavens, what a dark and twisted mind."

"Thank you, princess." The half smile returned in all its glory. "The *New York Times* said as much in its review of my last novel."

"I didn't mean it as a compliment. And please don't call me princess."

Bob intervened at that point.

"Children, children . . . let's play nice, please. What if we put the Twitter incident down to a simple misunderstanding? The main thing is that Baxter Books is going to bring together two of its authors on an unprecedented project. You are free to write whatever you please. As long as it isn't offensive, of course," he added. "Oh, and it should be inclusive, ideally; that's the kind of story that sells these days."

Marcel let out what sounded like a gasp of indignation.

"You editors! You talk about diversity as though it's just a box to check on a list of good intentions," he said, berating him.

For the first time that morning, Siobhan agreed with him.

"I think what Bob means is that fiction can be a way to address situations lacking adequate representation," Alex said.

"Exactly. Apart from that, the only thing I care about is that you keep to the deadline stipulated in the contract. Page four," said Bob, tapping the documents.

A feeling of general irritability settled in the room before a strange chain reaction started: Alex, who had already started to review the papers, raised his eyes and exchanged a silent glance with Marcel; Marcel looked at Siobhan; Siobhan looked at Alex, and he closed the circle with Gunton.

"End of September? That gives them only three months, Bob. With all due respect, I don't think that's realistic."

"Depends how you look at it. I understand it didn't take Siobhan long to write *With Fate on Our Side*. Or am I wrong about that?"

She didn't like being used as an example because she knew exactly what would happen next.

"You're not wrong, but the thing is . . ."

Marcel shook his head, his eyes issuing sparks.

"You don't get it, Bob," he snapped. "It's wonderful that Little Miss Speedy Pen can type up her fairy tale in five minutes, but I'm not going to allow my name to appear on the cover of some tearjerker crap that's sold on the supermarket shelf. Three months isn't enough to plan a crime novel under the best of circumstances. Even less so if I have to take the time to explain the basic rules of the genre to the cowriter."

"Might I remind my cowriter, in case he has forgotten, that the novel has to be romantic too," said Siobhan.

Type up.

Fairy tale.

Tearjerker crap.

Why did he hate romance so much? Despite that, he wasn't wrong. How could they write a novel in three months when they couldn't stand the sight of each other? How could an inexperienced writer like her meet the expectations of such a demanding author? And there was another small detail to consider, one that no one had mentioned yet: Siobhan worked full-time. How would she find the time to work with this man?

Suddenly, the editor's face clouded with annoyance.

"Jesus, Marcel! I'm offering you a very generous advance, and you do nothing but complain like a spoiled child." He rubbed his face in his hands. "I'm fed up with your capriciousness. Sort it out however you like, but I want a decent manuscript by the end of September. Period."

"You mean a manuscript that pleases Letitia Wright."

Gunton ignored him.

"What do you think, Siobhan?"

Despite all her reservations, her career was on the line. She knew there was only one answer.

"I'll do everything I can to make it work."

"Finally, someone showing a bit of common sense! Do you have any concerns about the contract?"

"Now that you mention it . . ." Siobhan flipped over the document and pointed at a figure: "Is this correct? I mean . . . isn't seventy-five thousand dollars too much for an advance?"

"Oh come on!" said Marcel. "Where did they find you, princess? Neverland?"

"Can't you at least try to treat me like an adult?"

"An adult wouldn't make a dumb comment like that."

Alex gave him a reproachful glare.

"Can I give you some advice?" he said, turning to Siobhan. She nodded. "Never tell an editor they're paying you too much, or they'll take you at your word. Taking things literally is common in this industry. No offense, Bob." Bob raised his hands and shook his head. "Believe me, it's not too much. A publisher like Baxter can afford it. Besides, it's much less than Marcel usually gets."

"That's all I need," he muttered. He seemed very sure of himself, while Siobhan struggled to clear her throat.

Alex Shapiro's openness was comforting. Nevertheless, a twinge of frustration niggled at her. She had scarcely been there twenty minutes and she had been made painfully aware of how little she knew. Who was she trying to kid? She knew almost nothing about this business.

"Thanks for the advice."

Alex smiled.

"Well, if there are no objections, let's get on with signing this thing," Bob said, handing Siobhan a pen. "I have tickets for *The Phantom of the Opera*, and I promised my wife I wouldn't be late."

"One moment."

Bob sighed.

"What now, Marcel?"

"Seeing as I'm the one putting my reputation on the line with this . . . publishing experiment, I demand a fairer division of the royalties. Ten percent for me and two percent for her."

"But—"

"It's nonnegotiable," he said, implacable as a steamroller.

What a bastard.

"It's okay, Bob. I understand," Siobhan said. "I'm not doing this for the money, so I don't mind if he takes the greater share of the profits."

"In that case, you won't mind if we make a slight adjustment to the advance, either? Four hundred and seventy-five thousand dollars for me, twenty-five for you."

Siobhan felt the bitter taste of humiliation in her mouth.

"Wait. You're pocketing four hundred and twenty-five thousand dollars and you're haggling just to annoy me?"

She could feel a pulse in her temple again as Marcel tried unsuccessfully to hide the terrifying smile of a psychopath.

"Something like that."

Bastard! That's too good a word for him.

She sighed with pure exhaustion.

"All right. Twenty-five thousand dollars is still a more-than-generous amount for a new author."

"Marcel, rein it in a bit, can't you?" murmured Alex.

"Are you my agent or Miss Harris's?" he said. "I'm not finished yet. Given that I am by far the more experienced of the two, I want a clause in the contract specifying that I decide on the working dynamic. And one more thing: I'm not leaving Manhattan."

That was no surprise. Manhattanites were known for their unwillingness to leave the island.

"Teamwork really isn't your thing, is it?" said Siobhan. "Do you have some kind of social phobia or what?"

"You got me," he admitted. Then, he stood up so abruptly that the chair almost tipped over. He caught it by the back just in time and tucked it under the table. "Bob, make sure you change the figures and include that clause if you want me to sign this lousy contract. And now, if you'll excuse me, I'm leaving; I've had enough for today. My agent will call you, princess. In the meantime, lay off the sugar."

He slammed the door as he left the room, making Siobhan jump. The room fell silent.

"Does he always do just as he pleases?"

Alex looked at her almost pityingly.

"Ninety percent of the time."

"And the other 10 percent?"

"He's asleep. Some time ago I compiled all his eccentricities into an Excel sheet. I can send it to you. You know, so you can get used to him."

How lovely.

◆ ◆ ◆

Paige's face appeared in the upper left-hand corner of her cell phone screen.

"Hey, hey, hey," she said. "How was the meeting? I'm dying of curiosity."

"Me too," said Lena, in the lower right-hand corner. "Tell us everything."

"Sorry, girls, I can't breathe a word. If I break the confidentiality agreement, they'll pluck me like a chicken. Mr. Black," she emphasized ironically, "is obsessed with preserving his secret identity. It's classified information."

"Mr. Black? So he's an old-timer," noted Paige, as she checked for split ends in her attractive red mane.

"Well, no, not an old-timer."

"So, how old is he?"

"I'm not saying a word."

"But his age doesn't reveal anything about his identity," pointed out Lena.

"Could you at least tell us whether he's attractive?"

"He can't be," said Lena. "If he was, he wouldn't have maintained his anonymity. Appearance is only an Achilles' heel for women—if you're not good-looking, they dismiss you; too good-looking, and no one takes you seriously. But no one would call into question the literary quality of a male writer just because he's attractive; on the contrary, his looks would be a wonderful strategy for selling more books."

"Are you suggesting I'm not good-looking?" asked Siobhan, feigning indignation.

"Of course you are, Shiv. Although you don't have that kind of over-the-top beauty that makes men dislocate their necks to look at you in the street. Thankfully," she emphasized. "Yours is a more . . . serene kind of beauty."

"Serene."

"Mm-hmm. Much less problematic. If you ever decide to leave the dark side to embrace the light, I have a bunch of girlfriends who would be happy to show you the way."

Siobhan laughed.

"Hey, being straight is cool too," Paige protested. "Can we focus on Marcel Black for now, please? Come on, Shiv, don't leave us hanging. Is he handsome?"

Siobhan flopped back on her bed, holding her cell phone above her.

"Very. He's very handsome."

Paige squealed.

"I knew it! Didn't I tell you both? Why do you never listen to my female intuition? Okay, so, on a scale of one to ten, how good is he?"

"Hmmm . . ." Siobhan bit her lower lip. "Eleven. And he doesn't look a bit like Philip Seymour Hoffman in *Capote*. You were way off the mark."

"Eleven? Wow. Damn. Things are getting interesting."

"In fact . . . ," she said. "The moment I saw him I blurted out, 'You're sexy.' It was mortifying."

"Whaaaaaat?"

"Nooooo!"

"I've never been so embarrassed in my life," she said, blushing as she recalled the scene. "He must have thought I'm some kind of crazy stalker who has no filter. And no wonder. Normal people don't go around telling strangers they're sexy. It just popped out. I suppose I wasn't expecting such a hot piece of ass."

"Okay," said Lena. "Is this going to make it hard to write this novel together? I mean . . . you know. The fact that you're attracted to him?"

Siobhan let out a strangled laugh.

"To that joy-sucking narcissist? Me? Hell no! His looks were impressive, but I got over it as soon as he opened his mouth. He's even nastier than he was on Twitter. You know what that jerk called me? Princess."

Paige ground her teeth.

"What a cocksucker."

"Handsome, arrogant, and rude. Bleurgh. He's like the hero of an aughties novel, the kind that idealizes toxic relationships and characterizes women as emotionally dependent. No doubt he's loaded too," added Lena. "You know, you don't have to go through with this. There's still time to back out. No one would blame you."

"The thing is I've signed the contract. And now we've got three months to deliver the manuscript. Three. Lousy. Months. I honestly don't know how I'm going to do it. Oh god." She sighed and covered her face with her hands. "Please tell me I haven't made a huge mistake."

"Of course not. You did the right thing," Paige reassured her. "It's a golden opportunity. You're going to write a novel with an internationally renowned author! He might be a pig-headed asshole. But, in the Olympus of literary gods, this guy is Zeus."

"More like Hades," Lena said.

"But he hates romance novels! He says they're sappy nonsense, and he doesn't even regard it as literature. I just don't understand why he agreed to do it. What does he get out of it?"

"Think of it as cross-pollination. He helps you make your name, and you help him make money, simple as that. You'll find a way to manage the situation, you'll see."

"Have you heard of *kairos*? In all lives, even the shittiest, the universe gives you at least one opportunity to change things. *Kairos* is the decisive moment that you can't let slip through your fingers. Even if it's only a very brief moment. And life doesn't give second chances," explained Paige.

"What is it with you and the Greeks?" Lena asked.

"Oh, I watched *Troy* again last night. What I mean to say is that this could be your decisive moment. So forget about the vertigo, okay? You have more than enough talent, Siobhan Harris."

"Totally agree. Anyway, be careful. I don't trust people who reject emotional relationships; it's highly likely this guy is hiding some kind of trauma. Oh, and if he dares to cross the line during these three months, I'll be sure to start a defamation campaign on the internet that he'll remember for the rest of his days."

"I'm all for that. I like fucking with people's reputations," said Paige.

When the call ended, Siobhan lay on her bed for a while, thinking. Marcel Dupont's beautiful features burrowed into her thoughts again. What was his story? Why had he chosen to be anonymous? She opened Twitter and started inspecting his account. He hadn't posted anything since that fateful night, nearly a week ago now. It was clear that she wasn't going to find anything of interest there. She rummaged in her purse for the copy of *An Ordinary Man*, which she had bought in a bookstore in Union Square after leaving the meeting. Marcel Black's first novel had run to nineteen editions so far. She stroked the cover gently, almost respectfully. She hadn't read anything of his—she hadn't ever read a crime novel, in fact—and she felt it was important to do so. If you can't beat them, join them. She opened the book and took a deep breath. She was impressed by the opening line.

William J. Knox had everything and nothing at all.

How much of himself was there in those words? She read the first page. Then the second. Then, a few more, to the end of the chapter. She read another, then another. She skipped dinner to keep reading. When she finally finished the book, it was three in the morning. Her heart was racing. She was shaken, overwhelmed. The strength of his writing style had impressed her.

Marcel was good.

He was more than good.

He was brilliant.

And he was playing in a much higher league.

PART TWO

Conflict

Chapter 7

Siobhan

The Saturday after signing the contract, Siobhan slipped into her favorite floral dress and ordered an Uber. Alex Shapiro had invited her to meet Marcel in an Upper East Side bistro for their first brainstorming session.

"My assistant has reserved a table for you," he had told her on the phone a few days earlier. "It's a discreet place but very expensive. Make sure you hang on to your receipts."

"Don't tell me you're leaving me all alone with Shrek."

Alex laughed knowingly.

"You'll be fine. Believe me, this ogre isn't as offensive as he looks."

That remained to be seen.

The driver stopped in front of Café Boulud about ten minutes before the meeting was due to start. Siobhan gave her full name at reception, and a waiter led her to a small private room. It wasn't hard to imagine the odious Mr. Black sitting there, sipping coffee from a tiny Limoges porcelain cup with his little finger sticking out. As she waited for Mr. Bestseller to appear, she ordered a cappuccino, which arrived almost immediately, accompanied by some macarons on an elegant rectangular slate. The arrangement was so absurdly charming that she couldn't resist taking a photo and posting it on Twitter.

Click.

> **Siobhan Harris** @siobhan_harris 1m
> Which of these delicacies shall I sink my teeth into first? I'll decide while I'm waiting for @InvisibleBlack in a super-secret location on the Upper East Side. Today is our first session together! Wish me luck 🤞
> #CrimePlusRomance

It had been a crazy week. Baxter Books had made the big announcement about the collaboration between the two authors. The sensation of the season was due to arrive this fall—this fall!—and the internet was talking about nothing else. If announcing the launch of a novel that wasn't even written yet was meant to be a pressure tactic, it was working; for her, at least. The notifications on her account kept flooding in, with new followers by the dozen. Whether they were congratulating her or wishing her luck, Siobhan spent more than two hours a day responding to messages. And then there were her own readers, who grew apace with her popularity; even more so after Letitia Wright had publicly announced that *With Fate on Our Side* was the most beautiful romance novel she had read in a long time. It was overwhelming, but the least she could do was appear grateful. Marcel hadn't even bothered to acknowledge it. It was clear that she would have to be the visible face of the project, which had its advantages and disadvantages. Who would the critics tear into, once the book was published? The highly respected crime author or the aspiring writer of love stories?

The balance could only swing one way.

This had also been the week of her first negative review. Although calling it *negative* when she could say *painful as a paper shredder* was being generous. Siobhan knew the theory all too well. *Don't let it affect you. It's just an opinion. Your book isn't Henry Cavill, not everyone is going to like it. Blah blah blah* . . . But theory was one thing, and practice was quite another. She had known this moment would come sooner or later—Bella had warned her about first negative review syndrome—but she still wasn't ready for the reality of it. When Paige and Lena found out, they hotfooted it to her apartment with a Baskin-Robbins ice cream cake and a bottle of vodka for damage control.

If that wasn't friendship, she didn't know what was.

"Whoever wrote that crap doesn't know what they're talking about," said an affronted Paige. "Buckley might be a lot of things, but he's not manipulative. He's just a first-degree jerk with serious commitment issues."

"You mean Damon," Lena corrected her.

"Damon is based on her ex. Or don't you remember? Anyway, in the hypothetical case of Shiv having created a dark male Hardin Scott–style protagonist, what would be the problem?"

"I guess dark is a euphemism for possessive and controlling."

"Wake up, Lena. It's fiction. F-I-C-T-I-O-N. If all the characters behaved impeccably all the time, there would be no conflict."

"Systematically reproducing certain behaviors, even if only fictitiously, merely serves to perpetuate said behavior. The message behind stories like *After* is that it's okay for a man to control even the clothes you wear because that means he loves you."

"Come off it! The message behind *After* is that there is no message. Two college students who spend more time partying than in class start screwing like rabbits. He's off his frickin' rocker and surprise! So is she. It turns out women can behave reprehensibly too. Have you seen *My Best Friend's Wedding*? Julia Roberts couldn't be more toxic in that movie. Did she really have to ruin Dermot Mulroney and Cameron Diaz's big day?"

"Spoiler: in the end she doesn't ruin it."

"Because she knows that her chances with him are precisely zero, not out of any sense of sisterhood. Anyway, it doesn't matter. Getting back to the point, the reading comprehension of whoever wrote this review is nil. How dare she say your style is boring?" She snorted. "We've read different books."

"She's just a hater," said Lena. "I've looked at other ratings she's given, and it's a pattern. Maybe we could get her blocked."

Siobhan disagreed. Much as it hurt, she had to be professional about it. And being professional involved swallowing her pride and accepting that not every story is right for every reader all the time. No drama. Unfortunately, that crappy comment had arrived just when her self-assurance was starting to wobble.

It was a maddening fact of life that a single negative opinion could drown out dozens of positive voices.

She checked the time with a sigh. That prize imbecile was late. She was about to pop a macaron in her mouth but changed her mind. As tempting as the colorful treats were, she wasn't about to risk her colleague—could she call him a colleague?—appearing and catching her off guard. She could almost hear Lena's voice: "Why do you straight women feel vulnerable about a man seeing you eat? It's ridiculous." And it was. The problem: Marcel was just too intimidating. And not just because he was attractive, but also because of that kind of avenging angel's halo that surrounded him and which he was somehow able to convey in his writing. After devouring *An Ordinary Man* and impulse-buying the next three in the series, Siobhan felt even more daunted, intrigued, and attracted than she had been on seeing him for the first time. She still hated him, of course. She sipped her cappuccino and tucked her hair behind her ears. As she did, she noticed her palms were sweaty. *Calm down already!* she berated herself. *This isn't a date, it's a work meeting. And he's nothing more than a man with his ego in his underpants. You can handle it.*

Okay, perhaps thinking about his underpants hadn't been the best idea.

Then her cell phone rang. Unknown number.

"Are you crazy or what?" a voice shouted the moment she answered.

Siobhan immediately recognized the unmistakable Southern drawl.

"Good morning to you too. Don't worry about being late, I have all the time in the world."

"Quit the crap. Why the hell did you post that tweet?"

A thin veil of sweat broke out on Siobhan's upper lip. She didn't know how to answer and hesitated for a moment.

"Which tweet?"

"I think you know."

"Ah, you mean *that* tweet," she bluffed. "Don't tell me you're pissed about that."

"The term *pissed* doesn't even come close to it at this precise moment. It would be more accurate to say livid, furious, or completely and utterly apeshit."

"Gosh, your lexical range is surprisingly broad."

Marcel exhaled indignantly.

"You think you're so clever, don't you, princess? Well, let's see if you still want to joke about it when you realize you've infringed on the confidentiality agreement."

Siobhan frowned.

"Hey, stop right there. And don't call me princess! What do you mean, I've infringed on the confidentiality agreement? I don't see the problem," she said, defending herself. "The only thing the tweet says is that I'm waiting for you somewhere on the Upper East Side."

"Exactly. Somewhere whose name can be clearly seen in the photo you posted."

Something exploded in her brain. Her eyes swiveled to look at the wall. Only then did she realize that right next to the door of the small private room was a huge sign with the bistro's logo. "Café Boulud" was spelled out in black lettering against a white background. She squeezed her eyes shut.

This was a fuckup of epic proportions.

She swallowed before murmuring:

"Oh."

"Yes, *oh*." Marcel let out a sigh that seemed to go on forever. "I knew this would be a mistake. It makes no sense for us to write a novel together; we're too different. This is just a game to you."

This statement lit a fire inside her; even so, she was too ashamed to deny it.

"I'm sorry, all right? I didn't even realize the sign was there. If I had . . . Well, I suppose it doesn't matter now. I'll delete the tweet right away."

"Don't bother on my account. I'm not coming anyway."

"What do you mean, you're not coming?"

"It's too risky. And I'm not in the mood. The meeting will have to wait. Alex will call you."

"But—"

Too late, he had hung up. Suddenly, Siobhan felt very selfish. Okay, so Marcel was paranoid, and it would be quite a coincidence for anyone to find him right here, at this precise moment, just because of her tweet. But life was full of coincidences. She shouldn't have posted it. Whatever the reason, his secret identity was fundamental to him. Siobhan didn't understand why, nor did she need to; all she had to do was respect his wishes and stick to the contract. The conversation still reverberated in her eardrums. Something halfway between a sigh and a groan escaped from her throat. She hated to admit it, but Marcel was entirely right. It made no sense for them to write a novel together. She thought about the events of the morning, about what would crop up next, about the terrible summer she was about to spend with him. She took a breath and decided to call Alex to see if he could help salvage the situation. Whatever happened, time was not on their side; they couldn't afford to waste another day. And contrary to what that ogre thought, this wasn't a game to Siobhan.

Ding.

A text message popped up on her phone.

212-500-0303

Can I trust you to be the responsible adult you claim to be? M.

Siobhan's eyes widened and she read it again. Did this mean all was not lost? It certainly seemed so.

Siobhan

Absolutely 😬

And a moment later.

212-500-0303

1010 5th Ave. Tell my concierge when you get here. And please, try not to publish my address on Twitter.

Chapter 8

Siobhan

Located across from the Met, the building had a limestone facade typical of the Upper East Side. She braced herself as she pushed open the door and entered the luminous marble lobby. A huge glass chandelier hung from the ceiling, radiating a dazzling light. The doorman, a Latino of around fifty, watched her from the other side of his curved desk.

"Can I help you, miss?"

"I'm here to see Marcel Bla—Dupont." She forced a smile. "Marcel Dupont." It was the first time she had uttered his name out loud, and she liked the way it sounded. "My name is Siobhan Harris."

"Yes, of course. Mr. Dupont told me he was expecting you. Go right on up to the penthouse."

"All right. Thanks."

On the way up, she inspected her appearance in the mirror of the elegant, gold-buttoned elevator. Hair in place, yes. Bits of food between her teeth, no. Dress sitting smoothly, yes. Sweat stains under her armpits, no. With a gentle shudder, the elevator came to a halt on the top floor. Siobhan took a deep breath, pressed her lips together to redistribute the lip balm she had just applied, and made for the solid walnut door. She rang the bell and waited, holding a Lady M Mille Crêpes cake that she had picked up as a peace offering on the way over. An unfamiliar sensation sprang up in her chest; she couldn't tell if she was excited or annoyed at her excitement. When Marcel appeared before her, a hint of expensive perfume wafted around her. He was wearing a dark shirt, open at the neck, allowing a glimpse of his brown skin beneath. He studied her with that disconcertingly intimate gaze that made her wonder if he could read her mind. Was she an open book to him?

What a terrifying possibility.

Siobhan cleared her throat and took the initiative.

"Before you say anything, I want you to know I'm really sorry about what happened. I'm grateful to you for inviting me here because that means you're trying to build a bridge between us. And to show that the goodwill is reciprocal . . . ta-da! I've brought you a cake," she announced, holding it out in front of her.

When she heard the hopeful note in her voice, she knew she had made a mistake.

Marcel remained impassive, not even blinking.

"I don't like sweets. I thought I'd made that clear if nothing else. And don't get excited, princess. You're only here because we've signed a contract."

What a prick.

Marcel had addressed her with such indifference that Siobhan ground her teeth. She wasn't expecting him to get down on his knees, but a bit of civility would make a nice change. Why was she demeaning herself for an asshole like him? Someone who turns their nose up at a Lady M cake deserves to go straight to hell.

"All right, all right. You know what? I can handle you not liking me. In fact, I'm not that into you either."

Marcel's full lips curved into a smug grimace.

"Quel dommage," he lamented. "You'd better come in."

Suddenly an electric tingle ran down her arms and legs. The idea of being alone with Marcel, on his turf, made her feel as vulnerable as a deer on a hunting reserve. His success didn't change the fact that he was a complete stranger. A tall stranger surrounded by a dangerous aura. Her face burned with shame. Or perhaps something else.

"Are you planning to stay out here all day, Siobhan?"

Despite everything, there was something warm about the way he said her name.

"Don't tell me you're afraid of being alone with a Black man?" he said, eyebrows raised in feigned concern.

The jerk-o-meter suddenly went up five points.

"You're a bit obsessed with the color of your skin, aren't you?"

"So speaks white privilege."

"Look who's talking about privilege," muttered Siobhan, entering the apartment with a sigh.

The living room was stunning. Spacious, light, and decorated in pure New York style. Pale neutrals with the odd splash of color, designer furniture—perhaps some ex had picked it out—hardwood floors, a vast leather sofa, and spectacular views of the city and Central Park. There were vinyl records and books everywhere. Siobhan wondered what the detestable Mr. Black read when he wanted to escape from his own world of heinous criminals. Crime novels or something else?

"Do you live alone?" she asked, still looking around her. Interestingly, she couldn't see a single photo to give her clues about Marcel Dupont's history.

She instantly regretted her question. He would think she was prying. Or even worse, that she was interested in his personal life.

"Mm-hmm."

"And your vanity needs all this space?"

The only way to overcome her curiosity was to be as unfriendly as him. (Curiosity = attraction.)

Marcel clutched his chest, as though mortally wounded by her remark.

"You're hardhearted for a romance novelist."

"I'm not the problem here; it's you and your preconceived notions. What is a romance novelist supposed to be like? Enlighten me, please."

"I don't know." He frowned. "Extremely sensitive?"

"Better to be sensitive than insensitive, I would say."

"Are you suggesting that crime writers are insensitive?" He tutted. "And I'm the one with prejudices."

"You must be. How else could you write about things as twisted as torture, rape, or murder and not give yourself nightmares."

"The world's misery is a huge rock that can crush you if you take it personally. You'll learn that as you grow up."

"Ha. Tell me something: Has anyone ever fallen in love in one of your books?"

"Why do you attach such importance to love? Love is a social construct devoid of any real meaning. It's no more than hormones coinciding at the right moment. Oxytocin, to be precise, which is released during copulation. Without it, the human race would have died out long ago. What really brings couples together is a matter of biology, nothing more and nothing less."

"What an aseptic way of looking at it," said Siobhan.

With his pronounced blink, Marcel gave her to understand how little he cared about her opinion on the matter.

"All right. I'll stop talking."

"You, stop talking? I doubt that. You suffer from incurable verbal diarrhea. Give me that."

"What?"

"The cake."

"I thought you didn't want it."

"I don't. I'm just going to put it in the refrigerator for a moment so it doesn't collapse. I wouldn't want you to ruin my $15,000 sofa."

Siobhan grudgingly handed him the box.

"You know there are more important things in life than money, right?"

"Oh yeah? Don't tell me . . . I'll be right back. Make yourself comfortable in the meantime. And don't touch anything."

As he turned around, Siobhan had to fight two impulses:

1) The impulse to throw any sharp object she could find at his departing figure. And

2) The impulse to check out his ass.

The first was easy to control. As for the second, well . . . Let's just say temptation won and scored a home run. *Wow . . . he has an incredible ass.* She immediately shook her head as though trying to erase the image from her mind. She perched on the cherished $15,000 sofa—how could he spend that much on a sofa, when there were people going hungry in the world? It was indecent—and distracted herself by flicking through the books that were sitting on the table. She noticed they were full of annotations in pencil, and she couldn't help but snort. *He's so vain he thinks he has the right to correct other people's work.* Although she had to admit, he was talented. Very talented. She was painfully aware of how good that man was at what he did. His work went straight for the guts from the first sentence. Not a word was wasted. His style was sharp, fierce, almost ruthless, like Marcel himself. And he knew how to get the reader hooked on the story like an addict on their drug of choice. Of course, Siobhan would have rather given a pound of her own flesh to Shylock before admitting that to him.

If a man's ego could be measured in degrees, his would spark wildfires.

Marcel returned to the living room with a bottle of water and two tumblers on a tray, which he set down on the table. He was wearing glasses that gave him a sexy university professor look. Naturally Siobhan berated herself for her wild imagination. What on earth was happening to her? First she checked out his ass, and now she was fantasizing about a private tutoring session. Great. As if it wasn't humiliating enough to be attracted to a guy who had made a point of showing his superiority on multiple occasions. He might be a literary genius, but he was also nasty and hypocritical, and from the way he behaved it was clear he believed he was the only author able to write decent books in the whole of America. Or maybe even the whole world. He sat at the other end of the sofa. Siobhan smiled, her polite way of calling him an idiot. From her purse, she took out a pen decorated with a Christmas motif—yes, she loved Christmas, so what?—and a brightly colored notebook with the phrase "Unicorns Do Exist" on the cover. Marcel's expression said it all: he was judging her. *Just remember, he never misses a chance to exploit someone's weakness.* At least he refrained from verbalizing whatever he was thinking.

"I have some ideas," announced Siobhan, spreading the notebook open on her lap like a diligent pupil.

"If they have anything to do with vampires or millionaires with sadomasochist tendencies, I'm not listening to them."

"Oh please, Marcel. Toxic masculinity went out of fashion in . . . 2014? Paige would probably argue about the date, but it's a fact. Paige is my best friend. One of them," she explained.

"Toxic masculinity. Okay," he repeated, trying to assimilate the concept. "So, let's talk about these ideas of yours."

"What do you think of this: a Brooklyn police officer falls in love with his female patrol partner."

Silence.

"Is that it? Where's the conflict? There is no conflict. And I hate Brooklyn."

"What's wrong with Brooklyn?"

"Apart from the fact that it's New York's largest borough and therefore the place where most things happen? Oh nothing, nothing at all. Except it's a fucking cliché."

"You don't like clichés."

"Very good, you're catching on."

"Well, there are always some in romance novels. From enemies to lovers, from friends to lovers, love triangles, second chances, forced marriage, fake relationships . . ."

"What's the point in faking a relationship?"

"It's very useful if you want to make your ex jealous."

"No comment," muttered Marcel.

"Okay, next idea. A police officer from"—she shook her hand—"from wherever, falls in love with a murder witness."

Marcel fell back against the sofa cushion, sighing in boredom. He crossed his arms behind his head and spread his legs wide like the lousy alpha male he thought he was. He looked at Siobhan with a strange glint in his eye and asked:

"Why don't we make him fall in love with the murderer?"

"Are you crazy? No way. Everything has its limits, and this limit is moral integrity. People fall in love with someone's goodness, intelligence, passion, or courage."

"And can't those qualities be extrapolated to a criminal mind? Or, in your opinion, bad people are bad by definition, and the good are paragons of virtue." He laughed through that ridiculously perfect nose of his. "You'd be surprised at how relative things are, Siobhan. Anyway, I didn't know the writer had an obligation to incorporate the rules of real life into fiction. I thought literature was a way to explore, not to correct, the world. Let's suppose for a minute that the police officer doesn't know the woman is a murderer. Let's imagine he finds out later. Would his feelings be justified in that case?"

"Possibly, although we still wouldn't have a plot for the novel."

"Why not?"

"Because then a happy ending would be impossible. I mean, no one marries a murderer, no matter how loved-up they are. Think about the societal pressure of something like that. And one of the characteristics of the romance genre is precisely that. Happily ever after." She tapped her pen in emphasis.

Marcel raised his eyebrows as if he couldn't believe what he had just heard.

"Bullshit."

"Pardon?"

"It's ridiculous to limit the development of a novel by forcing it to have a prefabricated ending, just because consumers of the genre are immature and still believe in fairy tales."

"This has nothing to do with fairy tales. It's about not perpetuating a cycle of misfortune," countered Siobhan, annoyed.

"Oh please! All the great love stories have a tragic ending. *Romeo and Juliet*, *Wuthering Heights*, *Madame Bovary*, *Anna Karenina*, *Tristan and Isolde*, *The Age of Innocence* . . . even *Beauty and the Beast* ends badly. Jeez."

"*Beauty and the Beast* does not end badly."

"So it might seem. But what kind of future can you expect from a relationship born of an abduction? That girl has full-blown Stockholm syndrome. What's the matter, Miss Harris? Had you never considered that? No, of course not." He smiled condescendingly. "Do me a favor and revise your position on toxic masculinities, because I'd say you need an updated version."

Siobhan felt a hot wave rising to her cheeks. She took a calming sip of water. When she had composed herself, she said:

"Whether you like it or not, the rules are what they are. A romance novel has to have a love story driving the plot and a happy ending."

"Who says so?"

"RWA. And we aren't about to break the rules just because your heart is tougher than old shoe leather."

Marcel tried unsuccessfully to hide his laughter with a cough. He shook his head and countered:

"The heart is just an organ. It has no sensibility, conscience, or feelings; it simply beats and keeps us alive. Did you miss biology class that day, princess?"

"I don't know why you can't get it into your skull that every genre has its own conventions. A crime novel where the crime isn't solved by the end would be inconceivable, don't you think? And I've told you several times," she said, her voice rising, "not to call me that!"

Her patience was wearing extremely thin. The man riled her every time he opened his mouth. She rubbed her temple. She felt a headache brewing, and there was still a long day ahead.

"We'll see. Where's your sense of humor?"

"The same place as your feelings. Oh wait." She gave a fake smile. "You don't have any!"

He raised his hands, as if surrendering. She noticed a hint of defeat in the slight tension in his eyes, in the vague gesture of his lips. It served him right.

Then a silence fell.

A minute passed.

Two.

Three.

Neither one of them said a word. Siobhan drummed her Christmas pen on her notebook, casting the occasional sideways glance at Marcel, who was pacing like a caged panther. His left hand was plunged into his jeans pocket, while the right stroked his stubble. *He's very handsome when he's thinking; he should do it more often.* He had rolled his shirt sleeves up to the elbows; the veins of his powerful forearms reminded her of rivers on a map.

He stopped abruptly, looked down at her, and said:

"What if the murderer was a kind of female vigilante who only takes down bad guys?"

"Like in *Dexter*?"

"Something like that. Could we use that?"

"That wouldn't excuse her from her crimes. Although readers might find it easier to empathize with her."

"Since when has it been necessary for readers to empathize with a character?"

"Well, it's kind of a given in romance novels."

Marcel took off his glasses and gently massaged the bridge of his nose.

"We've spent a half hour trying to come up with a decent plot, but it turns out the ten commandments of the FFTA are a fucking pain in the ass. A happy ending, perfect characters . . . God, this is torture!"

"The FFTA?"

"The Friends of Fairy Tales Association. We still haven't discussed the crime, and might I remind you there has to be at least one." His tone dropped until it reached the pitch typical of men when they want you to do as they say. "Why don't we stop circling round this romance nonsense and focus on the important part?"

If there was a perfect moment to put him in his place, this had to be it.

"For $475,000, surely you can take care of the important part on your own," Siobhan said, her chest brimming with a malevolent joy.

How sweet the taste of revenge.

He clenched his jaw as she had noticed him doing before. It had been a low blow, but what the hell, he deserved it.

"I need to go to the bathroom," she said then.

Release the bomb, let it explode, and get the hell out of there—an advanced survival technique.

"Upstairs, second door on the right. Try not to make a mess."

She climbed the modern L-shaped stairs, cursing inwardly, and locked herself in the luxurious bathroom. His cleaner deserved every dollar; although no doubt that miser only paid a pittance. She turned on the faucet, wet her face to refresh herself, and then dried it. She dried the splashes of water around the basin too, just to be on the safe side. *Try not to make a mess nah nah nah . . . I don't like sweets nah nah nah . . . The heart is just an organ nah nah . . .* Beauty and the Beast *ends badly nah nah.*

"Argh!" she groaned. "He's driving me up the wall!"

This was going to be much harder than she had thought. She sighed in resignation and left the bathroom. Passing the next door along the hallway, she couldn't help a furtive glance inside. It was Marcel's bedroom. She had never liked nosing around other people's rooms. As a child, she had seen *The Texas Chain Saw Massacre*, and she knew what might happen. But it was undeniable that you could discover a great deal of information from someone's bedroom. If she had gone in and looked through the window, she would have been able to look down on the highest point of Roosevelt Island, with its strange geometry of low brick buildings. She would also have seen a king-size bed with a dark satin cover—was he allergic to color or something?—the pile of books sitting on his nightstand next to a minimalist lamp, and a cavernous walk-in closet. And then there were all the things that couldn't be seen, that remained concealed in drawers, in the walls, between the sheets. Dark but latent, trapped but alive.

So many secrets.

She knew who Marcel Black was. But she doubted she would ever really know Marcel Dupont. But then . . . did it matter? They would write this lousy novel and then never see each other again. Destiny would carry her in the opposite direction from his unbreachable wall of privacy. And if at any point she dared to cross that threshold, even just with one toe, Mr. Black/Dupont was quite capable of kicking her down, literally.

A shudder ran through her as she headed down the stairs.

Back in the living room, he was waiting on the sofa.

"Something has occurred to me," he announced. "It might be a tad complicated to bring together, bearing in mind how little time we have."

"I like complicated. Go ahead, I'm all ears."

"Time travel."

She could barely contain her laughter.

"Ha ha. In Scotland, right? With warring clans, kilts, and all the rest of it. I'm sorry, I think Diana Gabaldon got there before you," she said.

"What? Who the hell said anything about Scotland? If you could allow me to explain my idea, perhaps we could actually get somewhere and be done with this once and for all. I don't particularly want to spend the rest of my day here with you opening and closing doors like in that Monty Hall paradox." Siobhan sighed and gestured for him to continue. "Okay. The protagonist is a late-nineteenth-century crime novelist who—"

"Crime novelist. Seriously?"

"There's a reason, you'll see. Let's say our man accidentally travels to New York in the future and—"

"New York? God, how dull! What if we made it London? I love London!" said Siobhan. "Notting Hill, the British Museum, red telephone boxes . . . Oh, it's so romantic."

Marcel furrowed his brow. His feline features adopted a mocking expression.

"Romantic? Don't make me laugh. The British Museum represents the greatest archaeological plunder in the world, and the phone boxes smell of piss, the few that are left. Perhaps Bridget Jones could stop interrupting me, please?" Siobhan closed an imaginary zipper across her lips. "Thank you. Okay, let's see, where was I? Our own Raymond Chandler suddenly wakes up in the twenty-first century. New York is deep in a devastating financial and social crisis where the rich are getting richer and the poor are getting poorer. The system is riddled with corruption. Criminals impose their own law on the street. A climate of prerevolutionary violence prevails in Manhattan."

"Like in Gotham City."

"Our man, let's call him . . ."

"Jeremiah."

". . . meets a stubborn journalist who decides on her own initiative to investigate a blood-curdling murder case that's . . . kind of old school. As he tries to adapt to this new setting, Jeremiah helps . . ."

"Felicity."

"Felicity? Jeez. Can't you come up with a less ridiculous name?" Siobhan narrowed her eyes for a second; long enough for Marcel to see. "Okay, whatever," he said. "Jeremiah helps Felicity solve the case."

"And falls in love with her."

"Whatever. In any case, we'll complicate things. We'll make everyone look suspicious to throw the reader off the scent. Each character will try to trick the others, and the truth will only slowly become clear through the haze of deceit, like in the classic novels."

"Their relationship will be complicated too. They are very different people and constantly clash. Of course, therein lies the key. Opposites attract," stated Siobhan. "And what happens at the end?"

"They catch the killer. And the dollar depreciates significantly as a result of the economic crisis."

"But presumably, once the investigation is wrapped up, he has to return to the nineteenth century. Unless . . ."

"He has nothing in his own time to go back for," concluded Marcel.

"Exactly. Maybe Jeremiah lost his wife to a fever shortly after they married. He drinks to escape from it all, and, to the great consternation of Mr. Pemberly, his editor, he isn't able to write a single word. And if that wasn't enough, he squandered the last cent of his fortune in a gambling den. The debts are piling up, his creditors are after him."

"Bad business."

"A very bad business. So the door to the future opens at just the right moment. As for Felicity, she's a hopeless romantic."

"But she's a journalist," Marcel objected.

"So what?"

"Didn't you say people who live surrounded by mundane evils are insensitive by default?"

"I've changed my mind."

Marcel smiled, showing a row of perfect white teeth. And that smile, even though it only lasted a second, made him slightly more human.

"Why is it so important that she's a romantic?"

"We need it for the plot," explained Siobhan, as though it was obvious. "Let's say that her way of understanding relationships is rather . . . traditional. Hence the fact that she's had no luck with the men she's met up to that point. Deep down, she dreams of meeting a gentleman to sweep her off her feet."

"Or a crime novelist," he said.

For the next few hours, Siobhan took notes like a madwoman. They worked out a good part of the plot, identified the most significant twists, and called out details as they thought of them. Incredibly, things were finally starting to flow between them. Marcel organized the project. He would take care of the chapters narrated from Jeremiah's point of view, and she would do Felicity's. The story would start with her in the present day. Once she had completed the introduction, Siobhan would leave the file in a shared folder on the cloud so that Marcel could read and edit it before picking up the thread himself. And so on.

"We'll work more efficiently that way, and we won't even have to see each other again," he said.

"We won't see each other again?"

"Why would you want to see a man you're not that into?"

"No reason," she answered quickly. "No reason at all."

A spark of something she was unable to identify seemed to light up in Marcel's gaze.

"That's what I thought. I'd say that's enough for today," he said, checking his watch. "I'll ask my assistant to look up some books or articles that might be useful to us. In the meantime, get as much down on paper as you can."

"You have an assistant?"

"Actually, I have two. But I'm not about to share either one with you. I'm too . . . toxic," he said. "I'll see you to the door."

She gathered her things and stuffed them in her purse. Why was she suddenly sorry to be leaving? She didn't understand her unexpected frustration. She followed Marcel to the door. He placed his hand on the knob and looked at her. He emanated a kind of dark brilliance that she was unsure whether to trust. Those eyes shimmered like deep lakes beneath his long lashes. Neither of them moved for five long seconds. Maybe ten. Or maybe more. The tension in the room almost crackled.

"Okay, well . . . see you sometime, I suppose. Although you've made it perfectly clear that won't happen, so . . ."

"Siobhan."

It was almost a whisper. Her heart leaped in her chest.

She noted a stifling heat in her cheeks.

"Yes?"

How could she explain the sweet tingling that was running through her from head to toe?

"You talk too much. Try to keep your internal monologue where it should be—internal."

She felt as though the sun had disappeared behind a thundercloud.

Marcel opened the door, and she left with a bitter taste in the back of her throat.

Chapter 9

Marcel

The next day, Marcel rose early as usual. He threw on his workout clothes and went out for his run around Great Hill, at the north end of Central Park. The park wasn't busy at that time of day; only the footsteps of other early-bird runners interrupted the Sunday-morning tranquility. Later in the day, the hill would fill up with families enjoying a picnic beneath the elm trees, folks playing Frisbee on the grass, and some jazz musician or other. He was listening to jazz as he ran. "Take Five," by Dave Brubeck; one of his all-time favorites. Listening to it transported him to New Orleans: nights in the Spotted Cat, the taste of a Sazerac, and those erratic summer storms that caught him off guard and forced him to pin himself against a wall while the water splashed his ankles. That morning, however, Marcel's mind was distracted by something closer to home.

Or someone, to be precise.

Siobhan Harris.

The naive, insolent, and insufferable Miss Harris.

He grunted as he lengthened his strides. He was running so fast it was like he was trying to flee something. When he had decided to knock off William J. Knox, he never imagined he would end up involved in a situation like this—one in which he found himself about to write a novel he didn't believe in, just because his idiotic editor had threatened to let the cat out of the bag. He would have a draft in three months, no question, but he had a deep hatred of obligation. If working under pressure wasn't his strong suit, doing so as part of a team was even less so. This young woman who looked like she was about to attend her first English lit class had altered his internal chemistry, and it was irritating. A spark of fury tightened his cheeks; then he calmed himself, grudgingly admitting that his mood, somewhere between ill humor and excitement, could be explained by the bond of sorts that had sprung up between them without Marcel realizing or intending it to. The fact that he couldn't stop thinking about her disturbed him. For god's sake, they didn't even get along! Hours after she had left his apartment, he could still discern her disconcertingly pleasant aroma of fresh coconut. He was surprised by his desire to savor it until it dissipated. His heart rate increased as he pounded up the path to the top of the hill. He thought of her sitting on the sofa, resolved not to let her nerves show, although her body language gave her away, with that stupid rookie's notebook on her lap and that frightfully ordinary dress she must have bought at Macy's. Good lord, her style couldn't be more off-putting. Even so, she was natural. And attractive. God, yes. She had beautiful blue eyes that observed everything around her with vitality. She hadn't realized he had been studying her. The way she played with her bracelets. The way she tucked her hair behind her ear or chewed on her pen with that mouth as tempting as a bowl of cherries. He was a writer, so he loved the details. A worrying thought flitted through his mind. Marcel's face contorted in genuine concern before he relaxed again. *No, what nonsense. You don't even like sugar,* he told himself reassuringly. He smiled in relief. He had met far more attractive women in his life. No matter how much she had intoxicated him, it was manageable. You don't get drunk on just one sip. No sir. Marcel knew he could break the spell whenever he wanted, just by snapping his fingers.

Siobhan Harris didn't interest him in the slightest.

An hour later, he stepped out of the shower. He slipped into a white shirt and a pair of jeans and decided to have breakfast at home for once. As he waited for his coffee to brew, he called Alex.

"What time is it? This had better be important. I was in the middle of an incredible dream about Scarlett Johansson in Tokyo. She was wearing a pink wig and I—"

"Wait, don't tell me. You were Bill Murray."

"With much more hair."

"Not that much more."

"Asshole."

Marcel smiled. Annoying Alex was one of his great pleasures in life.

"Well, you'll be pleased to hear that this asshole has worked out the plot of the next Baxter Books moneymaker," he announced. He took a sip of his coffee.

"Really? Tell me everything."

"Oh I will. When you invite me to dinner at one of those swanky fusion restaurants in Tribeca. But to give you a hint, the story centers on time travel."

"Seriously?" Alex sounded skeptical now. "Hasn't that kinda . . . been done already?" he asked.

"Don't worry, my friend. Our novel isn't set in Scotland, if that's what's worrying you."

"Our? As in the plural? Wow. This is what I call a small step for humankind and a great step for the ego of Marcel Black. So you and Siobhan are compatible after all?"

Marcel swallowed. He felt like he'd been slapped in the face: surprised, vulnerable, or a combination of the two.

"Don't talk nonsense, please. The princess and I couldn't have less in common. She's indiscreet and mouthy, and she talks a mile a minute and her worldview is that of a ninth-grader. Heck, she has a notebook with the phrase 'Unicorns Do Exist' on the cover! That girl represents everything I loathe. Would you believe, she showed up at my place with a cake? Shit. Just a sec. The cake. She didn't take it," he muttered.

He opened the huge stainless-steel refrigerator and confirmed that the white Lady M box was still where he had left it the day before.

"Wait, wait, wait. Rewind a moment? I think I've missed an important part of the movie. Did you say Siobhan went to your place? Heavens, you must have been impressed. As far as I know, the only woman you've ever allowed into your luxurious penthouse has been paid in advance. And I mean the cleaner," he hastily clarified.

"Listen, I can assure you that my interest in Siobhan Harris is purely contractual. Once we've finished the novel, it's over. In fact, just yesterday we agreed not to see each other anymore. We'll write separately. End of story."

"Was the experience so bad?"

"Bah . . . even worse than you can imagine."

"Poor girl."

Marcel huffed, affronted.

"You know what? You and Miss Harris are a lot alike in one regard: you're both absolute ball breakers," Marcel said.

"But you invited her to your home."

"Only because the stupid . . ." He frowned and held back the expletive. ". . . blabbermouth decided to tweet a photo of Café Boulud while she was waiting for me. Desperate times call for desperate measures. We don't exactly have a lot of time. And if she doesn't stop making a problem out of everything . . ."

"Are you sure she's the one who's been making problems?"

"Goodbye, Alex. I'm hanging up."

And he did.

The coffee was already lukewarm, so he poured it down the drain. He remembered Siobhan's cake. What should he do? Call her and ask her to come get it? Send it via messenger to wherever she lived? Take it to her himself? All the options seemed ridiculous. Just as ridiculous as Alex had been to insinuate that . . . He wasn't even entirely sure what Alex had insinuated.

"Compatible, like hell," he muttered.

He decided to get rid of the lousy cake and put an end to the matter. It would be fun timing how long it took to drop down the long metallic chute to the building's trash room. He was just opening the refrigerator when the bell rang.

How strange. He never received visitors without Gonzales warning him on the intercom first.

Who could it be?

A neighbor?

When he opened the door, he was hit by that cursed scent of coconut again. This was no neighbor. Siobhan was waiting on the doorstep with her irritating Girl Scout smile. A few strands of her coppery hair had freed themselves from her messy ponytail and fell haphazardly around her oval face.

"What the hell are you doing here? And why didn't the concierge warn me you were coming?"

He wanted her to go away.

Or did he?

"I asked him not to. I figured you wouldn't have let me come up."

"You figured right," he replied coldly. "What do you want?"

"I've brought this," she said, holding out a classic Bloomingdale's "medium brown bag." "Seeing as you've never read a romance novel, I thought it would be good for you to familiarize yourself with the genre. I picked out a few of my favorites for you."

"Lord have mercy on me . . ." Marcel grabbed the bag with one hand, took a deep breath, and started to pull out one book after another. "*And Then He Kissed Her*, *I Dream of You*, *The Mad Earl's Bride*, *Time of the Rose*, *The Duke and I* . . . Jesus, these titles. Tell me you haven't come just to torture me, princess." He slipped the books back in the bag. "Because if that's the case, you're wasting your time. Go home, take this with you, and get writing. Now."

His tone was brusque and verging on rude, but it was necessary.

Siobhan dropped the bag to the floor between her ankles.

"The thing is . . ."

Marcel raised a thick dark eyebrow.

"What?"

"I can't do it," muttered Siobhan. "I'm sorry."

Marcel folded his arms. *If she has the gall to turn up here with such a feeble excuse, let's hear what she has to say.*

"Explain."

"You see, yesterday . . . The whole thing was so clear in my head. I could hear the dialogue and visualize full scenes. It was like Felicity had come to life, like she was a real person. My brain was fizzing with ideas. I was desperate to get home and write. I hadn't felt like that since I used to publish on WriteUp. And then when I got home . . . I had a blank. The ideas, the dialogue, the scenes . . . It all just suddenly vanished. I . . ." She bit her lip, embarrassed. "I haven't been able to write a word."

"What do you want me to do about it, Siobhan?"

"Teach me."

"No one can teach you to write. It's something you have to learn on your own."

"Please, Marcel. I've swallowed my pride and dragged myself over here knowing you hate me, and you'd rather never see me again, because you're the only one who can help me out of this impending existential crisis."

"I'm not . . ." He clenched his jaw. "I'm no Mother Teresa. You should have thought of that before signing the contract."

"You think I like this situation?"

He looked at the distraught face before him, the delicate, nervously fluttering hands, the agitated breathing, the rapid blinking. For a moment he wanted to run his fingers around the outline of that precious face, though he quickly rebuked himself. What was he thinking? That would only give her the wrong impression. What should he do? Remain stony and implacable? Or help her? After all, like it or not, they had to get this book written.

He exhaled slowly.

"I need caffeine. And I'm guessing you do too," he said.

Siobhan nodded, visibly relieved, and entered the apartment. At his indication, she left the bag of books next to the door and followed him to the kitchen, where she sat on one of the metal stools around the island while Marcel got the coffee ready. He selected another capsule, a balanced arabica blend, and inserted it into the machine.

"I must seem ridiculous to you."

"One of the most common mistakes a new writer can make is assuming that just because you've written one novel means you can write another."

"Is that supposed to encourage me?"

"Would you rather I sang you the Muppets song?" he replied. He turned around and placed a steaming coffee in front of Siobhan. "I've given you a load of sugar. I know how much you like it."

"How considerate." Siobhan held the cup between both hands and took a sip. "Can I tell you a secret?"

Marcel furrowed his brow. "I didn't think we were that close."

"We aren't. I just need to vent to someone who understands. And since you're the only writer I know, I'm afraid that person is you. I'm sorry for you, Mr. Black. If you'd been lucky enough to get tangled up with Danielle Steel or Nora Roberts, I can assure you they wouldn't have come knocking at your door."

"You're breaking my heart, princess," he said. He let out a theatrical cry of pain and shrank back with his hand clasped to his chest before bursting out laughing; he had to admit, the girl was witty. He perched at the island and said: "Go ahead, I'm all ears."

Siobhan took a deep breath before plunging in.

"*With Fate on Our Side* was based on my own relationship. She is me. And he's . . . my ex. We broke up last year."

Fascinating. A character-shaping kind of tragedy.

"I changed the ending so the protagonists ended up together; you know, happily ever after and all that. The rest was based pretty much on real life. I assume you have no intention of reading my novel, so you won't mind if I give away the plot. I met Buckley in college, like in the book; I fell for him right away, like in the book; we moved into a Brooklyn apartment with all the charm of a Soviet missile base, like in the book." At that point, she sighed in frustration, a buried sadness in her expression. "And, like in the book, he just abandoned me one day, with a note stuck to the refrigerator. He also left me a bunch of debts, but I decided to leave that part out."

What a jerk. And what kind of a name is Buckley? God, it's pathetic, thought Marcel, making an effort to hide his disgust.

"The difference between the novel and what happened in real life is that Buckley never came back. And even now, I still don't understand why he left."

He felt like saying, "You see, Siobhan? Love is an illusion. One day it's blooming, and the next it's all frosted over." But he decided to keep that verbal ammunition for another time.

"But you still believe in happy endings."

"A story that ends well is a story that never ends."

Marcel could discern in her glittering pupils the fire of a powerful, uncontainable passion. Seeing that, he was overcome by the feeling that he was gravitating too close to the edge of an active volcano.

"I expect you're enjoying all this," Siobhan said, without lifting her gaze from the coffee cup. "I know how much you hate me."

Something resembling guilt tore at his conscience. After a brief silence, he replied:

"*Hate* is too strong a word for someone I've only known a couple of weeks. What is it exactly that concerns you?" he said to change tack.

"What if I can't do it? I went along with all this quite happily, believing I knew what I was doing, but it turns out I don't have the faintest idea. You were right: I'm just a third-rate wannabe writer. What the hell was I thinking when I signed that contract? I'm clearly not capable of writing anything that isn't based on my own stupid personal experience."

She seemed genuinely distressed.

Good lord.

Why is she baring her innermost fears to a stranger?

Why me?

"The thing is everything in literature is personal. Any detail from reality can be reshaped to become an essential element in a novel. A conversation on the subway, a newspaper headline, a still from a movie, or the last words of a loved one before they die."

Pause.

For a moment, Marcel's mind flew to the labyrinthine undergrowth of his own past. His heart was pounding; a brutal reminder of the fragile state of the levee holding his own emotions at bay.

Siobhan's gentle voice brought him back to the present.

"I read *An Ordinary Man.*"

"Really? I thought you weren't interested in crime fiction."

"I'm not. But someone once said you need to know your enemy."

"Not 'someone.' It was Sun Tzu. In *The Art of War.*"

"I knew that. Don't you want to know what I thought?"

"No. I'm not interested in opinions, good or bad." A half-truth. "Readers tend to read the book they want, not the one you wrote."

Judging by the expression on her face, Siobhan didn't seem particularly convinced by that argument.

"So why do you do this, then?"

"Because I have a publishing contract that makes me a shitload of money?"

"Oh come on! I'm not buying that. There must be more to it."

Marcel tensed. His reasons were too personal to divulge lightly. Even so, there was something in her innocent gaze that invited him to share confidences with her.

"Because the act of writing gives structure to the chaos of existence itself. And believe me: there's nothing so agonizing as having a story inside you that you haven't told yet." With that phrase he had revealed much more than it first appeared. "What about you?"

Siobhan threw her head back and frowned as she pondered her response. The light fell on the curve of her throat; to Marcel, the view was magnificent.

"I suppose . . . it's nice to be able to play tricks on destiny once in a while."

"That sounds like a good reason," he agreed, without averting his gaze.

She smiled. A wonderful smile.

He felt off-kilter, confused, out of place. A sudden weakness devastated every last muscle. He had let down his guard for a second, and Miss Harris had disarmed him with her crushing frankness. It was clear you couldn't judge a book by its cover. Or could you? What was happening here? He didn't know, although the sensation felt like walking along a ridge of shifting sands: if you stepped in the wrong place, you would sink irrecoverably.

Which was a problem.

"Well, that's enough fairy tales for today, princess. If we're going to do this, let's do it properly."

Chapter 10

Siobhan

Marcel Black's study, the impregnable fortress where the world's most mysterious crime novelist hatched his sinister plans, was protected by a four-digit security code, like the vault of a Swiss bank. As Marcel made a point of telling her, no one had ever entered his private Cave of Wonders—not even Alex—which made Siobhan feel more privileged than Aladdin. Unlike the rest of the house, this room conveyed a sort of controlled disorder. There was a certain chaos in the arrangement of the books—so numerous that they lined the walls from floor to ceiling—although it was funny to see a copy of *The Maltese Falcon* competing with *The Getaway*, while *The Talented Mr. Ripley* pushed against *The Given Day* to maintain equilibrium. The desk was in the center, dominated by an impressive iMac and a chair that looked extremely comfortable. And expensive. There was also a retro couch next to a coffee table with an old typewriter sitting on it. Siobhan would have loved to take a photo of it to post on Twitter, but she could imagine what Marcel would say, in the hypothetical case that she asked permission.

Nothing good.

"Vinyl records in the living room and a typewriter in the study. You have kinda old-fashioned tastes, don't you?" she joked. "And a couch in here?"

"What's wrong with that? Sometimes I lie down, look at the ceiling, and think. That's part of the writing process too."

"If you say so . . ."

"I see you still have a lot to learn, princess," he said. "Go on, sit down."

"You want me to sit in your chair?"

"Would you rather work on the floor?"

Siobhan rolled her eyes but acquiesced. He installed himself on the other side of the desk, arms folded across his chest. From that position he seemed even more intimidating.

And insultingly sexy.

"Well, it's very comfortable," admitted Siobhan, spinning around.

"And expensive. So treat it as though it were the innocent heroine of one of those literary marvels you brought me today. *The Chair and I: A Romantic and Ergonomic Adventure*. What do you think?" He wiggled his eyebrows. "Don't tell me that doesn't have a ring to it."

"Oh it does. You have an innate talent for titles."

Marcel started laughing. Suddenly, his face lit up like a million watts, and his features mellowed. A laugh like that could work miracles.

Good thing he didn't show it very often. Otherwise, she would become a gibbering wreck.

"Do you know the first virtue of a writer?" he asked, without seeming to want an answer. "Good buttocks."

Siobhan couldn't help snorting childishly.

"It all makes sense now," she murmured.

Marcel adopted a surprised expression.

"Have you been looking at my ass, Miss Harris?"

"Me?" She raised her hand to her chest, feigning puzzlement. "Pah. You aren't as irresistible as you think, Mr. Black."

"But I'm sexy. You said so yourself."

"If you're going to remind me of that dark chapter in my life at every possible occasion, I'll have no choice but to retract it. You are not sexy."

"The color of your cheeks would disagree."

"The color of my cheeks is perfectly normal given the heat at this time of year. Can we get back to your buttocks?" *Shit.* She blinked and tried to rectify the disaster: "I don't mean your . . . actual butt, but your metaphor."

She could tell by the way he was looking at her that the bastard was enjoying this.

Thankfully, he soon regained his serious expression.

"Writing requires physical and mental discipline," he explained. "You have to do it every day, without exception, so as not to break the narrative rhythm. Between four and six hours a day is ideal. Eight is even better."

"Eight hours? You're right about the buttocks."

"A comfortable chair is important, but not crucial. You know what *is* crucial for a writer, Siobhan? Patience. Have you ever played poker?" She nodded. "Good. Well, this is a lot like it. When you don't have a good hand, you withdraw. And when you're sure you're going to win the game, you raise the bet. But you never stop playing. What I'm trying to say is that you can't fall apart at the first sign of difficulty. You have to try again. That's how this works. You fall, you get up again, you brush yourself off, and you go back to square one. Failure is part of life. Success teaches you squat because it's based on other people's perceptions. Failure, on the other hand, helps you become stronger. More pragmatic. More ambitious."

"I'm not the ambitious type."

"Well, you should be. A good author is one who constantly challenges themselves."

"Is that why you accepted Letitia Wright's proposal? Because it was a challenge for you? Did you want to reinvent yourself as a writer or something?"

Marcel's jaw tensed before he replied:

"Bingo."

Something shifted inside Siobhan, as though she had detected an anomaly. He had said it so lightly that she didn't quite believe him.

"The most difficult thing about this profession," continued Marcel, "is overcoming the barrier separating reality and fiction. Writing involves facing up to all kinds of emotions, pinpointing them, and letting them flow, which isn't always pleasant. It's not a case of just spewing them all out; instead you channel them through the right words. Your style will give the prose its own voice and make it more personal. But you have to find that style. And then, polish it, brush all the soil off. That takes time, Siobhan. Maturity."

"You don't think I'm ready."

"It doesn't matter what I think but what you think."

Siobhan shot him an incredulous look.

"You've become very generous all of a sudden."

"Not at all," he replied, with a disturbing indifference. "Bombastic slogans are for Adidas or L'Oréal, not for me. I only said it to encourage you."

"Okay, okay. I'll do what I can."

"Don't do what you can. Do it, period."

"Wow. And you say slogans aren't your thing. Are you sure you aren't in advertising? Perhaps you were, in another life."

"You never know. In any case, try not to divulge any of this when they interview you, or I'll hire a couple of hitmen to come after you. Come on, to work."

"We're going to write?"

"Not me, you." Marcel came around the desk and turned on the computer. He was so close Siobhan noticed her heart rate soaring. He smelled so good . . . He opened a blank document and said: "Write the first chapter. And stick to the plan, okay? Don't try to impress me, just be yourself. Or rather, be Felicity. I'll read it when you've finished."

"And what will you do in the meantime?"

"Make sure you don't get distracted tweeting nonsense."

Her skin blazed with shame.

"What? You aren't going to stand over me like I was in high school, are you?"

"You reap what you sow."

"Well, I'm sorry, but I won't be able to write with you standing here."

"Why not?"

Because she wouldn't be able to concentrate. His proximity set her on edge.

"Because . . . you breathe too loudly."

Marcel looked annoyed.

"Would you rather I didn't breathe?"

"That would be problematic and incompatible with staying alive; unless you were a vampire, and you don't look much like Edward Cullen, to be honest. I could do with a little bit of privacy. Please? I promise I won't go rummaging in your files. Anyway, I'm sure you have protected them with some extremely complex and indecipherable password."

He seemed to think about it for a moment.

"Okay. You win," he finally agreed. "I'll be in the living room."

And he disappeared.

Siobhan breathed a sigh of relief. She found it hard to believe she was in Marcel Black's study, sitting in his chair, about to use his personal computer. It was crazy. It was crazy that she had turned up at his house looking for help. It was crazy that he had churned out that motivational speech worthy of a Hallmark card. And it was crazy that she had agreed she could do this thing. For a while she sat there frozen, looking at the screen and wondering whether she would be able to give shape to everything that was in her head. Each blink of the cursor was a painful reminder of her status as an apprentice. But she hated disappointing people more than anything. Even if Marcel was a complete moron, Siobhan didn't want to let him down. She wanted to show him, and above all herself, that she had the makings of a writer. So, she closed her eyes and tried to focus on visualizing Felicity, the obstinate journalist from the *Post.* She thought about where she would be at that precise moment, what she would be wearing, what her voice would sound like, whether she preferred bagels or corned beef. And she thought how extraordinary it was to be in New York in real life and in fiction at the same time.

Abracadabra.

She began to type.

A fine rain was falling on Manhattan that February night.

The dull thud of the keys reminded her of a stream flowing toward an unknown destination; where it would lead her was a mystery that she could only solve by following her inner compass. She wrote and wrote, spurred on by the feeling of being on the right path. Perhaps she had finally found the fuel she needed to tell the story. When she typed the last period of the chapter, more than three hours had gone by. Five thousand words in total. Her back was stiff, her mouth was dry, and there was a hole the size of Lake Michigan in her stomach, but she was happy with the result. She stretched as she waited for the document to print and then made for the living room.

Marcel was on the sofa, with his sexy professor glasses and a book in his hand. And not just any book: *The Duke and I*, no less.

I can't believe it. He's finally succumbed to the pleasure of reading a romance novel.

Siobhan cleared her throat.

"I'm sorry to interrupt this historic moment, but I've finished."

"One second," he replied, without looking at her. "I'm in the middle of something important."

"Simon and Daphne's first kiss?" she asked mischievously.

"Even better: an overelaborate and poorly formulated syntactic construction. I wonder what the others you brought will be like," he mused. He closed the book and deposited it on the coffee table with his fingertips, as though it were a container of biological waste. "Of course, this has every chance of becoming my new paperweight."

"Ha ha. Carry on like that, and you'll get your own spot on Comedy Central."

Marcel gestured at the pages.

"All right, hand them over."

As he read, Siobhan scrutinized his facial expressions, trying to glean his reaction. Did he like it or not? She hoped so because she had put a lot of effort into gaining Marcel's acceptance. Then he picked up a pencil and started to mark the pages here and there.

He crossed something out.

Something else.

And something else.

The utter . . . He was being truly merciless.

"You don't like it."

"Have you ever heard of economy of language, Siobhan? You use too many words. Why say *fine rain* when you could say *drizzle*? Ration the information, or you'll overwhelm the reader. And all these adjectives to describe Felicity's appearance are too much. Limit yourself to highlighting a couple of features. The rest is just distraction."

"Well, that's your opinion. And opinions are subjective."

"Sure. What do I know, I've only written fifteen books, right?"

Siobhan sighed inwardly. *Having to put up with this isn't worth the $25,000 advance.*

"There is a principle in literature called Chekhov's gun. If a gun appears, you'd better make sure someone is going to fire it. Otherwise it's pointless. A gun or any other element. Chekhov is—"

"I know who Chekhov is, thank you."

"I'm glad because comrade Anton is going to be your best friend from now on. You've written *literally* three times in two paragraphs. Can you explain what the frickin' deal is with millennials and the word *literally*? God, I feel like starting a petition on change.org for it to be used properly. And this ending doesn't invite you to keep reading. Have another look, will you?"

Siobhan felt a nervous tic emerge in her eyebrow.

"Anything else?"

"No, just that."

"'Just'? I feel much better. Hashtag irony."

Marcel shot her a scornful look over the top of his glasses.

"Are you too proud to accept the constructive comments of an experienced writer? Hashtag mature and come back when you have something a bit more solid than this high school composition."

Her face burned with rage and frustration. Fine. Marcel was probably right, though he could have been a tad more lenient with her, given that she was a debut writer facing imposter syndrome. Somehow she had to free herself of that, and, since falling to pieces wasn't a viable option, she decided to be pragmatic.

"If you're going to keep me locked away in here all day, the least you could do is offer me something to eat. Writing on an empty stomach isn't good for creativity. And your hashtag is ridiculous, and too long," she added.

"You know what? That's true. How rude of me," he agreed. "Come with me."

What's up with him? Is he sick?

They returned to the kitchen. Siobhan couldn't believe her eyes when Marcel took her Lady M Mille Crêpes cake out of the refrigerator.

Untouched.

"It can't be true. Are you from another planet or something? I mean . . . you haven't even tried it?"

"It might be poisoned. The truth is I was going to . . . It doesn't matter." He cut a small slice and pushed it across the island to her. "Bon appétit."

Siobhan stared at the plate and then at him with a serious expression.

"You've got to be kidding. Do you want me to die of starvation in your kitchen?"

"The first step to beating an addiction is admitting you have one. Hi, my name's Siobhan, and I'm a sugar junkie. Say it with me; you'll feel better."

"Screw you, Dupont."

After the first mouthful, an involuntary murmur of pleasure emerged from her throat.

"God, I'm going to go into a diabetic coma just looking at you."

"You don't know what you're missing," she countered, before lifting a second piece to her mouth. "Mmmm."

"Well, since I'm not a sugar junkie, I suppose it won't do any harm to try."

Marcel picked up a clean spoon and without warning plunged it into Siobhan's cake.

"Hey! That's mine!" she protested.

"Not anymore."

She watched as Marcel raised the spoon to his lips and licked it clean with pleasure, oblivious to Siobhan's fascination. The glint of his tongue gliding over the metal dazzled her; she couldn't tear her eyes away. It was such a sensual moment that she thought she was the one going into a coma.

Is there a doctor in the house?

He raised his eyes and caught her watching him as though he was the last goddamn chocolate in the box.

"Is something the matter?"

Oh nothing.

Except that a man like you, a man who assures me he doesn't like sweets, has no right to lick a spoon in that way. It's indecent. And far too erotic.

Please, tell me you don't lick everything with that . . . dedication.

Siobhan tried to compose herself.

"I was thinking . . . We need a title. What do you think of *Two Ways to Solve a Murder in Manhattan*?"

"*Two Ways to Solve a Murder in Manhattan*," he repeated. "I like it. It's catchy. Why do you look so surprised?"

"I suppose I was expecting you to mock me the way you always do."

Marcel tutted.

"So that's what I always do, is it? For your information, I can be very considerate if I want to be," he replied. Then, picking up a napkin, he stretched out his arm and carefully wiped the corner of her mouth. "See, princess?"

It was like a caress.

A caress that set her insides ablaze.

Chapter 11

Marcel

Six in the evening.

When he finished the chapter, he switched off his computer and went out to stretch his legs. July had arrived with a vengeance. The air was completely still, and the asphalt gleamed like a pond in the intense sunlight, although New York was still a buzzing hive of movement even in the midst of a heatwave. Wearing a cap for protection, he spent the next forty minutes wandering around the Upper East Side—not the sad, gray part that eventually becomes Harlem, but the rich, white, conservative part. Though it was true that things had changed in recent years—he himself was an example of the increasing number of people in the neighborhood who didn't fit that description—a stroll along Lexington or Park Avenue was all it took to confirm that the stereotype was still based on a tenacious reality.

Regardless, neither the suffocating heat nor that depressingly familiar state of affairs could ruin his mood. He was euphoric, and for one very simple reason: he was writing again. Not just a couple of paragraphs, but two whole chapters. A surge of energy had inexplicably kept him glued to the keyboard all week. Delving into the miseries of the tormented nineteenth-century crime novelist Jeremiah Silloway had allowed him to rediscover that spark of creativity he had given up for lost. The words poured out effortlessly onto the blank page. He was shocked that he had recovered his excitement working on a story that, in theory, didn't interest him in the slightest. A story that wasn't entirely his own and would represent a permanent stain on his career. Despite all that, the desire to write it grew insatiable.

He wanted to write without stopping.

And that was precisely what he had been longing for.

Of course, there was one external factor preventing him from progressing at his own pace: Miss Harris. Why had she shown no sign of life all week? Was she too busy promoting her own novel? If she had time to tweet nonsense or record a ridiculous podcast about romance literature, she certainly had time to write. Not that he had been monitoring her activity on social media. Nothing like that. Well, perhaps a little. Maybe she had run into another mental block, which was a worrying thought. What if the same thing happened every time she started a new chapter? Marcel thought he had resolved the matter with his "motivational" chat the previous Sunday—at least, that's what he had thought when Siobhan finally handed him a third version of the introduction that met with his satisfaction—but now he was doubting his skill as a mentor.

He needed to light some fires.

What the experts call reverse psychology.

He took his cell from his pocket and texted her as he walked.

Marcel

Will you have managed to write your part before the earth succumbs to climate change and we all have to emigrate to some Martian colony owned by Elon Musk OR DOES MADAM NEED ANOTHER WEEK?

Siobhan replied one minute later:

Siobhan

sorry I'm on it doing all I can

"What? You gotta be kidding . . . ," muttered Marcel.

It seemed he hadn't been forceful enough, so he decided to counterattack with a second, even more incendiary, message.

Marcel

It's great that promoting your chick lit is so absorbing you don't have time for the mere mortals around you. Problem is, if you don't make progress, I don't make progress. And if I don't make progress, I become insufferable. So damn well focus and make sure you have your part ready for July 4. No excuses. And another thing: COULD YOU PLEASE USE CORRECT PUNCTUATION?

It wasn't entirely true that he had to wait for her, not yet anyway. He had only resorted to emotional blackmail to get results.

Siobhan

It would be impossible for you to become insufferable because YOU ALREADY ARE.

Siobhan

Why not do the world a favor and GO TO HELL? 🖕

Siobhan

You just don't get it 😠😠😠

Marcel would have liked to ask her exactly what it was he didn't get, but he decided to leave it. He had pissed her off, and that was positive. Siobhan Harris seemed like the kind of person who operated better under pressure.

"Is that all you've got? Please, Britney Spears can write song lyrics with more depth than this," he had said after reading the second version of her introduction.

He had exaggerated on purpose. Her style wasn't bad; it just needed pacing and precision. Perhaps he had been too hard on her, but in the end, he was doing her a favor; after all, she was the one who had shown up at his house whining. That day replayed over and over in his mind, and he couldn't stop it. The moment he opened the door and found her standing there with her bag of books, her constellation of freckles, and all of her fears. He hated to admit that he had lowered his guard. Not only had he helped her; he had also let her enter his study, sit in his chair, and use his computer. And the worst thing was, he wasn't sure he had done it entirely for his own benefit. Was he going crazy? If Alex knew how much he had ceded to this girl, he would mock him ruthlessly. And he couldn't help remembering that urge, as stupid as it was impossible to control, to wipe the crumbs of cake from her lips with a napkin. A heat spread across his skin as he recalled that fleeting moment, and his thoughts became explicit enough to make him feel uncomfortable. He blinked hard to free himself of the image branded on his mind and stuck his phone in his pocket.

He needed a distraction.

At Fifth and Ninety-Third, he headed for the Corner Bookstore. Visiting bookstores was one of his favorite pastimes. He loved rescuing classics from oblivion or coming across some little-known work that had been buried at the back of the shelf. Upon entering, he encountered a huge display showcasing his book *The End of Days* and Siobhan's *With Fate on Our Side.*

I don't believe it. They've paired us up already?

He walked up to the display and compared both covers. While his was sober and dark, hers looked like an invitation to a Victorian wedding, with one of those bands used to entrap gullible readers. "The writer of the moment," he read. He shook his head. He knew this absurd arrangement was down to a Baxter Books marketing campaign.

He took a photo on his cell and sent it to Alex, stating, The world is going to shit. Then he picked up Siobhan's book, flicked through it, and read her biography on the flap.

"Siobhan Harris (Mount Vernon, NY, 1987) studied Communications at NYU. She discovered romance novels at the age of fourteen and became addicted to happy endings. She believes in second chances above all else. She likes summer, traveling, chocolate chip ice cream, taking photos with her friends, and talking about books, particularly love stories." Marcel gave an ironic laugh. Ice cream, happy endings, second chances . . . She was so predictable. He continued reading. "She is very active on Twitter and loves interacting with her readers. She currently lives in Brooklyn and combines writing with her full-time job in a digital marketing company. *With Fate on Our Side* is her first novel."

Marcel's eyebrows arched in surprise.

"What the hell . . . ," he murmured.

Then it all made sense.

The reason Siobhan hadn't delivered her section was right in front of his eyes: a full-time job in a digital marketing company. He couldn't help feeling like an idiot, because he hadn't even considered that she might have a job. *What kind of snob have you become?* he thought, reproaching himself. He contemplated the idea of calling to apologize, but his pride prevented him. *She could have told me instead of flying off the handle.* He let his gaze drift to the author's photograph for a moment. Siobhan's eyes were friendly, her mouth voluptuous and perfectly curved. If he was honest, she wasn't predictable at all. Sometimes she seemed delicate and sweet; at others, like solid steel. She challenged him in a way he found both infuriating and intriguing. After more than a decade exploring the dark side of human nature, few things surprised him. But now some girl who defined herself as a hopeless romantic was causing a kind of fizzing curiosity in him that was proving hard to repress. Marcel remembered that Siobhan had told him her book was based on her personal experience. Then he did something he would never have predicted.

He bought it.

Never say never, or I'll never read a romance novel in my life.

"This one?" asked the salesclerk when Marcel placed the book on the counter to pay.

"Yes."

"Would you like me to gift wrap it?"

"It isn't a gift."

"Is it for you?"

There was an annoying tone of incredulity in the busybody's voice.

"Let's just say I'm doing some research," improvised Marcel.

"Of course, that makes sense. I thought it was strange, you buying it for pleasure. You don't fit the consumer profile for this type of book, to be honest. Did you know the author is writing a book with Marcel Black?" He gestured toward the display. "I don't know what will come of it. It's quite a strange combination, but publishers will release anything these days if they can make a quick buck out of it. Do you know Marcel Black?"

Yes, moron, like the palm of my hand.

"Vaguely."

"If you haven't read anything of his, I suggest you do. He has a really good series about a detective who's a bit of a troublemaker. You know the kind of thing." A disturbing sound, something like a pig's grunt, came out of the impertinent salesclerk's mouth. "I'm sure you'll like it better than this immature flash in the pan stuff. What do you say, my friend?"

Flash in the pan? Immature?

Those words felt like a kick in the stomach, and he couldn't explain why.

It was surreal.

"I think the only thing that's flash in the pan in here is your intelligence, *my friend*."

The assistant gawped at him.

"What?"

"You heard me. And if you don't want to find a feature in the *New Yorker* about the prejudice of the staff in this bookstore, you'd better shut your beak."

Then he dropped a twenty-dollar bill on the counter, grabbed the book, and left, certain that he would never set foot in this establishment again.

He spent the rest of the day wondering what on earth was happening to him.

Chapter 12

Siobhan

The Fourth of July, Thanksgiving, and Christmas were the three sacred holidays in the Harris household. She could spend the rest of the year however, wherever, and with whomever she pleased, but she had an obligation to be home on those dates.

Unless there was a force majeure to explain her absence, of course.

Situations the Harrises would be willing to consider a force majeure

A hurricane (category 3 or above)

The imminent impact of a meteorite against the earth (so imminent there's no time to take the train from New York to Mount Vernon)

The zombie apocalypse (only if bitten)

Situations the Harrises would NOT be willing to consider a force majeure

Having committed to writing the third chapter of a novel in progress

"What am I supposed to do with all this meat? I bought enough cutlets to feed an army," her mother said when Siobhan phoned her at the last minute to let her know they would have to celebrate the Fourth of July without her. Yes, she would miss the barbecue on the back patio, the fireworks, the fire department parade, the fair with its cotton candy and makeshift bars buckling under pails of chilled Budweiser. Of course, given the choice between disappointing her mother and incurring the wrath of the odious Mr. Black, she would prefer the former. And so, while most New Yorkers headed for Long Island, Fire Island, or the Hamptons, Siobhan sat sweltering on her tiny sofa in her tiny apartment in Brooklyn with her laptop on her knees and a chilled lemonade.

Getting started wasn't easy. In the third chapter, Felicity Bloom's profession played a key role, and all Siobhan knew about the inner workings of the world of journalism came from *Lois & Clark*—and she hadn't even seen all four seasons. In any case, she would need to ask her fairy godmother Google for help.

How to investigate a crime as a journalist.

How to investigate a crime as a journalist in Manhattan.

Most famous crimes in Manhattan.

Jack the Ripper copycats.

How long does it take the police to reach a crime scene?

How long does it take a journalist to reach a crime scene?

Best podcasts about true crime.

If it was true that the CIA monitored people's internet searches, every alarm in Langley should have been going off right then.

Seven hours later, Siobhan wrapped up what she thought was a decent draft of the chapter. She smiled, pleased with herself, and stretched. Her shoulders ached, and she was hungry, but it had been worth it. Dupont had better not take issue with a single thing or she would send him an envelope full of anthrax in the mail. Or even worse: sugar. Since sugar was just what she needed, she jumped up to refill her glass with lemonade. Her cell rang. It was a FaceTime call from Robin.

"Christ, Cheerios," her brother said when she answered. "Do you have a Jägermeister hangover or something?"

"Jägermeister? I haven't drunk that shit since the high school prom."

"Well, then, if you don't have a hangover, why do you look like you haven't slept since 1995?"

Siobhan raised her eyebrows.

"Wow. That sure is a nice way to tell a girl she looks awful. I'm exhausted. It's been a difficult week. Please, don't tell Mom. She's already pissed at me for not going home."

"Don't worry, she isn't pissed at you. She didn't even mention you during the meal. You know, I think she's forgotten she has a daughter at all."

"Ha ha. The good news is I've written the chapter, and I'm ready to send it to Mr. Black, as promised."

"Hey, this guy isn't exploiting you, is he?"

"'Exploiting'? Come on. It isn't his fault that my inexperience, combined with a lack of time, is holding us back. I signed a contract with Baxter Books, and I don't want to disappoint them. Mr. Black is depending on me; we're a team now." She liked the way that sounded. "The problem is my jerk of a boss always finds some reason to keep me late at work. When I get home, I'm so tired I don't have the energy to write. And then there's Bella, my agent, who keeps reminding me I need to stay active on social media and attend all the literary events I can and blah blah blah."

A long sigh rose from the center of her chest.

"The way I see it, Shiv, it's a no-brainer. Quit your job."

"I can't quit my job," she argued, pinching the bridge of her nose in exhaustion. "I have bills to pay. Living in New York costs a fortune."

"I doubt money is going to be a problem for you in the short to medium term."

"Did your Spidey sense tell you that, or did you see it in your crystal ball?"

"You do know that Netflix is making a movie based on this guy's books, right? And rumor has it Chris Hemsworth is going to play the lead?"

"Oh come on! Chris Hemsworth is too . . ."

"Brawny?"

"I was going to say Australian."

"The point is that his books sell like hotcakes, which means big bucks for you, once you've written this thing together." He rubbed his fingers together. "It's just a job, Shiv. If for some reason this doesn't end well, you can always look for a new one. People change jobs all the time."

"I don't know, Robin."

"I'm just saying that life is too short to waste time doing something you don't like when you could be doing something you love." He scratched his chin and glanced at the ceiling for a moment before returning his gaze to her. "Do you get what I'm saying? Because I'm not sure if I made it clear."

Siobhan smiled.

Of course she got it.

Loud and clear.

Chapter 13

Marcel

He had to put the book down. The scene he had just read put him on edge. It wasn't anything extraordinary in literary terms; on the contrary, you might even say it lacked depth. But simply visualizing Miss Harris as she was described on those pages, naked and moaning with pleasure, stiffened a certain part of his anatomy, which constituted a problem.

A very big problem, by all appearances.

He grimaced, feeling uncomfortable.

"Fuck. Just what I needed," he muttered, breathing heavily.

He knew that Siobhan herself was the protagonist of *With Fate on Our Side*. Why the hell did she have to tell him that? Now he couldn't get the image out of his head, and the very idea of getting turned on thinking about her tortured him. Marcel didn't want to fantasize about a woman who, in turn, fantasized about some Prince Charming who didn't fade after the first wash. A woman he didn't even particularly like, with whom he had nothing in common beyond a contractual agreement. He hid the book under a cushion as though it were a sinful temptation and decided he wouldn't bother finishing it. What for? For his mind and his testosterone to betray him? He had more important things to do than allow himself to be consumed by matters of the flesh.

He exhaled emphatically and stood up to free himself from the clutches of desire. He needed to move his body. He had spent a large chunk of the Fourth of July lying on the sofa reading a stupid romance novel. *You need to take a long hard look at yourself, boy.* In his defense, he had to admit that Siobhan wasn't too bad at building narrative tension, which had kept him turning pages. He noticed that it was getting late and wondered whether the little princess had kept her part of the bargain. He saw that he had a message from her but didn't manage to read it before an incoming call flashed up on the screen.

It was Charmaine.

He sighed and briefly considered not answering. Talking to his sister always ended up putting him in a bad mood. It was always problems, problems, and more problems. Of course, given how stubborn the eldest Dupont sibling was, he knew she would only keep trying to reach him.

"It's nine o'clock, Chaz," he said as he answered.

"Mm-hmm. So what? Is there a telephone curfew or something? And it's only eight in NOLA. Anyway, it's good to hear your voice too, little bro."

Marcel rolled his eyes.

"Spare me the sarcasm. Why are you calling?"

"I need a reason to call you now?"

"Chaz . . ." His voice betrayed the fact that his patience was wearing thin. "What's he done this time?"

Charmaine sighed.

"He's been acting up for a while. As soon as he sees me, he goes crazy. He acts like I'm out to hurt him and . . . Well, he tries to defend himself. I've changed nurses twice in the last month because no one can handle him for long. I'm desperate, Marcel. Why don't you come home?"

An irritating lump formed in his throat. The very idea of returning under these circumstances was inconceivable.

He swallowed.

"Impossible, Chaz. I've got a lot going on right now, with the novel and everything."

"Well, I need you to make whatever arrangements it takes for you to come help me out."

"Aren't you listening to me? I just said I can't. I live here, in New York." He paused, took off his glasses, and placed them on the coffee table. "Listen, if you need more money, you only have to ask," he added, massaging the bridge of his nose to relieve the tension.

"No, it's not about that. I . . . It's just that I can't take it anymore. This situation is too much for me. It's getting worse."

Silence.

"Well, you know what I think," Marcel said brusquely.

"Yes, and you know how I feel. I don't think abandoning Dad in this condition is a viable option."

"Admitting him to a clinic where he gets the round-the-clock care he needs isn't abandoning him. Think about it. I would deal with the bills, and you could get your life back. Anyway, the demented old goat doesn't even recognize you."

"Marcel Javarious Dupont! I forbid you from talking about our father that way!"

"Give me a break, Chaz. He got what he deserves. It's called karma."

A new uncomfortable silence settled over the telephone line.

"You're not coming, are you?"

"Not while the old man's still at home."

"You're so pigheaded! Can't you back down for once in your life? You weren't here for Thanksgiving or Christmas or Mardi Gras. I don't even remember the last time you honored us with your presence."

He remembered. And his memory of that trip to New Orleans wasn't exactly a pleasant one.

"No, Charmaine. I'm not going to back down. I'm not like you, okay?"

"Damn right you're not like me. You behave like a rich white guy who's forgotten where he came from."

A bitter laugh escaped his throat.

"How interesting. It doesn't seem to bother you all that much when you get the monthly check."

That had been a low blow, and he immediately regretted it.

"I'm sorry."

"I'm sorry too," she muttered, before hanging up.

Marcel expelled the very last drop of air from his lungs. He remembered all the times as a child when Charmaine had sat on the edge of his bed and told him stories. His favorite was about Rougarou, the wolfman of the Louisiana swamps. And all the times she had tended the wounds he incurred chasing swamp beavers. And all the times she had dried his tears.

His sister had been his mother, his father, and his friend.

His family.

And he couldn't help feeling like a swine.

But he needed some way to protect himself against everything that had turned him into damaged goods.

Chapter 14

Siobhan

When Marcel opened the door on the morning of July 8, Siobhan could see the unmistakable signs of confusion in his face: the furrowed brow and the half-open mouth. And he was blinking compulsively, as though trying to process what he was seeing.

"Where did this troublesome apparition come from and how do I block it?" he asked. He didn't appear at all happy to see her. Which made sense, given that their most recent text exchange had gotten rather heated. "I'm going to have to have serious words with Mr. Gonzales about this . . . new habit of not notifying me about visitors."

"See, I . . . I had a job," she blurted out. "A boring, poorly paid job in a digital marketing company that took up too much of my time. And I say 'had,' past tense, because I no longer have it." She smiled shyly. "I quit."

On sharing her news, Siobhan held her breath as she watched Marcel's expression, waiting for him to show a spark of recognition that never came.

"Mm-hmm. And you've come here for me to pat you on the back?"

That wasn't the response she was expecting, but never mind. She had felt so proud of herself for the last twenty-four hours that not even the odious Mr. Black's sarcasm could spoil her mood. She had done it;

she had dared to take the plunge. Most decisions, right or wrong, are not particularly momentous; some, however, are life changing. Siobhan had quit the day before. With no regrets. She was finally clear about her goals. Happiness and the pursuit thereof would be her number one priority from now on, even if that meant taking certain risks. Her brother was right: not only did she get nothing positive from her job, but it also robbed her of the energy she needed to write.

Work at something you love, and you'll never work a day in your life.

"Of course not. Can I come in, please?"

"Would it make any difference if I said no?"

Siobhan limited herself to shooting him a meaningful glare from beneath her heavy lashes. Seconds later, in the living room, she dropped her purse on the sofa so naturally that it didn't go unnoticed by Marcel, judging by his narrowed eyes.

"So . . . I'm finally free. Isn't that great? No more delays. From now on, I'm all yours." Marcel raised a quizzical eyebrow. "In the literary sense," she clarified hastily. She noticed herself blushing. Why did she always talk too much? It must be because of the glasses. It was undeniable—his sex appeal shot up whenever he was wearing them. "You know something? It took a lot for me to realize this was the path I want to follow. I've always been a delayed reaction kind of girl," she confessed.

"L'esprit de l'escalier," said Marcel.

She loved the way he pronounced it, with that soft, velvety cadence of French from the lips of a Southerner.

"I've decided to focus entirely and exclusively on writing."

Marcel folded his arms and looked at her suspiciously.

"So why aren't you at home right now doing precisely that? In *your* home," he stressed. "In Brooklyn."

"Brooklyn doesn't inspire me."

That wasn't entirely true. She was just laying the groundwork for what she planned to say next.

"Really. Well, that's no surprise. Have you tried going to a Starbucks? I gather it's the preferred workspace for hipsters."

"Too noisy."

"And the library?"

"Too quiet." She paused briefly and bit her lip. "I was thinking . . ."

"Heaven help us. Why am I getting a bad feeling about this?"

". . . that I could come here from now on."

She could almost see the cogs in Marcel's brain starting to turn and working up to full speed. He stared at her with wide eyes.

"What? No, no, no. No chance." His head and arms reinforced his adamant refusal. "I understand that I might seem like scintillating company to you, but it's not going to happen. Forget about it, Siobhan. I work alone. A-L-O-N-E. In case you hadn't noticed, I don't like people."

"Look at it this way: we'll make faster progress if we're together. The communication will be more fluid. You must admit that each of us working in our own homes has been a complete disaster so far."

"And whose fault is that, hmm?"

"All right, I'll accept my share of the blame. Will you accept yours?"

"I don't know what you mean," Marcel said.

"Well, I sacrificed the Fourth of July just to please you, and the only comment you've made about my chapter is that there's nowhere to fit it in."

Marcel shrugged.

"That's what I think. Should I apologize for being honest?"

"Of course not. But it would be nice if you could be a tad more specific, if you want us to get anywhere. How am I supposed to understand what you want me to do if you only communicate by smoke signal? That's why we need to change the work dynamic. Listen, I understand that geniuses need their own space to create." There was no ulterior motive behind this last remark; she genuinely believed it. "In fact, we don't need to be in the same room; I could write in the living room, and you won't even know I'm here."

"That's highly unlikely, Miss Harris."

"It would only be until we finish the novel. After that, I guarantee you won't see me again."

The prospect left a surprisingly bitter taste in her mouth. She wasn't sure what to think about Marcel. There was no doubt she was attracted to him, but she would have to think long and hard before saying whether she really liked him. And it was clear that he didn't like her.

"What do you say, Mr. Black? Do we have a deal?" she asked, extending her hand.

He met her gaze with those impossibly dark eyes and studied her intently. Suddenly, the air burned her lungs, and she felt like the walls were closing in on her. Her heart beat so fast she feared it might burst. When had she decided this plan was a good idea? Spending time with Marcel was something she feared as much as longed for; and yet, analyzing the situation objectively, there was no other way for this goddamn novel to come together.

They were condemned to get along.

"All right. You win, princess," he replied. "I hope I won't regret this."

When he took her hand to seal the deal, Siobhan experienced a curious sensation, as though a secret door was opening that would finally allow her to glimpse what was on the other side. She couldn't have explained why, but she was convinced that a crack had just appeared. Then, she realized the tip of her thumb was stroking that dark brown skin next to hers, and it made her go weak in the knees.

She pulled her hand away as though she had scorched it.

I hope so too, she thought.

Chapter 15

Marcel

Marcel was so used to doing his own thing that he found it hard to adjust to Siobhan's presence. She was always there, all the time; she had invaded his space and altered his routine. His living room had turned into something resembling one of those coworking offices for startup entrepreneurs in SoHo, with shared access to premium services like the bathroom—his bathroom—and the coffee machine—his coffee machine. And if that weren't enough, the princess was noisy.

"For crying out loud! Could you please turn down the volume or use headphones? It's bad enough having to tolerate your abysmal taste in music without putting my aural health in jeopardy!" he shouted one day from his study.

To which Siobhan replied:

"Sorry, I didn't know you were, like, sixty! And there's nothing wrong with my taste in music! For your information, Maroon 5 have evolved a lot since 'Moves Like Jagger'!"

Another thing that riled him: she didn't keep her phone on silent, and the notifications never frickin' stopped. How could she care so much about her likes and mentions on Twitter when the real magic was happening right there, on her computer screen? He would never understand this dependency on clicks. And her habit of constantly interrupting him with trivial matters like:

"Where can I charge my laptop? My battery is running low."

Or:

"You're out of milk. Do you have a preference? Whole? Skim? Organic? Soy? Oat? I'm asking because I'm going to go and buy a carton. And I was thinking, we should set up a shared kitty for that kind of expense, you know."

Or:

"Why do you print the chapter double-spaced and on one side only? You don't need to waste all that paper. Think of all the forests you could save."

And without doubt, the worst of all:

"Why is my book buried under the sofa cushions?"

Shit.

Rule number one in the crime writer's handbook: the criminal must always get rid of the murder weapon. Leaving it behind at the scene of the crime is not an acceptable option unless you're a rookie or a second-rate author.

Since he wasn't about to admit to having spent his money and a fair amount of time on a romance novel, his only options were to take advantage of his constitutional right not to incriminate himself by invoking the Fifth Amendment, or play dumb. He went for the second.

"I don't have the faintest idea how *that* got there."

The start of the most irritatingly triumphant smile appeared on Siobhan's lips, the kind of arrogant shyster smile that tends to follow a "No more questions, Your Honor" when you know you've won the case. She wasn't buying it, clearly, although Marcel was skillful enough to divert the focus back to where he would rather it stayed.

"How the hell do you expect me to concentrate if you won't stop interrupting me with your horseshit?"

The situation forced him to make the drastic decision to move Siobhan into his own study, where at least he could keep an eye on her, and, using his prerogative as the more experienced author of the two, he imposed four unbreakable rules:

1) No music
2) No cell phone
3) No talking
4) No moving around

"Can I use the bathroom, or is that forbidden too?"

He didn't even bother to hide his amusement as he replied:

"You can. As long as you don't call on me to pass you the toilet paper."

Siobhan tutted.

"You're about as fun as a pimple on the ass, Mr. Black."

The new dynamic only half worked. Marcel couldn't have imagined that spending an average of six hours a day in front of her would end up distracting him even more. The fact that she sat on the other side of his desk—so close that every time he stretched his legs they grazed against hers—was exciting and agonizing in equal measure. Sometimes, he found himself watching her over the top of his screen. He counted her freckles. He studied her gestures. The way she absentmindedly twisted a lock of hair around the index finger of her left hand as she stared pensively at the ceiling. The way she narrowed her eyes when an idea was floating around her and suddenly opened them wide to trap it. Instead of keeping his eyes trained on his own screen, he was spending his time watching her. Siobhan caught him on one occasion, and he couldn't help feeling like a creepy voyeur; it was humiliating. The worst thing was her scent, that striking fragrance of freshly cut coconut. She smelled like a summer's day, warm, wild, and full of promise. Her perfume hovered in the air even after she had gone and hovered over him all night, disturbing his sleep. But it wasn't just that. There was something about her that had wormed its way into his brain and all his senses.

Be careful, Marcel. Be very careful.

The days and weeks flew past. Over time, working with Siobhan didn't seem so bad. And he was no longer annoyed by her presence, not even when she hummed those stupid Top 40 songs or appeared every morning with a bag of freshly baked bagels and an enthusiastic smile that should be illegal at that hour. He discovered he enjoyed her company, more than he was prepared to admit. And he also discovered, despite his best efforts to ignore it, that a vortex of loneliness sucked him in when she left. He blamed it on those brief moments when it felt like they were really connecting. They say there's a way of getting to everyone, even the most impenetrable character; it's just a question of working out how. Perhaps the way to get to Marcel was through a passion for writing. And perhaps Siobhan had stumbled upon the secret. Being a writer isn't like having an office job that you forget about as soon as you turn off the computer. Writing requires a destructive mental detachment: being simultaneously in the world and outside it. You might say it's like decompression in diving. You don't surface quickly after a deep dive; you do it gradually. Sometimes, you get to a place where you feel too vulnerable to leave the waters of fiction. Other times, you don't want to get out. It's a matter of ego, pure and simple; after all, that world down there is yours, you've created it, and you govern it. That's why writing is so addictive. The other side of the coin is a constant feeling of isolation. Of course, it was different now. There was someone diving by his side, someone having the same experience with the same obsessive intensity. Someone with whom he could stay submerged a while longer, in spite of the world and its biorhythms.

And it wasn't all bad.

"You know what? I've figured something out. For authors, writing is both the illness and the cure," Siobhan said to him on one occasion.

In that moment, Marcel thought perhaps they weren't so different after all. Except that he had gotten used to living with that duality, and she was just discovering it.

"Not for authors," he corrected her. "For us. Plural."

Siobhan bit her lower lip, hiding a smile.

"You know, you're generally kinda obnoxious, but sometimes you're normal."

"I'm not normal, princess. I'm a fucking genius."

"And do you grant wishes too?"

"*Genius*, not *genie*. And it depends how you rub my lamp," he replied, winking mischievously.

That shared passion allowed them to progress extraordinarily quickly and reach the halfway point of fifty thousand words by the end of July. Without killing each other, which was an achievement. It seemed that the worst was over, although it hadn't exactly been a bed of roses. Marcel was implacable in the face of Siobhan's campaign to soften the story's violent tone.

"But why do you have to get rid of Felicity's police officer friend?" she asked him one day. "Isn't one corpse enough? God, it's depressing."

"Do I try to tell you how much kissing there should be? No, right? So, why the hell are you encroaching on my territory? It would be nice if you could stop arguing about every little thing for a change."

"Ha! As if you don't do the same to me."

"Only because you know nothing about crime novels." He took off his glasses and held them up to the light. "I mean, wanting Felicity to open a double-locked armored door just like that!" he said, cleaning the lenses on his shirttails. "As if she's Houdini's daughter."

"Now that you mention it, you don't have the faintest idea what's expected of a romance novel. To start with, you describe Jeremiah far too vaguely. He has to be more . . . attractive. A gentleman who'll make an impression on the readers from the moment he appears. Like Henry Cavill."

"That side of beef? You must be kidding."

"I'm warning you, Mr. Black: don't mess with Henry, or you'll have me to deal with."

Marcel threw his head back as if he had just been punched. Then he raised his hands in surrender and, trying to contain his laughter, asked:

"Since when is it essential to the plot for the protagonist to be handsome?"

"Handsome, tall, strong, and . . ."

"And white, of course. I get it."

Siobhan furrowed her brow.

"Why do you say that? William J. Knox is white too."

"But no one knows his creator is Black."

"Wait, wait. Don't tell me your secret identity is for racial reasons." She sounded surprised. "That's absurd, Marcel. It's the twenty-first century. Our previous president was a person of color."

"So what? The United States is still the most racist country in the world. Have you ever put up with more from a Black man than you ever would from a white man out of fear of offending him? That's what will happen if they discover who I am. People would be condescending toward me and my work. You can bet your life on it."

It was a rehearsed speech, a narrative devised for his own convenience to avoid the truth.

But there was no reason for her to know that.

They got into the habit of working in a comfortable silence with frequent interruptions. When she was tired, Siobhan would get up from her chair to stretch and walk around the study, scanning the shelves.

"There are so many books here I've never read," she commented one day. "I've never even heard of most of them. Would you lend me some? I promise to return them in a reasonable amount of time. I'm not the kind of monster who doesn't return books."

"Take all you want. Although I should warn you, you won't find any sugar or happy endings in my collection, princess."

"I'm not looking for happy endings, just . . . other perspectives."

He liked her answer.

It was as though a door had opened to reveal another Siobhan, one that was far more open-minded than the image he had formed of her in his head.

Sometimes, it was Marcel who broke their working rhythm. Like when he kept sighing, and Siobhan eventually had to ask what the problem was.

"Just something I can't resolve. Nothing's flowing. You have no idea of the battle I'm waging with this lousy paragraph," he said as he drummed his fingers on the desk.

"Perhaps a fresh pair of eyes . . . ," she suggested tentatively, as though fearing the idea that her assistance might be offensive.

And, to be fair, that would have been the case a month earlier.

"Sure. Take a look. I'd like to hear what you think," he said.

Their working days grew longer, peppered with conversations that were never simple, no matter how straightforward they seemed. One night, as Siobhan was gathering her things, Marcel asked her, with a casualness that was unusual in him, whether she would like to stay for dinner. And just as casually, she said she'd love to. Maybe she was just tired and hungry. Or perhaps there was more to it. They ordered Thai food, opened a bottle of wine, and sat on the balcony facing one another. It was hot, and the city lights flickered against the dark backdrop.

"Manhattan at night is one of the most stunning sights in the world," Siobhan remarked.

"I agree."

She put her hand on his forehead to see if he was feverish.

"You must be ill."

Marcel laughed.

That night, as they dug into their food, he discovered a lot about Siobhan Harris. Things he had already sensed. For example, that she came from a close family, that she was raised in Mount Vernon, and that Paige and Lena were her rock. He tried not to reveal too much. He limited himself to the obvious facts: he was from New Orleans—as if his accent hadn't already given him away—he'd been living in New York for more than fifteen years, Alex was his only real friend, Bob Gunton was an unscrupulous bastard with a tendency to infantilize authors, and Baxter Books was typical of the ecosystem of penny-pinching and power games in any large publishing company.

"Did you say fifteen years? So you weren't in NOLA during Katrina?"

Something churned in his gut. The air left his lungs momentarily.

"Well, no," he admitted, disconcerted. "But in 1992, when Andrew devastated southern Louisiana, my sister and I saw the cyclone tear up a thirty-foot oak tree from the backyard in a matter of seconds, right in front of us."

"I didn't know you had a sister."

"Why would you know?"

"Fair enough. I'd forgotten you were the hermetic man who never explains anything. Okay then, why New York?"

"I wanted to start from scratch. Where better than this city?"

When, after a brief silence, Siobhan continued asking about the reasons for his anonymity, Marcel limited himself to quoting Ovid.

"*Bene qui latuit bene vixit.* One who lives well lives unnoticed."

"Even so . . . the world has a right to know the author of Marcel Black's novels, and you have a right to be recognized."

"I'm not doing this for recognition, Siobhan. I do it because it's the only thing I know how to do. For me, writing has never been entertainment; it's total commitment. And, anyway, the truth is always disappointing. More wine?"

Siobhan nodded, and Marcel filled her glass. Perhaps he had said too much. Not that he had revealed all his secrets—far from it—but he had hinted that he had some, which was reckless for him. Yet, there was something about this girl with her sparkling eyes and generous laugh that made him lower his guard. Not enough to answer certain uncomfortable questions, but enough to allow her to glimpse the difference between Marcel Dupont, the man, and Marcel Black, the writer.

He noticed her grimacing slightly whenever she picked up her glass.

"Your hand hurts, right? Between the thumb and wrist?"

"Yes. How did you know?"

"Oh, I know that feeling well. The tendons get inflamed when you spend a long time pounding away at the keyboard. You should try to stretch before and after each session to prevent chronic pain. Let me show you."

Marcel took her hand and exerted a light pressure on her knuckles with his fingers. And suddenly . . . boom! Something warm darted across his skin.

Adrenaline.

Fear.

Revelations.

"This might be a bit uncomfortable, but you'll feel better afterward," he said, maintaining the pressure.

The atmosphere had suddenly changed. It had become intimate. He could feel it. His voice sounded hoarser than usual. Siobhan raised her eyes and looked at him as though seeing him for the first time, with a glint in her blue irises.

"Okay," she whispered, clearly agitated.

"Okay," he repeated like an idiot.

He couldn't avert his gaze from hers or let go of her hand. They stayed like that for a long time as the tension grew around them, coiling like a spring. Everywhere else, life was carrying on as usual, but on that balcony in Manhattan, time seemed to stand still. There's something strange about touching someone's hands, even more profound than sex. It's as though you could reach someone's soul through the thousands of nerve endings in the fingertips. Something suddenly sparked in his chest, and all at once his entire body was ablaze. Marcel thought he heard violins playing somewhere, but perhaps he had imagined it.

And only then, when he had realized the magnitude of the problem, was he able to release her hand.

Chapter 16

Siobhan

Alarm bells rang in her head when she realized she had spent the last twenty minutes deciding what to wear. Why did this feel like her prom night? She had only invited Marcel to dinner because Alex had let slip that it was his birthday, and a gift would have been far too personal. And there was another small detail: his friend was coming too. So choosing between a short dress with a very low back and ripped boyfriend jeans shouldn't have been such a major decision because this was categorically not a date. She would never go on a date with an insensitive, ungrateful man who had criticized the restaurant she had chosen because it wasn't up to his usual standards. The epitome of an insensitive and ungrateful man who had no idea of the lengths she had gone to, to get a table.

"Grimaldi's. For my birthday. Seriously? Couldn't you find anywhere less squalid?"

"'Squalid'? How dare you call Frank Sinatra's favorite pizzeria squalid? My god, your soul is twisted."

"I've always preferred Tony Bennett to Sinatra. Anyway, I see no need to go to Brooklyn for something as overrated as pizza. You know what the air smells like in Brooklyn? Sweaty balls."

Siobhan rubbed her temples. Just when her feelings toward him were starting to mellow, that idiot went and pissed her off all over again.

She counted her thoughts off on her fingers.

"Okay, so, number one: Didn't your parents teach you that it's good manners to say thank you? Number two: there isn't a single pizzeria in Manhattan with a wood-fired oven, but Grimaldi's has one. So, like it or not, tonight you're going to get your ass over to Brooklyn. And number three: I'm sorry I don't have the luxury of an Amex with no credit limit like you do, Mr. Bestseller of the Upper East Side. Next year, I'll reserve a table at Eleven Madison Park."

She wanted to impress him. But Marcel sounded anything but impressed when he replied:

"Pah. You can save yourself the two hundred and ninety-five dollars. I've had Chef Humm's honey lavender duck several times and it's no great shakes."

Two hundred and ninety-five dollars? For that price, they should be coating the ducks in gold before sticking them in the oven.

The strange thing was that, despite being together every day and the fact that the odious Mr. Black had an exasperating knack for infuriating her, the prospect of seeing him somewhere other than his penthouse was rather exciting. Was she some kind of masochist?

Probably.

About an hour later, Siobhan arrived in Dumbo, at the foot of the majestic Brooklyn Bridge. How many starry-eyed couples had strolled across it hand in hand on torrid August nights like this? How many promises had been made on that feat of engineering built over the fast-flowing waters of the East River? A hopeless romantic like her couldn't help but wonder about these kinds of things. The two men were waiting for her at the door, standing apart from the usual weekend line. Marcel was sporting a mid fade haircut and had shaped his stubble slightly; it was hard to imagine there could be a sexier man within a thousand-mile radius; he looked like he had just walked out of an Alicia Keys video. Noticing that he was looking at her and barely disguising the fact that those feline eyes were roving all over her body, she quashed any feelings of feminist guilt and was pleased she had opted for the short dress.

Alex welcomed her with a smile that lit up his whole face.

"The writer of the moment!" he exclaimed. They hadn't seen each other since the contract signing in the Baxter Books office, but they had exchanged several messages during that time. What's more, Alex Shapiro was the kind of person who made you feel like you had known them your whole life. "You look gorgeous. If you don't mind me saying so," he added. "Isn't she gorgeous, Marcel?"

Marcel shrugged and frowned.

"I couldn't say. She looks the same as ever to me."

But what . . . Was he serious?

"I would have thought you'd have learned to behave in company by now."

A sneer took shape on Siobhan's lips.

"I'm afraid your esteemed client has all the social skills of a bag of chips."

"I have a good ass too. It's interesting you didn't mention that," countered Marcel, directing a meaningful glance her way. The meaning being: *I know how much you like to look at it in secret.*

Five seconds. That was how long it took for Siobhan's cheeks to flush a deep shade of crimson.

She stuck out her tongue in reply.

"What a pair. It's incredible you're both still alive," said Alex, laughing. "Anyway, let's head inside. I'm starving."

Grimaldi's had a particular New York vibe, somewhere between a Hopper painting and *Once Upon a Time in America* with a louder color scheme. They sat next to one of the vast windows that looked onto the street, at a table with the typical red-and-white checkered tablecloth. The air smelled of tomato sauce, oregano, and flour. Alex and Marcel sat on one side, Siobhan on the other. A waiter—one of those Italian Americans whose English is inflected with the accent of their great-grandparents' country, despite never having set foot in

Italy—took their order. They asked for a bottle of prosecco and three Margherita pizzas that turned out to be so big only Tony Soprano could have finished one. The place was packed. Italian classics like "Tu vuo fa' l'americano," by Renato Carosone, and "Il mondo," by Jimmy Fontana were playing on the speakers so loudly that diners had to raise their voices to be heard. They toasted the birthday boy, who didn't appear to be particularly enthused by the celebration. Initially, Alex and Siobhan talked while Marcel limited himself to downing his wine, with a blank expression, as though he was holding back some kind of trauma that must never be confessed. By the second bottle of prosecco, Marcel had stopped studying his cuticles and started to participate. Every so often, Siobhan's gaze drifted to his hands. He had lovely hands. Strong but gentle, with long, slim, elegant fingers. When she found herself wondering what else he might be able to do with them apart from type, she rebuked herself and pleaded with her imagination for a silent truce.

"So, tell me. How's the bestseller coming along?" asked Alex as he folded over a portion of pizza to slot it into his mouth.

"You know I don't like talking about a book while I'm writing it. It diminishes the story," replied Marcel with the weary condescension of a teacher who has heard the same question a hundred times.

"Nonsense," Siobhan said, shaking her head. "Marcel's had quite the steep learning curve. But even so, I think we're making good headway. It's a mix between *Castle*, *Sherlock Holmes*, and *Kate & Leopold*."

"It's more *Sherlock Holmes* than *Kate & Leopold*," qualified Marcel.

"Mm-hmm." Alex finished chewing, swallowed, and wiped his mouth on his napkin. "Interesting. I mean, comparisons are horrible, but commercial success has a lot to do with the association of ideas. Your editor will love it."

"Well, of course he's gonna love it," spluttered Marcel. "Bob Gunton is the greediest man in publishing. That moron is convinced he discovered me. Sometimes he even takes the liberty of mentioning 'our books' when talking about *my* work. I mean, honestly." He pursed his lips and leaned back. "Who do you think paid for his beach house in the Hamptons? If *Two Ways* turns out to be a hit, he'll claim the whole thing was his idea."

Alex looked puzzled.

"*Two Ways to Solve a Murder in Manhattan.* That's the title of the book," explained Siobhan.

"Wow!"

"You like it?"

"You betcha. It's the kind of title that gives you a little jolt inside. Whose idea was it?"

"Hers," said Marcel.

"Both of ours," said Siobhan.

Marcel glanced at her but made no remark.

"Well, when the time comes, we'll meet with the design team at Baxter Books. We have to make sure they nail the cover design. The font is crucial. I think a sans serif that conveys both strength and elegance would be perfect. Readers have to be able tell at first glance that this is both a crime and a romance novel."

"Thank god!" Siobhan cried out, holding up her hands, palms outward. "Did you hear that, Marcel? *Crime and romance.* You don't need to leave your personal scent on each page like you're pissing around a tree trunk."

Alex spluttered with laughter.

"Tell me your ego is too big without telling me your ego is too big. I love this girl."

Marcel raised one of his thick, dark eyebrows. Those who knew him would have recognized that expression and run for cover immediately.

"If you didn't write like a groupie who's horny for Superman, I wouldn't have to correct everything you do—right down to your shopping list."

"Wow. Maybe it was too much to expect one of your dazzling metaphors, but you might have come up with something a little more poetic."

"The poetics are your department, princess."

"What's so bad about writing from the heart?"

"*That* is precisely your problem. A good author doesn't write from the heart or any other organ except for the brain."

"Why do you always have to be so rational? Sometimes I think you're made of stone. It's . . ." Siobhan mulled over a dozen ways to end her sentence. "Demoralizing."

"Then perhaps the most intelligent thing you could do would be to stop trying to understand me," he said, unable to mask the defensive tone in his voice.

This truth struck her in the face like a blast of cold air.

Well, I'll be damned if that wasn't a complete revelation.

She nodded in silence. Marcel was right. Trying to understand that evasive and mysterious man was like sticking her neck into the lion's den. Even so, the more time she spent with him, the more she wanted to get close to the beast. She wanted to both study him up close and never have to think about him again for the rest of her life.

It was genuinely crazy.

Just then, someone shouted her name and roused her from her trance.

"Shiv!"

It was Paige. Paige? Seriously? What were the chances of meeting someone she knew in all the thousands of restaurants in this city? Chance was a fickle thing. Naturally she was happy to see one of her best friends, but this was neither the time nor the place for socializing. And certainly not in this company. How should she introduce Marcel? What should she say?

They exchanged a fleeting glance that said, *We're screwed.*

"Paige! What a coincidence," she exclaimed. She got up from the table and hugged her friend at length, trying to gain time to build a reasonably solid story. "Let me look at you. You look . . . different. Have you done something to your hair?"

"Uh, no."

"Really? Because it looks more . . ."

"Loose?"

"Yes!"

"Oh, that," she said, and shook her precious red Jessica Rabbit mane seductively. "It must be my new hair mask. It's organic. No sulphates or parabens, you know. So, what brings you here?"

"I've come for dinner."

"Well, that's obvious."

"Yup."

There was an uncomfortable pause during which she could almost hear her own heartbeat.

"Aren't you going to introduce us?"

"What? Yes, yes! Sorry, I don't know what I'm thinking." She cleared her throat. "This is Alex Shapiro, literary agent."

"Paige D'Alessandro." She extended her hand. "Please, don't get up. Has anyone ever told you you look a lot like Aaron Eckhart?"

"The guy who played Harvey Dent in *The Dark Knight*? I don't think so. I would have remembered. But you've just given my self-esteem a nice boost."

"Well, make sure you keep it up there." She turned to Marcel. "And you are . . . ?"

Siobhan decided to take the initiative. This was the moment to test her worth as a professional storyteller.

"This is Ma . . . Michael. His name is Michael. And he's . . ." She counted to three in her head and released the bomb. "He's Alex's boyfriend."

Marcel clenched his jaw hard as Alex struggled to contain his laughter.

My god, this is going to get ugly, and we've only just started, I can feel it.

"Ah, I see. You make a lovely couple. And I don't just mean because interracial is, you know"—she made air quotes with her fingers—"'fashionable.' I'm all for diversity. Our friend Lena is Jewish, and she's dating a girl of Palestinian origin. I mean, technically, Noor isn't Black, but her skin is dark enough to fall under the BIPOC banner. Wait, can you still use the term *BIPOC,* or is it too broad? I mean, aren't we glossing over the particular characteristics of each group if we lump them all together under the same label? I mean, the history of African Americans in the United States is marked by slavery and segregation, which is very different from what Native Americans experienced. Correct me if I'm wrong, Michael."

"No, you're not wrong."

Over the course of the next few minutes, Paige jumped on the train of social conscience and made it clear she wasn't about to get off any time soon. She railed against Trump, the NRA, alt-right white supremacists, Friends of Abe, police violence, the tyranny of Wall Street, inequality, and poverty.

A vein was throbbing on Marcel's forehead.

"The Great Awakening of progressive white America. Thanks for the TED talk," he blurted out.

The slap echoed as far as Pensacola.

"Shit. That was quite the put-down. Are you always this friendly?"

"Not normally, no. This is your lucky day."

Alex hastily tried to change the subject.

"Don't listen to him. Michael's a bit . . . sensitive about certain topics. Hey, Paige, why don't you sit down and have a glass of wine with us? Shiv's friends are our friends. Right, babe?" he said, lovingly draping his arm around Marcel's shoulder.

While Alex seemed to be enjoying this comedy sketch, Marcel's vein threatened to burst at any moment and give the game away.

"I can't, I'm meeting my Tinder date for dinner. He's Italian. Well, technically he's from Bensonhurst, but you know what I mean." She checked her iPhone. "Where on earth is he? He should be here already. Has he never heard of the fifteen-minutes-early rule? I swear to god, if he's late, I'll send him straight to the friendzone. Anyway, how's the new novel coming along?"

"Oh. Pretty well. I suppose."

Paige looked at her curiously.

"Jesus, Shiv, you're acting weird tonight. Is it because of that psychopath Marcel Black? Has he threatened you or something? Don't tell me he's still got a pole stuck up his ass."

Siobhan swallowed. And Marcel had to swallow something else—his own anger, more than likely. All the while Alex was pressing his lips together so as not to erupt into laughter. Perhaps the moment had come to shout, *Earthquake!* and hide under the table.

"Well . . . things have gotten a bit better in the last few weeks."

"Just in case, always take pepper spray with you. And if he tries to kill you on the pretext of research, make sure you get his DNA under your fingernails. Never trust handsome men. Most of them are perverts who like sending dick pics."

"How do you know Marcel Black is handsome?" asked Marcel, in a tone suggesting genuine interest. "Have you met him?"

"That slippery bastard? Hardly. Shiv told us. Her precise words were *a hot piece of ass*."

It was official: she was going to have a heart attack.

An irritatingly victorious smile started to glimmer on Marcel's lips. The dimple under his stubble was unreasonably cute. Siobhan started to scratch her neck compulsively as she looked the other way. Her face burned with shame.

"I don't recall having used those exact words," she murmured.

But the damage was done.

"Well, it's great to see you," said Paige, taking her friend by the hands. "I know you're superbusy with the novel, but Lena and I miss you."

Siobhan's heart softened.

"Awww . . . And I miss you guys. Let's do something. We'll have a night out."

"Yes, let's! I know a new place in the Meatpacking District. It's gay friendly." She turned to face the two men. "You game?"

"Just try and stop me," enthused Alex, to Marcel's great consternation.

The sound of Paige's cell phone put an end to this drama. When she had left, Siobhan felt all the tension that had accumulated in her lower back rise to her shoulders and evaporate toward the ceiling. She fell back in her seat as though a tornado had just passed, and only then did she burst out laughing. Alex joined her.

"I don't find it remotely funny," protested Marcel. "And you, princess, couldn't you have thought up something better? His boyfriend. Come on!"

"Hey, I'm not all that bad. You heard Paige: I look like Aaron Eckhart."

"Yeah, and I look like Obama. Why the hell did you come out with that horseshit?"

Siobhan couldn't believe it.

"So, my friend calls you a psychopath, and what worries you is that I suggest you're gay. Really, Marcel? Sorry, I didn't know your masculinity was so fragile."

"Checkmate," murmured Alex.

Marcel looked up at the ceiling and sighed.

"It's not that, all right? It's simply not credible. Period. I'm sure your friend realized you were making it up as you went along. If she's quick-witted enough, she'll have put two and two together right away."

"Okay, and what did you want me to say? That you're in the witness protection program, and I couldn't reveal your identity?"

"You could have said we were together."

For a moment, Siobhan felt a slight tickle in her stomach that rose to her chest. She wasn't going to pretend she had never fantasized about the idea of walking hand in hand with Marcel along the colorful, leafy path of the High Line, the historic disused railroad that was now one of the most popular public parks in Manhattan.

But it was just that: a highly improbable fantasy.

"Together? You and me? Like on a date? Oh, please, don't make me laugh! That really would have sounded far-fetched."

"Why?" he asked with a note of disbelief.

"Because I wouldn't date you if you were the only survivor of an alien attack. I'm about as attracted to you as I am to Danny DeVito in a Speedo."

"Is Danny DeVito a hot piece of ass too? Wow, you have the strangest taste."

Again, that suffocating heat in her cheeks. *You and your big mouth, Paige,* she thought.

"It's possible that at some point I might have mentioned that your appearance isn't . . . Let's say . . . um . . . entirely unpleasant. Nothing more," she concluded. "So don't get your hopes up."

"Ha! That's rich! Hopes? With you? Little Miss Happy Endings? The queen of sugar? I'd rather ask Alex here to marry me."

"Don't be offended, Michael, but I don't want to be anyone's second choice," said Alex, who had been watching them as though he was at a tennis match. He started laughing and rubbed his face as he sighed. "My god, you two are so alike. Do you know, there are so many sparks flying between you that it's like Fourth of July fireworks? They can see you in Jersey right now."

Siobhan lowered her head and bit the inside of her cheek. She had noticed it too, or at least she thought she had. The night they had dinner together at his house and he massaged her hand to relieve the strain, she had definitely felt something. Heat. Static electricity. A shock. It frightened her to feel so attracted to a man like Marcel Dupont.

A man whose very existence could move her so strongly it might jolt her heart out of place.

"Just when I thought I'd heard everything . . . ," muttered Marcel as he stood up.

"Where are you going?" asked Alex.

"To the bathroom. I've got Jordan hanging on the hoop about to score a basket. Do I need to be more specific, *darling*?"

"Nah. Don't bother."

When Siobhan and Alex were alone, they exchanged a knowing look.

"He's such a shit."

"I know. Even so . . ." She bit her lip. "I never thought I'd say this, and if you dare repeat it in front of Marcel, I'll deny the words ever left my lips. The thing is I think I've started to get used to him. I like working with him. It's very stimulating."

"He likes you too, I'm sure of it."

"If he heard you saying that, he'd cut your balls off, dice them up, and turn them into fish food."

"You do know him well."

"Well, Marcel is a closed book in some regards and wide open in others. Did I tell you I found a copy of my novel hidden under his sofa cushions?"

"Nooooo!"

"You'd better believe it. And when I asked, he said he had no idea how it had gotten there."

"Typical of Marcel. But anyway, I think you're both doing a fantastic job. You make a good team." He smiled enigmatically and added: "Changing the subject, your friend . . . Does she date a lot of guys on Tinder? I only ask because . . . I'm on Tinder too and . . . I'd like to know what kind of guys she's into."

"Put it this way: if you vote Democrat and read Jonathan Franzen, your chances will increase substantially."

Alex opened his arms in a dramatic gesture.

"But you've just described me."

"Well, then, I'll tell her you've split up with Michael and you're rethinking your sexuality. That sound okay?"

"That sounds awesome. And please, don't forget to tell her I'm staunchly anti-dick-pic."

Marcel returned ten minutes later. He hadn't just taken care of his intestinal needs but had paid the check as well.

"That wasn't what we agreed," protested Siobhan. "It was supposed to be my treat for your birthday, but I guess you don't understand that it's a matter of female empowerment. Another reason I would never date you. You're the classic guy who feels morally obliged to pay for dinner."

"Heavens above." He pinched the bridge of his nose. "Can you turn off the protest switch for just five minutes and give me a break? I didn't do it because I'm a *guy*, okay?" He uttered the word as though it were painful.

Alex intervened.

"It's his way of apologizing for having been a jerk. What? Why are you looking at me like that, Marcel? Someone had to tell you."

"Have you been conspiring against me while I was in the bathroom? Come on, let's get out of here."

On the street, Siobhan suggested they go for another drink in the neighborhood.

"But I'm paying," she stressed.

"I can't," Alex said. "I have a pile of manuscripts this high waiting for me. You two go. I'm sure Marcel will want to keep celebrating his birthday with you. Isn't that right, my friend?"

Chapter 17

MARCEL

Note to self: kill Alex with my bare hands next time I see him.

He had done it on purpose. That bastard had taken off with the express intention of leaving them alone together. Manuscripts to revise—yeah, right. And what was that horseshit about sparks? Was it so obvious that he liked Siobhan? Because, if that was the case, he had an additional problem. As for her friend, would she have noticed, or was she too caught up in her display of rehearsed woke moralizing? Perhaps the reason he had been behaving like a boorish, immature asshole for most of the meal was precisely that: to hide his feelings from prying eyes. Although it seemed he hadn't tried hard enough, given the circumstances. Now that they were alone, his body was crying out for him to stop feeling irritated by everything and nothing at the same time. Though he didn't particularly want another drink, he did feel like enjoying her company for a while longer. So, in an act of part-generosity, part-selfishness, he suggested they take a walk.

"Are you sure the Brooklyn air won't make you vomit?" asked Siobhan.

"I think I can handle it."

They headed for the Promenade, a broad pedestrian walkway next to the East River. The air, thick and sweltering even in the evening, stuck cloyingly to his skin. The sky glittered under the mantle of lights reaching as far as New Jersey. In the distance, the Statue of Liberty waited impassively for a new day to arrive and with it, the hordes of tourists with cameras and green foam crowns. Beyond the dark waters rose the silhouette of Manhattan. For a moment William J. Knox entered his thoughts. He imagined him right there, in a turbulent summer in the 1920s, with the sun rising at his back, watching the dawn reflected in the urban skyline still under construction. Today, it was the most recognizable cityscape in the world. It was interesting to look at that changeable urban jungle from the opposite shore. It didn't seem real. Except that it was. He had walked along those blocks crammed with people who didn't care who he was or how he had gotten there. He had become just another New Yorker. The city had taught him how to become anonymous, to show what he wanted to show and no more.

"I don't really think you have a pole stuck up your ass," Siobhan blurted out.

Marcel gave a one-sided smile.

"And I don't think you write like a groupie. I mean, you're no Joyce Carol Oates, but I'm sure you have a great future ahead of you."

"Is that a compliment?"

"It might be."

"Wow! To what do I owe the honor?"

"Who knows. Anyway, don't get used to it. I'm not the kind of man who goes around handing out compliments to newbie writers."

"No shit," she replied. Then she smiled.

She was lovely when she smiled naturally like that.

"How's your hand?"

"Much better, thanks," she said, rotating her wrist to demonstrate. "I've been doing the stretches you taught me."

He would be lying if he said he hadn't been recreating that apparently insignificant gesture over and over in his mind since it happened.

It was ridiculous.

It was new.

"Well, princess. You need to strengthen your muscles if you don't want the pain to drive you crazy over the next few weeks. And believe me, we've got some really intense weeks ahead of us. The hardest part of the process is about to begin—the real rock 'n' roll."

Siobhan took a deep breath.

"You know what? Sometimes I think writing a book is kind of like sex: you need to put in the work if you want to climax." And then she added: "I mean the perfect, choreographed Hollywood kind of sex. In real life, you're more likely to get stalled along the way."

Marcel guffawed and gave a spontaneous clap. He was laughing so hard he had to stop walking for a moment and bend over.

"I think you need to change gender, sweetie," he said in a honeyed voice that made his accent even more pronounced.

Was he flirting?

Goddamn it if that didn't sound like a come-on.

They walked for a while, enveloped in a comfortable haze of silence. Marcel, with his hands in his pockets; Siobhan, gripping the strap of her purse. The red lights of airplanes starting their descent into LaGuardia and JFK flashed ceaselessly. Along the walkway, groups of teenagers were listening to rap, couples were making out, and tourists were all taking selfies with the skyscrapers in the background.

"How did you and Alex meet?"

"It's a long story. You'd find it boring."

"But your skill at summarizing is astounding."

Marcel sighed with resignation. He sensed that Siobhan wouldn't give up, so he decided to satisfy her curiosity.

"When I arrived here from New Orleans," he began, "I spent two years juggling various low-paid jobs to make rent while I was writing my first novel. I lived here back then. You know that?"

"You mean . . . in Brooklyn?" she asked incredulously, looking really quite astounded.

"Yup. In a filthy apartment in Bed-Stuy, between a Black salon and an old Baptist church converted into a rehab center for the worst drug addicts, whores, and dealers in the neighborhood."

"How inspiring."

"You can't imagine."

"So that's why you hate Brooklyn, because it reminds you of your difficult early days here, before you became a shining example of the American dream."

"Believe it or not, I've never forgotten who I am or where I come from. Money hasn't washed the melanin from my skin or turned me into an Oreo. I'm not Black on the outside and white on the inside, even though I live on the Upper East Side."

A long silence followed, long enough for Marcel to rewind and realize he might have been a tad hard on her. An imaginary BuzzFeed caption appeared in his mind, saying:

You've blown it, asshole.

He squeezed his eyes shut.

"I'm sorry. I didn't mean . . ."

"It's fine, Marcel. Honestly," she reassured him, patting his arm gently. And every single hard edge on him softened to her touch. "Go on."

"All right. I met Alex by chance. One of those lousy jobs was washing dishes in a diner in Hell's Kitchen. Sometimes, if it was really busy, I would lend a hand waiting tables. One night, I noticed a man sitting at the back. He caught my attention because he was reading, and well, you know, a diner isn't the kind of place you go to read. So I served him his house special hamburger and checked out the book he had on the table. Paul Auster's *New York Trilogy*. So, I tell him it's not bad, but *Leviathan* is much better because the plot isn't as linear as it first appears and blah blah blah. I remember he looked at me and then to either side, like he was searching for a hidden camera or something. It was very funny. I don't suppose he was expecting to hear literary analysis in a place that reeked of onion rings. And much less from a Black waiter with earrings and a Louisiana accent."

"No! I can't believe you used to wear earrings."

"Thankfully, I'm a reformed man," he added, touching his lobes. The holes had closed up over time.

"So, what happened?"

"He said, 'I'll let you in on a secret. I actually think Auster's a bit of a drag.'"

Siobhan raised both thumbs.

"Retweet."

"I liked him right away. When he explained he had just started his own literary agency, I thought it must be some kind of sign from the universe, and I decided to tell him about *An Ordinary Man*. The idea interested him. Even though all the publishing houses had already rejected it."

"Wait. What? They rejected you? You?"

"They did indeed. And each rejection was like a blow to the heart. But then, it was also the prelude to success."

Siobhan snorted disbelievingly.

"I bet those editors must have wanted to end it when they realized."

"Some of them really excel at letting golden opportunities slip through their fingers. You know how many publishers rejected Stephen King's *Carrie*? About thirty."

"Carnage."

"It's all part of the process. You, Miss Harris, are an extraordinary exception."

"I know. I'm aware of how lucky I am. Although Paige always says that luck is a relative concept. Anyway, it doesn't matter. What did Alex make of the fact that they turned down your novel?"

"Said I probably hadn't sold it well. 'Okay, so how am I supposed to do it?' I asked him. And he answered, 'Leave that to me.'"

"It sounds like the start of a beautiful friendship."

Marcel's mouth curved into a nostalgic grin.

"One thing's for sure: if it weren't for him, I wouldn't be where I am now. It wasn't easy, of course. The publishing industry is a complex ecosystem. But Alex is a very intelligent man who knows what he wants. If you ask me, you should get his agency to represent you. Nothing against Bella Watson. I'm just saying that Shapiro is the best in the business."

Silence.

"It's kind of you to be concerned about me."

Marcel snorted with laughter.

"Who said I'm concerned about you, princess?"

She responded with a mocking smile.

Near Fort Stirling Park, a saxophonist was playing "Summertime" under a streetlight in front of a small improvised audience. They stopped to listen, hanging a few steps behind the crowd.

"That's the way to play, brother," said Marcel, keeping beat with his fingers and nodding his head rhythmically.

Then, he noticed Siobhan pulling her phone out of her purse and getting ready to record a video. It infuriated him so much that he grabbed her phone from her hand impulsively and held it behind his back.

"But what . . . ? Why did you take my phone?"

"Because you have to learn to live in the moment. Without recording it."

"Bullshit. Come on, give it back."

"No chance."

"Please could you return my cell phone to me, Marcel?"

"Nope."

"Okay, you asked for it."

Everything that happened next seemed to happen in a haze. Siobhan stepped toward Marcel and started to grapple with him to retrieve the phone. The considerable height difference between them didn't make things easy. During the ensuing tug-of-war, she lost her balance and fell against him. Marcel caught her, one hand on her shoulder, the other around that slender waist.

The sax leaned into a sensual crescendo.

"I got you," he whispered.

"You got me."

Siobhan's eyes seemed to darken. Suddenly, in a stupid and rash gesture, Marcel slid his hand from her waist to the curve of her bare back, above the line of her dress. He wanted to touch her hot skin, run his fingertips through the embers, play with fire. Burn himself. She moistened her lips, and all intelligent thought had abandoned him. For half a second, the music, the people, and all the rest of it seemed to exist on the other side of a bubble.

And again, that goddamn feeling of vertigo fluttered in his stomach.

As though he was on the edge of a cliff, about to fall into sin.

The question was whether he would be able to step back in time.

Chapter 18

Siobhan

Try as she might, it just wasn't humanly possible for her to concentrate that morning. Every time she thought of Marcel's caress, the heat she had felt the night before spilled through her body like liquid asphalt. It had been special. Intense. So special and intense that she was convinced it had meant something. But when the last notes of "Summertime" faded, he had pulled away from her abruptly, and the feeling vanished. And now, all she wanted to do was dissect the before and after of that moment. Then there was the fact that Marcel had opened the door in his workout clothes—heavens alive, those running tights accentuated his muscular thighs, quite the sight for sore eyes—and soaked in sweat because he had inexplicably woken later than usual, and his morning exercise routine had been delayed. And finally, she couldn't help but think about the fact that while she was preparing the coffee, he was in the shower. Naked. Wet. With water cascading over his dark skin.

The imagination is a double-edged sword.

Later on, her conversation with Paige and Lena on the group chat only made things worse.

Paige

I'm NEVER sleeping with another man again. I am officially going into SEXILE.

Shiv

What happened?

Paige

The guy I was with last night let out an almighty fart right in the act.
A FART.
I'm traumatized.

Shiv

I don't believe it!

Lena

I could believe anything of a white cis hetero man.
I hope at least it was discreet.

Paige

About as discreet as a pipe bursting in the middle of the night.
For a moment I thought he had shat the bed.

Lena

Too much information.

Shiv

Gross!

Lena

Tell me he apologized.

Paige

Negative.

He started laughing with his prick still inside me and said they were OCCUPATIONAL GASES.

The brute didn't even seem embarrassed.

Shiv

NOOOOO!

Lena

So not only did the guy have dodgy pipework, he was a comedian as well. My god, Paige, you're onto a WINNER there.

Paige

I know, OK? I'm a frickin' weirdo-magnet.

Anyway, Shiv. Are you 100% sure your friend Alex is gay?

Because he couldn't stop looking at my tits.

Lena

Alex? Who's Alex? Have I missed something?

Paige

So, last night I bumped into Shiv at Grimaldi's. She was with two guys, Alex and Michael, supposedly a gay couple. And I say supposedly because I got the impression they were both MEGA-HETERO. Alex was charming, the kind of guy who's all smiles. As for Michael . . . well, I admit he's hot, but he's also SUPER-RUDE.

Shiv

He isn't all that rude. He's just . . . a bit tricky to handle.

Paige

Tricky verging on impossible.

Lena

And how do you know them, Shiv?

Paige

Alex is a literary agent. The other . . . I suppose he comes as part of the package. If they are actually a couple, that is.

Lena

Wait. Wasn't Marcel Black's agent named Alex?

Shit.

At that point, Siobhan dropped out of the conversation. Lena was the most intuitive of the three; Siobhan should have known Lena would figure it out right away.

This was another factor adding to the constant hum in her poor tormented head.

A couple of hours later, as her fingers were drifting erratically over the keyboard, she pressed the *M* key—*M* for Marcel, what a coincidence—and held her finger down until a line of *M*s appeared on the computer screen. Before that she had made and unmade a ponytail, tidied her side of the desk, emptied half a pack of Jelly Bellies into her mouth, stretched her arms over her head, and yawned at regular intervals.

It's a well-known fact that boredom changes the way we perceive space and time.

Marcel sighed heavily.

"You're making me anxious. Don't you have anything better to do? Like work or something?"

"Sorry. I don't know what's up with me today." She did know. "I can't concentrate. The words aren't flowing. I don't even feel like writing."

"Yeah. Me neither," he admitted, taking off his glasses and placing them on the desk.

Maybe he had the same image burned on his retinas, of the two of them in that magical and perfect moment under a streetlight, with the East River in the background. Maybe the sensuality of the sax was still ringing in his ears. And maybe he regretted having jumped into a taxi instead of staying with her.

Too many maybes and not a sure thing in sight.

"Why don't we take the day off?" suggested Siobhan.

"Okay," he agreed, massaging the bridge of his nose with an absent expression. "Go home and come back tomorrow with your batteries recharged."

"Actually . . ." She paused and bit her lip. "I was thinking we could do something together."

"You and I?"

"Yes, you and I. Perhaps we could . . . I don't know . . . go to the beach?"

Marcel looked at her as though she were an alien.

"You're kidding, right? The beach? In this heat?" He gestured toward the window.

"Come on, don't be a wet blanket. We haven't stopped for a month and a half. Don't you think we deserve at least one day of rest?"

"Well, yes, but . . . why the beach? It's mid-August. Everyone'll be packed in like sardines," he said. "If you want to see me in my swimsuit, I'll get changed right now. It's no problem."

Siobhan half closed her eyes and sighed.

"My god, you're conceited, Mr. Black. I just want to see the sea, that's all. Feel the sand between my toes and the sun on my skin. Come on, do it for me." She pouted and fluttered her lashes in an attempt to appear irresistible. "Please?"

Marcel tutted, notably irritated.

"How is it that you always get your way? Fine, we'll go to the lousy beach," he said, sighing with resignation.

Yes! She had won.

◆ ◆ ◆

They arrived at Coney Island at midday. Marcel had spent the twenty-nine stops between Seventy-Second and Ocean Parkway, at the end of the Q line, complaining as usual:

"A rickshaw would have been more comfortable . . . I don't like the New York subway, you know? There are rats everywhere . . . Do you have a wet wipe? I hate sitting in someone else's ass sweat."

It was the price she had to pay to satisfy her desires.

The sun fell heavily on the peninsula south of Brooklyn. As expected, the beach was mobbed. The broad strip of sand was speckled with colorful umbrellas and towels from the boardwalk to the water's edge, and the music from each outlet vied for dominance. The first song that reached Siobhan's ears was "Shape of You," by Ed Sheeran, which a few seconds later merged into "24K Magic," by Bruno Mars. Generally, the kind of people who visited Coney Island in mid-August were New York families, although that day there were also groups of boys playing Frisbee and girls taking selfies. And, of course, a bunch of tourists. A light aircraft flew overhead trailing a long Budweiser advertising banner.

Siobhan took out her cat-eye sunglasses from her purse and put them on.

"Let's go?"

"Where?"

"To see the sea up close."

Marcel pulled down his dark cap and folded his arms across his chest like a petulant child. His disgust was palpable.

"I can see it perfectly well from here, thank you. And I'm pretty sure there are sharks."

"But you're from Louisiana."

"What does that have to do with anything?"

"Are you shitting me? Everyone knows that folks from Louisiana have gators on their porches."

"Yes, of course. And we eat them at Thanksgiving because the meat tastes better than turkey."

Siobhan laughed. Then she grabbed Marcel by the elbow, and he allowed himself to be pulled along, against his better judgment. They dodged a group of inline skaters, the wooden walkway vibrating beneath their wheels. They went down the stairs onto the sand and wove their way through the beach umbrellas and deck chairs. A foot here, another there, step to the left, step to the right; it was like playing Twister. The place stank of sunscreen. Three seagulls were perched on the lifeguard station. The waves rolled in constant low ripples. At the water's edge, Siobhan took off her sandals and let the Atlantic lick her feet. A sense of well-being flooded over her right away. The scent of the sea reminded her of the happiest times of her childhood. Marcel took off his shoes as well.

"Isn't it amazing?" she asked, her gaze fixed on the horizon.

"What, that a crummy beach like this is jam-packed with people? Oh yeah, amazing."

"I mean this," she gestured toward the ocean. The blue sky met the sea in a perfect line in the distance. "I don't know what it is, but watching it makes me feel like I'm in harmony with the world. I remember when Robin and I were little, and my dad taught us to fish."

"There are studies showing the neurological benefits of the sea. Just being near water reduces stress and improves mental clarity. It releases endorphins. It's a natural painkiller."

"See? It was a good idea to come here," she said and then splashed water over Marcel with her foot.

"Did you just splash me?" he said, fixing her with a glare of feigned indignation. "Did you seriously dare to splash me?"

She splashed him again in reply.

"Are you . . . ? You want war, huh, princess? Very well, I'll give you war."

He crouched, grabbed a fistful of sand and lobbed it at her knees, just below her denim shorts, with a speed she didn't see coming.

"Hey, New Orleans! That was uncalled for. Pearl Harbor fell after much less. Take this!"

No sooner said than done. Her revenge was a huge ball of sloppy sand that landed right in the middle of Marcel's thin T-shirt. From his crazed expression, Siobhan knew she should run. But he was faster. When he caught her, he trapped her in his arms and smeared her with sand. They started to laugh and couldn't stop. Marcel was charming when he laughed: he threw his head back and revealed those marble-white teeth. It was a spontaneous and genuine gesture, which spread right across his face. The unthinkable had occurred: they were having fun together. Laughing! Who would have thought it would feel so good. The hum of the waves increased in intensity, decreased, increased again. The laughter gradually petered out, although they remained tangled together. Siobhan stretched out her hand to touch the point, just below his Adam's apple, where the sand had dried to form a small crust. She used her thumb to brush it off and then, on an impulse, slid her thumb down and hooked it over the neck of his T-shirt. His skin was such a beautiful color she would have liked to tell him so, but it would have been inappropriate. Marcel's intense gaze roamed to her eyes. Then, to that rebellious strand of hair across her face. And finally, to her lips. An electric current flowed between them. The fire she had seen in him the night before returned, glowing behind his jet-black eyes.

"You're going to burn," he warned her, with that hoarse voice that came out in intimate moments, emphasizing the natural musicality of his accent.

"I don't care," replied Siobhan, almost without thinking.

Marcel gave a lazy smile.

"I doubt those lily-white shoulders of yours would agree. Come on, let's find a bit of shade. I'll treat you to an ice cream."

Siobhan let out her breath very slowly, trying to release the tension in her ribs. She wanted to beat her head against a wall.

"I'm not five years old," she protested. "But then, if they have mint chocolate chip . . ."

They went to Nathan's—you don't go to Coney Island without visiting the legendary Nathan's. They ordered sodas and hot dogs, which they devoured under the capacious parasol at one of the tables on the boardwalk, with the emblematic Ferris wheel and the Cyclone, the mother of all roller coasters, forming the backdrop. At that time of day, the attractions were closed, but later, when the last rays of sun had dissipated and the horizon had adopted an orangey hue, the place would erupt in an explosion of noise, neon lights, and glittering bulbs.

"Well, well, well. Do you realize that's two days in a row you've forced me to come to Brooklyn? I assume you've thought of a way to make it up to me," remarked Marcel, before sinking his teeth into his hot dog.

"Now that you mention it, I don't recall having put a knife to your throat at any point. Could it be that you enjoy my company?"

"When you're being quiet."

"Ha! You're lucky the ketchup dispenser is four tables away," Siobhan said and stuck out her tongue.

Marcel's lips tightened into a sarcastic grin. As he took a drink, she was spellbound by the way his cheeks sunk in as he sucked the liquid through the straw.

My god, he's so ridiculously hot in every way. It's so unfair.

An ice cream and an espresso later, they were still sitting in the same spot. Neither of them seemed to have any intention of moving. The sea breeze, the sun's caress, and their full stomachs kept them rooted to the spot.

Siobhan pushed her sunglasses onto the top of her head and rested her cheek in her palm.

"Tell me something about yourself that I don't know," she asked him.

"You already know lots about me. More than most."

"That's because you live like you're a double agent in *The Americans*."

"To control the narrative."

"Come on, don't play hard to get," she pressed him, flapping her hand impatiently.

"All right." He interlaced his hands on the table. "But you have to do the same for me."

"All right. I'll start. Let's see, I went to NYU. Where did you go to college? In New Orleans, I expect, so Loyola or Tulane?"

"I didn't go to college. Everything I know about literature I learned on my own. I'm 100 percent self-taught."

Fascinating.

"A self-made man, and a talented one at that."

"Talent is all well and good, but it's no use without determination and hard work. If there's one thing you need to be successful as a writer, it's resilience. Always remember that, Miss Harris. Come on, next question."

"Okay. What was the last book you read?"

A mischievous smile played at the corners of his mouth. He raised a hand to his lips as though about to unveil a secret and leaned forward with an air of mystery.

"You know which one," he whispered.

Siobhan's mouth dropped open.

"You mean the one I found hidden in the sofa, which you denied having bought because you were ashamed to admit you could read a romance novel without dying in the attempt?"

"Mm-hmm. It's possible we're talking about the same book. Do you want to know whether I liked it?"

"And see you take pleasure in destroying my self-esteem? I'd rather commit hara-kiri."

Marcel shook his head.

"If you're going to let just anyone destroy your self-esteem, you'd better find another line of work. We don't write for people to like us, but to find meaning in what we don't understand." He scrutinized her with a stern expression, allowing her to take in his words. It wasn't a platitude or a reprimand. It was important. "And for your information, I think you have what it takes to be a writer."

"Wait. Can you repeat that last bit?"

"In your dreams. And now it's my turn to ask. Do you sing in the shower?"

"What kind of a question is that? Everyone sings in the shower."

"I don't."

"Oh, what a surprise. Given how jovial and joyous you are."

"*Jovial* and *joyous* are synonyms." Siobhan rolled her eyes. "Have you already forgotten our lesson from that first day? Economy of language, honey." The prick of annoyance she felt turned into something else when she noticed how naturally he had called her *honey*. "All right, next. The movie you've seen the most times?"

"*When Harry Met Sally*. And before it occurs to you to ask, no, I'm not going to emulate Meg Ryan faking an orgasm in Katz's." Marcel's face seemed to say, *What a pity.* "Favorite food? Let me guess. Filet mignon or Iranian caviar."

"Almost. Jambalaya."

"That's a Cajun dish, right?"

"Wrong. It isn't just any Cajun dish, it's *the* Cajun dish."

"I've never been to New Orleans. What's it like?"

"Well . . . ," he began. He took off his cap and played with it. "I'd say it's almost too intense. A mix of whites, Blacks, immigrants, Cajuns, and Creoles. A chaotic city, where great poverty exists alongside great wealth, sometimes on the same street. Ideal for drunks and dreamers who don't wake up before noon."

"Sounds good. Particularly the sleeping until noon. Any secret hobbies?"

"I like to sit in the hall of Grand Central Terminal, watching people and imagining their lives. It's one of my favorite places in New York. What's yours?"

"My favorite place?" She pushed her hair behind her ear as she pondered her reply. "The skating rink at Rockefeller Center at Christmas."

Marcel snorted involuntarily.

"I might have known."

"Are you judging me?"

"Ha! God forbid," he said, raising his hands in defense. "What would be your perfect day?"

"One spent with my nearest and dearest. And you?"

"One spent writing."

"Is there really nothing you like more than writing?"

"Of course not," he replied, as though it was obvious. "Not even sex. I mean, sex is very good, but writing is much more personal. Speaking of sex, what's the strangest place you've ever done it?"

Siobhan blushed. She could feel a blaze of shame furling over her neck and shoulders. Unable to meet his eyes, she averted her gaze.

"Well . . . um . . . in the back row on a Greyhound bus to Philadelphia."

Marcel's eyebrows shot up.

"Seriously?" He seemed genuinely surprised, and Siobhan couldn't help but feel offended by his reaction. What did he take her for? A prude? Just because she didn't sleep with the first man she met in the street didn't mean she was incapable of enjoying sex and being a bit daring. "Whoa, princess. Who was the lucky man? A college fling?"

"I don't . . . I don't have flings. It was Buckley, my ex. His family lives in Philly." She cleared her throat. "But that was a long time ago, when we first started dating."

Silence.

"Do you still think about him?"

Good question. Siobhan suddenly realized she couldn't remember the last time Buckley had crossed her mind. She also realized that the only man occupying her thoughts for more than two months had been Marcel.

Day and night.

A casual attraction had turned into an intense and unbearably dangerous sensation that made her skin bristle. And it wasn't just physical.

Every conversation with him revealed something new that made her like him more.

Much more.

So she said:

"All the time."

And she wasn't talking about her ex.

"It's terribly cruel when someone you love hurts you, and yet your feelings don't just fade," he replied. He sniffed and averted his gaze, his eyes narrowed, as though the glare of the sun was bothering him. Or perhaps something else was bothering him. "That's why I'd rather be alone, to avoid the distress."

"Well, I think solitude is unnatural. Everyone needs to love and be loved."

"My god, who still says horseshit like that? Love is nothing like the idealized vision you have in your head. It isn't something shiny and perfect that makes you recite Shakespeare sonnets in a field of lavender under a rainbow. Love upsets the balance and causes infernal pain." He looked at her disapprovingly. "As if there could ever be a happy ending in real life. It never happens."

Another silence, this time rather more tense.

She would have loved to stop to analyze him and search for clues about his personality and his past in each comment.

But she was becoming far too interested in this man.

"Are you speaking from experience?"

Marcel ran a hand over his face, exasperated.

"I'm not interested in relationships lasting longer than a night. I only take calculated risks."

"You're assuming that feelings can be controlled. They can't. They just emerge, and that's that. Sometimes you know it's going to fail, and you rush into it regardless. Have you never been in love, Marcel?"

"Okay, that's enough," he said, cutting her off and gesticulating wildly. "What kind of man talks about these things? What's next? Making s'mores and braiding our hair? I'll pass."

"You don't need to get all defensive. I'm just asking because sometimes you seem a bit resentful, that's all."

"All right, whatever. Can we change the subject, please?"

Siobhan nodded, and Marcel relaxed. The nerves settled, and the conversation continued to flow like before.

At least, until Siobhan asked:

"What are your parents' names?"

She found it strange to think of Marcel having a family and reconciling the idea that, before becoming a tall, antisocial cynic who didn't believe in happy endings, he was probably an adorable child. Not for the first time since she had met him, Siobhan considered how little they had spoken about his private life.

"Father. No mother. His name is Bernard. He lives in New Orleans with my sister, Charmaine." He swallowed and added: "He's been fighting Alzheimer's for a while now. She takes care of him."

Siobhan felt a lump form in her throat.

"I'm really sorry. I had no idea. That must be terrible."

"I haven't been to see them for a year. The last time . . ." He blinked. "See, my dad isn't in his right mind, and he does stuff that . . . Chaz refuses to place him in memory care. And I refuse to return to New Orleans while that man is still at home."

And in that fraction of a second, she saw it all clearly.

This was one hell of a revelation: Marcel Dupont was a human being who felt pain, sadness, confusion, and loneliness.

They looked at each other for a long time, without blinking. An invisible thread stretched from her eyes to his, and she felt as though electricity was crackling along that thread.

Suddenly, a voice broke the magic.

"Excuse me, are you Siobhan Harris?"

When she turned around, a group of teenage girls was surrounding the table.

"Um . . . yes."

The girls squealed. Siobhan and Marcel exchanged a sly glance.

"We've been watching you for a while, and we weren't sure if it was really you, but your face is, like, unmistakable," claimed the girl who seemed to be the leader of the group. "Oh my god, oh my god, oh my god. You're so much prettier in real life!"

"Thanks?"

Marcel frowned and lowered his head to hide his suppressed laughter.

Another girl said:

"We're superfans!"

And another:

"Yeah, *With Fate on Our Side* is our favorite book."

"Can we take a photo with you? Please, please, please?"

"Of course. Would you mind, Marcel?"

"No problem."

The girls posed next to Siobhan, making peace signs with their fingers. Click, click. Then they swarmed around her, flushed with excitement, and barraged her with questions. Siobhan started to feel rather uncomfortable and exposed, but she didn't know how to deal with the situation without being rude.

And being rude to those girls was the last thing she wanted to do.

Luckily, Marcel knew what to do.

"Darling, didn't you want to take a walk before we go home?"

It worked.

Perhaps the odious Mr. Black had more social skills than she'd thought.

And he had called her *darling*.

"Wow . . . That was . . . I don't know what to say. Do you realize those girls just recognized me? It's amazing!" she said once they were alone. "I felt a bit, I don't know, like Kim Kardashian," she continued. "Although I don't have her ass."

"I said you'd go far, and I wasn't wrong. As for the ass . . . Well, it's a matter of perspective."

"Sure. Well, thanks for rescuing me."

"Anytime."

Marcel gave her a warm, slow smile. Siobhan felt so absurdly happy just then that she would have liked to capture the moment in her hands and lock it in a safe so she would never lose it.

Then a notification sounded on her phone. What she saw made her go pale. She covered her mouth with her hand, knowing that her happiness was going to be short-lived.

Chapter 19

Marcel

"What's up? You've gone all pale. Have you lost a follower?" joked Marcel, his sarcasm tempered with a wink.

"I think . . . you have to see this," said Siobhan, passing him her cell phone with a trembling hand.

> **Grl18** @grl18 1m
> My friend and I just met @siobhan_harris at Coney Island and . . . WOW ♥ It was incredible! She's lovely and so pretty in person. FEASTYOUREYES. #PASSIOBHAN

Marcel raised his eyebrows.

"Wow, proper fangirls. It didn't even take them ten minutes to post the photo. I bet this . . . @grl18," he read from the screen, "was writing that tweet while she was posing with you, instead of enjoying meeting her favorite author. When I say social media is a form of modern slavery—"

"Read the whole thread," Siobhan said.

> **Grl18** @grl18 30s

By the way, Siobhan was with a FINE PIECE OF ASS 🔥
FEAST YOUR EYES ON HIM TOO.

Marcel's eyes practically popped out of their sockets.

"But, what the hell . . . ? Those girls took our photo without us realizing?"

Siobhan swallowed.

"There's more. And you're not going to like it."

Grl18 @grl18 20s
His name is Marcel. LIKE MARCEL BLACK.
Coincidence?

Lady Herondale @LadyHerondale_85 10s
Maybe @siobhan_harris and @InvisibleBlack are an item. See how they're looking at each other. 😘

Grl18 @grl18 7s
Well, that's possible because he did call her DARLING.

Lady Herondale @LadyHerondale_85 3s
OH. MY. GOD. 😱 I LOVE IT! #SHIPPING

"Fuck. Fuck. Fucking hell!" he shouted. He just managed to restrain himself from smashing Siobhan's phone on the ground, placing it instead on the table, next to his cap. That goddamn cap! Why the hell had he taken it off? He put his hands on his head and started pacing back and forth. "They took my photo! Without my consent! And they published it on that fucking hellsite Twitter!" He glared furiously at Siobhan, who was watching him from behind the safety of her sunglasses. "You know what this means? Now half of America knows who I am. It's unbelievable. Unbelievable. I manage to keep my identity hidden for more than ten years, and now these pseudo-paparazzi come along and screw it all up." He clenched his fist, raised it to his mouth, and groaned.

He wanted to shout.

He wanted to break something.

Break it all. This was definitely not part of the script.

"If it's any consolation, the image is very poor quality," she argued. "You could be anyone. You could be . . . I don't know . . . Denzel Washington but twenty pounds lighter?"

Unfortunately, her effort to assuage him just lit the fuse of his anger.

"You think this is funny? I know, you want your moment of glory, right, princess? Well, congratulations." He applauded. "It looks like you got it."

Siobhan's cheeks reddened. She took off her sunglasses and gave him a reproachful look. For god's sake. She was even more beautiful with the sunset reflected in her eyes.

"What the hell are you saying? Calm down. You're stressing me out."

"*I'm* stressing *you* out?" he said, tapping his chest incredulously. "Ha, that's rich."

"Might I remind you that you're not the only one in the lousy photo."

"But your image is public and mine isn't."

"That doesn't mean I like people speculating about my private life. And much less insinuating things that aren't true, like the nonsense that we're"—she gestured contemptuously—"an item."

Of course. In case your dumbass ex sees it and gets confused, thought Marcel. And the very thought made him grind his teeth.

"You and I, an item," he jabbered. "That's the most bizarre thing I've heard in a long time."

Siobhan looked at him.

"Well, if you hadn't called me darling, perhaps they wouldn't have jumped to that conclusion."

"And if you hadn't called me Marcel!"

"How is it my fault if that's your name?"

He opened his mouth to reply and held it like that for a few seconds, like the imbecile he was, before closing it. He exhaled.

"You know what? Forget about it," he murmured, putting his cap back on his head. "I'm tired of these stupid games."

"What games?"

They stared at each other for a few seconds. The electricity was palpable, except that this time it was generated by fury.

"I knew it was a mistake to come here. I knew it would be a mistake to write this goddamn novel. And what's more, I knew it would be a mistake to get involved with someone like you."

Something acidic burned his throat. He could see the disappointment in her half-closed eyes, in the grim set of her lips. He had never seen Siobhan look so crushed as she did at that moment, and a wave of guilt broke over him.

But the damage was done.

"Well, why the hell did you accept? For the money?"

"Money?" he repeated contemptuously. "You think I need to waste my time with you to earn money? I only accepted because Gunton threatened to leak my identity if I didn't!"

Siobhan massaged her temples as though making a superhuman effort to understand the situation. She adopted a serious expression and asked:

"What are you hiding from, Marcel? Have you killed someone? Are you a fugitive from the law or something?"

He snorted.

"Of course not."

"So? Why do you get like this because of a stupid photo that doesn't even show your face clearly?"

"Do me a favor. From now on, mind your own business." Then he took his phone from his pocket. "End of discussion. I'll order an Uber, and we'll get out of here."

"I'll go back on the subway. I wouldn't want to . . . What was it?" She tapped her finger on her chin. "Ah, yes: be involved with someone like you for a minute longer."

Those words hit him like a punch in the gut. Even so, he tried to conceal his frustration as best he could.

"Do what you like," he muttered, without lifting his eyes from his phone.

"Fine."

"Fantastic."

"Great."

Siobhan turned on her heel and disappeared from sight. Marcel suddenly felt profoundly alone, in a way that he hadn't for a long time.

And the feeling overwhelmed him.

"Calm down, man," said Alex, pouring him a double whiskey. "You're making a mountain out of a molehill. The image isn't even hi-res. That's what happens when you take a photo on a phone and zoom in too far."

Marcel frowned.

"You too, Alex? I'm grouchy as fuck, so I would advise you not to contradict me for the rest of the year."

He hadn't gone to his friend's penthouse to listen to sermons. He had asked the Uber driver to take him to Tribeca because he needed to vent. The journey from Coney Island had been hellish. Against his principles, he had downloaded Twitter to his cell to monitor the real-time development of @grl18's tweet, which was going viral at breakneck speed.

Refresh.

Refresh.

Refresh.

How was it possible that there were already memes circulating? Although some users had the courtesy to ask for confirmation that the man in the photo was indeed him, the majority took it as fact. Some praised his appearance and were happy to finally see the face of the mysterious Marcel Black, even just from a side angle. Others accused him of racism, as if being Black limited an author to telling only Black stories. And then there were the romantics who were going wild over the possibility that he and Siobhan had gone from enemies to lovers in real life. This group tweeted their feelings on the subject using the hashtag #Sioblack.

Alex placed the whiskey on the coffee table in the living room and sat down facing Marcel.

"You must admit the hashtag is ingenious. Right now, you and Siobhan are like the lead characters in a Shonda Rhimes series, and all your fans have set that photo as the background on their cell phones. Isn't that frickin' amazing?"

"That's right, you laugh. Mock me all you like," Marcel said reproachfully. "Can't we take legal action against the account that posted it?"

"But she's a child, Marcel! You really want to sue a teenager? Besides, that would only confirm that it's you in the photo. The best thing to do is nothing at all. Believe me, in a few days everyone will have forgotten about it. *TMZ* will give them a juicier story."

"People might. But Google? Google doesn't forget."

"Hey, you focus on finishing the novel and—"

"No," he said abruptly. "I've decided I don't want to continue. It's over. Call Gunton right now and tell him I'm out."

Alex's strawberry-blond eyebrows knitted together.

"What? Give me that whiskey," he said. He grabbed Marcel's glass, drank almost half in one gulp, and handed it back, ignoring his friend's disconcerted expression. "I don't think you quite know what you're saying. Did you get sunstroke at Coney Island or something? Take a deep breath." He waved his hand gently. "Inhale, exhale. Inhale, exhale. Inhale, exha—"

"What the fuck are you doing? This isn't a yoga class."

"I'm just trying to get you to calm down before you make"—and here the pitch of his voice went up an octave—"a very bad decision in the heat of the moment. To begin with, you've got a contract with Baxter Books. And for the love of god, Marcel, think about Siobhan. You can't do this shit to her."

Siobhan, Siobhan, Siobhan. He didn't want to think about Siobhan. His life had been fine until that little princess appeared, with those gentle blue eyes and that goddamn voluptuous mouth, stirring him up and derailing everything. He wished he had never met her.

"Fuck that. It's thanks to her that I'm in this mess. If that . . ." He clenched his teeth to stop himself from uttering any insult he might regret later. "If she hadn't called me by my name in front of those girls . . ."

Alex shook his head, visibly concerned.

"Don't tell me you argued over it."

Before replying, Marcel bit the inside of his cheek.

"I wouldn't call it arguing. All right, maybe . . . I went slightly overboard and shouted . . . a few things that were . . . not very nice."

"You gotta be kidding me."

Guilt twisted at his guts like a corkscrew.

"You don't understand."

"What don't I understand?"

Marcel rubbed his hand over his face as he exhaled. He heard Alex make a kind of murmur of acknowledgment before replying to himself: "Okay, I get it now. This whole business has made you realize how much you like this girl, and now you're pissed because you don't know what to do."

A grunt of indignation emerged from the depths of Marcel's throat.

"What? Bullshit," he replied. He rubbed his chest where he could feel a kind of dull pain.

"No bullshit, amigo. I've seen the way you look at her. Why do you think I left you two alone last night?"

"I knew it! You're a fucking traitor."

"Yeah, and you're a fucking idiot for not making a move. Admit it, man: you're smitten with Siobhan. And that scares you because it clashes head-on with your policy of one screw and bye-bye. Am I wrong?"

Silence.

Marcel squirmed on Alex's designer sofa, wondering whether it had always been this uncomfortable. Suddenly, his phone started to vibrate inside his pocket, and he tensed.

"Is it her?" asked Alex anxiously.

"My sister," he said as he checked the incoming number. "I'll call her later." He put his phone away. "And you're wrong, all right? Completely wrong. Siobhan and I have nothing in common. She's . . ." He shook his hand contemptuously. "A chatterbox and absurdly cheerful. She isn't my type. She loves Christmas, and her favorite movie is *When Harry Met Sally*." He stuck two fingers in his mouth and pretended to vomit. "What's more, she looks like the type to get infatuated and follow you around always wanting more; emotionally dependent in every way."

Not to mention that she was still hung up on her ex.

Alex gave a sarcastic little laugh.

"You don't like her, but you go spend a day at the beach with her? Yeah, that makes perfect sense. Come on, call her." He pointed a finger at him. "Now."

"Call her for what?"

"To be honest with her. I can tell by the way you're looking at her in the photo, eyes shining like two candles on a birthday cake."

"Fuck you, Shapiro. Didn't you say you can't even see my face?"

"Call her," insisted Alex. "If you don't have the balls to tell her how you feel, at least apologize for pulling this little stunt. She deserves it. That girl has more passion in her little finger than most established writers have in their entire body. And a lot of guts. For agreeing to write a novel with you, for not throwing in the towel, not to mention putting up with you day after day." Marcel placed his hand on his chest with an affronted expression. "Come on, stop playing the victim and call her."

Should he call her or not? Part of him wanted to wipe the slate clean and let everything go back to normal. To *his* version of normal. And another part of him wanted to be really honest with Siobhan, more than he cared to admit. He sighed and rubbed his face.

Then his phone rang.

It was Charmaine again.

Chapter 20

Siobhan

It was ten o'clock by the time Siobhan fell into bed in her tiny apartment. She felt slightly dizzy. Maybe the two craft beers she'd had at Brooklyn's open-air food market, Smorgasburg, hadn't agreed with her. Or maybe her head was just spinning from trying to make sense of the day.

I knew it would be a mistake to get involved with someone like you.

Those words echoed loudly in her ears. She pictured Marcel under the huge parasol at Coney Island, glowering down at her contemptuously. She hated feeling so small. She hated being blamed for what had happened. And she hated the fact that things had gone sour between them after the wonderful day they had spent together. That infernal Twitter photo had ruined everything.

She'd summoned Paige and Lena, and they'd met up at East River State Park. Dozens of wooden tables were packed with hipsters digging into ramen burgers, spaghetti donuts, and truffle fries and posting their #foodporn experiences on Instagram. She told her friends everything.

"So . . . it's really him? Marcel Black?" Paige asked.

Siobhan nodded slowly.

"I knew it! I knew that guy wasn't gay! And to be honest, he didn't look like a Michael either," she added, dipping a tortilla chip into organic guacamole.

"Yeah, maybe I . . . lied to you a bit. And maybe I kind of . . . like him. A lot."

She nearly choked on her own tongue admitting it.

Lena's eyes widened, and she held out her hands as if she didn't understand.

"What? You're kidding, right? What kind of person is attracted to someone who goes through life brandishing a nail-studded baseball bat? Hooking up with him would be like going to the dark side. Are you Kylo Ren? No, you are not Kylo Ren."

"Hot but stupid. What a pity. Guys like Marcel What's-his-name are a double-edged sword," agreed Paige.

"Dupont. His name is Marcel Dupont, and he's from New Orleans." When Siobhan realized she had probably said too much, she lowered her voice. "I don't need to remind you that if either of you gets loose-tongued, his lawyers will turn me to pulp, right?"

Paige snorted.

"I prefer to use my tongue for more interesting things, thanks," she replied, appearing offended that her friend might even consider the possibility.

"Just in case. As for the other . . . Well, I admit that 90 percent of the time he's standoffish, but . . . the other 10 percent, he's charming and interesting."

"The question is whether it's worth making things complicated for that 10 percent," said Lena. "I mean, was it really necessary to make such a fuss about this?" She gestured at Siobhan's phone, which was sitting on the table. "Just because he's obsessed with maintaining his privacy doesn't give him the right to raise his voice at you."

"Not to mention that the only thing you can tell from the photo is that he's African American," added Paige.

Siobhan took a deep breath. The tightness in her chest still wouldn't go away.

"You're right," she conceded. "He's a real asshole." A brief pause. "The problem is that . . . sometimes . . . he looks at me in a way that makes me feel confused. At least when he's a jerk, I know where I stand with him. But when he isn't . . . Today, for example. We were having a great time together . . . There was a real connection between us." She placed her hand on her heart and noticed it was racing. "I even forgot about my phone. I . . . I don't want to like him, but I do and . . . Oh god, this isn't good."

Paige patted her arm comfortingly.

"What are you going to do?" she asked.

"Nothing. I'm just going to finish my part of the novel. Anyway, I doubt we'll see each other again once we've delivered the manuscript. Marcel and I . . . We're too different. I can't get hung up on a man who's only interested in one-night stands; it would be emotional suicide."

"That's the smart way to look at it, Shiv," agreed Lena. "You suffered enough when Buckley left. Life is supposed to be fun. Otherwise, what's the point? To hell with men, and to hell with relationships. This is your moment, yours and nobody else's."

"Damn right," said Paige. "Wanna know what I think? I'm going to get another round of beers. We need to get drunk in the name of group support."

Gazing at her bedroom ceiling, she wondered whether she should return to Marcel's house the next day and pick up her routine as though nothing had happened. Was it wise after today? She honestly doubted it. The asshole would almost certainly still be angry and might not even open the door to her. He would never be the one to relent, ever. His true identity and his reasons, whatever they were, for keeping it secret seemed to be the cornerstone of his very existence. But then, Siobhan was angry too. And hurt. So, given that there was little chance of receiving an apology from the odious Mr. Black, she decided they should go back to the way things were at the start.

From now on, we'll work separately. He'll be in his apartment, and I'll be . . . in Starbucks.

She sighed despondently and hugged her shoulders, before wincing with pain. They were red hot, just as Marcel had predicted. What was he doing right now? Thinking about her? She chased the possibility from her mind and tried to distract herself by looking at her phone. A catastrophic mistake, given that the first thing her treacherous index finger did, as if it had a life of its own, was to open Twitter, search for the photo that had caused so much grief, and download it. She enlarged the image until Marcel's blurry profile filled the whole screen. God, he was so handsome. And he looked so relaxed in that moment. Comfortable. Calm. Happy? Yes, he was even smiling! It was as though he was enjoying her company.

As though he liked her.

Did he?

"No. Not a chance," she said to herself out loud.

Ding.

A message from Marcel.

Marcel
Are you awake?

The protocol in these circumstances is very clear: you have to wait at least ten minutes before replying so as not to seem desperate. But Siobhan conveniently forgot all about protocol and immediately typed a succinct yet hasty answer:

Siobhan
Yes.

Of course, it could have been worse. She could have inserted a humiliating party emoji.

Then her phone rang.

Oh my god. He's calling me? He's calling me!

She waited three rings—there was no way she was skipping protocol twice in a row—and answered on the fourth. Her heart rate soared, her hands trembled, and her mouth went dry. She closed her eyes for a second, a knot forming in her stomach. She was a bundle of nerves.

But she had to stay firm.

"Hi."

"Hi," he replied in a whisper.

Siobhan squeezed her eyelids shut. She hated that he had such a deep, sexy voice. And that goddamn melodious Louisiana drawl infused even the most insignificant word with sensuality.

To hell with being firm.

"I wasn't entirely honest," he said abruptly. After a brief pause, he continued. "Earlier, when you asked if there was anything I liked more than writing . . . I . . . I said no and . . . Well, that's not true. There is something I like more than writing, Siobhan."

Every time he uttered her name her whole body trembled.

"I see. And what might that be?"

"Writing with you."

Silence.

Her heart expanded in her chest.

"Are you still there?"

"Yes," she replied in a thin voice. She cleared her throat. "I'm still here. Why do you like writing with me?" she asked, trying not to sound too emotional. "I thought you couldn't stand me."

"You may have driven me up the wall early on."

"Because we're so different and all that, right?" she said.

"I've come to the conclusion that we're not that different after all."

A mischievous smile played on her lips as she twirled a lock of hair like a lovestruck teenager.

"Oh no?"

"No. Tell me something. Why do you write romance novels?"

She filled her cheeks with air, then released it very slowly before answering the question.

"Well . . . I suppose I like unraveling the mysteries of the heart. And you? Why do you write crime novels?"

"I like unraveling the mysteries of the human mind. See? It's all a matter of perspective."

"Mm-hmm. All right, put Alex on the line."

"Alex?" He sounded confused. "But he's not here."

"So who's slipping you your lines, then?"

The sound of laughter caressed her ears through her phone.

"I don't need anyone for that. I'm kind of good with words. More than good. I'm a fucking machine."

"Are you apologizing or teasing me?"

"I'm being honest. Apologizing is the next step."

"Okay, seriously now. Whoever you are, I don't have the money to pay a ransom for Marcel Black. You'd be better off calling Bob Gunton."

"Very funny. Hey."

"What?"

Marcel exhaled at the other end of the line.

"About earlier: I shouldn't have shouted at you. What happened wasn't your fault. To be honest, it wasn't anyone's fault. I suppose . . . my circumstances are complicated. I'm sorry. I was a jerk."

"Wait. Can you repeat that? There was a bit of interference, and I'm not sure I heard you clearly."

Siobhan heard Marcel laugh again.

"You're cruel, princess."

"I have the best teacher. And now that you mention it, yes, you were a real jerk."

"You're still mad at me, I can tell."

"Well, yes. But less than I was five minutes ago," she added after a brief pause.

"Well, that's something. Will you come over to my place tomorrow?"

He hadn't said *to work* or *to write*. He'd said *to my place*. And Siobhan found herself savoring his words.

"To that prison camp? I still haven't decided," she lied.

"Okay. Let's see. What if I buy you a basket of muffins and some flowers?"

"I feel dizzy. You would do that for me?"

"No, not really."

"You're such a dumbass, Dupont."

She only said that because she needed a way to recover some control. She had miscalculated how easily that Southern snake charmer was able to soften her up.

"Listen, Siobhan. I hate this situation. I know I'm the one who caused it, but . . . I don't like it. I . . ."

Say it.

Say it.

Come on, say it.

"Yes, Marcel. What were you going to say?"

"Nothing. Just that I like your company. Professionally speaking," he hastily clarified, rather too vehemently. "I think we make a good team. I take care of the sordid stuff, and you do the sweet stuff. I'll understand if you need space, but . . . this novel won't get finished without you, so . . . I'd love it if you came over tomorrow."

That was nice.

And disappointing at the same time.

"Fine. I'll come over."

"Really?"

"But only because I've just realized my laptop is at your house."

"I'll take that. Thank you for understanding."

"Yes, well, good night, then."

When she hung up, she was besieged by a strange feeling, almost like loss. All the things she wished they had said to each other floated across the quiet expanse of her room.

Barely five minutes later, the sound of another call interrupted the silence. Siobhan furrowed her brow.

It was him again.

"What's up? Guilty conscience not letting you sleep?"

"No, it isn't that. See, I was wondering . . . Would you like to come with me to New Orleans?"

Chapter 21

Siobhan

The first thing to hit her when she stepped off the airplane at Louis Armstrong International Airport, some fourteen miles outside New Orleans, was the heat. It was seven in the evening, and the sun was sinking below the horizon. The sultry air clamped around her like a vise. Marcel had warned her: "In NOLA, when it's hot, it's really hot. And when it rains, it rains hard." So, she had packed for all eventualities, including a swimsuit, mosquito repellant, sunscreen, boots, and a raincoat. Although they were supposedly there for work, Siobhan had no idea what the week would bring. During the flight she had wondered several times how it was possible that the man reading James Ellroy in the seat next to hers had gone from thinking that getting involved with someone like her was a mistake to suggesting she accompany him to his hometown. And not just that—he had also offered to pay for first-class tickets and put her up in his own home. Did this generous invitation stem from a desire to make things up to her, or was it something else? He didn't seem to be the same Marcel as before—the one who regarded empathy as a manufacturing defect and not a human trait. Either way, there was no point in getting too excited. Before leaving, he told her that his sister had agreed to have their father placed in a memory care center. Although that was probably the reason he had decided to make a trip to New Orleans just then, she had no idea why he had wanted to take her with him. But it was a change of scene, and she figured it would be good for them, given everything that was going on. A few days of keeping a low profile, and, with any luck, everyone would forget about #Sioblack.

Low profile, in Mr. Black's language, meant:

1) No social media until further notice.

"What, not at all? Not even to post a picture of the airplane wing? But Bella gets annoyed if I don't tweet at least a couple of times a day."

"For the love of god. Forget about her. Believe me, you'll be happier when you decide not to be at the mercy of the"—and here he made air quotes—"obligations of popularity."

2) And go unnoticed.

"Don't you think spending the whole flight in sunglasses and a hat is a bit much? It's not like we're Brangelina."

"Speak for yourself. I'm the spitting image of Brad Pitt. In fact, I get mistaken for him all the time."

They collected their luggage and headed for the exit. A Black woman with short hair and huge hoop earrings was smoking a cigarette next to a ruby-colored Chevy Silverado parked outside the revolving doors. She was tall and robust, but there was something in her features, a kind of symmetrical delicacy, that reminded her of Marcel. Siobhan guessed this was Charmaine Dupont.

They walked over to her.

"That shit will kill you," Marcel said, berating her.

The woman tossed her cigarette to the ground and crushed it with her platform sandal. She exhaled the smoke with an almost offensive lack of urgency.

"Is that how you greet your sister, you little brat? Marcel Javarious Dupont, give me a hug right now, or I'll make sure that scrawny Black ass can't sit down to write for weeks."

Siobhan pursed her lips to avoid laughing.

The siblings embraced warmly.

"You're looking good, Chaz."

"You'd know that if you came to visit more."

Marcel snorted.

"I'm a busy man, you know that."

"Pardon me, Mr. President of the United States." She narrowed her eyes and slapped the air. "Well, then, who's this lovely thing? The first lady?"

A stifled laugh gave Siobhan away: she liked this woman's sense of humor.

"I'm Siobhan Harris." She extended her hand and Marcel's sister squeezed it warmly. "It's lovely to meet you, Charmaine. And if I ever get that far, I'll hire you to keep my office in line."

Charmaine threw her head back and let out a guttural laugh that offered a glimpse of a slight gap between her upper incisors.

"Oh, she'd be a natural at that, believe me," agreed Marcel.

"Don't listen to this idiot, honey. And call me Chaz, won't you? So you're the one who has the privilege of witnessing the great American crime author attempting to write a romance, huh?" she said, and a wicked smile appeared at one side of her mouth.

"Half romance," he clarified.

"My god, how on earth do you put up with him? He's insufferable."

"I wonder that myself."

"Well, you'll grow fond of him in twenty years or so."

"Seriously?"

"No, not really."

Both women laughed, and Marcel shook his head.

"You've known each other for five minutes, and you're best friends already. Unbelievable," he muttered.

"It's called sisterhood," replied Charmaine, and then she winked at Siobhan.

"Whatever. Come on, let's go."

They stuck their bags in the trunk and got into the pickup. Up-tempo jazz music filled the air when the engine started. They left the airport and headed toward the city. Although the air-conditioning was set to igloo temperature, Siobhan could feel the heat in her body like the onset of a night fever. She rummaged in her purse for a tissue to dry the sweat beading on her forehead.

Charmaine glanced at her in the rearview mirror.

"First time in New Orleans?"

"Mm-hmm."

"August isn't the best time to come, of course. The weather is crazy at this time of year: it's either torrential rain or infernal heat. But I think you'll like it. The Big Easy has a lot going on."

"As long as Entergy doesn't cut off the electricity supply, of course."

"Brother dearest, that's the kind of reductionist point of view that gives the state of Louisiana bad press. What will our New York friend think of us?"

"Our New York friend thinks we have gators on the porch, Chaz."

"You're kidding."

Thanks a lot for making me look ignorant in front of your sister, you bastard.

"That was only a joke!" Siobhan protested. "Anyway, everyone knows that New York and New Orleans have a lot in common."

Marcel turned his head and glanced at her over his shoulder.

"Do you mean they both seem friendly and hospitable, but deep down they're classist, violent, and racist?"

Charmaine sighed.

"You really are a glass-half-empty kind of a guy, aren't you?"

"I call it a capacity for critical thought, sis."

"Yeah, and I call it being a real pain in the ass."

Marcel's response was to raise the volume of the radio and hum along to a few bars.

Siobhan concentrated on looking at the views flashing by outside the window. The sun hadn't quite sunk below the horizon, and the last rays of light bathed the battered highway in a twilight splendor. The landscape was not particularly attractive: factories, cranes, gas stations, and superstores scattered here and there—the usual. In the distance she could make out fields of sugarcane and sweet potato, occasional ruins of stately mansions, and willows bent over by the wind. They left behind the causeway linking New Orleans to Covington across Lake Pontchartrain—twenty-three miles, once the longest in the world—and headed toward Mid-City. The panorama changed as they penetrated deeper into the city. As was the case in many other American cities, there was a clear gap between the suburbs and the urban center, although here you got the feeling the inhabitants cared less about those class distinctions. Traditional shotgun houses rubbed shoulders with French architecture and traces of Spanish colonial style. There was color everywhere: purple to represent justice, green to represent faith, and gold to represent power; the colors of Mardi Gras. They turned right, onto the busy St. Charles Avenue, with the metallic clank and hum of the old trams in the background, and made their way to the Garden District, where the streets became tree lined and the houses considerably larger.

After a few minutes, they parked.

"We're here," announced Charmaine.

"This one?" asked Siobhan, stretching her neck to get a good look at the pale yellow mansion.

"Mm-hmm."

She whistled, unable to hide her surprise.

"Wow!"

"Anne Rice lives right across the street," Marcel said, pointing.

"Are you shitting me?"

"Who can say?" He shrugged. "Things aren't what they seem in this city. Didn't Bon Jovi have a song about that?"

The Dupont residence was in a quiet neighborhood lined with nineteenth-century mansions and colorful trees with roots erupting through the sidewalks. Guarded by an ancient oak tree that had most likely been there since the days of Jean Lafitte, the columned, two-story house had spacious balconies on both levels; the upper held a couple of rocking chairs, and the lower had royal ferns hanging from the arches. Four large windows flanked by shutters looked onto a front yard with exuberant vegetation. Bougainvillea, banana trees, and crape myrtles. A mixture of fecund tropical beauty and elegance.

Charmaine opened a gate topped with a row of fleur-de-lis, the symbol of New Orleans. Siobhan followed the siblings inside, where the house was even more impressive: hardwood floors, high ceilings, a vast spiral staircase coming down to the entrance hall, moldings, French windows, and decor that betrayed the large amount of money invested in the property. She tried to imagine Marcel as a child running around this house, but she couldn't picture it.

"Have you always lived here?"

"Not at all. We used to live in Tremé. You might have heard of it. It's famous for being the birthplace of jazz and the oldest Black neighborhood in the country. So old that it was here before the United States became the United States."

Marcel moved closer to Siobhan as though about to share a confidence and said:

"Actually, it's famous because of the HBO series, but my sister is an idealist." Charmaine swiped at the back of his neck with her open hand. "Hey, what's with the violence?"

"Shut your beak if you don't want me to get really violent. And take our guest's bags. Do something useful for once, can't you?"

"The things I have to put up with," protested Marcel.

This week was full of promise. Siobhan could feel it in every cell of her body.

◆ ◆ ◆

The backyard was a small paradise with an illuminated pool, a three-person swing seat, and a barbecue area. The table was set. Marcel took the lid off the pan sitting on a wooden board in the center. A column of steam rose from inside and floated in the air. It smelled wonderful.

"I can't believe you made jambalaya, Chaz. My god, it's a miracle." He stuck his hand in with the intention of grabbing a prawn, but his sister gave him a dissuasive slap.

"Where are your manners, young man? Have you left them in Manhattan?" she asked in a pretentious nasal tone, imitating a New York accent. "Come on, let's sit down before it gets cold. You have to eat this as soon as it's cooked. Siobhan, I hope you like it."

"It looks amazing. What's in it?"

"Rice, chicken, sausage, prawns, and a shitload of pepper. It's the star of Cajun cuisine, honey."

"I know. And Marcel's favorite."

He glanced at her and gave her a warm smile, one she had never seen before. Siobhan felt like she might disintegrate into a million pieces right then and there.

Charmaine's eyes, outlined in black, wrinkled in satisfaction.

"I see you know my brother well."

They ate unhurriedly as they chatted about trivialities. It hadn't rained for two weeks, and the temperature had shot up to 104 degrees. The garbage collectors were on strike, and apparently every single fly in America had decided to come south. Burnell's grocery store on Caffin Avenue and the renovation work at the Riverfront, along the banks of the Mississippi. In New Orleans, there's an unspoken rule that forbids talk of politics or work at the table. The problems of the world are of relative importance, and none of them warrants ruining a good meal. Food—in addition to jazz, Mardi Gras, and the Saints—is sacred.

"In NOLA we always say we haven't finished one meal before we're thinking about the next. And it's true," Marcel said in a low voice that brought out his Southern drawl. Charmaine murmured an *mm-hmm* every so often, as though listening to a church sermon in Harlem. "When the heat closes in, and the air is so suffocating it's hard to breathe, all you can do is try to trick your palate. Hot spices, dark stews, and cold cocktails are your salvation. Just like music."

Siobhan listened, rapt, her cheek resting in the palm of her hand, feeling like she could spend her life listening to him talk.

"Amen. At last you're saying something sensible about your place of birth," agreed his sister.

"They're just words, Chaz."

"Sure. I forgot you make a living from them."

Night fell and brought with it the croaking of tree frogs and the hum of mosquitos, which had started to attack their ankles mercilessly. Once they had finished eating and drained their glasses of Pimm's, the conversation started to wind down. Siobhan knew the Dupont siblings needed to talk. Either their father was a taboo subject, or they didn't want to discuss their family situation in front of a stranger. Either way, this was the moment to leave them to it. She excused herself, claiming she was tired from the flight, and went upstairs to the guest room, which was twice as large as her apartment and decorated in French style, with an en suite bathroom and a canopy over the bed. She took a shower, put on a white nightshirt, and dropped onto the springy mattress like dead weight.

"My god, this is comfy."

She rolled one way and then the other. Then she took a selfie, which she sent to the group chat. The time had come to update her friends.

Shiv

I don't want to make you jealous, but I've just had the most intense gastronomic experience of my life and right now I'm lying in a bed that would fit the entire crew of the Titanic. INCLUDING JACK #JusticeForJackDawson

Paige

Amazing! Just make sure you don't spend the night like Rose. 😴

Shiv

Meaning?

Paige

ALONE.

#JusticeForSioblack

Shiv

Ha, funny. Whose side are you on?

Paige

I'm on the side of anyone who blows away the cobwebs down there FOR ONCE, honey👉👌💦

Shiv

My cobwebs and I are fine, thanks.

Paige

Like hell.

Lena

My brain is going to explode. Wasn't Mr. Black a bastard only interested in one-night-stands ten seconds ago?

Shiv

It's Paige's fault, she's an undercover troublemaker.

Lena

I know. Did you get to NOLA ok?

Shiv

Lena

Cool. And what about the sister?

Shiv

She's AMAZING.

She's super friendly and has a great sense of humor.

And the best thing is, she knows how to put Mr. Black in his place.

Paige

I LIKE HER.

Lena

I do too. So, what are your plans for tomorrow? I hope you aren't going out to the woods to practice voodoo and predict the future with chicken bones.

Paige

Why don't you ask him to take you to St. Louis Cemetery? They say it's haunted. And apparently Nicolas Cage had a huge white mausoleum built there in the shape of a pyramid that's always covered in lipstick marks.

Shiv

SERIOUSLY? Gosh, how macabre.

Paige

Perhaps it's a nod to National Treasure.

Lena

Or perhaps old Nicolas is a member of the Illuminati.

Paige

Anyway, getting back to the SUBJECT, I think it's really something that you're in New Orleans with him.

Lena

With Nicolas Cage?

Paige

No, for god's sake. With MARCEL. And I admit I have contradictory feelings about it. A week ago I thought he was a hot idiot, but this plot twist has removed most of his idiocy from the equation. What if he's just hot?

Lena

You aren't objectifying him, are you? Because that's what it sounds like.

Paige

What I mean to say is that maybe we misjudged him. Maybe he isn't a jerk. And maybe he likes you, Shiv.

Shiv

He doesn't like me, Paige. Or if he does, only as a friend.

Paige

Yes, but . . . would you take someone who's just a friend to meet your family?

Lena

Damn right. And I have to admit you make a good couple. If you get together, it would be like a fairy tale ending.

Shiv

My god . . . 😂 How many romance novels have you been reading? I think I'm a bad influence on you. I'm going to bed. ALONE.

She shook her head.

Although she was tired, she knew she wouldn't fall asleep anytime soon with so many emotions whirling in her mind, so she decided to Google New Orleans.

It was a way to bring her a bit closer to Marcel.

Jazz.

Hurricane Katrina.

Tremé.

Legends of New Orleans.

After a while, someone knocked on her door.

"Come in."

It was him.

Siobhan put her phone down and sat up in bed.

"I saw the light was on, and . . ." He rubbed his hand over the back of his neck. "Well, I just wanted to make sure you hadn't been devoured by a gator or anything."

"Unlike the mosquitos, I don't think the gators are finding me too tempting at the moment. Maybe they're vegan."

"Vegans in Louisiana. Nah. That's highly unlikely."

They both laughed. Lovely little wrinkles formed around his eyes.

"I like Charmaine. Are you sure you're siblings? You don't seem much alike."

Marcel bared his teeth.

"You're so kind. I think I might change your return ticket to New York to tomorrow morning." Siobhan stuck out her tongue, and he laughed. "Okay, I'm going to bed. If you need anything, Chaz's room is downstairs and mine is right next door to you. Sleep well." He turned on his heel but immediately swiveled to face her again. He rested his hand on the doorknob, moistened his lips, and said: "I'm really glad you're here."

There was a confessional note to his voice.

"I'm glad too."

For a moment, he remained frozen, enveloped in a dense cloud of awkward silence. He looked at her intensely. She had never been with a man able to convey so much without saying a single word. And that look betrayed an internal conflict.

The same one she was experiencing.

"Good night, Siobhan," he said at last.

"Good night, Marcel."

Everything seemed the same.

But everything seemed different.

Chapter 22

Siobhan

When she opened her eyes, she watched the ceiling fan spin until she could no longer focus on the blades. Her eyelids were heavy as if she was waking up from anesthesia, and it took her a moment to remember where she was.

"New Orleans," she said out loud, sitting up abruptly.

She opened the shuttered sash window and took in the view of the balcony and part of the house next door. Sunlight flooded in, highlighting the dust motes floating in the air. She stretched, then dressed quickly, ready to embrace the promise of a new day. Fifteen minutes later, face washed and hair pulled back in a messy ponytail, she went downstairs. She could hear activity in the kitchen. Mrs. Robicheaux, the cook, told her that Charmaine was in the backyard and pointed to the open door. She pulled aside the mosquito screen and stepped out. The birds were warbling, and the air was impregnated with the scent of magnolias. Siobhan recognized the click of a lighter and an inhalation of smoke followed by a long exhalation.

"Good morning, Chaz."

Charmaine sat in a wicker chair, drinking a cup of coffee and reading the *Times-Picayune*. She lifted her eyes from the paper, smothered her cigarette in a crystal ashtray, and tried to waft away the smoke with her hand.

"Good morning, honey. How did you sleep?"

"Like a baby."

"I'm glad. Come, sit down. I'll ask Mrs. Robicheaux to fix you some breakfast."

Siobhan sat opposite her. There was no breeze, and the tops of the palm trees were perfectly still. She felt a drop of sweat trickle down the back of her neck. *Great,* she thought. *And it's not even midday.*

"Where's Marcel?" she asked, fanning her T-shirt.

Charmaine frowned.

"He went out early for a run. That ingrate would rather overheat than spend time with his sister."

"Don't take it personally. He does the same thing in New York. Every frickin' day, without exception."

Mrs. Robicheaux brought out her breakfast though the word *breakfast* didn't quite do justice to the array of dishes that appeared. There was a plate of scrambled eggs with bacon, French toast, grits with butter, pancakes drowning in syrup, a bowl of fresh fruit, and a cup of steaming coffee.

Siobhan whistled in amazement.

"I guess you don't go in for half measures in New Orleans," she joked.

"Mm-hmm. There's no hurry, eat at your leisure. You aren't marching a Starbucks latte from one side of New York to the other. Although . . ." She raised her index finger to emphasize her point. "Did you know that the disposable cup was invented right here in Louisiana?"

Siobhan laughed. She picked up a slice of bacon and raised it to her mouth. It crunched pleasingly between her teeth.

"When was the last time you were in the Big Apple?"

Charmaine leaned forward as if about to share an intimate confession.

"I've never been to New York, honey."

"You've never been to visit your brother?" she asked, trying not to sound judgmental.

"I've spent the last few years caring for our dad." Charmaine was about to light another cigarette but paused. "You mind if I smoke?" Siobhan shook her head. "You know he has Alzheimer's? Advanced." A swirl of smoke hovered a few inches from her mouth. "You can't imagine how demanding it is caring for someone so sick. And frustrating. You can't plan anything. You can't go anywhere. Your days consist of cleaning up feces, putting up with insults, and having pills spat in your face. Look." She raised her left arm to reveal a large bruise the color of ripe plums. "His goodbye present."

Siobhan stared at her, horrified.

"Your dad did that?"

Charmaine shrugged. Her cheeks sank in as she took a drag of her cigarette. She held in the smoke for a few seconds before expelling it loudly.

"He recently got it into his head that I was trying to poison him. Witnessing a man losing his sanity to the point that he doesn't recognize his own children and not being able to do anything about it is . . ." She blinked heavily. "Terrible. I didn't want to send him to the clinic. No sir." She shook her head and frowned to emphasize her words. "Where could be better than his own home? Who would care for him better than me? But my brother persuaded me. He said: 'Chaz, it doesn't matter what sacrifices you make. Dad's life is only going to get worse; it's time you started living again.' And you know what? I think it's the best decision I ever made. Now I feel . . . relieved." She paused. "Do you think I'm a bad person?"

"Of course not. It's only natural for you to feel that way. It must have been a really difficult situation. I'm sure your dad will be well looked after."

"Oh, you can bet on it. Marcel shelled out a fortune to get him admitted to Lakeview House. If they don't look after him properly, he'll raise Cain."

"Marcel's paying for the clinic?"

Charmaine smiled indulgently and stubbed out her cigarette against the ashtray.

"Honey, everything you see here has come straight out of his pocket: this house, the syrup on your pancakes, the coffee, the clothes I'm wearing, even this pack of cigarettes. My brother is a very generous man. If it weren't for him, I don't know what would have become of us."

"What do you mean?"

In the five seconds it took Charmaine to fill her cheeks with air and exhale slowly, Siobhan realized just how little she knew Marcel Dupont.

"Let's see, where do I begin . . . Marcel and I come from a poor family. My father owned a small carpenter's shop in the Ninth Ward, which is the largest in the city. The business was attached to what we called home at that time, four streets from the Industrial Canal. I crunched the numbers, answered the phone, that kind of thing. You were probably still a child when the Ninth Ward showed up in every news report in the country. The media portrayed us as the very definition of a Black ghetto." She counted off the examples on her fingers: "Crime, gang fights, unemployment, poverty, drug addiction . . . I mean, the neighborhood wasn't any kind of utopia, but we had the highest rate of home ownership in NOLA. And I'll tell you another thing: no one locked their door when they went out. You could be out all the livelong day, and the worst you'd find when you came back was the neighbor's cat prowling around your kitchen. Of course, the white trash on Fox News preferred a simpler narrative that could be easily assimilated by their mosquito-brained audiences. No offense. About the white trash. It's just a figure of speech."

"None taken."

"Anyway, the Ninth was built below sea level, squeezed in between the Mississippi, the bayou, and a canal. So in 2005, when Hurricane Katrina almost destroyed New Orleans, it was one of the worst-hit zones. And the lowest part of the ward was completely swept away."

Siobhan lowered her gaze to her hands, interlaced around her coffee cup, and muttered:

"It must have been terrible."

"Yeah, it was. Katrina is a stain on the history of this city. And it's still here twelve years later. Some stains won't come out no matter how hard you rub."

"I just can't make sense of it. Sometimes nature is too cruel."

Charmaine raised an eyebrow quizzically, the way her brother did.

"Nature?" She let out a humorless cackle. "The hurricane was a natural disaster. But the flooding of New Orleans . . ." She shook her head. "That was an epic failure that could have been avoided if the federal government and the local authorities had given a single solitary fuck about this place. And I swear to god, I won't tire of saying that."

Her words had taken on a belligerent tone. Siobhan stretched out a hand and touched Charmaine gently. The physical contact seemed to calm her. She continued her story.

"A week earlier, they were talking about a tropical storm crossing the Florida Keys and the possibility that it might head north. But it's the same story every August, and most people don't even bat an eyelid. Three or four times a season, we hear alarming reports on the news about hurricanes heading straight for the city, but they always seem to change course or abate in the Gulf of Mexico. If any storm reaches NOLA, it's usually already weakened, and all we get is another gray and rainy day. In Louisiana, we're used to the routine of hurricanes and their litany of preparations. Then, the NHC raised the category of the hurricane to 2 and people went crazy buying plywood. Mayor Nagin, Governor Blanco, and FEMA advised us to leave the city and head further inland. But of course, that would have meant abandoning homes, jobs, commitments . . . My dad was too stubborn to give in to the climate, so we stayed. And we weren't the only ones."

"Marcel told me he wasn't here when Katrina struck."

"No. Thankfully, he'd gone to New York long before. On August 26, the NHC declared that Katrina would soon reach category 3. They were talking about winds of up to 150 miles per hour. There was a possibility of the levees giving way, and if that happened, we could expect waves up to twenty feet high. But that scoundrel Ray Nagin didn't order the evacuation of the city until two days later, shortly after it was classified as category 5. Yes, you heard me. When the authorities informed us that the Superdome would be open as a 'shelter of last resort,' I was horrified just thinking about it; the previous year, with Hurricane Ivan, that same plan had been an abject failure."

Siobhan recalled the horrifying images that she'd seen on television: hundreds of people trudging toward the infamous city stadium laden with coolers, blankets, and suitcases; trees torn up by the roots and electrical poles flattened; vehicles floating in torrents of filthy water; destroyed houses, some missing their roofs, marked with a large *X* on the front wall, or what remained of it; and loads of tents.

"In the end, it went down the way it was always going to," continued Charmaine, playing with her lighter between her fingers. "The levees didn't hold, and the river reclaimed its own. I remember I heard a roar, like an explosion, and then I saw a swelling mass of water about to engulf our house."

"Christ!"

"The water burst through doors and windows. Flattened everything. My dad broke through the ceiling with the ax and we took shelter on the roof; I still don't know how we managed it. We were up there for eight hours, waving flags we improvised from our own clothes, until the rescue teams put us in a boat and got us out of there. That was August 29, 2005."

"Where did they take you?"

"The Convention Center. We were supposed to be transferred to other nearby towns, but the buses took six days to arrive. So we had to live alongside corpses in 95-degree heat for six goddamn days. With no food, no drinking water, and no way to attend properly to the wounded. The poor of NOLA were left to our fate. Some of us stayed there, others set out on foot, heading west along the interstate."

Siobhan took a long drink of coffee, hoping the liquid would dissolve the knot in her throat.

It didn't.

"Were you able to contact Marcel?"

"No. Eighty percent of the city was waterlogged. All of it except for the French Quarter, which only suffered wind damage and a burst pipe under the wax museum. Because the precious French Quarter never floods. Convenient, right?" she added sarcastically. "There was no electricity, no running water, no fuel, no stores open, and of course no phone lines. The sewage system had overflowed, so walking through the city meant stepping through filth. Until we got to Baton Rouge, we had no way of communicating with my brother, who didn't even know whether we were alive. After the storm, some people were just never seen again; they simply disappeared. God, it was hell . . . ," she murmured, massaging her temples.

"When we came back a few weeks later, it was a mess. One out of every four or five houses had been flattened to a pile of rubble, or was about to collapse at any moment. Our house was pretty much destroyed. The structure was still standing, but that mud bath made it uninhabitable. It stank of mold. There was trash everywhere. The carpenter's shop hadn't survived either. We lost it all." She exhaled. "We were left with nothing, and the insurance people washed their hands of it. The bastards said our policy didn't cover flood damage. Can you believe it? As though we had left the faucet running in the bathroom. It was Marcel who saved us. First, he helped us move to Tremé. And then, when my dad got sick, he bought this house. The Garden District is a neighborhood for rich white folk; people here don't mix with Blacks or Creoles. Even so, my brother wanted the best for us. He's a good man, Siobhan. Did you know he started writing when he was eight?" Siobhan raised her eyebrows in astonishment. "He loved ghost stories, headless pirates, and the terrifying creatures of the bayou. The darker and more twisted, the better. He had a wild imagination. And he was very observant. He still is, in fact." A smile crept onto her lips. "I always knew he'd go far."

"Your brother is a terrific writer, Chaz. He has a unique way of describing the world."

"Oh, I know. Believe me, I know. I've read all his books. I've even kept an album of press clips from the bestseller list, ever since his first novel came out. My dad never forgave him for leaving, but if he hadn't, he wouldn't be the man he is now."

"Why did he leave?"

The question had just slipped out.

"Look, this place swallows you whole if you're not careful. I've seen what New Orleans can do to people more times than I care to admit. Let's leave it at that. And Marcel has done a lot for this city since Katrina. Every year, he donates thousands of dollars to its recovery."

An icy shock ran through Siobhan. The man Charmaine Dupont was describing didn't sound at all like the man she had met in Manhattan a few months earlier.

Marcel Dupont was generous.

Marcel Black, on the other hand, had screwed her over by renegotiating the advance and royalties for the book in his favor.

She was confused.

"Are you serious? I thought he hated New Orleans!"

"He doesn't hate it. It's just that . . . You see, my brother had a very difficult childhood. He spent half his life standing outside the candy store staring in through the window. Marcel is a wounded bird, Siobhan. And all wounded birds return to their nest sooner or later."

Siobhan swallowed to free herself of the lump that had suddenly lodged in her throat.

"What happened to your mother? He never mentions her."

"He didn't tell you about her? I thought he would have. I can tell he trusts you."

"I don't know, Chaz. There are a lot of things I don't know about him. He hasn't even told me why he uses a pseudonym. Not long ago we had an argument because . . ." She waved her hand. "It doesn't matter. I've asked him several times, and he's always evasive. Marcel is very reserved. It's as though he has a 'No Entry' sign hanging around his neck."

Charmaine sighed.

And in that sigh, Siobhan thought she detected something like empathy.

"Well, you know what I say? No more talking about bad stuff. As we say in these parts, *laissez les bon temps rouler*. Now, I want you to tell me all about your novel, *With Fate on Our Side.* Please?"

"How did you know . . . ? Did Marcel tell you?"

"Honey, Marcel didn't tell me a thing. Do you think he's only uncommunicative with you?" Siobhan tried not to smile. "Let's just say . . . I've been researching you. How could I resist, when you're the first girl that dumbass has ever brought home?" she said, with a tone of female complicity. "Anyway, I follow you on Twitter. I'm @renew_orleans2005, if you want to follow me back."

Chapter 23

Marcel

I'm glad you're here.

Last night's confession tormented him as he jogged along the path at the edge of the swamp. He paused to take a drink of water and then emptied the rest of the bottle over his head; it was hot, despite the early hour. Why the hell had he said that? Quite the plot failure. It wasn't like him. His father had warned him repeatedly: "Stay on top of your feelings. The day your feelings get on top of you, you're dead." He felt a suffocating sensation in his chest. This tended to happen whenever the old man entered his thoughts. He took a deep breath, bent double, and channeled the air out slowly. The smell of mud licked his face. The reeds shone thick and green in the dappled light; the water lilies were in flower and their leaves were dotted with drops of dew; the sun was poking out above the tree line. New Orleans had a contradictory effect on him: the farther he was from the city, the more he needed it, and the closer he was, the more he felt adrift.

Come to think of it, Siobhan was having a similar effect on him.

His visits weren't becoming less frequent for no reason. Part of it was that he struggled to cope with the sensation of leafy dirt that he couldn't scrub off whenever he was there—perhaps it was true that Manhattan had made him bourgeois, like Charmaine always taunted him. And part of it was that he couldn't stand being in the same room as his father. But something was different this time: a lightness in his mood that he had initially attributed to the old man's absence and which he saw reflected not just in his sister's good spirits but also in the tranquil feel of the house now that it was finally divested of illness. But when he returned from exercising that morning and looked through the kitchen window to see Siobhan in the backyard, he experienced something unfamiliar.

It felt closer to a home than anything else he could remember.

A home with the lights on and the doors open.

And that only heightened the feeling that he was losing control of the narrative.

"I'm sorry, but I disagree," said Siobhan, as she flicked through a book from the Duponts' extensive library. She returned it to its place and came back to stand next to Marcel, who was watching her from the desk. "A romance novel without at least one erotic scene makes no sense. It's like . . . I don't know . . ." She searched the ceiling for the right analogy. "Going to McDonald's and ordering a salad."

Marcel laughed. He took off his glasses and set them down beside the laptop. Then he leaned back in his chair, arms crossed behind his head.

"Is it really so important for you to know how big Jeremiah's . . . appendage is? Do readers beg for that kind of thing?"

Siobhan sighed.

"It's not about that. A well-written erotic scene doesn't have to be a study of anatomy. You've never read J. R. Ward, have you? No, of course not; stupid question," she said. "Intimate encounters between the two protagonists give the story realism." Marcel looked at her with genuine interest. "I mean, when a man and a woman fall in love, in the beginning . . . there's that passion that . . . Well, you know what I mean, right?"

Of course he knew. He wasn't stupid. The fact that emotional relationships didn't interest him didn't mean he couldn't understand the mechanics of them. But he found Siobhan so delightful when she was embarrassed that he decided to play with her a bit.

He frowned.

"Well, no, I have no idea. Why don't you explain?"

"Well, you see . . ."

The fun ended the moment Charmaine appeared in the library. The good news was that she was carrying a tray of food.

"I've made you a snack," she announced. "You've been in here for ages; you must be hungry."

"Damn right. Thank god you think of everything, sis."

"Yes, thanks, Chaz. You're really kind," added Siobhan.

"Don't mention it." She left the tray on the desk and urged them to dig in. "Come on, eat."

Siobhan approached and glanced at the tray. There were a couple of fish po'boys smeared with Creole mustard, a basket brimming with fries, and two chilled bottles of Jax beer.

Marcel handed one of the sandwiches to Siobhan and wolfed down the other. A long murmur of pleasure broke out from deep inside him.

"Ah ha!" exclaimed Charmaine. "Looks like someone has been missing Southern food."

"Believe it or not, we have sandwiches in New York too," he said.

Siobhan raised her hand to her mouth to hide a laugh as she chewed, and Marcel winked at her.

Charmaine tutted.

"These aren't sandwiches, my boy. This is a way of life. Okay, what are your plans for this afternoon?"

"Keep working," answered Marcel. "We're in the middle of something important, and we aren't going to leave it half-finished because I hate leaving things . . ." He stretched out and grabbed a fry from the basket at the same time as Siobhan. Their fingers grazed against each other for a second, and the sensation ran through him like a drug. He swiftly pulled away. ". . . half-finished."

"But overthinking kills creativity," said Charmaine.

"Oh yeah? Says who? The Kardashian sisters?"

His sister threw him one of her formidable glares.

"Cut the crap. Why don't you move your ass for once and take our guest out to see the city? You're a terrible host, you know that? You should be ashamed."

Marcel sighed, frustrated.

The first thing that hit them when they got out of the car was a strong stench of rot, a reek that rose from the ground itself, having seeped into the stonework and asphalt long ago. Siobhan grimaced, which made him laugh.

"Welcome to New Orleans, princess."

They started the tour on Canal Street, the city's main artery. Marcel explained that Mardi Gras took place here, and that it was not just a party, but a symbol of the city's identity.

"Of course, if we expended the same energy solving this place's endemic problems as we do tossing strings of beads in the air, we might be better off," he said.

They turned onto Royal Street, with its antique shops, galleries, and fern-filled wrought-iron balconies, and plunged into the popular French Quarter. The nauseous stench soon became overpowering. Siobhan looked as though she wanted to absorb every last detail, her fascination evident on her adorable face. Although he normally looked down on Bourbon Street and its excessive hedonism, he agreed to show her the city's claim to fame—the street with the most bars, restaurants, sex shops, strip clubs, and street musicians per square yard in the United States—just to satisfy her curiosity. He had to admit, he would have done anything she asked. The smell of beer mixed with the tang of sweat, the temperature seemed to be rising, and music burst out deafeningly from the bowels of every venue. People were drinking from plastic cups, laughing, smoking, singing, celebrating bachelor parties, birthdays, and all kinds of events. Black, white, Creole, or Asian, all had surrendered to the joie de vivre of the Big Easy. Many wore beaded necklaces, hats adorned with feathers, and costumes.

Then, someone pushed against them by accident and doused them in beer.

"Assholes!"

Marcel remembered why he avoided Bourbon Street at all costs.

"Can we get out of here? There are a lot of weirdos around here, and I'm going to end up punching someone. Don't laugh, I'm deadly serious."

"I'm not laughing," she replied with feigned sincerity, unable to hide a giggle.

She was so lovely when she laughed like that.

"I must admit, New Orleans gets under your skin in no time. It could certainly inspire a novel or two," remarked Siobhan, strolling past a group playing bluegrass next to the fountain.

"Is the Tourist Office paying you?" Marcel raised an eyebrow. "You can say that because you don't live here and you don't see how it's coming apart at the seams day after day. I mean, it has the highest rates of both violent crime and municipal licenses for public festivities. Quite the paradox, right?"

"Well, all cities are complicated. But there's something about the faded beauty of this place that makes it different from any other."

"Ladies and gentlemen, the romance of decay. If I could give you a 'like' right now, I would for sure."

She laughed unapologetically and bumped her shoulder against his arm in a gesture that seemed entirely natural. Marcel hadn't felt so at ease with a woman in his entire life.

They strolled on to Café du Monde. Going to New Orleans and not having a café au lait with beignets on the banks of the Mississippi would be sacrilege. It was always full, no matter what time of day. Inside, the air-conditioning was going with the strength of an industrial refrigerator. They sat at a table next to the window, where they could watch the river, Steamboat Natchez sitting at the pier, with its dance band playing on the deck for the tourists, and the sky marbled with the color of burst plums. A very elderly waitress, with a smile that unashamedly revealed her precious few teeth, served them the house specialty: freshly made pastries with a generous dousing of powdered sugar and coffee that was well worth the trip.

Marcel sipped his with gusto, a smile of satisfaction lighting up his face.

"Finally, a proper café au lait. Not sixteen ounces of boiling milk with a finger of dirty water in a depressing disposable cup."

"So you've made your peace with your city, huh?" Siobhan broke off a piece of beignet and chewed it. "Mmmm . . . God, this is good. You have to try it."

"As if I don't know what beignets taste like. Anyway, I've told you a hundred times that sweets—"

Siobhan let out a great sigh. Without a word, she slotted the piece of pastry into his mouth, and, against all odds, Marcel ate it up willingly. This woman was throwing him right off track.

"See? It's not so bad," she said, as she wiped the powdered sugar from his stubble with her fingers. "There is a person in there and—spoiler alert!—he's not as bitter as he seems."

He watched her with a mix of bewilderment and delight. He was afraid her charms would weaken him even further, so he hid behind his shield of sarcasm as he recomposed himself.

"Why are you suddenly seeing me in such a positive light? Have you hit your head on something, princess?"

"Chaz told me some things this morning."

The air got trapped in his windpipe for a few seconds.

"Wow. My sister doesn't waste time. What exactly did she tell you?"

"That Katrina destroyed your house and the carpenter's shop but that you helped them get back on their feet. And also"—Siobhan paused and bit her lip—"that you're a wounded bird."

A torrent of fear rushed through him. He lowered his gaze and focused on his coffee cup.

Don't ask, please. Not here. Not now.

"I want to ask you something, Marcel. I'd like to see where you grew up. Would you take me to the Ninth Ward?"

Marcel looked at her, perplexed.

"It's really depressing. The storm destroyed it, and it hasn't improved much since then. There's nothing to see there except misery and poverty. Stick with the pretty face of New Orleans. Snap some photos for Instagram."

"I don't want photos. To hell with Instagram and to hell with Mark Zuckerberg. The only thing I want is"—she stretched her hand over the table as though searching for physical contact that wasn't forthcoming—"to know who you are."

"You know who I am, Siobhan."

"Only partly. There are still lots of pieces of the puzzle that haven't fallen into place."

A solitary lock of hair fell over her face, and Marcel was tempted to tuck it behind her ear. Siobhan had said the protagonists of romance novels did that all the time. She had even wanted Jeremiah to do it in a scene in *Two Ways*, but Marcel vetoed it because he found it ridiculous. "Explain why on earth he has to put Felicity's hair behind her ear? Can't she do it herself?" he remembered saying. "Because it's tender, Marcel. And there's nothing more pure and true than a tender gesture," she had argued.

She was right. He knew that now.

Except that he was not the hero of a romance novel.

So he restrained himself.

"I asked you to stop trying to understand me," he muttered.

"If that's the case, then why have you brought me to New Orleans?"

It wasn't a reproach. There was something else in the question, something he couldn't answer.

He found it difficult to meet that gaze that was able to plunge to the very depths of his soul. He lowered his eyes to Siobhan's hand, which was still on the table, and slid his own toward it until their fingertips touched.

"All right. I'll take you to the Ninth Ward tomorrow."

Chapter 24

Marcel

When he decided to take a beer out to the backyard in the middle of the night, naked from the waist up, he wasn't expecting to find Siobhan there. She was sitting in the swing seat, legs crossed and computer in her lap. Surprised, he lingered in the doorway for a few seconds, watching her. The moonlight glittered on the pool and projected flashes of blue over her beautiful frame. Her hands hovered indecisively over the keyboard. They typed, deleted, typed again. He smiled, transfixed. Everything about her seemed to fascinate him: the gentle flutter of her nightgown, both innocent and seductive at the same time; her nervous manner of wiggling her big toe; and even a resounding slap on her neck to scare off a mosquito. Was he losing his mind, or did he only notice this kind of detail because he was a writer? The most sensible course of action would probably have been to turn around and take his beer elsewhere, but . . .

To hell with being sensible.

He quietly slid aside the mosquito screen, went down the steps, and walked up behind her.

"Are your muses keeping you busy?" he asked.

Startled, she turned her head. Her eyes shone like embers when she saw him shirtless. She seemed entranced for a few seconds, then averted her gaze.

"More like they won't let me sleep."

"You want company?"

"Sure, why not?"

He sat down next to her. Her perfect naked knee brushed against his leg, and a flash jolted through him. Luckily a barking dog in the distance brought him back to his senses.

"Tell me, what are you writing?"

"The scene where Felicity tends to Jeremiah's eyebrow wound after the fight with those drunks and—"

Marcel finished her sentence:

"They end up in bed together."

"Yes, well, first they kiss," she explained. "I know we haven't come to an agreement on this part, but I wanted to try it. I don't like the way it turned out."

"Let me read it."

"Hell no. It's garbage."

"Come on, I'm sure it's not that bad. Your style has improved a lot."

Siobhan exhaled.

"If you say so."

She swapped her laptop for his beer, and, while Marcel read, she swung on the seat and downed his chilled bottle of Jax.

When he finished, he gave a low whistle.

"You're right. It's garbage."

The tiny spark of emotion he had seen in Siobhan's eyes disappeared behind a mask of fury.

"Bastard," she muttered through her teeth. "You're quite the diplomat, aren't you?"

He accepted the reproach with a sly smile.

"The way I see it, there's something about the spatial arrangement that doesn't work. Look at this." He pointed at the screen. "'Felicity sat on Jeremiah's knee holding a cotton wool pad moistened with alcohol and leaned in slightly to clean the blood oozing from his left eyebrow,'" he read out loud. "Sitting on knees is what Heidi did with her grandfather. There's no sexual energy in that position. There's no anticipation. There's no . . . fire."

"Okay, so how is Felicity supposed to sit to create . . . fire? Straddling him?"

"That's too explicit. Look, fire only needs two things to grow: fuel and oxygen. Let's give them a bit of both. Make it Jeremiah who pulls her onto his knee and kisses her when he can't hold back any longer."

Siobhan lifted her index finger to her lips pensively.

"Let's try it," she suggested finally. "Let's do some role-play. Then we'll know whether it works or not. What do you think?"

Curiosity burned in her eyes.

Marcel blinked several times.

"Let me get this straight. You want us to pretend we're Jeremiah and Felicity in the prelude to the erotic scene?" he asked doubtfully.

"It would be for the sake of the novel. Anyway, we don't have to kiss for real. It will be theater. You know, like we're actors on Broadway."

Say no.

Say no.

Say—

"All right. What do you want me to do?"

"Let's see." Siobhan placed the beer and the laptop on the ground and stood up. "Open your legs to give me room. That's it. Now I'm going to lean over you and clean your wound. Lift your head a bit." She held his chin gently and pretended to dab at his brow.

His heart rate soared. She was too beautiful, and that nightgown, too thin. Marcel was so agitated he didn't know where to put his hands without giving himself away. He noticed his palms were damp and cursed inwardly.

"Ow," he protested. She frowned, puzzled. "Just making it more realistic. You know we men are wimps," he explained.

Siobhan laughed.

"Now, sit me on your knee."

Let's go, champ. Forget that your hands are just the right size to grab her around the waist. And that when she looks at you the way she's doing right now, all you can think about is kissing her until neither of you can breathe. You're Marcel Dupont, man. You'll survive.

But as soon as he felt the touch of her ass against his thigh, he feared his banks would burst as catastrophically as the levees during Katrina.

"Okay?"

"I feel like Santa Claus, for Christ's sake. Ho ho ho!" he crooned.

"I don't think Santa has pecs like that. Let's try something else. What do you think about me straddling you?"

What did he think? That he was heading straight for self-destruction, that was what he thought.

"Sure," he murmured, although it was more of an exhalation than a word.

When Siobhan changed position, Marcel stayed still, grinning and bearing it. The full weight of her body fell on his thighs, causing a hot, sharp pain; admittedly, it would be even worse farther up. If she shifted forward, even just a couple of inches, all was lost.

"Can you hold me? Like before." Siobhan took his hands and lifted them to her waist. "Like this."

"And now what?"

"Now I should . . ."

Then she moved and . . . God. A shudder ran up and down his spine. Marcel held his breath for ten seconds. Unconsciously—or perhaps not—he gripped her more firmly, and her nightgown tightened across her stomach. The friction intensified through his pants. The blood pounded in his head, and somewhere else.

He was turned on.

Very turned on.

And she was only wearing tiny panties under her nightshirt.

"I don't want to be rude, but you're crushing my balls."

Crushing was the polite way of putting it.

"Oh, I'm so sorry."

"I have an idea. Why don't . . . ?" He gestured for her to lean back, and she did as he asked. Marcel placed an arm on either side of her body and angled himself over Siobhan just enough. The seat lurched. "Much better, don't you think?"

Much better now that I'm the one in control.

"Y-yes," she replied, her eyes darting over the swollen veins of his tensed muscles. She cleared her throat. "What do you think Jeremiah would do now?"

The night hung heavy and humid. Marcel took a deep breath before answering.

"I suppose . . . ," he started to say, as he gently brushed a lock of hair off her lips, "he would caress her here . . ." He ran his fingers down the line of her neck to the hollow of her throat, which contracted obscenely. "And here."

Siobhan's breathing deepened. Marcel noticed the contrast between his dark skin and hers, white and creamy and so sensitive to his touch that the hairs were standing on end.

"And then?"

"Then . . ."

He lowered his head and brushed her lips with the tip of his nose, imitating the gesture of kissing her without actually doing it, which was torture. Siobhan let out an involuntary moan, and he became aware of the faint note of beer on her breath. Her chest expanded with each inhalation.

"And what else, Jeremiah? What else would you do to me?"

"I'd do it all, Felicity."

This was a very dangerous game, and he knew it. But by this time, the boundary between fiction and reality was beginning to fade, and Marcel clutched on to that trump card so he could keep playing.

"Do you want me?" she asked, as she timidly ran her fingers up his arm.

"You bet I do. From the moment I saw you."

Siobhan licked her lips, and a thousand images flitted through his mind: kissing her, ripping off her nightgown, sucking her nipples, slipping his hand inside her panties . . .

My god, he was going to explode.

"Do you think about me?"

"Every goddamn second," he confessed. He ran his eyes over her face, consumed by lust, from her eyes to her mouth, from her mouth to her breasts, her hardened nipples starting to show through the almost-transparent fabric. He slid his finger over the buttons delicately, barely grazing them, and continued down toward her belly. He stopped there. The fabric was burning his hand. "Should we take this up a level?"

His voice came out hoarse and rough.

She nodded silently, then added:

"Just for the sake of the novel."

"Purely and exclusively for the sake of the novel."

Marcel lay down on his side, grabbed her deftly around the waist, and pulled her toward him until her back was nestled up against him. His heart was beating so hard she must have felt it between her shoulder blades. He buried his face in her hair and breathed it in. His insides felt like a house burning to the ground, and he wanted her to feel the full force of that. He wanted her to know how hard he was. He stroked her hip under her nightshirt. God, her skin was so soft. He began to trace circles on that tiny piece of blazing skin, and in response Siobhan rocked her hips sensually. He felt like he was getting lost in the sensation of her, in her scent, in the way she moved.

He thought it might drive him crazy.

"I want to touch you," he whispered in her ear. He slipped his hand from her hip to the inside of her thigh. "God . . . I want to touch you so bad."

Siobhan pressed her buttocks against his erection. It was a subtle movement, but powerful enough for him to throw his head back, aching with anticipation, close his eyes, and gasp.

"Keep talking," she said.

"Does it turn you on when I talk dirty? Yeah, sure it turns you on. Sure that sweet pussy of yours is ready for me to fuck you right now."

Then she suddenly went rigid.

"What did you say?" she whispered, bothered by something.

Shit. I've offended her. This is where she turns around, twists my balls, and tells me I'm a pervert. Christ, man, you've screwed up big-time.

He squeezed his eyelids together and swallowed to get rid of the lump rising in his throat. She turned her head and scrutinized him with a puzzled look. She made a sound that seemed halfway between a taunt and a grunt, which turned into laughter—a cackle that could have come from a goddamn hyena. Marcel needed to blink several times before his eyes remembered how to focus.

A wave of clarity dissipated the fog that had weakened his senses and made him sit up suddenly.

"Might I ask what the hell is so funny?"

His voice came out strangled.

"You said *pussy* and *fuck*! Do you realize, Marcel? *Pussy* and *fuck*!" she repeated, still laughing. "Jeremiah can't talk like that. I mean, he's from the nineteenth century. Oh, this is hilarious."

And she kept on laughing.

Oh yeah, funny as fuck.

He ran his hands over his face angrily. He would almost rather have offended her than have to tolerate this humiliation. Nevertheless, he had the dignity to pretend he found it as amusing as she did.

"Honestly, how could I think of saying that instead of *virtue*, *fornicate*, or some other equally erotic word? What was I thinking?" His usual sarcastic tone had returned. "Although I'm pretty sure a nineteenth-century detective would have used a bit of rough language. Anyway, do you want to continue the role-play or . . . ?"

"No need. I think I have enough material to write a scene with plenty of . . . fire. But thanks for the help," she said and gently pinched his arm. "It was really useful."

"Sure, no problem. Whenever you like."

Siobhan stood up, smoothed down her nightgown, picked up her laptop from the ground, and vanished.

What had just happened? And why did he feel like some kind of lousy guinea pig? Disconcerted, he lowered his gaze to the bulge in his pants and let his head drop back against the swing seat, sighing despondently.

Someone needed to take a cold shower urgently.

And to jerk off. That too.

Chapter 25

Marcel

Spying on her through the kitchen window was becoming a worrying habit. He felt like a voyeur, watching as she swung her legs lazily in the water, perched on the edge of the pool. The sun was toasting her shoulders and lighting up her faraway smile. A strange prickle ran across his stomach. Was she thinking about last night? Marcel hadn't slept a wink. Half of him was annoyed at having gone too far; the other half, at not having gone further. He wanted to sleep with her, to have her in his bed, to see what that beautiful copper hair looked like against his pillow. Which was kind of problematic, because a woman like Siobhan would want something more than just a roll in the hay, and he wasn't prepared to give her that. He closed his eyes for a second to get his thoughts in order. He shook his head as though coming back from a trance and emptied half a bottle of sports drink down his throat. All right, he shouldn't have gone along with the game, but criticizing his temporary madness after the fact wasn't going to do him any good. He had to be practical, cold like steel. He would act like nothing had happened, pretend it had all been innocent role-play and that he let himself get carried away because . . . Well, damn it, he was human. He would behave completely normally, although inside he was reaching the end of his tether. And if she raised it, he would play dumb. *I don't know what you're talking about, princess. I was just playing a part. Weren't you?*

"She's a great girl, isn't she?"

Charmaine's hoarse voice burst into the kitchen. Marcel tensed suddenly, like a child caught with his hand in the cookie jar. A trickle of sweat made its way down his back in a solitary trail toward the base of his spine.

"I see you've become great friends in my absence," he replied, screwing the cap back on the bottle.

"Yes, we have. And you'd better not jerk her around, or I swear on the Bible, I'll take her side."

Marcel turned around and looked at her closely.

"What do you mean by jerk her around?"

"I mean what I mean."

"Wow. You should have been a public speaker," he said.

Charmaine flapped her hands violently.

"Don't you change the subject, young man. When are you going to tell her?"

"Tell her what?"

"All of it. About the pseudonym, about Mom . . . All of it. You haven't told her shit. You're still hiding behind that whole melancholic, mysterious act."

A feeling of unimaginable resentment swelled up in his heart. Marcel lowered his gaze and played with the bottle. For years, he had been gluing the pieces of himself back together. Time had lessened the pain of certain memories, but the prospect of unburying them made him feel sick. His stomach churned just thinking about it.

No chance.

He was a lone pilot and had every intention of continuing to be.

"Digging up the past isn't going to fix anything."

"What doesn't fix anything is bottling up all that resentment. And, anyway, now that you've invited her into your little tormented writer bubble, the least you could do is be honest."

"I didn't invite her. I can assure you she gate-crashed the party all by herself."

"Perhaps only because you left the door ajar. Think about it."

"I don't have anything to think about, Chaz." He opened the refrigerator decisively and put his drink inside. "What the hell is going on with you? What is going on with everyone? First Alex, then those crazy women on Twitter, and now you. Siobhan is . . . a temporary colleague. Period." He adopted a bored expression. "What do you want me to say? When we finish writing the novel, she'll go her way, and I'll go mine."

A melodic and prolonged *mm-hmm* emerged from Charmaine as she nodded her head.

"Try saying that again like you mean it. Like you believe it," she said. Marcel narrowed his eyes and sighed noisily. "Okay, whatever, right now I don't have time to help you mature emotionally. I'm going to Lakeview to see Dad. You should come. There's a lot of paperwork still to go through."

"I'll drop by later. I promised Siobhan I would take her to the Ninth Ward. I'll need the Chevy, so leave me the key before you go."

A thunderous cough rose from the depths of Charmaine's chest.

"Ninth Ward? Couldn't you think of anywhere better for sightseeing?"

Marcel shrugged.

"She asked me."

"No way . . . So you're going back to that shithole just because she asked you. Well, well, well. She's really got you by the balls, huh?" she exclaimed, winking to soften the blow.

"Cut the crap, will you? It's your fault for talking too much." He pointed his index finger at her. "If you hadn't taken it upon yourself to resurrect the wonderful family story of the Duponts and their post-Katrina feats, Siobhan wouldn't even know what the Ninth Ward was."

"Maybe. Anyway, you're going to take her. I think the white queen has closed in on the black king, and he's about to be checkmated," she speculated.

"Ha! My god, Chaz. You have no fucking clue about chess. The queen can't checkmate on her own."

"Oh my lord," she murmured. "For such a smart guy, you're a real dumbass sometimes. Well, have fun in the burbs. And don't forget to go see Dad today. Till later, Kasparov."

◆ ◆ ◆

The Chevy Silverado slowed to a stop at the corner of Caffin and North Galvez Street. Marcel lowered the windows and pointed out a small patch of dry grass in the middle of nothing. The sunlight beat relentlessly against the asphalt.

"It was there. That was where the house was before the storm destroyed it. And that plot over there used to be a movie theater," he said.

There was a note of sadness in his voice.

For someone who didn't know New Orleans, the Ninth Ward might pass for a neighborhood on the rise, with some new buildings and well-tended yards. But that image only represented a small part of the reality. It only took a stroll around the streets to realize that, twelve years later, the tragedy of Katrina still lingered in the foundations, stones, abandoned houses, deserted blocks, shuttered businesses, and roads devoured by weeds and deformed by potholes. For every newly built house there were four or five empty plots and a dilapidated car sitting forgotten next to a gas drum on some porch. On the facade of one ruined building, orange spray paint, faded by time, declared:

FIX

EVERYTHING

MY

ASS!

The initials explained everything. That slogan, perfectly expressing the discontent at the lack of effective response by FEMA, had become very popular in the weeks following the flood and was still present in collective memory.

Siobhan removed her sunglasses and took it all in from the passenger seat.

"There's nothing left," she said. She seemed confused. "Charmaine said the house was still standing."

"It was demolished by a contractor from Texas. All this was houses," he continued, turning off the engine and unfastening his seat belt. "And now there's nothing but weeds. Around eight hundred thousand people left after Katrina; it was the largest migration in the US since the Dust Bowl exodus in the thirties. And lots of plots just stayed empty. A while back, the local government started to expropriate the ones that were overgrown to auction them off, but our city government is slow and ineffectual; an endemic problem that's not helped by the corruption, of course. Let's just say that most of the apples in the city barrel are rotten."

"Yes, but . . . how can it still be like this after twelve years? It's an outrage," she said. "And I thought the recovery of the World Trade Center after 9/11 was slow!"

Marcel sighed with resignation.

"There's something you should know about NOLA." Siobhan turned her head to give him her full attention. "Everyone loves the music, the food, the colonial architecture, Mardi Gras . . . As for the people . . ." He gave a dramatic pause, embellished with a shake of the head. His features hardened. "And speaking of 9/11, the Federal Reserve coughed up millions to rebuild New York after the attack. Same after the earthquake in San Francisco. What did Bush do for New Orleans? They put people in trailers and shut down access to subsidized housing so they had to live like goddamn refugees in their own country. Fucking bastards," he muttered.

Siobhan put her hand on his arm in a gentle caress that set his skin on fire. And yet, strangely, it calmed him.

"Um . . . are you okay?"

He nodded silently. He felt more and more comfortable talking to her. It was like she had the power to release the anger that he'd been bottling up for years. And the feeling gave him a sense of relief.

"I haven't been here for a long time, that's all. You know what? Sometimes I dream about New Orleans, and when I do, I'm always in the city during the flood," he confessed.

It was the first time he had ever told anyone.

"I guess coming back to search for your family must have been really tough."

"It was worse for them. After all, I had my life in New York. Baxter Books was going to publish my second novel, and Alex was already negotiating the contract for the third; things were starting to go well. But yes, it had a profound effect on me, seeing with my own eyes that the news reports were true. The storm didn't just destroy the homes we grew up in; it destroyed our memories and the spirit of the neighborhood."

"Chaz mentioned that the insurance company behaved terribly toward you."

He laughed indignantly.

"You know how much they offered my father in compensation? Four hundred and ninety-five dollars."

"What? That can't be right. You're kidding me."

"I wish. Those sons of bitches claimed the policy covered damage caused by the hurricane but not the flood. Anyway, he was one of the lucky ones. Most folks in the Ninth didn't have insurance at all, or if they did once, they had stopped making the monthly payments. In case you hadn't noticed, this neighborhood is poor and Black."

"And the state did nothing to help?"

"There was a program called Road Home, but it still wasn't enough. In the end, I managed to find a decent place in Tremé for them. It cost me an arm and a leg, thanks to speculators, but . . ."

"You weren't about to leave them out on the street."

"Precisely."

"To your credit."

"I just helped them get back on their feet. Anyone in my situation would have done the same. I mean, I never got on well with my dad, but he's still my dad. As for my sister . . . Well, I owe pretty much everything to Charmaine."

"It's interesting—she says the same about you. When we first met, you did nothing but brag about your $15,000 sofa, but I know you bought the house in the Garden District and that you donate a lot of money to the city's recovery."

"She told you that too? I think Chaz and I need to have some words tonight."

"Don't you dare, you hear me? Or you'll have this New Yorker to deal with."

"Pah, you don't scare me, Brooklyn princess."

It was admirable that he could hold her gaze as he uttered such a bare-faced lie.

Because, in truth, he was scared of Siobhan.

Not of her exactly, but of her light.

That blinding light that suddenly prevented him from seeing the right path.

"If I were you, I wouldn't underestimate me, Mr. Black." Her reply cut through the air like a sharpened knife. God, he loved this woman. "Speaking of Brooklyn, did you stay down here for a while?"

"No. I got out of here as soon as I could. Things got ugly. Shootings, thefts, holdups, gang fights, police brutality . . . The National Guard were patrolling the streets as if this was fucking Fallujah. They even implemented a curfew. I'm not surprised people took to the bottle, or OxyContin, just to get through it."

The echoes of a cheerful melody floated through the air. Suddenly, a brass band of African American musicians in uniform appeared, marching across the street, followed by a funeral cortege, dancing to the rhythm of the music. The parade gave off a carnival atmosphere as it snaked through the cracked, weed-speckled streets.

Siobhan stuck her head out the window.

"What's this?"

"A funeral, Big Easy–style. We call it *second line*."

"Sounds great. A perfect way to say goodbye."

A melancholic smile appeared on Marcel's face.

Perhaps that was New Orleans's strength: despite everything, there was always something to celebrate. Although maybe that was also its weakness. Whatever happened, the city always found a way to carry on, no matter how hard things got. And, in some way, that gave him some peace.

"You know what, Miss Harris?" he said, drumming his fingers on the steering wheel. "You're in luck. Tonight, you're finally going to learn what real music is."

◆ ◆ ◆

A few hours later, they settled into a small restaurant in the heart of Marigny, one of the city's most charming old Creole neighborhoods. Night had just started to descend, and the lights of the bars and restaurants twinkled as they came on.

"See, gumbo is like jazz: a cultural emblem of New Orleans," explained Marcel, smoothing the napkin across his knees. "A music critic once said that gumbo is culinary jazz and jazz is musical gumbo. August isn't the best month to eat blue crab though; maybe we should have ordered the smoked meat," he mused, more to himself than to her. "Anyway, it doesn't matter. Bon appétit."

Siobhan nodded and sampled a spoonful of the stew they had just been served along with a chilled bottle of white wine.

"Mmmm." She savored the mix of rice and crab with her eyes closed. "Delicious," she said, to her companion's great satisfaction. She ate another spoonful before asking: "How do they make the broth so thick?"

"Dark brown roux, okra, and sassafras leaves, a contribution from the Choctaw natives," he explained. "Some see this dish as a connection to the okra soups of Africa; others link it to French bouillabaisse, or even to the Cajuns, the French Canadians who settled in Louisiana after being expelled from Acadia by the British Crown."

"That's a lot of influences."

"It makes sense, given New Orleans's colonial past."

"You should write a novel set here, Marcel."

A conspiratorial smile appeared on his face.

"Actually," he said, his voice lowered confidentially, "that's what I was thinking of doing after . . . you know"—he glanced to either side to make sure his words didn't reach the wrong ears—"killing Willy."

"Seriously?"

"Well, yeah. A thriller set in a dystopian future, with a New Orleans almost engulfed by water and devastated by climate change, and a serial killer striking fear into the population. Alex didn't like the racial focus I wanted to give it. He said it was too sensitive for the times, blah blah blah. Anyway, I'm planning to write that novel one day."

He paused, realizing it was the first time he had ever spoken to anyone about his projects, apart from his agent or his editor.

Of course, Siobhan wasn't just anyone.

Siobhan was Siobhan.

The only person who truly understood his passions and frustrations.

"So, it's true that a wounded bird returns to the nest sooner or later."

"What?"

Siobhan shook her head.

"Nothing. I was getting sidetracked. It's a brilliant idea, Marcel. Really. I suppose you would be getting deep into your thriller right now if I hadn't appeared on the scene, so . . . I'm sorry to have ruined your plans."

She looked genuinely sorry; Marcel knew her well enough to be sure she was.

"Well, technically the first to arrive on the scene was Letitia Wright. And anyway"—he averted his gaze and focused on his plate, unable to meet those disarming blue eyes—"to be honest, I had had a bad bout of writer's block. I hadn't written a single line since I finished *The End of Days*. Nada. Zilch. I had a terrible fear of not living up to expectations. And to top it all off, Mira Yamashita wrote a dreadful review in the *New York Times* that nearly finished off my career."

There was a silence.

Siobhan broke it.

"A critic is just a critic. They shouldn't have the power to prevent a good novel from occupying the place it deserves, or to drain the soul of a brilliant author."

He noticed a muscle tensing in her neck. If only he had the balls to kiss her right then. But all he could do was whisper, "Thanks," under his breath before hiding behind a slug of wine.

What a coward.

"Why are you thanking me? For telling the truth?"

"No, Siobhan. For helping me recover my ability to tell a story. If it weren't for you and *Two Ways*, chances are good I'd still be lost."

If someone had told him weeks before that he would be thanking Little Miss Happy Endings for getting him out of his creative rut, he would have laughed in their face.

"Don't you think that's a bit drastic? Sooner or later you would have gotten unstuck. You were born to write, Marcel. It's in your blood. I know you started as a child. Chaz told me."

Marcel sighed.

"Of course she did," he murmured.

"What I'm trying to say is that you have no reason to thank me. I haven't done anything. I'm not important. You would have had the same experience with any other romance writer who crossed paths with you."

What he was thinking at that moment was:

Like hell. Of course you're important. There's no one like you, Siobhan Harris. Shit, can't you see? There's not a woman in the world who could hold a candle to you. You . . . You're special.

What he said was:

"You wanna try the pecan pie?"

A bottle of wine later, the world seemed somewhat less complicated. The night was just getting started, and the lively Frenchmen Street exuded a chaotic energy, embodied by the go-cup culture of drinking in the street, playing in the street, dancing in the street. The bars and restaurants alternated with jazz clubs—perhaps not as elegant as Preservation Hall, in the French Quarter, but much more authentic—which were the very essence of the city.

Marcel stopped at the door of the Blue Nile, bathed in blue neon lights, and said:

"This place is the epitome of what a New Orleans jazz club should be. It'll be packed to the rafters in half an hour. So, if you'd like to discover some real music, it's now or never. Do you want to? Please say yes."

"Of course I do."

Inside, the temperature was quite pleasant. On the stage, a band was playing renditions of stomp classics, marking the up-tempo beat by stamping on the floor; it was impossible not to join in. They walked up to the bar. Marcel asked what she would like, and she went for something strong: a Sazerac.

"Well, well, well. It would appear that Miss Harris has grown up," he joked.

"Oh come on. I'm not a porcelain doll."

People kept flooding in, and space was becoming tighter, so they had to squeeze together while they enjoyed their drinks.

"So, is there live music in all the venues in this neighborhood?" asked Siobhan, stretching up to direct her question past Marcel's shoulder.

Her breath tickled his earlobe and he liked the sensation. Why deny it?

"In all the major ones, yes. And the musicians always play, audience or not. Ragtime. Dixieland. Blues. Hot jazz. All sorts of things."

"Living here is like being at a party that never ends. Don't you miss it, even a tiny bit?"

"Nah. I have all I need in New York," he said.

He looked her in the eye.

He felt a scorching heat creeping up from his stomach to his solar plexus. And he knew it was all starting to fit together.

Or fall apart.

It was her.

Her and nothing else.

Siobhan drained her Sazerac and returned the glass to the bar with a decisive bang.

"Let's go," she ordered.

"Where?"

"To dance."

"But . . ."

"No buts, Mr. Black." She raised a finger to her lips. "Not tonight."

Marcel laughed like an idiot and allowed her to lead him onto the dance floor. The musicians were so close you could feel the energy of the trumpet, the rhythm of the clarinet, and the sensuality of the saxophone emanating from the lights and shadows of the stage. Siobhan started to sway to the sound of "Basin Street Blues," and . . . God, she was a good mover.

"That's the way, girl!" he called out, cheering her on.

The rocking of her body fascinated him. At what point had the naive Miss Harris turned into this impossible blend? Siobhan seemed to be all the elements at once: water, earth, air, and a lot of fire. He couldn't recall ever having wanted anyone so intensely. He decided to join her and follow her steps. Hip to hip. Fingers interlaced. Arms up. Turn to one side. Turn to the other. And start again. Her joy for life was infectious. His face seemed to ache with happiness—was that even possible? Feeling like this was a balm for the soul.

Then the mood changed, suddenly becoming much more intimate.

The first chords of "Anyone Who Knows What Love Is" announced that it was slow-dance time. Marcel stretched out his arm, palm up, in a gesture that Siobhan understood perfectly. He took her by the waist, and she interlaced her fingers around his neck; both were soaked with sweat, but neither cared in the slightest. He looked down at her from his height with low-lidded, penetrating eyes. The crowd around them became blurry and irrelevant as they turned in small circles on the dance floor.

"Why are you looking at me like that?" asked Siobhan, tilting her chin slightly, beautiful in her uncertainty.

"How am I looking at you?"

"Like I was two scoops of ice cream. Just like last night."

Marcel tried not to show the inner smile that glowed in his chest.

"Last night? I don't know what you're talking about."

Siobhan smiled, beautiful and fierce.

"So we're going to keep pretending nothing happened, are we?"

Which in reality sounded more like: *It's an irrefutable fact that we were about to get it on in the backyard of your house last night. Just because we've spent all day avoiding the subject won't make it go away.*

"Nothing happened."

Which in reality sounded more like: *The irrefutable fact is that if you hadn't gotten the giggles at the crucial moment, I would have given you the ride of your life in the pool.*

In an attempt to deflect, he said, "Come on, let me enjoy the moment."

"Wait, wait. Enjoy? Who are you, and what have you done with my friend?"

Friend. He shook his head. "How flattering. I don't know if I'm ready for that level of commitment."

He caught the skepticism on Siobhan's face and grabbed her tighter, contradicting his own words; she ran her fingers along the hairline at the back of his neck with a delicacy that made his skin bristle.

"Well, I don't think you'll have to play the role of 'friend' for much longer. Luckily, we're nearly finished with the novel," she said. And she fluttered her lashes deliberately to lower his defenses. It worked quite well.

"Good thing too. Because being your 'friend' is starting to become unbearable," he replied, fixing his gaze on her mouth.

It would be so easy to forget everything and stay in that moment forever.

With her.

◆ ◆ ◆

The taxi dropped them back in the Garden District at around two in the morning. Marcel got out of the car and grappled to extract Siobhan, who could barely stand. She staggered, but he caught her around the waist in time.

"Ohhh . . . Thanksshhh," she said between hiccups. "You're like a nineteenth-century gentleman, Mr. Black. A gentleman—hic!—rescuing a damsel in dishtress." She tried to curtsy and very nearly ended up on the ground.

"Very good, damsel. It's time to go sleep it off. Come on."

Without releasing his grip on her, he pushed open the gate. Siobhan started singing "Fever" at the top of her lungs.

"Shhh . . . Lower your voice. You'll wake the whole goddamn neighborhood."

"But this is New Orl—!"

She couldn't finish her sentence. Marcel covered her mouth and gave her a warning look. She brushed his hand aside.

"Okay, okay, don't—hic!—be like that. You know something?" she asked as they moved toward the porch. She lost her balance again, and Marcel caught her. "Oopsss . . ." She giggled drunkenly. "Fighters first, lovers later," she chanted like a little girl.

Marcel laughed. She really was a very funny drunk.

"And . . ." She stopped in front of him and put her arms around his neck provocatively. "You like me. You're crazy about me," she assured him, despite her difficulty getting the words out.

"What?" He moved away, trying to repress something like a nervous smile. "What makes you say that?"

"Only the fact that I have eyes in my head," she replied, opening her eyes wide. Marcel pried her hands from his neck. "I know you want to"—she pointed at her chest—"the word beginning with *F*. Me."

"Is that so? And what is the word beginning with *F*?"

Siobhan moved her lips to his ear and whispered:

"F-U-K . . ." She stopped and scratched her neck thoughtfully. "Hang on, I think I forgot the *C* . . . Hic!"

"My god, Siobhan. You're in no state to be spelling."

"Hey!" she said and slapped his shoulder. "Don't mess with me. The thing is I like you too. You're," she started to say, although her tongue tripped her up again. "I like ev—hic!—I like everything about you."

Then she leaned forward, grabbed him by the cheeks, and boldly kissed him on the lips. It was an innocent kiss, a clumsy brush of the lips, but damn it if that tiny gesture didn't stir something inside him. It was like drinking a glass of bourbon in one gulp. Of course, that insignificant peck shouldn't really have made his heart race, nor did it explain the fact that he suddenly felt quite blurry.

Marcel placed his hands over hers, still on his face.

"Why did you do that?"

"Because I can. And because I want to. And because you're very handsome. And tall. And sexy."

"And because you're drunk."

"Yup, that t—hic!—that too."

Siobhan started to laugh hysterically and resumed her singing, so Marcel had no choice but to hoist her up and throw her over his shoulder. He grasped her by the calves and made for the porch.

"Party's over. Let's see if you're still laughing when I tell you about this tomorrow morning."

"There's a great view from here," she murmured, before prodding his buttocks with her index finger.

"Did you just touch my ass?"

"No, no, just a bit."

"Without my consent."

"Oh, I think I'm getting dizzy . . ."

Marcel quickly lowered her and took her in his arms.

"Hey. Hey, Siobhan. Are you okay?"

She made a small noise, leaned her head on his chest, and closed her eyes.

Charmaine appeared in the doorway just as they were about to enter.

"What the hell is all this racket? Do you know what time it is?" she said. Then her brow furrowed with worry and she asked: "What's wrong with Siobhan? Is she ill?"

"Ill? She's drunk as a skunk."

"But what did she drink?"

"You'd be better off asking what she didn't drink."

"Why did you let her drink herself senseless, idiot?"

"So now it's my fault? I'm not her nanny. Stop with the sermonizing and stand aside. My back's killing me."

Charmaine shut the door and urged him to take Siobhan to her room. Marcel ran his eyes up the staircase and wondered how best to manage the situation.

"You're kidding, right? I can't go all the way up there with her in my arms."

"Come on, man, get on with it. It's only about four steps."

"Oh yeah? Well, you carry her, then, Superwoman. Let's see if you can get past the third."

Charmaine tutted.

"All right. She'll have to sleep in Dad's room."

"No way. I'll take her to the sofa. Do me a favor—could you bring pillows and clean sheets? And some water. She'll need to hydrate."

Marcel went to the living room and lowered Siobhan carefully onto the sofa. He sat next to her and unfastened her sandals and put them on the floor, next to her purse. When his sister returned with sheets and pillows, he used one set to make her comfortable and the other to improvise a bed on the floor.

"You're sleeping there?" she asked in surprise.

"Of course," he replied as though it was obvious. He removed his shoes. "You don't want me to leave her here alone, right? What if she wakes in the night feeling nauseous? Someone will have to hold her hair back . . . or whatever you do."

A very irritating little smile took shape on Charmaine's lips.

"Didn't I tell you, little bro? This queen has crushed the king."

Marcel sighed with pure exhaustion.

"Go to bed, Chaz."

Alone at last, he sat down again next to Siobhan, who was sleeping soundly, oblivious to Marcel's inner torment. He watched the rise and fall of her chest as she breathed. Her serene expression gave him a rush of tenderness that threatened to drown him in emotion. He brushed a strand of hair off her face and stroked her cheek with the back of his hand. And as he watched, he wondered what might have happened if he had met her at some other time in his life.

But the answer was that there was never a right moment to meet a woman like her.

"Happy endings don't exist. Happy endings don't exist," he repeated like he was trying to convince himself of a mantra.

Siobhan moaned, murmured something unintelligible, and turned over.

Chapter 26

Siobhan

Daylight struck her right in the eye. Groaning, she tried to lift her arms to cover her face, but they felt weighed down, like there were sandbags on top of them. Her mouth felt furry, almost anesthetized, and the jackhammer in her head wouldn't let up. The air stank of alcohol. Correction: *she* stank of alcohol. She pried her eyelids apart with difficulty. It took a few seconds for her eyes to focus. She was staring at the ceiling of . . . of somewhere. The Duponts' living room? What was she doing in the living room? Why had she slept on the sofa? A fuzzy image swam up from the depths of her brain and surfaced; even then, she couldn't remember a thing. She tried to get up slowly, holding her temples to minimize the pounding of her head. Little by little, the events of the previous night slipped into order in her mind. She had gone out for dinner with Marcel, and then they had a Sazerac. They had danced, together, very close together; she remembered that much.

And after that, nothing.

"Good morning, princess," he said, coming into the living room. How could he be fresh as a daisy when she felt the way she did? "How are you feeling this morning? Much of a hangover?"

"My head is pounding."

Marcel gave a slight smile.

"I'm not surprised. Here." He held out a glass of fizzing water. "I brought you an aspirin. I thought you might need it."

"Thanks. Did I really drink that much last night?"

He shot her a skeptical look.

"Don't tell me you don't remember," he said, folding his arms over his chest.

"Well, I know we went out for dinner and then to a jazz club and all that, but . . . how did I end up sleeping on the sofa?"

"It's quite simple: you passed out. Chaz wanted me to carry you to your room, like I'm some kind of goddamn Marvel superhero with the ability to climb forty stairs with a dead weight in my arms and not break my back. By the way, how much do you weigh?"

"A hundred and fifteen pounds. So, Chaz saw me in that state?" She sighed and stared down at the glass of water, which she was clutching with both hands. "Oh my god, how embarrassing. I'm never going to drink again in my life," she said, before downing her medicine.

"It was no great drama. The most interesting bit was when you kissed me, but apart from that—"

Bubbles shot out of her mouth. She almost choked.

"I did what?" she asked, eyes wide like saucers.

"You kissed me."

"What? No! I didn't . . . ! It can't . . ." Her ability to produce syntactically coherent sentences had melted in her brain, so she made an effort to gather her composure and maintain a reasonable and calm tone. "Are you being serious? Please, tell me you're not being serious."

"One hundred percent."

Siobhan hid her face in a cushion and wished for a meteorite to land right on top of them.

"I know. Dutch courage, I guess." His "no big deal" attitude should have calmed Siobhan, but it only increased her panic. "Oh, and you touched my ass," he added. He appeared to be enjoying this moment a tad too much.

A fresh wave of humiliation broke over Siobhan like a tsunami.

"It's not true! You're making it up!"

"You kissed me. Without my consent. And you touched my ass. You know I could sue you for that? And I could sue you for snoring like a buzz saw."

"I don't snore," she grumbled.

"Oh yes you do."

"There's no way you heard me from your room."

"Who said I slept in my room?"

"So, where did you sleep?"

"Right here," he pointed at the floor. "What? I couldn't leave you unsupervised. Do you know how much my dry-cleaning bill would have been if you vomited on the rug?"

Siobhan ground her teeth. She felt like her jaw would break she was clenching it so hard.

"Okay, but in the end I didn't vomit." She suddenly grimaced with horror. "Did I?" Marcel shook his head, amused, and she felt instantly relieved. After a brief pause, she glanced at him slyly. "Was it good, at least? You know"—she licked her lips—"the kiss."

Marcel's eyes darted around her face for a few seconds, and she could have sworn she saw something like adoration flickering in his gaze. Her chest inflated as though she were holding a deep breath.

"Mmm. It wasn't bad, although I've had better, princess."

"You jerk," she burst out, her pride wounded, before throwing a cushion in his face.

"A jerk who's handsome, tall, and sexy, to use your precise words," he replied, as he caught the cushion midflight. Siobhan opened her mouth to protest and then closed it again. "Hey, don't take this the wrong way, but you stink like a distillery. Why don't you take a shower before breakfast? I'll tell Mrs. Robicheaux to make you something restorative. Nothing like some Southern-style pork chops to cure a hangover."

The nausea rose in her throat in an instant.

The shower managed to wash away the smell of the booze but not the shame or the shakiness in her legs. She had kissed him. She had kissed Marcel. And she didn't know what was worse, the fact that she had done it or the fact that she couldn't remember it. While the water rinsed off the last traces of soap, she brought her fingertips to her lips and tried to imagine what that kiss would have been like. Soft and gentle? Or fiery and passionate? Her mind rewound to the night of the role-play. She was tormented by what might have happened between them if not for that silly fit of the giggles. And more to the point, had it been laughter or fear? She still wasn't sure. And she had no sense of whether it had been as real for him as it was for her or simply a game. She had spent every minute of the next day debating whether or not to raise the subject, trying to act normal and hide the fact that her knees went weak every time she visualized Marcel on top, under, behind her. And now . . . that kiss she couldn't remember. Goddamn alcohol and lousy hangover! Kissing that man had been at the center of her fantasies for a long time. This was not the way she had imagined it: it should have been *he* who kissed *her*. And it would have been a movie kiss. She couldn't imagine it any other way; not after sensing how passionate he was up close. The very idea of Marcel kissing her, first on the lips and then on the neck, caressing her breasts and then grabbing her buttocks to squeeze her against his half-naked body while he whispered obscenities in her ear . . . That image turned the spark into a flame and the flame into a furnace. She had to press her hands to her chest to try to slow the beating of her heart.

For god's sake, Siobhan. Calm down.

She stepped out of the shower breathless from that exquisite torture. She put her erotic thoughts on hold, but the aspirin and the fact that he had slept on the floor so as not to leave her alone played on a loop in her mind. In his own way, Marcel was concerned about her. They had a connection. They got on well. They had fun. And sometimes, he looked at her in a way that made her feel dizzy. She couldn't allow herself to think about him romantically—the notion that he might harbor some feeling for her was absurd—but then, he wasn't the same arrogant and reserved man she had met in New York. She dried her hair and pulled it back into a messy high bun. She glanced at her watch: 10:00 a.m. There was no chance of her feeling any fresher than this, so she put on a floaty dress and went downstairs for breakfast. The voices coming from the kitchen made her stop short: Marcel and his sister were arguing. She knew she shouldn't eavesdrop on other people's conversations, but she couldn't fight her instinct. There were too many pieces in the Dupont family puzzle that she didn't know how to fit together. So she stood still and trained her ears on their argument.

"The only thing I asked you to do was to go and see him, for Christ's sake. Once. One lousy visit. Is it really so much to ask? You've been here four days, Marcel. You expect me to believe you still haven't found time?"

"I don't give a damn what you do or don't believe, Chaz."

"But yesterday you promised me you'd go."

"No, I didn't promise shit. I just said that—"

"Your obligation—"

"Stop there, Charmaine. Don't go down that path. Don't do it." Siobhan held her breath. Marcel's tone had suddenly become more serious. "Don't talk to me about obligations because I think I've more than fulfilled mine."

"Are you throwing something in my face?"

"I'm not throwing anything in your face. For the love of god! Have I ever? You're my sister. You know I'd give my life for you. But do you think I would have come back home if the old man was still here? You really think that? The last time was hellish. Or have you forgotten? He hit you, goddamn it! Right in front of me."

Siobhan silenced a cry with her hand when she heard Marcel's words.

"Dad is sick. He's not himself. He's lost his mind."

"Stop making excuses for him! Healthy or sick, that man has made your life a misery. He made both of our lives a misery. I don't want to see him. What for? If I couldn't stand being near him before, I certainly don't want to now. I'll pay whatever it takes for him to live out his final days with as much dignity as possible, but don't ask me to feel sorry for him, because I won't."

"One day, Marcel Javarious Dupont, that pride of yours will give you a good smack of reality. Pride or rage, I don't know which will hit you first."

Marcel laughed, a loud, sarcastic laugh.

"Tell me something, Chaz. How long has it been since you had a night out? How long have you thought about nothing but the well-being of a man who sucked you dry over the years like a fucking parasite? First, Mom. Then the carpenter's shop. Then the fucking storm. Then his wretched illness. And now the clinic."

"And so what? Were you here, by any chance? No! You weren't here. You've never been here. You hotfooted it to New York at the first sign of trouble and left me alone to deal with him. You think you were the only one who suffered over Mom? Okay, so you put the money on the table, but I've had to bear the cross of being the daughter who stayed behind. I'm the one who had to put up with his bitterness and his bad temper all these years, the one who cleaned up the shit, who turned the other cheek, again and again. And the one who feels guilty for sending him away, despite it all. You've achieved your big dream of being a successful writer and living in Manhattan, but . . . what about me, Marcel? What do I have? Nothing."

"You have me. Although apparently that's not enough for you."

Then Siobhan heard footsteps approaching. It was Marcel. He saw her there, next to the staircase, but he walked right past her. He seemed to be looking at something in the distance. An uncomfortable leaden feeling formed in her stomach when she noticed he was holding the car keys and heading for the door.

"Are you going to Lakeview?" shouted his sister, who appeared before he had time to unlock the vehicle. Her eyes and chin had a stubborn set to them.

Marcel turned around. He exhaled and rolled his eyes as though he had just lost his final ounce of patience.

"No, okay? I'm not going to Lakeview. Not today, not tomorrow, and not the next time I come to New Orleans. If there is a next time. Happy?"

The slam of the door as he left shook Siobhan to the core.

Charmaine squeezed her eyes shut.

"Go with him, please," she asked. "Don't leave him alone."

Chapter 27

Siobhan

Marcel drove in silence along Route 90 to Bayou Sauvage. When they reached the wildlife refuge, he parked by the trailhead and unfastened his seat belt. He remained still for a few seconds, his hands limp on the steering wheel; he seemed deep in thought.

"Are you okay?" asked Siobhan.

"Yes," he replied after slightly too long a pause.

The faint tremor in his voice made her doubtful. She could see that he was swallowing down whatever it was he had contemplated telling her.

The thirty-minute journey had been the longest, tensest, and most uncertain of her life. They had barely exchanged a word since they got in the car. He didn't seem annoyed to have company—quite the opposite in fact—but he had hardly said a word the entire time, except when they stopped at a gas station to fill the tank, and he asked if she wanted a soda or a coffee. It was understandable but nonetheless worrying.

He expelled his breath toward the ceiling, and his jaw seemed to relax—a truce, at last.

"Come on, let's go and breathe a bit of fresh air," he said decisively. "It'll be good for your hangover. This is where I come to run in the morning while you're still in REM mode. Except when you get drunk, of course."

"I don't know what you're insinuating."

"Me?" He raised his hands in defense. "God forbid that I should insinuate a thing."

The Marcel she knew seemed to be back. His comment about fresh air must have been ironic too because it was horrendously hot, sticky, and dense. They made for a wooden walkway surrounded by lush vegetation that followed the irregular outline of the wetlands. Sweat flowed from every pore. At a bend in the path, the foliage opened out into a swamp. Rays of light penetrated between the branches of the trees that formed a protective cupola over their heads. The atmosphere was slightly less oppressive in the shade. She could smell the lichen growing on the bark, and the only sounds to be heard, over the twigs snapping beneath their feet, were the birdsong and the humming of insects. There was a chipped wooden bench at the foot of a majestic cypress whose gnarled roots formed a lattice stretching to the water's edge. They sat at either end, staring at the water. The lake gave off the fug of stagnant water.

Siobhan took a breath. She desperately wanted to think of something to say, but what? She bit the inside of her cheek as she tried to find the right words but failed spectacularly.

"Nice place. Perfect for escaping the stress of the city and enjoying nature."

"Yes."

There was an uncomfortable silence.

"Hey, Marcel . . ."

"Listen, Siobhan . . ."

They looked at each other and smiled.

"You first," he said. "What were you going to say?"

"I'm sorry I eavesdropped on your conversation. I shouldn't have done that. You?"

"I'm sorry you had to witness such an unpleasant scene."

"Well, it was no big deal," she said, trying to downplay the situation. "I argue with Robin too. Sometimes, I even allow myself the luxury of imagining I'm strangling him with my bare hands. You have no idea how exasperating my brother can be. You know, when he was ten, he made me believe my parents had found me in a garbage can? I was traumatized for most of the school year." Marcel's lips curved into a smile; things seemed to be improving. "The thing is, however much we argue, we always make our peace in the end. It's the cycle of sibling existence: argue, make peace, argue again, make peace again. Anyway, I'm sure Chaz wasn't being serious. People say things without thinking all the time."

"I know, I know, I know what she's like. That's not what worries me."

"What is it, then?"

Marcel ran his hand over his stubble and breathed out hard, as though wanting to empty out everything inside him.

Things weren't getting better after all.

"The other day I saw a gator. Right there." He pointed at the water lilies and reeds. "It stuck its head a few inches out of the water, and I just sat speechless watching it."

Siobhan shot him a look of amazement.

"My god. You saw a gator and you didn't run off screaming?"

"They're fascinating animals. Unlike other reptiles, gators care for their young until they're adults. Not all humans can say the same," he added, with a touch of bitterness.

She knew he was talking about his father.

"Look, I don't know what happened between you, and I don't want to stick my nose in, but perhaps you should listen to Charmaine and go visit your dad before—"

"Before he rots in hell forever?"

The certainty and conviction of his tone surprised her.

"You don't really think that, do you?"

"Sure I do. My dad did nothing but screw up our lives, ever since we were kids. I don't have very good memories of those days. Just lots of arguing, punishments, and the odd beating." His voice was strained, as though this wasn't a topic he was used to broaching.

"He hit you?"

"Only when he was drunk, but that was about half the time. The other half he didn't even come home; the only thing that mattered to him was that shitty carpenter's shop," he said, flapping those beautiful hands contemptuously. "I'll never understand how Charmaine was able to forget everything he did to us."

Siobhan felt a huge weight in her gut as she imagined Marcel as a child.

A child abused by his own father.

"I'm sorry," she muttered helplessly. "I'm really sorry you had to go through that. Was your mother . . . ?"

Marcel's body instantly transformed. His shoulders tensed until the muscles were perceptible beneath the fabric of his T-shirt, and he clenched his jaw. He turned to her and shook his head slightly. Siobhan couldn't help searching his eyes for signs of the story he had started to tell her, perhaps unconsciously, some time ago. Years of rage, sadness, and solitude bottled up inside him, threatening to burst forth. Then, he slipped his hands beneath his thighs, lowered his head, and focused on the shapes he was drawing in the dirt with his sneakers.

"She abandoned us. She left when I was eight and my sister was twelve," he said.

After this admission, he seemed to relax. Siobhan, on the other hand, felt a lump form in her throat, and she couldn't say a word.

"Claudette," continued Marcel. "You asked me her name once. That was it."

The lump constricted her throat and strangled her voice, which sounded weak when she asked:

"But . . . why? Why did she leave?"

"Honestly? I don't know. I don't know what could possibly lead a mother to abandon her two young children. I suppose she must have been very unhappy. Even so, that doesn't justify her leaving. She left a note. Just like your ex and the protagonist of your novel; apparently cowards love doing that." The saddest smile in the world broke through his anguished expression. "It said that she didn't expect us to understand her decision because we were still very young and that one day she would come back for us." He paused briefly. "I believed her, and that's why I sat waiting for her on the porch steps, day after day. But she didn't return. I never saw her again."

The story provoked multiple emotions. Siobhan had to blink repeatedly to hold back her tears. *Don't cry. Not now. This isn't your moment.* She sat perfectly still, assimilating what Marcel had told her. She looked at him, sitting hunched on the bench, and for the first time since meeting him, she understood there was something broken inside. She averted her gaze and released the very last drop of air from her lungs, overwhelmed by the significance of his revelation.

"I . . . I don't know what to say. That's terrible."

"The note also asked us to forgive her, but I've never been able to. I was very angry for a long time; I think I still am, in a way. Something like that changes everything." Then he raised his head and looked up for an instant. The clouds that had started to congregate in the sky were making the temperature shoot up. His gaze returned to some point in the dense swamp. "When someone abandons you, your childhood ends."

Siobhan felt a stab of pain in her chest. She moved closer to him until their knees brushed together. Neither of them moved apart.

"So you took refuge in literature."

A hint of a smile appeared on his lips.

"Nice way of seeing it," he said. "Some people drink to forget, like old Bernard; I wrote stories about monsters and mysterious creatures."

"Was that when you became a fan of crime novels?"

Marcel nodded.

"There weren't many books at home, so I borrowed them from the library. Agatha Christie, Dashiell Hammett, Poe, Wilkie Collins . . . Reading those authors helped me discover worlds where the limitations of real life didn't exist. And with time, I realized that describing other people's tragedies is a very useful way to forget your own. Writing has a great therapeutic power." He turned to look at Siobhan. "I'm sure you know what I mean, though your specialty leans more toward the light than the darkness." A timid laugh slightly eased the pain in her chest. "I got excited about creating a reality where I'm the only one making the rules. I suppose that's why I decided I wanted to become a writer."

"But your dad had other plans."

"The old man wanted me to learn the trade so I could take over the family business at some point. I would rather have blown my brains out," he admitted, pointing a finger at his temple like a gun. "Writing? That was no use to anyone. It was something for slackers with their heads in the clouds. Though I never heard him complain when he started receiving the checks a few years down the line. You know what he did when he found my first notebooks? He ripped them up. Right in front of my face. With his bare hands. Just like that. Since then, I've always kept my writing somewhere secret."

That explains his mistrust and the fact that the study in his apartment in New York has a security access code. Although he let me in when he barely knew me, mused Siobhan.

A tear sat on the tips of her lashes, but she refused to let it fall.

"At least he didn't destroy your dream."

"No, but he wrecked a lot of other things. When my mom left, he took to the bottle. He became this mean, bitter guy who warned his children that no one would ever love them. 'People always leave, just like your whore of a mother.' That was his catchphrase. He didn't even allow us to have friends, for Christ's sake. Why do you think my sister and I are so dysfunctional?" He exhaled. "It was Chaz who took care of me. *She* was the one who made sure I wore clean clothes to school and put hot food on the table. *She* was the one who came running to my bed in the middle of the night when I had bad dreams. All my dad did was tear up my notebooks and hit me. Why on earth would I want to see him?" he asked, and his dark gaze drilled into her like a corkscrew.

"The title of Father doesn't come included with the goddamn sperm; you have to earn it. You can't take out your frustrations on your kids and expect them to respect you. Things don't work that way."

"You left because you couldn't take any more."

"And I don't regret it. You know what I do regret though? Not taking my sister with me. She decided to stay, which I'll never understand. Maybe"—he raised his hands and let them drop limply against his thighs—"I wasn't persuasive enough. Maybe I should have found a way to make her see that if she stayed, she would be unhappy."

"Charmaine made her own decision. That's what adults do. You can't blame yourself for that."

Siobhan believed she finally understood why Marcel Dupont was a solitary and hermetic man who claimed he didn't believe in love. And it had nothing to do with romance being corny or the absurd idea that men shy away from commitment. It was because of his childhood. It must have been the solitude of that childhood with so few emotional bonds, with an abusive father who only made his mother's abandonment worse, that had forged his fierce individualism.

"Siobhan."

"Yes?"

"You once asked me why I hide behind a pseudonym." He took a deep breath and said: "I don't want my mother to find me, ever. That's all. Now you know the pathetic truth."

Suddenly, something clicked in her brain, and the loose pieces of the puzzle all slid into place. Marcel's armor was built of fear. A traumatized fear of abandonment, of loss, of there being nobody there to hold him if his nightmares returned. He was terrified by the idea of going back to being that kid sitting on the porch. What would happen if his mother returned? He could reasonably assume she would leave again. As would anyone else he got too close to. Because *people always leave.* How would he cope if something like that happened again?

Marcel Black was just the shield he needed.

And Claudette, his mother, the cause and effect of its creation.

It was the saddest, most complicated story she had heard in her life.

"Hey," Marcel whispered with unexpected tenderness. "Are you crying?"

"Sorry, I'm an idiot," she apologized, wiping away her tears with her hands.

"You're not an idiot, all right? You're anything but that. You're sensitive. You're generous. You're special. And you're important. To me, at least. And to a lot of other people. Look at me." She sniffed and raised her head. Marcel dried a tear with his thumb. "You have beautiful eyes, you know that?"

The temptation to hug him was unbearable.

"Say that again."

"That you have beautiful eyes?"

"No, that I'm important to you."

"You're important to me."

"How important?"

"Important enough to share things with you that I've never shared with anyone. Does that sound like the right level of importance?"

"Yes."

"Good."

An uncontrollable desire to touch him swept over her, and she gave in. Light as a feather, she caressed every corner of his perfect face, making the symbolic gesture of trying to smooth out the worry lines. Marcel closed his eyes and let her do it. As she ran the back of her hand over his skin, his lips opened slightly, his Adam's apple bobbed in his throat, and his nostrils flared, as though his pulse was quickening.

She lowered her hand to his chest and placed it over his heart. She could feel it beating quickly beneath her palm.

"What's going on in there, Marcel?"

"I don't know, Siobhan. I don't know," he whispered, a tormented look on his face.

Then he took her by the cheeks and rested his forehead against hers. They breathed each other in. Siobhan grabbed his T-shirt and felt the scorching heat of his skin through the fabric. She thought he was going to kiss her; she was sure he would. Until a bolt of lightning split the suddenly leaden sky in two and a fat raindrop landed on her face.

"Shit!" he said, glancing upward. "We gotta go. It's about to pour down."

Pity. It would have been romantic if he had kissed her in the rain.

And she deserved a kiss she could remember.

Curse destiny for having other plans.

And curse Louisiana's crappy weather.

The rain fell furiously, without warning. It wasn't a drizzle that gradually increased in strength but a torrential downpour. By the time they reached the parking lot, they were covered in mud and soaked to the bone. The return journey was difficult. Marcel was silent, concentrating hard on driving. The rain pounded so hard on the Chevy's roof it sounded like it would burst through. Gridlock, blasting horns, and a few crashes brought traffic to a standstill while the lightning flashed and the clouds gathered menacingly across the gulf to the south.

"My god. It's like the apocalypse," murmured Siobhan as the windshield wipers swept away sheets of water.

He glanced at her and took her hand. They stayed like that, hands clasped over the gearshift, for the rest of the journey.

Back in the Garden District at last, with the Chevy sheltering under the carport, they left the vehicle and ran the short distance to the porch. Then Marcel stopped abruptly in the rain.

"Siobhan!"

She stopped short, turned around, and covered her head with her hands like an umbrella.

"What?"

"I just . . . I just wanted to say . . ." He swallowed. "I'm glad I told you. I've never been good at talking about things close to my heart, but . . . you . . . you make it really easy. When I'm with you, everything inside me seems to loosen up, and the words just spill out."

Siobhan said nothing. As he stood before her, dripping from head to toe, breathing hard, eyelashes heavy with water droplets and wearing his heart on his sleeve, she thought he was the most fragile, most beautiful creature on earth. She couldn't control the urge to throw herself at him and hug him with all her strength. After hesitating for a few seconds, Marcel enclosed her in his arms, and she closed her eyes.

It's not about who kisses you in the rain.

It's about who hugs you during the storm.

The final veil that had been obscuring her feelings dropped. And she finally understood the truth: she was hopelessly in love with Marcel.

She loved that broken boy to the very depths of his soul.

The sound of a branch lashing against the side of the house woke her with a start. It was midnight, but the storm hadn't abated yet. There had been power outages, and many streets remained dark. The wind blew in great gusts, rattling the shutters, and the rain beat ferociously against the roof. Siobhan was worried. A series of images of natural disasters paraded before her eyes like one of those Discovery Channel documentaries narrated in highly alarmist tones. Hurricanes. Earthquakes. Tsunamis. Floods. The very crust of the earth splitting unstoppably like the bark of the crape myrtle in summer. A thunderclap rumbled outside. She drew in her feet and pulled the covers up to her head to try and calm down, but it didn't work. There were too many things bursting, prowling, and flitting through her mind, not all of them related to the rain. She tried to push away the tangle of emotions—Marcel's confession, the long embrace in the storm, the chaos outside, the chaos inside—but they only seemed to grow stronger.

Something compelled her to get up. Before she knew it, she was outside Marcel's door, wielding her cell phone like a flashlight. She opened the door slowly, her heart racing. She approached the bed and shone the phone light at it. He was fast asleep in his underwear. Those tight ones that show everything. Absolutely everything. *God, this should be illegal,* she thought. She cleared her throat, leaned over him, and touched his arm gently.

"Marcel," she whispered. "Marcel, wake up."

He grunted and turned over, which gave her an interesting view of his anatomy. That back was so broad you could have written the whole Dark-Hunters saga across it. And that ass . . . She shook her head. *You didn't sneak into his room in the middle of the night to check out his ass, stupid.*

"Marcel," she persisted. "Marcel!"

"What? What? What's going on?" he shouted, sitting bolt upright. He held his arm up to shield his eyes from the light, looking disoriented. "Siobhan, what's . . . ? What are you doing here?"

"How can you sleep when modern civilization is about to be swept away out there?"

"How should I know? Because I'm from Louisiana? Hey, would you mind not shining that thing in my face, please? You're blinding me."

"Yes, sure, sorry." Siobhan turned off the light. "I envy you, you know that? I wish I was from Louisiana, then I wouldn't be shit-scared right now because of this lousy hurricane."

"It isn't a hurricane, just a storm," he said. "It will have passed by tomorrow. Go on, back to bed."

"Yeah, but . . ."

She heard him sigh.

"But what, Siobhan?"

"I was wondering whether . . ." She wrinkled her nose. No, it was completely stupid. She must have been crazy even to enter his room. "You know what? It doesn't matter. Leave it. It's silly. I'll go. Good night."

"Hey. Come here."

"Do you mean . . . *there* there? With you? Both together? In the same bed?"

Marcel laughed.

"Isn't that why you came?"

"Well, no. Or rather, yes. But . . . I mean, it isn't—"

"Miss Harris, this offer will expire in five, four, three—"

"Okay, okay, I'm coming."

Marcel lifted the sheet to make room for her. She lay on her side, rested her head on his chest, and let him put his arm around her. It was spontaneous, as though embracing were the most natural thing in the world for them. The beating of Marcel's heart pounding in her ear was comforting and drowned out the storm outside. Pum-pum. Pum-pum. Pum-pum. The warmth of his skin singed her cheek. She breathed in his natural scent.

"Better?"

His chest vibrated when he spoke, and the tremor ran right through her.

"Much better."

"Good. This is a safe space for you and your irrational fear of storms."

"Irrational? I've seen the pictures, you know."

"We're safe here."

She liked him using *we*. It made her feel like she was part of his life. Maybe it wasn't a big deal, but she and Marcel had something, and perhaps they could keep that something after *Two Ways*. She knew her relationship with him would only ever be platonic. She slid her fingers over his abdomen. His muscles were so well defined that she started to count them, tracing a line downward, then over and back up, and again, a few more times.

"Are you feeling me up, by any chance?" asked Marcel.

"What? No! I mean, what?" she said, embarrassed, hastily withdrawing her fingers. "I was just counting your abs. How many do you have? Like, twenty-four? That's crazy. Normal people only have a couple if they're lucky."

"You really are something else. First you kiss me, and then you fondle me on the most absurd pretext in history. I'm going to have to think seriously about getting a restraining order, princess," he said teasingly. Then, he sank his nose into her hair. "Particularly because you smell so good," he whispered, in a tone of false existential angst. "What the hell do you use to smell like that?"

"It's an organic . . ." Siobhan had to clear her throat because her words got stuck when she felt Marcel stroking her back between her shoulder blades. ". . . coconut shampoo. From Bath & Body Works."

"Yeah, well, your goddamn organic coconut shampoo is driving me crazy, you know that?"

Siobhan felt as though something was melting inside her and pressed her lips together to repress the giggle that threatened to erupt.

"I'm so sorry. Next time I'll try rolling in dung to give your soul some peace."

"That's very considerate."

"And another thing. Can I just say that your skin is intolerably soft?" As she spoke, she started to caress that torso in a downward direction. "For god's sake." She continued moving down until she reached his navel, where she entertained herself drawing tiny circles. "What are you made of? Kitten fur?"

"Siobhan . . ."

There was a strange warning note in the way he said her name.

"What?"

"You're kind of touching an erogenous zone, and . . . well, I'm not made of stone."

"Oh." She stopped right away. "Sorry, I didn't mean to make you feel uncomfortable."

Siobhan heard the muffled sound of something like a laugh beneath his rib cage.

"*Uncomfortable* isn't really the best adjective for my state at the moment. *Horny as hell* would be more fitting."

He trotted the words out without hesitation. So clearly they sounded strangely elegant. And exciting.

So exciting that something throbbed in her belly and began to melt a little bit lower down.

"Wow, that's . . . problematic," murmured Siobhan.

"Agreed."

"Because we can't . . ."

"Of course we can't."

"It would be . . . out of the question."

"A disaster of unquantifiable magnitude. Worse than a hurricane." Pause. "Are you?" he asked.

"Y-yes."

"How much?"

"A bit. A lot," she replied in a hoarse voice.

"Shit, Siobhan," he whispered in the darkness, almost like a sigh.

They were moving into murky terrain. Again. How many more times would they end up in a situation like this? And how long before one of them lost control?

Marcel brushed his hand against her breast but swiftly retracted it.

The tension in the room thickened. Siobhan moistened her lips. A wave of heat ran through her from throat to pelvis, brutal, painful, and almost paralyzing. Fleeting images of the night of the role-play flashed through her mind like fireworks; the sparks fell and burned her all over. She wondered how it was possible to want someone so desperately despite being certain it was a mistake.

"But what would happen if . . . ?"

"It isn't a good idea, Siobhan. Believe me," he said resolutely.

And with that, all the sparks suddenly fizzled out.

To tell the truth, she felt slightly disappointed. And then she was furious with herself for feeling disappointed. Desire and shame coursed through her entire body. What had she done? Why had she even suggested it? He was probably just as confused as she was. If they crossed that line, there would be consequences. She would fall even more in love with him, and he would push her away.

"You're right, it's a terrible idea," she said at last. "I should probably go back to my room."

Against all odds, he squeezed her against his body with an intensity that suggested he didn't want her going anywhere, which was disconcerting and glorious at the same time.

"You can stay. As long as you promise not to take advantage of me while I sleep." Siobhan punched him on the shoulder. "Ow!" he protested.

"I have no intention of taking advantage of you while you sleep, idiot. Sadly, I can't make any promises about not drawing a cock on your face, taking a photo, and posting it on Twitter."

"Go to sleep. And no snoring."

"I don't snore, smart-ass. Good night."

The echo of his laugh thudded in his chest.

"Good night."

Thirty seconds later:

"Marcel?"

"Mmmm?"

"Do you think Jeremiah and Felicity should end up together?"

"What kind of question is that? Didn't you say a happy ending is essential in a romance novel? Wait. Don't tell me you've finally seen the light."

"No, it isn't that. See, I think they should end up together. Not because it's a rule of the romance genre, but because here, inside"—she touched her heart, although she knew he couldn't see—"I feel like they deserve it. Have you never felt like you were falling hopelessly in love with a story and its characters while you wrote it? I know it sounds strange, but . . . Well, it doesn't matter. I want to know what you think. That is, in the hypothetical scenario of Jeremiah and Felicity really existing and not being fictional characters, in the very hypothetical scenario of Jeremiah being able to travel to Manhattan in the future, meet Felicity, and develop feelings for her . . . would it work?"

"Honestly? I doubt it. They're very different people. Setting aside the fact that they come from different eras, there's the fundamental problem that Jeremiah is a broken soul."

"But broken souls can be mended. Like a porcelain vase dropped on the floor. You just have to stick the pieces back together. The Japanese do it. What's it called?"

"*Kintsugi*. Anyway, even if you repair it, the cracks are still there, and the vase will never be the same."

"That's where you're wrong. The vase is still a vase, which is the key thing, but it's also even more beautiful."

"How can something full of scars be beautiful?"

"Because the scars are proof that even the most fragile materials can be mended. The wound is where the light comes in."

Marcel remained silent. If she had raised her head, she might have seen a gleam in his black eyes. He hugged her tightly and held her hand. Siobhan couldn't have escaped his clasp, nor did she want to. At that moment, she simply adored this man. With all of his layers, fears, and complications.

Chapter 28

Siobhan

In the morning, when Siobhan awoke, she learned that Marcel had gone to see his father at the clinic. Charmaine told her as they ate breakfast in the kitchen because the backyard was muddy and strewn with fallen branches after the storm.

"I don't know what you said to that pigheaded boy, but whatever it was, you managed to persuade him," said Chaz, as she filled a cup with coffee and hot milk at the same time, New Orleans style. "You're clearly a good influence on him, so I hope to see you back here again soon," she added, giving her a conspiratorial look. "Next time at Mardi Gras, so you can have the full NOLA experience. What do you think?"

"I'd love that!" Siobhan exclaimed. But the enthusiasm drained from her face as she realized something. "But the novel will be published by then, and I doubt Marcel . . ." Charmaine nodded very slowly, as though urging her to finish the sentence. ". . . would have any reason to bring me."

Charmaine lit a cigarette and took a long drag. Siobhan watched it consume the paper.

"Honey, like 95 percent of men, my brother doesn't know what he wants. Not yet anyway," she added. "But you." She gestured at Siobhan with her cigarette. "You're an intelligent woman; I'm sure you'll work out how to point him in the right direction."

"Which is . . . ?"

"Make him see that the only thing that matters in this life is the present. And it just so happens that you're a part of his."

"Only temporarily."

Charmaine's black-rimmed eyes flashed in a way that Siobhan didn't understand.

"That remains to be seen," she replied, before exhaling the smoke noisily. "Anyway, you can come visit whenever you like, honey. With or without Marcel. You're more than welcome. If that lousy storm yesterday hasn't put you off NOLA, that is. What a deluge."

Siobhan bit her lip, remembering how, where, and with whom she had slept. And then she realized she was smiling like an idiot.

An idiot with burning cheeks.

"Oh, it was no big deal."

Later, she took a taxi to Canal Street to do a bit of shopping. The morning was mild; the sun sparkled in the sky, and the air seemed clearer than ever. The worms had taken over the sidewalks and lay there lazily, not even bothering to coil up, steam rising around them. A few workers were moving a palm tree that had fallen across the tram rails. The city appeared to have largely recovered from the storm. She wandered for a while among the zigzagging mass of shoppers, strollers, and tourists. The street was buzzing with life. In front of the old Maison Blanche building, now the Ritz-Carlton, a preacher was pontificating on the atonement of sins, and, right next to him, someone was handing out leaflets for a dubious-looking club called Paradise. Siobhan smiled. She would miss this unique and contradictory place. Despite its ramshackle streets and its faded glory, she was enchanted by it all. She bought a few souvenirs: some oil paintings by a street artist, a bouquet of red lilies for Charmaine, and a book on the art of kintsugi that she found by chance—wonderful chance—in a bookstore on Decatur Street. She thought it must be some kind of sign and decided to give it to Marcel. Then, she hopped on a tram to picturesque Audubon Park and strolled around.

Back in the Dupont house, she went up to her room to pack while she waited for Marcel. She didn't know what kind of mood he would be in when he returned from the clinic, and she was worried that his reunion with his father might be upsetting.

"Hi."

Siobhan turned her head and saw him standing in the doorway, with that perpetually furrowed brow and his hands in his pockets.

"Hi."

"You went shopping?" he asked, nodding at the bags of souvenirs scattered over the bed.

"I did. And I bought you this." She picked up one of the bags and handed it to him. "I stumbled on it in a bookstore in the French Quarter, and I thought you might like it."

"For me?"

"Well, it was really for Anne Rice, but there's doesn't seem to be anyone home across the street."

He rolled his eyes, though the slight twitch of his lips gave him away. He took the book out of the bag. When he saw the cover, illustrated with a broken vase whose fractures had been repaired with powdered gold, his expression went from one of confusion to surprise—and then it transformed into a beautiful and brilliant smile, the kind that spread across his face.

"'The Art of Kintsugi,'" he read aloud. He turned it over and scanned the back cover. "Well, well, what an . . . interesting coincidence."

"Is that all you have to say? My god, Dupont. You're the dullest man on the planet."

"Dull?" he repeated slowly. His voice sounded sharp, as though he was offended. "Maybe I am dull, but at least I'm not scared of rain. A few drops, and you come running to snuggle up against me."

"I didn't run to snuggle up against you, smart-ass," she protested. "Although . . ." She paused for a moment, and her annoyance evaporated. "I'd be lying if I didn't admit I missed you in bed this morning."

Oh no. No, no, no.

She instantly regretted saying it. Now he would think she thought the fact that they had shared a mattress meant they could play house, when she knew there wasn't the smallest chance of that.

Great, Siobhan.

But then, they hadn't just shared a mattress.

They had slept in each other's arms all night, which was something else altogether.

Marcel ran his hand over the back of his neck.

"I went to Lakeview," he said. "To see my dad. Or what's left of him."

"How did it go?"

"As well as can be expected, given that he's got Alzheimer's," he said and shrugged, perhaps with the hope of shaking the image from his mind.

"I understand. And how are you?"

"Honestly? Pissed. And relieved. I don't know when I'll be back, so this might be the last time I see him alive. If you can call that decrepit state alive. He's in a bad way." He went quiet for a moment, and his face took on a pensive look. "Have you ever wondered why a person starts going downhill? What is it that triggers the fall? Is it fate? Or our actions? I've always believed you reap what you sow, but today I felt . . ."

He couldn't finish the sentence.

"Compassion?" she said. Marcel nodded. He seemed troubled. "It's natural for you to feel sorry for him. He's still your father. And you're a human being. Don't be too hard on yourself, all right?"

"All right," he replied, more calmly. He smiled. "You know what? I think you should try writing a self-help book. You ought to broaden your horizons."

Siobhan huffed and pushed him toward the door.

"And you have to pack your things, so beat it."

"Sure. The flight doesn't leave until eight, so I've booked a table at Commander's Palace. Ready for one last Southern feast, princess?"

"I doubt I've got any space left in my stomach. But what am I saying—of course I am."

"That's my girl."

His girl.

It's incredible how a couple of words can sound so promising.

The siblings had made their peace. They laughed, told anecdotes, and teased each other, and Siobhan was happy to witness their reconciliation On the way to the airport, she felt sad. She didn't want to return to New York. It had been a wonderful week, and she was sure a piece of her heart would stay in New Orleans forever.

She was important to him.

And he was definitely important to her.

At departures, the siblings said goodbye with a hug and promised not to leave it too long before seeing each other again.

"And don't even think about coming back without this girl, or I won't open the door," Charmaine warned him.

Siobhan pressed her lips together to contain her laughter.

"The things I have to put up with," murmured Marcel, shaking his head.

"You think you can deny me my legitimate right as your older sister to embarrass you in front of your girlfriend?"

"Siobhan isn't my girlfriend. She's my—"

Charmaine flapped her hand dismissively.

"Yeah, yeah. Temporary colleague, I know. Anyway, take care, won't you?"

"You too, Chaz."

As he was taking the baggage from the trunk, Charmaine turned to Siobhan, took her by the elbow to move her away a few steps, and said in a low voice:

"Can I ask you a favor?"

"Sure, Chaz, anything."

"Be patient with my brother. He's the right guy for you. And I'll bet my bottom dollar that you're the right girl for him. Marcel doesn't know it yet, but he will. Sooner or later, he'll realize."

Siobhan had to make a titanic effort not to burst into tears right there.

A spark of hope warmed her heart.

Chapter 29

Siobhan

"I don't believe it!" said Paige, as she ran on the treadmill. She returned the phone to Siobhan, who was at the next machine, jogging at a considerably slower pace, and added: "I had to read the message twice. How dare that lousy wretch show up again now?"

"That's not the question," argued Lena, running alongside them. "The question is why. Why now and not eight months ago."

"Isn't it obvious? Because he's discovered that Shiv is a winner, and he wants her back. Period. Come on! He even followed her on Twitter and had the nerve to like her pinned tweet!"

"A pinned tweet that mentions her novel."

"A novel inspired by him."

"Precisely."

"Get lost, Buckley!" they chanted in unison.

Siobhan sighed. She was starting to question whether this democratic approach to deciding her emotional future had been such a good idea.

"Girls, you're not helping," she said. "What do I do? Do I meet him? Do I ignore him? Do I send him a link to buy my book and a friendly invitation to rate it on Goodreads?" She realized she was struggling for breath. She lowered the speed a couple of points and wiped the sweat from her forehead with the back of her hand. "Christ! Isn't there anywhere else we could meet on a Sunday morning other than the goddamn gym? I'm dying here."

"Hey, you're the one who complained about having eaten like an Arctic whale all week," Paige said. "That's why we're here instead of working on our tans in Central Park."

"It's not like I need any more vitamin D. Have you seen my freckles? The sun in Louisiana is brutal."

"I think they look cute," Lena reassured her.

"You're not exactly objective. But thanks anyway."

Paige cleared her throat.

"Getting back to the important item on today's agenda, I think you should ignore your ex. The guy disappears overnight after . . . how long? About a century together? He goes off with no explanation. He blocks you from his socials. He leaves you with a bunch of debts. And let's not forget the most important thing: he breaks your heart. And now he crawls out of the woodwork and wants you to go out for dinner with him. Tell me that's not the most absurd thing you've heard in your life."

"Well, maybe we should ask Shiv how she feels about it," Lena said.

That was the problem: she didn't feel anything at all. She hadn't felt butterflies in her stomach when she opened her inbox the previous day and saw Buckley's email. She didn't feel dizzy or even need to understand why he had left her all those months ago. She wasn't angry or hurt. Puzzled, perhaps. But there wasn't a shred of emotion. Even so, shouldn't she at least hear what he had to say? Buckley had been an important part of her life. On the other hand, dining with her ex was pretty much the last thing she felt like doing.

"I still haven't decided," she admitted.

Paige shook her head energetically, her long red ponytail swinging wildly from side to side.

"If I were you, I'd be perfectly clear. It makes no sense for you to see each other. Especially after everything that happened in New Orleans."

"But nothing happened in New Orleans," said Siobhan.

"Except you kissed Marcel."

"I was drunk."

"And you slept in his bed. Cuddling him like he was your teddy bear," Paige countered. Lena coughed, trying to disguise a laugh.

"Because I was shit-scared. Do you have any idea how terrifying the summer storms are in Louisiana? It rained like the world was coming to an end."

"So, I suppose the part where you nearly hooked up doesn't count either?"

"We were just—"

"Don't tell me. Doing research for the novel?"

"Bingo! How did you guess?"

Paige pressed the button to stop her treadmill, and as it slowed down she turned to face her friend.

"Shiv, look at me."

"I can't look at you, Paige. If I turn my head, I'll wind up on my ass."

"Is it so hard to admit you've fallen for him?"

Lena stopped too.

"You're. Shitting. Me. Okay, are we sure about this? I mean, on a scale of one to ten, how intense are your feelings? Because looking for a quick roll in the hay isn't the same as *liking* liking someone, you know?"

"I don't know . . . Six?"

"Twelve and a half," Paige corrected her, as she dried herself with a towel. "She *likes him* likes him. Actually, she *loves him* loves him."

Siobhan's eyes narrowed, and her mouth pursed into a tight knot.

"You don't know what's going on in my head," she muttered.

"I don't need to. I know you well enough. You would never kiss a guy if you didn't feel anything for him, even if you were wasted. And since when have you been scared of storms?"

"Yeah, but, in Louisiana—"

"Not to mention that, since you returned from your honeymoon in the South, your eyes light up every time you mention Marcel. Honey,

I'm sorry, but you're more transparent than Halle Berry's 2002 Oscars gown."

Siobhan sighed.

"Okay, you're right. I do like him. I even . . . love him."

"Oh. Then, this is serious," said Lena, stretching her quads.

"Pretty serious, yeah." Siobhan gave up on the exercise session. When the machine came to a stop, she bent double to recover her breath. "But he's made clear he's not interested in a relationship, so the best thing we can do is forget about it and pretend this conversation never happened." She straightened up and drank a gulp of water. "Can we go to the sauna now, please?"

"Did he tell you that?" asked Paige.

"Are you crazy? Of course not. I just know."

"Well, his sister doesn't seem to think that's the case."

"It doesn't matter what Chaz thinks. Marcel isn't the kind of guy to commit. Let's leave it at that. Are we going to the sauna?"

In other words: *I'm not prepared to fall in love with a man who doesn't believe in happy endings.*

"That doesn't mean he doesn't have feelings for you, Shiv. He takes you to New Orleans, introduces you to his sister, tells you his secrets, and lets you into his bed because you're scared of a lousy storm."

"I told you already, the storms in Louisiana are"—she gesticulated in exasperation. "Oh never mind."

In other words: *Marcel's life is complicated, and I'm not the heroine of a romance novel. I can't mend all his cracks just by existing.*

Lena stepped off the treadmill and stood in front of her friends.

"What if all Marcel needs is a wake-up call?"

Siobhan furrowed her brow.

"I don't follow."

"Tell him Buckley's back on the scene. Tell him you're going to dinner with him, and let's see how he reacts. The best way to find out whether he feels anything for you is to put the ball in his court."

It wasn't a bad idea.

Except for one small detail. She wasn't about to lie to Marcel to put him to the test, so there was nothing she could do but accept Buckley's invitation.

◆ ◆ ◆

Siobhan cleared her throat, glanced at Marcel over the computer screen, and said:

"I need to ask you a favor. Two, in fact."

"Sure. Go ahead."

"Well . . . I have a date tonight, in a couple of hours, to be precise." Marcel's expression was impenetrable. "Can we leave it here for today?"

"No problem. What else do you need?"

"To take a shower. And get ready. In your bathroom. For logistical reasons. It just doesn't make sense to go all the way back to Brooklyn," she explained.

"So it's an important date, huh?" he asked, scrutinizing her with a flash of interest in his eyes.

"You could say that." Siobhan took a deep breath as she prepared to drop the bomb. "I'm going out for dinner with . . . Buckley. In Gramercy."

Marcel raised a quizzical eyebrow and folded his arms over his chest.

"Buckley? Buckley, your ex? The same Buckley who left you hanging with no explanation and almost plunged you into poverty? That Buckley?"

"You sound just like Paige. You two would get along well."

"I didn't think you kept in touch with that guy."

"I didn't. Until Saturday night, when I got a message from him."

"Seriously? Wow, what a coincidence, right when a photo of the two of us starts circulating out there," he noted. "I hope at least he's taking you to the Rose Club and not some crappy hamburger joint."

The photo.

She and her friends hadn't considered that possibility.

And Siobhan found it disconcerting that Marcel was the one who raised it.

"I very much doubt Buckley can afford the Rose."

Marcel laughed contemptuously.

"Yeah."

"What's wrong? Are you pissed that I'm going out with him?"

She asked the question in the hope that he would say yes. Which was completely irrational, not to mention kind of old-fashioned.

A deep vertical furrow formed between Marcel's thick black brows.

"What? Of course not. Your private life is none of my affair, princess. Just promise me that, if you get back together, you'll post it on Twitter so that the #Sioblack fans leave me in peace once and for all."

Your private life is none of my affair? Seriously? After the week they spent together?

That had been a low blow. And, like all low blows, it hurt double.

"Don't worry, I'll post every detail of the night," she countered.

"Perfect. I can hardly wait."

"So, are you going to let me use your shower or not?"

"Go ahead. Use it all you need. Would you like me to lend you a tie as well? In case you feel like strangling your boyfriend in the middle of dinner."

"He's not my boyfriend. And I don't think I'll need to strangle him."

"Pity. It would be a great plot for a crime novel."

Siobhan stood up with all the dignity she could muster and left the study, unsure how she was supposed to feel.

After her shower, she dried her hair and decided to leave it loose. From her backpack, she took out a set of black underwear, a tight strappy dress, and a matching pair of peep-toe shoes. She had picked them out the night before, after receiving an overly enthusiastic message from Buckley: Thanks for replying, Shiv. Glad we can still work things out. I'll meet you tomorrow at nine at Pete's Tavern. Can't wait to see you. Buck. She dressed slowly, as though wanting to delay her departure for as long as possible, and made up her face: mascara, matte powder, red lipstick, and a few drops of perfume. The girl looking back at her in the mirror seemed more confused than ever. What was she doing? She didn't know. She sighed. When she was ready, she went downstairs. Marcel was in the living room, pacing as he typed something into his phone. As soon as he raised his eyes and saw her, he stopped. Open-mouthed, he looked her up and down.

She got so nervous that the only thing she could think to say was:

"Do you mind if I leave my backpack here? I don't think it goes with the dress."

Marcel shook his head in silence and returned his attention to his phone, which made her feel stupid, frustrated, and terribly disappointed. As though she had been expecting something that would never arrive.

Aren't you going to say anything, Marcel? We've slept, danced, laughed, and cried together and . . . now you're going to let me leave, just like that. Are you really going to push me into another man's arms?

"Siobhan, are you listening to me?"

"What? Sorry, I got distracted."

"I was saying I've hired a Blacklane car for you. You can use it all night."

A nice gesture on his part. But still, it annoyed her. It hurt, to tell the truth. Why did it hurt?

"Thanks, but you didn't have to."

"Oh, it's nothing. Do you want a drink while you wait? To calm your nerves."

"I'm not nervous," she replied brusquely.

"Well, you look it."

"Well, I'm not," she insisted. She exhaled slowly and suddenly blurted out randomly: "I miss New Orleans. I miss the breakfasts in the backyard, the jazz, the ridiculously rich food, the sticky heat, the rain, Chaz."

I miss being with you the way we were in New Orleans.

Marcel smiled.

"How is that possible when we've only been back four days? You didn't get bewitched in one of those voodoo stores in the Vieux, did you?"

Siobhan gave him a gentle punch on the biceps.

"You're an idiot," she said, shooting him an annoyed look.

His smile widened.

"I know."

"And you don't deserve a temporary colleague like me."

"I know that too."

They looked at each other for a moment, protected by a bubble in which only the two of them existed, along with everything that united them: their jokes, New Orleans, Coney Island, "Summertime," their routine of writing together in that Upper East Side penthouse, *Two Ways*.

It was magical.

Unfortunately, his phone pinged and burst their small bubble. The magic vanished. Marcel pressed his lips together, closed his eyes, and looked pained for a moment.

"The car's here. Go now, or you'll be late."

"Okay."

Then he said her name in such a strange way.

"Siobhan."

There was something contained in it, something that couldn't quite reach the surface. A feeling of depth.

Of possibility, perhaps.

"Yes?"

Marcel took a breath. His shoulders rose and fell with her own heartbeat.

"You look beautiful tonight," he said. "Really. And if that guy can't see it, he's a jerk and a coward."

There was sincerity in the low pitch of his voice.

Desperation.

And something else that Siobhan couldn't or didn't want to identify that threatened to destroy her from within.

She nodded, opened the door slowly, and left with a lump in her throat. In the elevator she fought to keep the tears stinging her eyes at bay. Why did she feel as though someone was using a knife to cut the rope that was keeping her from falling into the abyss?

As if Marcel himself was cutting it.

A Mercedes A-Class with tinted windows was waiting on the street. The driver greeted her and invited her to make herself comfortable inside, before setting off. Siobhan leaned her head against the window and let her gaze roam along Fifth Avenue. Eight months ago, if Buckley had come back, she would have forgiven him without a second thought. They would probably have ended up eating popcorn on the sofa watching *Jeopardy*. They would have fallen asleep, without even a reconciliatory screw, but it wouldn't have mattered because at least they were together. The problem was that none of that felt right anymore. Her heart remained cold and unchanged at the thought of seeing him again. She took out her phone and scrolled through the image gallery looking for something, a memory, to make her feel something. But what she found was a blurry photo of her and Marcel in the Blue Nile the night she got drunk. He must have taken it, because she hadn't seen it before. Marcel was smiling at her while she stuck her tongue out. She enlarged the image and studied his face, that perfect, angular face that she had caressed with her own fingers. She observed the crow's feet forming around his eyes, the white teeth beneath those lips whose taste she couldn't remember, the spark in his gaze, the confident posture, the natural laugh, the closeness of their two bodies . . .

Then something clicked in her brain.

She remembered all the times Marcel had been there for her, all the times he had helped her, all the times he had been concerned about her well-being, even if he hid it with sarcasm. She recalled all the gestures, the looks, the touches, and the veiled insinuations. She remembered how desperate he had sounded when he called to apologize, the day they argued at Coney Island. She remembered the first night in New Orleans. The second. The third. She remembered how he had protected her from the drunks on Bourbon Street. She remembered their long embrace in the rain, their long embrace in bed, the contained and latent desire. And she remembered how he had poured his heart out to her when he told her about his past.

You're important to me.

Marcel felt the same way she did; she could only see it clearly now.

Siobhan knew what she had to do, and going to dinner with Buckley wasn't it.

"I've changed my mind. Could you turn around, please?" she asked the driver.

Chapter 30

Marcel

Marcel paced the living room like a caged animal, the ice clinking in his bourbon. As he listened to the opening chords of "Anyone Who Knows What Love Is," his thoughts turned to the night he saw her dance, when he first realized how screwed he was. Siobhan was like the best kind of jazz: she hooked you with the first notes. But he had let her go. He hadn't fought for her; he hadn't so much as lifted a finger to encourage her to stay, and now his whole body hurt. His head. His guts. He wondered whether she was with that guy already. The thought of them together riled him. Then he got annoyed at himself for caring about something that had nothing to do with him. Jealousy wasn't a familiar emotion to him; it was a very different feeling from the solitude that had enveloped him since the age of eight. Why hadn't he asked her to stay? Because Siobhan deserved better than the broken man he was. That's why he had tried to push her away every time they got close. He had held back his desire more than was humanly tolerable.

And now he was going crazy.

Even though he had done the right thing.

Or so he thought.

When the bell rang, his pulse soared. He cursed, knowing it was her. He took a deep breath and opened the door. There she was, like a dangerous drug that kept tempting him. Him, with his heart in his hands, crying out for her to break it. Yes, he knew what she had come for.

So he raised his defensive walls.

"What are you doing here, princess? Did you leave your lipstick in your backpack?"

"We need to talk."

Marcel blocked her way.

"This isn't a good time. I'm with someone," he improvised. "A woman."

Siobhan nodded as though acknowledging the validity of his argument. But she didn't seem convinced.

"For a good writer, you suck at lying."

Goddammit.

"Go home, please," he said, with a mixture of exasperation and indulgence.

Ignoring him entirely, she crossed the threshold. His brain and reflexes were responding in slow motion. He watched as Siobhan slipped off her shoes and left them at the door next to her purse. Her expression betrayed her relief.

She gestured to the bourbon in his hand.

"Could I have one of those too?"

"One. And then you're going," he said, with a note of veiled warning.

They went into the kitchen. Marcel poured a meager measure into a glass with ice and handed it to her. Siobhan's eyes darted from the glass to his face and back again with a look that said *You've gotta be kidding me.*

He shrugged.

"We all know what happens when you drink too much, princess. So, why aren't you in"—he flapped his hand dismissively—"wherever it was with your boyfriend? Did you stand him up or what?"

"Buckley isn't my boyfriend. Stop saying that he is. And, for your information, I sent him a message to tell him I wasn't going, okay?"

"Okay, okay. Jesus . . . Hey, why are you getting mad at me?"

Before replying, she took a long slug of bourbon and slammed the glass down on the counter.

"No. Why are *you* so mad at me that you don't even want me here?"

"I'm not . . ." He closed his eyes and rubbed his face. "I'm not mad at you, Siobhan. I'm . . . some other things, but not mad."

"What other things?" she insisted, moving closer to him.

"Well . . . tired. So, say what you have to say and go home. I'm serious."

She stared at him as though trying to figure him out.

"Why did you ask me to go to New Orleans with you?" Marcel shot her a disconcerted look, visibly confused, and opened his mouth to reply; he promptly closed it again when he saw Siobhan raise her hand in warning. "Please, spare me the excuses. I know you. I know you're going to say you invited me so we wouldn't break the rhythm of our writing, but I'm not buying that. Not anymore. I want the truth. I want to hear it from your lips."

"We're not having this conversation, okay? Forget it."

"Why not?"

"Because . . . because . . . Argh!" He emitted something like a groan. "Fine. You want the truth? Okay. The truth is I asked you because it was the right thing to do after what happened at Coney Island. I was a jerk, and I felt guilty. End of story."

Siobhan shook her head.

"That's not true."

Marcel's mouth curved into a bitter smile.

"What's up, princess? Didn't you like the answer?"

"An honest answer would be a good start."

"Okay, what do you want me to say? That I asked you to come because I can't bear to be away from you? Is that what you want to hear? Should I get down on my knees too?"

"I just want you to tell me how you feel about me!"

Her words struck him like an arrow in the middle of his chest.

And he felt like he was bleeding.

He.

Couldn't.

Take.

Any.

More.

"For god's sake, Siobhan! Isn't it clear what I feel? You think I was pretending the night of the role-play when I said I think about you every goddamn minute of the day?" He swallowed. He wanted to stop, but he couldn't. The words burst out uncontrollably from inside. "You really think I was talking to a fictional character and not to the flesh-and-blood woman right next to me? Couldn't you tell I was dying to . . . be with you? To be inside you?" His voice came out strangled. "Couldn't you feel it when we slept together? Didn't you hear my heart pounding? I . . ." Desperation contorted his face. "I'm living in real agony, for Christ's sake. Do you think I was pretending when I said you were important to me, that I shared things with you I've never shared with anyone? You think I fake the electricity that gives me goose bumps when I look at you, when I touch you, when I smell your coconut shampoo, when I hear your voice, or when you say my name? Or this stupid feeling of fullness I get just from being by your side. You think I'm faking it? Do you really think that?"

He stopped speaking, his pulse racing and his blood pumping through his veins, overwhelmed by vertigo at having admitted it all to himself.

At having said it all aloud.

"No, Marcel. I know you're not faking it; I know that very well. That's why I came back."

"Fine. Well, now that you know, you should leave."

Siobhan moved closer, so close that Marcel could see the tiny flecks in her blue irises, her thick lashes, the capricious scattering of her freckles. He averted his gaze, focusing on her mouth, which didn't help much, because he knew the taste of those soft, shining lips, even though it had only been for the briefest of moments. He didn't pull away when she took him by the cheeks. He couldn't. And with each moment that passed, he felt his self-control eroding a little more.

"I'm not going anywhere, and I won't let you push me away. I'm staying, Marcel. Can't you see that it makes no sense to build a wall between us?"

"You don't want this, Siobhan. You really don't," he whispered, his eyes lowered, fixed on her mouth.

"I know perfectly well what I want. And you know it too. The question is whether you're going to keep fighting your feelings."

He tried to speak, tried to tell her that it couldn't be, that it was a mistake, but she kissed him gently and thwarted any attempt. The warmth of her lips was his downfall. Marcel pulled away, stunned, his breath agitated, unsure whether he would ever be able to calm himself. He cast his eyes tremulously around the beautiful oval of her face and wondered whether he could bear to hold out for a second longer.

Whether all he was feeling was real or just the metaphysics of desire.

Whether it was worth ruining the story.

But in real life, as in literature, some stories have to be ruined before they turn into something really good.

Then, it happened. Something surged uncontrollably inside him and burst his levees. And that wild deluge propelled him inevitably toward those silky lips, both shipwreck and safe haven. His ability to reason had abandoned him. He was no longer the same person he had been. Or perhaps he was more himself than ever before. All he could think was *At last, at last, at last*, as he surrendered to the play of their tongues, the taste of bourbon in Siobhan's mouth, his hands gliding urgently over her neck, her arms, her back. Kissing her was like the sun hitting your face after a cold, dark night. Then, everything went blurry. He lifted her up onto the island and fitted himself between her legs; she grabbed him by the shoulders. Their passion danced around their bodies like licking flames. Marcel kissed her jaw and then her neck and very slowly lowered the straps of her dress. Realizing that he was about to leave behind those days of repressed desire, he gave in to the urge to press himself against her. When he massaged her breasts, Siobhan moaned, and the sound sent him spiraling.

"The things I want to do to you . . . You can't imagine," he whispered, as he stuck his thumb into her bra and stroked the smooth peak of her rosy nipple.

She moaned again.

"Marcel . . ."

It sounded as though she had dragged his name from somewhere deep inside her.

Logic told him that his excitement must have a limit, but, if that was the case, he hadn't reached it yet. He leaned over her and kissed her breasts hungrily. Then he slid his hand under her dress, between those soft thighs, and moved it toward her panties. He brushed his finger across the fabric, which was already moist; Siobhan shuddered and instinctively pressed herself against him. Marcel's desire became atomic, it overwhelmed him, and he quivered as he hooked his index finger around the elastic and pulled the lace to one side. Touching her was like sinking his hand into warm caramel.

"God . . . Were you this wet the night of the role-play?" he asked, very close to her mouth.

"Y-yes."

"It's a pity I missed that," he said, without stopping his caresses. "Tell me, did you do anything to resolve it?"

Siobhan bit her lower lip and nodded.

"Show me, baby. Show me what you did."

"Ma-Marcel, please . . ."

"Show me. I want to see," he said again.

He left a trail of kisses from her earlobe to her neck and moved back slightly to watch her. She looked more beautiful than ever, her mouth half-open, a pinkish glow to her cheeks, her face contorted in a grimace of pleasure that gave him no peace. She took off her bra and started to rub her nipples with her fingers.

It was a gift to his eyes.

A blessed gift.

"You did it like that?"

"Mm-hmm . . . And I touched myself there."

"Here?" he asked, gently pressing her clitoris.

"Yes . . . God . . . Yes. Right there. But a bit faster."

"Faster, huh? You're quite the little pervert, princess." Siobhan made a sound that was a mixture of laughter and pleasure. "And what were you thinking while you touched yourself?"

"I wanted . . . I wanted you to come to my room and—"

She couldn't finish her words. She was too short of breath.

"What, baby? What did you want?"

"For you to fuck me. I wanted you to fuck me, Marcel. Every which way. Hard and gentle and sweet and dirty."

Marcel exhaled fiercely. He was going to explode. She was getting wetter and wetter, thicker. And he ached all over with the desire to put something besides his finger in her.

"How inconsiderate of me not to have satisfied your desires."

"Yes. Very. Very inconsiderate."

"To make up for it, I'm going to fuck you right now. Every which way. Hard and gentle and sweet and dirty. Does that sound good?" Siobhan uttered something that sounded vaguely like a yes. "And I want you to know," he whispered in her ear, "I'm going to make every second count."

The moan that escaped her lips when he stuck his finger inside her was his alone. Siobhan was tight, and anticipating what would come next made his vision go blurry.

But not yet.

He still wanted to take her a bit closer to the edge.

As he did, she tried to undo his shirt. She struggled with the third button, so he pulled the tiresome thing right off, and it landed on the kitchen floor next to her bra. The caress of those lips on his naked torso awoke every last nerve ending in his body. Siobhan ran her hands down his back and he shuddered. When she grabbed his buttocks, he smiled in satisfaction.

"You were dying to touch my ass, huh?"

"It's your fault for having such a perfectly pert one. God, it drives me crazy."

"All right, then, let's see if that's the only thing that drives you crazy," he said. And then he took her hand and placed it over his huge erection.

Siobhan started to fumble with his fly. Marcel threw his head back and gasped with pleasure when he felt those delicate fingers sliding into his underwear and closing around his hard shaft.

"Fuck," he murmured.

A few seconds later he had to ask her to stop.

"Don't you like it?" she asked, sounding confused.

He took her gently by the chin and smiled, gazing at her.

"It really gets me going. That's why you need to stop. Or it will all be over."

He kissed her again passionately, and then, without warning, he knelt between her legs. He slid his lips from her knees up her inner thighs, their entire surface warm and damp. He pulled her dress down; the garment slid down her legs to the floor. He was about to take her panties off, but then she said:

"Wait. Rip them off."

He raised his head and looked at her, half-surprised, half-amused.

"You want me to rip off your panties?"

"Don't worry, they're from the Gap, they're not expensive. It's . . . In a novel by Christina Lauren, the guy ripped the girl's panties off every time they did it, and . . . well, I thought it was hot."

Marcel burst out laughing.

"You're something else. All right. Move your legs further apart. Here I go." He grabbed the fabric at the edges and tried to rip it. No luck. "Damn it. They might be cheap, but they're strong. What the hell are they made of? Valyrian steel?" Her tinkling laugh caressed his ears. He tried again. Nothing. "Shit. I didn't know ripping off panties was so difficult. But, you know what? If a fictional character can do it, I can too. Mind you, that bastard had practice," he muttered to himself. He tried again, this time with more force; the veins tensed from his neck to his forearms.

The fabric finally gave way.

"You were right. Really fucking hot," he whispered, his flashing eyes taking in the thin strip of light fuzz that covered her pubis. "I'll keep this, for my efforts." He slipped the shred of fabric into the back pocket of his pants. "And now . . . I think my hard work deserves a reward," he announced, grabbing her by the hips and burying his face between her thighs.

"What are you . . . ? Marcel . . . Oh my god . . ."

She tasted incredible, out of this world. His tongue licked, entered and withdrew, traced circles around the exact center of pleasure; he drank in her sweet scent through his nose. He lifted his gaze and saw her trying to maintain eye contact with him as she leaned back on the kitchen island, her toes tensing on his shoulders.

"Marcel, please," she begged.

He pulled his face away slightly.

"Have a bit of patience, girl," he said, and started to blow gently on her glistening wetness.

"I have no patience. I don't want to wait. I can't—"

She raised her hand to her mouth and let herself fall back, arching her spine. She climaxed quickly. As she convulsed, moaning, he watched her again over her pubic mound; head to one side, eyes rolling in pleasure, lips shining.

She had just orgasmed, and she was beautiful.

His entire life seemed to converge into that moment.

He was dying to be inside her, but he wasn't going to do it on the kitchen island. He stood up and took her nimbly in his arms. Siobhan gave an adorable little cry that made him laugh. He carried her up the stairs without difficulty.

"You're not complaining about my weight today?" she asked slyly, caressing the swollen veins of his biceps.

"A man's physical strength is multiplied by three when he's horny. Didn't you know?"

"Really?"

"Not really, no," he admitted, laughing.

"Idiot."

"But this idiot ripped off your panties, girl."

"Yes, on the third attempt."

"Better late than never."

They entered the bedroom laughing, and Marcel placed her down gently on the bed. He knelt at her feet and ran his gaze over her naked body.

"You're so beautiful," he whispered, bewitched.

He caressed her lips with his thumb, and then devoted himself to running his mouth over all the possible pleasure zones—neck, throat, breasts, stomach, hips—on his torturous descent, heading down there without quite getting there. She separated her legs a bit more, perhaps an involuntary gesture, and begged him with a moan:

"Marcel, please, I need you closer."

He didn't make her wait. He lowered his pants and underwear clumsily and fell on top of her. Siobhan grabbed his penis at the base and rubbed it against her moist slit. A hoarse cry of pleasure broke out from deep inside; this was high voltage.

"Shit, Siobhan . . . I can't . . . I'm going to get a condom right now and fuck you till the sun comes up."

He stretched out his arm to the nightstand, opened the drawer, and took out a box. He was so eager it slipped from his fingers and fell on the floor.

"Shit!" he exclaimed.

He got up to collect it, and while he was urgently slipping on a condom, he heard Siobhan laughing behind him.

He turned to glance at her over his shoulder.

"What's so funny, princess?" he asked with mock outrage.

"It's just . . . I find it very funny to see you so flustered and with that"—she pursed her lips and gestured between his legs—"huge cock."

She could barely contain her laughter.

Marcel tutted.

"So that's where we are, is it? Okay, let's see if you're still laughing when I put this *huge cock* right inside you, baby."

And having said that, he lay on top of her again and entered her. The laughter became a sigh and finally a moan that kept pace with the creaking of the bed beneath their bodies. He was gentle with her; even so, he could tell she was holding her breath as she sank her fingers into his biceps. He looked at her, her coppery hair strewn messily across the pillow.

He had dreamed of this moment so many times that he could barely believe it was really happening.

But it was happening.

He was inside her.

And he didn't ever want to leave.

Lust overflowed inside him, saturating his brain. She clamped her legs around his hips, and he took her by the calves to get deeper inside. A world of pleasure condensed in Siobhan's face as she tilted her pelvis, grabbing his buttocks. He pumped away without stopping.

"Is this . . . still . . . funny?" he whispered, his voice faltering against her neck. She moaned and shook her head. "What about . . . this?" He pushed further in. She cried out, and he felt he had only a few minutes of life left in him when he felt her walls enclosing around his cock as though trying to keep it there forever. He wanted more, he wanted everything it was possible to have, he wanted to disappear inside her and never come back. He rested a hand between her beautiful head and the headboard and thrust harder; the bed struck the wall again and again. "Or . . . this?"

"Marcel . . . Mar . . . cel . . ."

Through the fog of lust, he heard her utter his name falteringly and knew that she was coming for the second time that night. The certainty of her pleasure made him lose what little control he had left. Marcel exploded right away. His body no longer belonged to him, and his mind splintered into a thousand pieces as they both reached climax together. It was intense, urgent, and so devastating that all he could do was bury his face in her neck and let her scent cradle him in that sweet shuddering. When he had calmed down, he kissed her collarbone. They were both breathing erratically and hoarsely in the silence of the room, trembling with the release. Suddenly, it all made sense. From the moment he met her, he had known she would shatter his armor. He lifted his head to look at her, brushing a damp lock of hair from her forehead, and started to laugh. She did the same.

Stretched out in bed, facing one another, hands interlaced on the pillow. Marcel looked at her in a way that he had never looked at a woman before. Siobhan was smiling. She was beautiful after sex; her eyes glowed, her mouth glowed, her skin glowed.

"Stay the weekend," he said suddenly.

"Are you worried we're running behind?"

"I don't mean for writing. I mean to be together. Alone. You and me."

"The whole weekend?"

"All of it."

"I don't have a change of clothes."

"You don't need clothes for what I have in mind," he whispered and then raised her hand to his lips and kissed her fingertips one by one.

"And what do you have in mind?"

"A wild, relentless sex marathon? No, god! What do you take me for?" He feigned indignation, which made Siobhan laugh. How was it possible that seeing her happy warmed his heart like this? He had definitely lost his head. "Actually, I was thinking of cooking and watching movies. I don't know the protocol in these cases, especially in the trial period, but I imagine that's the kind of thing that"—he swallowed—"couples do." He paused and frowned. "Actually, if you have the same terrible taste in movies that you do in books . . ."

He didn't see it coming when Siobhan launched a pillow at him. And she didn't see it coming when he pounced on her in a swift movement and immobilized her with the weight of his body.

"We'll rule out movies."

"Then we'll have to cook."

"I don't object to my girl cooking something for me."

Siobhan snorted.

"Pardon? That sounds terribly sexist."

"You didn't let me finish. I was going to say I don't object to my girl cooking for me while I cook something for her. A Southern specialty, the kind of thing I know you like. Deal?"

"Depends what you mean by cooking. Does opening cans and emptying them onto a plate count?"

Marcel laughed.

"Well, to be honest, I'm not exactly a virtuoso at the stove myself. So, let's rule out movies and cooking, that just leaves . . ."

"The wild, relentless sex marathon."

"I'm afraid we'll have to make do with that," he agreed, gently biting her neck.

Then Siobhan gently pushed him away and scrutinized him with a confused look in her eye.

"You said, 'My girl.'"

A mischievous smile appeared on Marcel's lips.

"Did I?"

"Yes."

"I don't remember."

"Well, you said it. Twice. And you said we were in a trial period. Like a couple."

"My subconscious betrayed me."

Something glinted in Siobhan's eyes.

A glint of triumph.

"Ha. But the subconscious doesn't betray; it just gets rid of our inhibitions to allow us to express our innermost thoughts. Doesn't that phrase ring a bell, Mr. Black?" Marcel returned her gaze, disconcerted. She gave him a slight smile and narrowed her eyes scornfully. "That's what you said to me when we met, and I blurted out that you were sexy."

Marcel shook his head.

"What an arrogant bastard."

"Number one in the category of most arrogant bastard on the planet. I didn't like you at all, and the very idea of having to spend the summer writing a novel with you made me ill."

"I didn't like you much either, Miss Harris. You struck me as an unbearable goody-goody. Just look at us now," he added, interlacing his fingers with hers.

"Why haven't we done this before, Marcel?"

"Because this plot twist wasn't in the plan, honey."

And then, they tangled into each other once again. And this time, their passion wasn't like a forest burning out of control, but a steady and inextinguishable flame.

Because this time the fire was raging in their hearts.

PART THREE

RESOLUTION

Chapter 31

Siobhan

Marcel wasn't in bed when she woke the next morning. She stretched out her arm and ran it over the wrinkled sheets, which still held the warmth of his body. In the light of day, the previous night seemed like a fever dream. But her aching thighs, the lingering feel of his stubble grazing her neck, and his smell on the pillow reassured her that it was all real. She rolled over on the mattress feeling stupidly happy and buried her face in the traces of his scent. It had been amazing. All of it. What Marcel had done in the kitchen, what they had done twice in a row in bed, and what she had done to him later, with a determination she hadn't known she had in her. "You're no princess, you're a fucking goddess," he had whispered, surrendering to the pleasure of her mouth, as he stroked her hair. When she remembered his confession, she shivered. *Do you think I fake this stupid feeling of fullness I get just from being by your side?* How strange that a man who claimed not to believe in love was able to define it so well. The fact that he had suggested spending the weekend together was irrefutable proof that he felt the same way she did. And she couldn't have been more delighted. Good thing she had trusted her instincts. Going out to dinner with Buckley would have been an unforgiveable mistake.

She heard a noise downstairs and decided to get up. She missed Marcel, even though they had spent all night in each other's arms; so incomprehensible, unclassifiable, and unpredictable is love. She was naked. When she realized that her dress was still lying where she had abandoned it on the kitchen floor, she gave a naughty giggle. And what had become of her panties? Or rather, what was left of them. Had he kept them as a trophy? The idea seemed sordid and exciting in equal measure. Since her backpack was downstairs, she took the liberty of going into Marcel's walk-in closet and looking for something to wear. She selected one of the few white shirts he had. It came down to her knees, but she felt comfortable in it. Before going downstairs, she went into the bathroom to pee, wash her face, and straighten her hair. A penetrating aroma of freshly made coffee wafted toward her as she walked down the stairs. Marcel was in the kitchen, his back to her, with his arms outstretched and palms on the counter; he seemed to be waiting for something. Or someone. Siobhan entered stealthily, circled that island of lust and sin, and embraced him from behind, interlacing her fingers over his firm abdomen. He smelled of soap.

"Good morning, Mr. Black. You're always such an early riser. For a moment I thought you'd gone out running. As if we didn't get enough exercise last night," she joked, with a broad smile. "So, you've made coffee for your girl, huh? Admit it: you were going to bring it up to me in bed."

Marcel tensed.

He didn't take her hands as she expected.

He didn't mention that she was wearing his shirt.

He didn't turn to kiss her.

Something wasn't right. She took a couple of steps back and asked:

"Marcel, what is it?"

He sighed, let his head drop forward, scratched the back of his neck wearily, and finally turned around. He broke her to pieces before he even started to speak, just with the forlorn way he looked at her. She saw shadows under his eyes and tension lines marking the rigid set of his mouth.

She saw regret.

And suddenly everything became clear.

"I'm sorry, Siobhan. I can't do this. You and me . . . I can't do it, I really can't."

Her heart sank. And that wasn't a metaphor. She really felt as though it had sunk into a very deep, black hole.

"I don't understand. What's changed since last night? What on earth could possibly have made you change your mind, when last night you seemed hellbent on being with me?"

"It's not you, Siobhan. It's me."

She gave a bitter laugh.

"You could at least have come up with less of a cheap cliché. You're making me feel like a loose end you've finally been able to tie up," she replied stonily.

Two parallel furrows appeared between Marcel's eyebrows. He shook his head.

"That's not fair. Everything I said last night is true, I swear."

"But?"

"You deserve someone who's able to give you what you need."

It felt like someone had thrown her off a cliff.

"What I need is for you to stop pushing me away," she said.

Marcel ran a hand over his face, disconsolate.

"I'm going to screw it up. I know I'm going to screw it up. You want something out of a romance novel, and I—"

"I don't want anything out of a romance novel!" she cried. "I want real love! Real and mature love. And I don't care how complicated it is. Relationships can be solid and precious even if they're not perfect. Do you think I'm a china doll?"

"Of course not! You're an incredible woman. But I know what would happen if we had a relationship. It would be like driving over bumpy ground, and you'd break in the first pothole, because of me, because I'm defective."

"And that's why you've decided to slam on the brakes. Thanks for sparing me the trauma."

"I'm not what you're looking for, Siobhan. I never have been. And I couldn't bear to hurt you." He paused to swallow. "Not you."

"You couldn't hurt me as much as you are right now, Marcel."

Her voice trembled, muffled by the tears that threatened to break her pride as well.

"I'm really sorry to hear that," he muttered, head lowered.

Perhaps she had been too hard on him. The problem was that she had gone to bed as the girl who believed in happy endings and woken up with her illusions torn to shreds.

"Why risk loving or being loved? It's better to break up before we even begin," she said, trying to keep her tears at bay.

"You don't understand, Siobhan. I don't believe in love. I don't believe in saying 'I love you.' The most important lesson I've learned in my life is not to trust those three empty words."

He had summed up the situation with the surgical coldness of a heart hardened by the cruelty of the world. It could only mean one thing: Marcel believed that she would leave him too.

It was understandable.

But no less hurtful.

"You're scared," said Siobhan.

"And can you blame me, knowing what you know about my life?" he said, sounding pained.

"No! I blame you for not being braver. I blame you for not trying. I blame you for not at least giving us a chance. And I blame you for fighting against what you really want."

"What's the point in being brave? Brave people are the first to go into battle, and that's why they're the first to fall."

"So, this is the end?"

He remained quiet, jaw clenched. Siobhan watched him and knew there was nothing she could say to change his mind. Marcel had given up. The man who had carried her to bed in his arms the night before and the man standing before her now were not the same person. They were two different people whose paths had crossed, heading in opposite directions.

"You aren't going to say anything, are you?"

Marcel didn't move or make a sound.

"Okay, I get it."

Her dress and bra were neatly folded on one of the kitchen stools; it struck her as the saddest sight in the world. She grabbed them and left the kitchen. She retrieved her backpack from the living room and headed into Marcel's study. She was emptying her side of the desk when he entered. He caught her by the wrist. Siobhan raised her eyes slowly and fixed her teary gaze on him.

"Why are you taking your things?"

"Because I think it's better if we finish the novel separately. There isn't much left. We can wrap up the last few chapters on our own, and then I'll have disappeared from your life, just like you wanted."

Her voice broke. And he, who seemed to be wavering between moving closer and keeping his distance, eventually released her.

"You think I like the way things have turned out, Siobhan?"

"I don't know," she said with a sigh. "And frankly, I don't want to know. I just want"—she rubbed her temples—"to go home. So please, don't make things any harder."

Marcel nodded silently.

"If you don't mind, I'll go up to your room to get dressed."

"Sure. Take all the time you need."

It didn't take her long to erase all traces of her presence in the apartment. She was struck by a feeling of unreality; she had both found and lost everything within the space of a couple of hours. It was one thing to break someone's heart and quite another to shatter their pride. If she had to lose him, better for it to be quick, like ripping off a Band-Aid.

When she was ready, she trudged back downstairs. Marcel was waiting for her, leaning against the door, with a crestfallen air about him. She looked him in the eye; there was anguish in his gaze, confusion, and a mountain of words left unsaid. Better not to ask. Better not to put his weak will to the test. He drew her toward him and wrapped his arms around her in an embrace so long, so intense, and so true that she lost herself in it. She wanted his protection to last an eternity and for it to swallow up the pain.

She was too in love to leave.

And she was too in love to stay.

She summoned every last ounce of strength to separate herself from him and, in a reedy voice, said:

"Goodbye, Marcel. I don't know what will make you happy, but whatever it is, I hope you find it."

Marcel blinked as though he was only just realizing that everything—whatever it was they had had—was over between them. Siobhan turned the door handle with a single thought in her head: she wouldn't cry. She. Would. Not. Cry. She took a deep breath and left. Later, she regretted not slamming the door. The tears flooded her eyes before she reached the elevator.

The wound was deep.

Bloody.

Real.

Chapter 32

Marcel

"Can you explain this, please?" Alex demanded from the other end of the phone line.

"You know what it means," answered Marcel. The glare of his computer screen reflected in his glasses. "Surely you don't have trouble with reading comprehension. If so, might I suggest a change of profession?"

"Ha, ha, ha. And I thought you'd chilled out a bit in Louisiana. I see you're still just as much of an asshole."

"An ill weed grows apace, as they say."

Alex sighed heavily.

"Okay. Look, it's too early in the morning to keep up with you. All I want to know is why you emailed Bob Gunton, copying me in, asking him to reverse the percentage of royalties for *Two Ways*. Do you really want Siobhan to take 10 percent and leave you with 2 percent, or did you undergo some kind of voodoo ritual in New Orleans?"

"No voodoo. I would simply rather she keep the bigger slice of the cake, that's all."

"Yes, but *why*? And why now? As I recall, when you signed the contract, you were very specific. 'It's my reputation on the line, so I demand the higher percentage of royalties.' Those were your literal words. I'm not making it up."

Marcel's gaze wandered to the other side of the desk, unbearably empty for the last three days, three interminable days and nights, and he was besieged by a feeling of sadness.

"I changed my mind."

"You changed your mind," repeated Alex, dubious. "Very well. All right."

"Hey, if it's your earnings you're worried about . . ."

"What the hell do you take me for? A Wall Street broker? You're talking to me, Alex, your friend. The only one you have, if I'm not mistaken. And if you suggest something like that again, I'll revoke all your friendship rights. I don't give a damn how much I earn with this book. I just want to be sure you know what you're doing."

"I know what I'm doing."

"Fine. In that case, I'll tell Legal to draw up a new contract for you and Siobhan to sign."

"No," replied Marcel, unequivocally.

"No?"

"Leave Siobhan out of this. She can't know. If she finds out, she won't accept; I know her too well. She tends to confuse pride and obstinacy with empowerment."

"So how are we going to do it, then? Forge her signature?"

"How the hell should I know!" he shouted. "Why don't you do your goddamn job and think of something?"

An irritated sigh filled the telephone line.

"What on earth is going on with you? Why are you treating me like your frickin' assistant? Am I to blame for whatever's bothering you?"

Marcel squeezed his eyes shut. He took a deep breath and then released it very slowly.

"I'm sorry. I went too far."

"Are you going to tell me what this is all about? What's really going on, Marcel?"

What was going on was that he was struggling to concentrate.

The walls were closing in on him without her there.

He missed her so much it took his breath away.

He was listening to that lousy song they had danced to together at the Blue Nile on repeat because those days in New Orleans had been the happiest of his life.

He couldn't stop wondering whether he had done the right thing in letting her go.

He hated that the answer to that question might be yes.

Because he didn't want to hurt her.

But he couldn't bear to lose her.

"I've screwed up big-time. That's what's going on," he finally admitted.

"With Siobhan?"

"Yes."

"Okay, what have you done this time?" he asked, in the tone of a parent who has run out of patience with their kid's hijinks. "Have you been criticizing her writing again? I hope the novel isn't at risk because of your bullshit," he warned. "I mean it."

"There's no problem with the novel, so breathe easy. And you'll be happy to hear that I have no reason to criticize her writing style. Siobhan has evolved a lot as a writer. Sooner or later, she'll find her own voice, I'm sure of that. She's good. And she has that fire that makes this vocation worth the effort."

"So, what happened?"

Silence.

A very eloquent silence.

"You're shitting me. You slept with her?"

Another silence.

"You slept with her!" exclaimed Alex. "I knew it! You slept with her, and then you got scared, and now you feel like a bastard, and you're looking for any way to assuage your terrible guilt."

"I don't know if you're aware how incredibly twisted your theory sounds."

"Like hell. I noticed you felt something for her on your birthday. And when you took her to New Orleans, it only confirmed my suspicions."

"That was no big deal, Sherlock. You came with me once too."

"The difference being that I had to stay in the Dauphine."

"Different circumstances, man. My father was still at home back then. And why are you talking as though we were away on vacation? We were writing, you know."

"Oh yeah, sure." Marcel heard his agent snigger. "I bet you were nonstop while you were there."

Marcel hesitated before saying:

"The truth is it was a very . . ." He blinked several times as he searched for the right word. "Intense trip. For both of us. And not for the reason you're thinking. Nothing happened while we were there."

"It doesn't matter where, but what. You slept with her, and then you got scared, and now you feel like the bastard you are. Admit it. It's the first step to redemption, my friend."

"I didn't get scared, all right? But she wants something I can't give her. End of story," he said definitively and placed his hand on his chest as though suffering the pain of his own words. "And for your information, I didn't decide to reverse the royalties because I feel guilty. It's just that . . . Siobhan is the soul of this novel. She deserves all the recognition. She deserves to . . . shine."

"Man, sounds like you're hopelessly in love with this girl."

Marcel noticed a sudden scratch in his throat.

No, that wasn't it.

Not at all.

He couldn't fall in love.

"Alex."

"What?"

"Take care of the contract, will you?" he said.

And he hung up.

Chapter 33

Siobhan

The first day, she didn't even feel like leaving the sofa. She cried an ocean of tears, wolfed down the bag of Reese's that she kept on hand for extreme crises, and binge-watched the first season of *This Is Us*, which turned out to be a terrible idea as it only worsened her dark mood. Between episodes, she checked her phone, but the sign she was waiting for never came. At night, she tried to silence her demons by writing. They say that melancholy is a writer's best friend and that inspiration flows easily from states of deficiency. All she achieved, however, was to end up curled on the sofa with a glass of cheap wine that reflected the unbearable glow of her computer screen. She knew perfectly well what she had to write, but she didn't know how. All the words sounded hollow, and the details rang untrue. Nor did she get much rest, her sleep eroded by the same undefined anxiety that oppressed her during waking hours.

Her mind moved in zigzags. Marcel. New Orleans. The kiss in the kitchen. The sheets tangled around their naked bodies. The echoes of pleasure. The plans. The day after. The goodbye. Their *Two Ways.*

On the second day, she made a titanic effort to get on top of things. She peered through her tiny kitchen window and noticed hints of fall looming. She thought about calling Paige and Lena but wasn't ready to talk about her feelings. Besides, talking about it wouldn't change anything. And the prospect of hearing phrases like *All cis-hetero men are the same: it's all promises, promises until they get it, and once they've got it, they're gone* (that would be Lena), *You can't trust a man who sleeps in the same bed as you and doesn't lay a finger on you. For god's sake, it's unnatural* (that would be Paige), or *You have to forget about him and broaden your horizons* (that could be either of them) just seemed too discouraging right now. She didn't want to forget him. What had happened between them, although brief, had been intense, strong, and unforgettable. Marcel had helped her get to know herself better. With his help, she had learned to write looking outward, toward the world and other people's stories. Yes, she was thirty years old, and her heart was in tatters. She was sad and furious because she loved a broken man who didn't want to mend himself. But life and literature had to continue.

Of course, her dream—that meteoric literary career that had launched as if by chance—would only come true if she continued writing the novel.

Or the part she was writing, at any rate.

On the third day, she showered, forbade herself from having ice cream for breakfast, grabbed her laptop, and left her apartment with its worryingly noisy air-conditioning unit and stench of desperation. After such a crushing blow, it was hard to imagine ever feeling better. But little by little, so slowly she hardly noticed it happening, she reconnected with her purpose. Siobhan found it again in Café Grumpy on Twentieth Street, on the quiet and pleasant patio. She returned on the fourth day and again on the fifth and the sixth. Because, eventually, her rage dissolved and transformed into the courage she needed to put herself in the shoes of Felicity Bloom. Not the sadness—that was still there—but she took refuge in her writing.

On the seventh day, her phone started to vibrate on the café table while she was working. When she saw Marcel's name on the screen, she stifled a cry with her hand. One week. It had been exactly one week since they had said goodbye. Writing without him was complicated, lonely, and less stimulating. But it was also true that a small part of her had started to become accustomed to his absence. What if answering the phone set her back to the emotional precarity of the first day? Her equilibrium was hanging by a very fragile thread because, after all, she was human and in love. What did he want? Why was he calling her? She looked at the phone, debating whether to ignore the call. But then, she wasn't made of steel, particularly not when it came to Marcel.

She summoned all her courage.

"Hi."

"Hi, Siobhan." Hearing his voice was like someone beating her and tending to her bruises at the same time. "I was going to leave you a message. I didn't think you would answer."

"Me neither."

"I understand. How are you?"

"I've been better." It just slipped out. Perhaps she should have made an effort to sound less pathetic, to give the impression she had barely thought about him over the last few days. She swallowed and added: "And you?"

"I don't even know what day it is."

There seemed to be an insurmountable distance between them, and neither one could reach the other.

"Why are you calling?"

"Something's happened, Siobhan, something big, and I'm . . . I don't know . . . in shock. I need to talk. Do you think we could see each other?" he asked. "I'll go to Brooklyn or wherever."

"I'm in Manhattan right now. I can meet you at your apartment if you like."

"Yes. Yes, please. That would be . . . I just . . . I know I don't deserve it, but I need you. Just come, please," he said, tripping over his words.

"I'll be right there," she said, reaching out to close her laptop. She heard his anguished sigh at the other end of the line, and she shuddered. "Can you at least tell me what happened?"

"It's my mother, Siobhan. She's back. And she's here, in New York."

Marcel had dark bags under his eyes, his stubble was getting unruly, and his expression said he was carrying the weight of the world on his shoulders.

"Thanks for coming," he said in a tense voice as he opened the door. "It means a lot to me."

Siobhan nodded timidly. Merely being in his presence again divested her of all the layers of protection she had made for herself over the last few days. She plunged her hands into her jeans pockets and followed him into the living room, feeling like she was coming apart at the seams. But she was there because he needed her, so she took a couple of deep breaths to calm herself. She didn't understand why Marcel crouched on the floor at the foot of the sofa, nor did she ask. She sat down, pulled her knees up, and hugged them to her.

An intense quiet stretched out between them. A couple of interminable seconds passed before Siobhan dared to turn to meet the fragile depths of his gaze. Marcel sighed and ran his hand over his face. The rough sound of his stubble gave her goose bumps.

"What I told you on the phone is true. Claudette is in New York. And she wants us to meet."

"But wh—? How did she find you? Wait. Don't tell me she saw that photo of us on the internet and recognized you."

Marcel laughed bitterly. His expression hardened.

"I wish. But no. It's because she's been in touch with my sister ever since Katrina."

"What?" Siobhan's eyes widened in perplexity. "You mean your mother . . . ?"

"Has known all along who Marcel Black is."

"I don't get it," she said, rubbing her temples in an effort to assimilate the information.

"And I don't get why Chaz betrayed me like this. She even gave her my number! Can you believe it?"

"Have you spoken to her?" she asked, hesitantly.

"Not yet. I'm too pissed. Pissed, shocked, hurt . . . I don't even know how I feel. I wasn't expecting this from my own sister. After all we've been through! It feels like I've been living a lie for the last twelve years."

"I meant, have you spoken to your mother."

"Oh, yes. Two hours ago. I don't usually answer calls from unknown numbers, and I wish I hadn't. As soon as I heard her, I just shattered, Siobhan. She said, 'Marcel, it's me. Mama.'" His voice broke. And it can't have been the only thing breaking inside him, judging by his expression and his body language. "How can she call herself that when she abandoned us the way she did? God, it's ridiculous."

Siobhan put a hand on his knee, hoping the physical contact would somehow console him.

"Did she say why she wants to see you?"

"I hung up before she had the chance. And I hope she never calls again. I just don't have it in me to see her." He gesticulated vehemently. "Why did she have to appear right now? What the hell does that woman want from me? To be a mother to a thirty-six-year-old man? It's too late for that. I can look after myself."

A shadow of doubt loomed over her. Whatever the reasons that had impelled Claudette to do what she did, Marcel needed to know what they were. He needed to hear the truth from his mother's lips, not the version twisted by resentment that he had formed in his mind.

"If I've learned anything in the time I've been writing with you, it's that a story unresolved in the past always turns up again in the present," said Siobhan delicately. "It's like . . ." She wiggled her fingers in search of the right phrase and snapped them when she found it. "Like Chekhov's gun. Well, something like that." He gave a weak smile. "What I mean to say is that maybe, just maybe," she clarified, "you should consider the possibility of seeing her."

Marcel looked at her as though she had plunged a dagger into his back. A tense fury spread across his face, from his forehead to the dimple on his chin. He shook his head.

"No. There's just no way. I'm not doing it. That woman destroyed my life. Mine and my sister's, even though she seems to have forgotten that. Which I suppose is only to be expected of her."

Although his tone was firm, Siobhan noticed a touch of confusion in his eyes, so she decided to go all in.

"Aren't you tired of hiding, Marcel?" She squeezed his knee. "Go and see her."

"And say what?" he muttered, unable to contain the pain dominating his voice.

"Maybe you don't have to say anything. Maybe it will be enough to listen to what she has to tell you. Whatever it is, I know you can face it. If Charmaine could, you can too."

"No, no I can't!" he shouted. "She'll destroy me again! I know she will! She abandoned me, Siobhan! My own mother abandoned me!"

The deep cry that rose from his guts startled her. But there was worse to come, when Marcel started beating his head with his palms as though his brain was about to explode. That really frightened her. Shaken, she rushed to him and tried to contain him with all her strength, begging him to stop. His eyes, black as onyx, flooded, and his tears fell without restraint, gut-wrenching sobs contorting his face. All the things he had taken such pains to bury so long ago rose to the surface. His outburst eventually ran its course. Exhausted, he buried his face in her chest, holding on to her as though he was on the edge of a precipice. Siobhan said nothing. She simply let him cry as she stroked his back gently. After a while, a contained calm, punctuated by erratic sighs and the odd hiccup, replaced the crying.

"I'm sorry," he whispered.

"You don't have to apologize for crying, Marcel. It doesn't make you weak; it just makes you human."

Marcel raised his head, and they looked at each other. Then he kissed her. It was a passionate, urgent, and heartrending kiss. A free fall.

Agitated, she placed her palm against his chest and gently pushed him away.

"We can't, Marcel. Neither of us needs this right now. It will only complicate things."

Although he seemed disconcerted, he nodded.

"You're right. Sorry. I'm really sorry, honestly," he said, moving away from her and leaning back against the sofa. "I don't know what came over me. I suppose it was just a moment of weakness. Another one."

That *just* pierced Siobhan's heart like an arrow.

That *just* made it clear that there was nothing complicated between them.

She sighed and rummaged in her purse. She found a pack of tissues, pulled one out, and handed it to Marcel.

"Do you feel a bit better?"

"Yes, thanks." He blew his nose and stuck the tissue in his pocket. "Why are you so good to me, Siobhan? You should hate me, and instead you're here, putting up with my pathetic crying."

"It isn't pathetic to cry. And I could never hate you. I'll be here whenever you need me."

The look Marcel gave her contained so many emotions that Siobhan couldn't identify them all.

"I lied before. I said I was sorry for kissing you, but the truth is I'm not sorry at all. I would do it again. I would kiss you again right now without thinking twice, if I wasn't sure it would hurt you. I . . . I'm a mess. I don't know how to stay here. And I don't know how to leave," he confessed.

Siobhan felt her eyes narrow. Her throat. Her veins. Her heart.

"I'm not a musical instrument you can play to console yourself whenever you're feeling down. I'm a woman. And I have feelings for you, Marcel. Very intense feelings that I can't express in words because

I can't bear you rejecting me again. You're confused, and I get that, but please, don't keep confusing me."

Marcel tensed his jaw.

"You deserve someone better than me. And I'm sure you'll find him eventually."

I don't want anyone better than you. I love you, with all your cracks, your fears, your tears. I want each and every one of your imperfections. I want to be by your side to catch you when you fall. Is that so difficult for you to understand? she thought.

Why bother saying all that when she already knew the answer?

"I think I should go."

"Wait. Can I ask you one last favor?" She nodded. "I'd like you to write the end of *Two Ways*. I know you'll give our story the ending it deserves."

"And what about *your* story? How does it end?"

"I . . . I don't know," he muttered. "Maybe mine will have an open ending."

Chapter 34

Marcel

The human mind works in unpredictable ways. When he glanced through the windows of Minetta Tavern and saw the Black woman sitting at a table, a whole series of images he thought were long forgotten paraded before his eyes. It wasn't so much the sight of her that made him anxious but the memories flowing uncontrollably inside him. The scent of marigold and talcum powder, the taste of rice and beans, and the lyrics to "A Peanut Sat on a Railroad Track," a song that took him back to his childhood, stuck in his head.

He considered turning around and walking away. He was angry, terrified, and agitated. His pulse was racing, his palms were sweaty, and his mouth felt gritty. The everyday sounds on MacDougal reverberated in his ears like a distant echo. Fresh doubts and fears assailed him. He shook his head, trying to get his thoughts in order. It had taken a lot for him to come this far; three days overcome by Shakespearean indecision. To give in or not to give in; that was the question. But Siobhan was right. A story unresolved in the past always shows up again in the future.

And this was his story, waiting for him in a restaurant in the Village to have dinner.

He took a deep breath and opened the restaurant door. The aroma of roast meat and béarnaise sauce would have whetted his appetite any other day, but that evening it provoked a profound nausea. He walked with determination through the low light, trying to step only on the white tiles on the checkerboard floor; he wasn't sure why. He went past the long bar and the red leather booths until he reached the table occupied by the woman who must be his mother. He barely recognized her. The person watching him, her face contorted by emotion, seemed a complete stranger. Wearing a ridiculous straw hat, she had more gray hairs and wrinkles than he had expected. It was in her profoundly dark eyes that he finally found the essence of Claudette Dupont.

"Hello, Marcel."

Hearing his name in his mother's mouth sent a shudder down his spine and almost rendered him senseless.

"Mrs. Dupont," he replied, in the long silence that followed.

"I'd rather you called me Mom."

"I'm afraid you lost that privilege a long time ago."

"Well, then, call me by my first name, if you don't mind." She gestured at the empty chair. "Sit, please."

Marcel sat opposite her with a rigid, haughty posture. He folded his arms over his chest and slid one leg under the table. He averted his gaze, looking anywhere except at the person before him.

"I'm glad you came. You're very—"

"Different from when I was eight?" he broke in. He couldn't disguise the sarcasm in his tone.

"I was going to say handsome. Although you always were, from the day you were born. You were a beautiful baby."

He narrowed his eyes and sighed.

"Spare me the cheap sentimentalism, will you?"

Claudette nodded with a sigh.

"I took the liberty of ordering iced tea while I waited." There were two highball glasses with ice and lemon on the table. His mother held one out to him, keeping the cardboard coaster underneath. "You loved it when you were little."

"I don't want tea," replied Marcel. "And I'm not staying long, so say what you have to say, and then I'll be on my way. I'm a busy man. Of course, thanks to my treacherous sister, you already know that."

"Please don't be mad at Charmaine," she said, adopting a maternal air. "I just want the best for the family."

"Sorry, what family are you referring to? The one you abandoned twenty-eight years ago?"

"Son . . ." Claudette stretched her hand over the table and tried to reach Marcel's, but he jerked away.

Then he did look at her.

"Don't touch me."

A silence laden with shards of glass fell between them.

"I know you feel resentful toward me, and you have every right to. All I ask is that you hear me out, Marcel. I owe you an explanation."

"Why now?"

"Because this is when you need it most."

"Who? Me or you?"

Claudette removed the ridiculous straw hat and set it aside.

"Your father made me very unhappy. And I'm sure you know I'm not lying about that," she said, dabbing the sweat on her forehead with the corner of a napkin. "I only married him because I was pregnant with Charmaine, and my parents—your grandparents—had cut me off. That was my first mistake. The second was believing I could settle for the life that awaited me with him." She paused to take a sip of iced tea. "I always wanted to be an actress; that was my dream."

"I had no idea," said Marcel, giving her a surprised look.

"There are lots of things you don't know about me. Anyway." She flapped her hand. "When you're a Black woman in the poorest neighborhood in New Orleans, opportunities to fulfill your dreams don't come along very often," she said. A spontaneous sound of agreement left Marcel's lips before he was aware of it. "Bernard didn't support me either. To him, actresses were little more than whores, tarts who wiggled their asses for the camera to provoke men. He wanted me to stay at home waiting for him to return from the carpenter's shop, with clean clothes, dinner on the table, and legs open. And I did that. And eventually I forgot about my dream."

Marcel squirmed in his seat. He identified with certain aspects of the story. The old man had tried to quash his dream of being a writer too. But feeling sorry for the woman who had abandoned him with nothing more than a carelessly scrawled note, like something you would scribble before running to the corner store, wasn't part of his plans, so he berated himself immediately for any sympathy he felt toward her.

"To cut a long story short, one day you got tired of playing the submissive wife, and you left."

"It isn't as simple as that, Marcel. Your father made my life a living hell when I asked for a divorce."

"And what do you think he did to us after you left, huh?" he asked.

A tear was caught on Claudette's eyelashes, and she blinked it away.

"I swear, there hasn't been a single day when I haven't regretted leaving you with that man, but I couldn't take you with me. If I had, he would have accused me of kidnapping you. Being involved in something so sordid would have been traumatic for you."

"'Traumatic'?" The word churned his stomach. "It was traumatic enough waiting for you day after day on the porch, not knowing why you had left or whether you would ever come back. It isn't fair, you know that? Parents are supposed to weather life's blows so their kids don't have to. That's the deal."

The woman's eyes filled with tears. Marcel felt an inexplicable distress seeing those drops spilling over her cheeks. Although he wanted to remain dispassionate, he couldn't.

"Here, clean yourself up," he said, handing her his own napkin. "Your mascara's running." His mother nodded gratefully. "Can I ask where you went?"

"First to Houston. Then to Los Angeles."

"The movie mecca. Did you get a role?"

"Not one. Turns out I was a terrible actress, after all that." She sniffed. "Although I worked as a maid for Marsha Hunt for fifteen years; that's as close to fame as I ever got or ever will. Now I live in Napa."

"Did you ever try to contact us?"

A furrow of anguish formed between her brows.

"Not until after the flood. I went back to New Orleans to look for you both. You might not believe me, but it's the truth. The storm had destroyed the house, of course. I looked all over, even under the rubble. No one knew a thing, no one had seen a thing. I didn't even know if you were alive. Then, one day, divine providence led me to your sister in Tremé. She told me all about you. What you did for a living, where you lived, what you called yourself, and how badly your father had treated you since I left. That man"—her lips contorted in resentment—"he's gotten what he deserves. I felt so guilty I wanted to take the first flight to New York, but Charmaine asked me not to. You didn't want to be found. Your writing career was just taking off, and my return might have thrown you off-balance. So, I resigned myself. I don't know if that was the right decision. I only know that all your sister and I wanted was to protect you. So I returned to Los Angeles and got on with my life. Since then, I've stayed in touch with her in secret."

Marcel felt his head hammering so badly he could barely think, and his vision grew blurred.

"What do you want from me?" he asked, grimacing with pain from that sudden migraine.

"I want you to stop suffering on my account."

"Please, don't," he cut her off. "You don't know anything about me."

"I know that you're one of the best writers in North America and that you've sacrificed a lot to get where you are. I know you're a generous man who has helped people who probably didn't deserve it. I know you've been furious at the world since you were a child, and you don't allow anyone to get close. And I also know that you're not happy."

Marcel let out a sarcastic laugh.

"Who the hell do you think you are to show up after all these years and spout this shit?" he replied, with such force that people turned to look at him.

"The woman who brought you into the world, Marcel. And nothing can change that, however many mistakes I've made."

"If you came to New York thinking you can play mother to me, you can get right back on the plane to Los Angeles or wherever the hell you live."

"Napa. And I'm not going back. I've decided to stay here."

"Here?" he said, incredulous. "Wouldn't you be better off going to Louisiana and living with your daughter?" he said. "She'd be delighted to have you. She's a great one for forgiving parents who have systematically fucked up their kids' lives."

"Marcel, I get where you're coming from. Just try to see it my way, please. You're my son, and I want to be near you. I'm not asking you to allow me into your everyday life—or even for you to forgive me. I'll be happy to breathe the same air as you and know that you're making good decisions." She paused. "Look, Charmaine told me everything. I know there's a special girl, the first one. Don't let her slip through your fingers just because your mother couldn't do any better. Keep going."

He lowered his gaze and fixed it on his right hand, which was drawing meaningless shapes on the palm of the left. He remained silent, wondering what would have become of their lives if his mother had never left. And for a moment, the briefest of moments, he thought he understood why Claudette was there, why now and not before.

"I think I should go," he announced after a confused silence, standing up from the table.

"Fine. You have my number. Call me whenever you want. I'll wait as long as it takes."

When he got home, his head hurt as though he had been beaten with a lead pipe. He took a couple of pills, switched off his phone, and got into bed. Before long he was fast asleep. That night he dreamed he returned to New Orleans to rescue his mother and sister from the flood after Katrina.

And then he dreamed that Siobhan was rescuing him.

Chapter 35

Siobhan

The end of September arrived, bringing with it the fiftieth anniversary of Baxter Books. The much-anticipated celebration would take place at 1 Oak, one of the most exclusive nightclubs in New York, whose regular celebrity clientele included Rihanna, Leonardo DiCaprio, Beyoncé, and Jay-Z. Rumor had it that Baxter Books had coughed up an outrageous sum to rent a room. Everyone was invited—directors and associate editors, assistants, designers, literary agents, influential Bookstagrammers, a few journalists, and, of course, the authors. They were allowed two guests each. There would be bottles of Dom Pérignon, luxury catering, and a DJ flown in all the way from Mykonos to get the party going. Paige was delirious with excitement, not just at the prospect of going to 1 Oak—it was easier to travel to the moon with Elon Musk than to get into that club—but also of meeting Alex Shapiro again, now that she was sure he wasn't gay. And Lena was thrilled at the possibility of meeting Margaret Atwood and sharing some opinions with her. As for Siobhan . . . let's say she was making an effort to appear enthusiastic about the party.

Give our story the ending it deserves.

The last few weeks had been difficult. Writing the final chapters of *Two Ways to Solve a Murder in Manhattan* had been harder than she anticipated. For one thing, she had to be sure that there were no loose ends and that the finale was up to the standards of a respected crime writer. For another, Marcel lingered in her thoughts so obstinately that she could hardly focus on Jeremiah Silloway and Felicity Bloom. How was it possible to miss someone so much? There were days when she couldn't stop checking her phone, and when there was nothing but an enduring silence from him, she had to summon all her strength not to call him. She was worried. She couldn't rid herself of the image of him sobbing, clinging to her as though for dear life. Sometimes that image mixed with other more pleasurable ones before she could stop herself. So, she decided to move back in with her parents in Mount Vernon and close herself away in what had been her teenage bedroom to finish the novel in peace. She was more aware than ever before of how lucky she was to have grown up in a home she could always return to whenever she needed it. She cried as she typed *The End*. Not only was it emotional to finish her second novel, but it was liberating and sad as well. Jeremiah and Felicity ended up together, but she had had to renounce the man she loved.

As she reluctantly got ready for the party, she thought about the last time she and Marcel had had anything resembling a conversation. It had been a few days earlier, after Siobhan had sent him the ending of the book.

Marcel
I've read it.

Siobhan
And??

Marcel
It's very good. Just as it should be. And it's not corny at all.

Siobhan
Really?

Marcel
Yes. Congratulations, princess. You're going to be a big success.

Siobhan
Don't forget we wrote this novel together, Mr. Black. We both deserve recognition. I know you don't want to be associated with romance, but don't do yourself a disservice. Will you make any changes before the proofs?

Marcel
I doubt it. But give me a couple of days to reread the whole manuscript. If I don't find any glaring errors, you can send it to Gunton yourself.

Siobhan
Great! 🙂
Hey.

Marcel
What?

Siobhan
I really liked working with you. I'll miss our chats.

Marcel
And I'll miss everything about you, Siobhan Harris.

Siobhan
Do you think we'll ever see each other again?

Marcel never replied.

A week later, Bob Gunton emailed them both, copying in Alex and Bella, to congratulate them. Nice work, this is going to be a hit, you might want to think about a sequel, yada yada yada. As a reward, he invited them to spend a weekend in the Hamptons, all expenses paid, but neither Marcel nor Siobhan showed the slightest interest. Gunton set the Baxter Books machinery in motion to make sure *Two Ways* would be ready on the scheduled launch date. As it was the big release of the fall, the marketing plan included a tour. Siobhan would be the face of the book, the only face. Thinking of what was to come made her feel dizzy. But the thing she found hardest to bear was that she couldn't share any of it with him, the other half of the project, her other half. Marcel would have no part in any of it.

She sighed, disheartened.

"You can do it, princess," she told herself, trying to summon some enthusiasm as she checked her appearance in the mirror.

She had picked out a long black strapless dress with a slit that allowed a glimpse of one slender leg. Actually, Paige had chosen it for her. She had copied the idea of pulling her hair into a tight bun from an It girl, although it hadn't been the easiest do to achieve. As soon as her Uber arrived, she slipped on her uncomfortable but glamorous stilettos, grabbed her stylish but not remotely practical clutch, and left the apartment. When the car pulled up to the club about a half hour later, her friends were waiting impatiently at the door.

"I don't know about you, but I still can't believe we're about to go into this place," said Paige. "Can someone take a blood sample and check for hallucinogenic substances, please? Are you aware that people go without eating to be able to afford a table here? Literally. What if we meet someone famous? That would be out of this world!"

"Shiv's famous," pointed out a slightly calmer Lena.

"I'm not famous."

"Yes, you are. You've even got your own hashtag! Anyway, I wasn't meaning that kind of famous. Someone more like . . . Leo DiCaprio."

Lena narrowed her eyes.

"Keep dreaming, Paige. Even if you do meet Leo, you're over twenty-five, so you won't be on his radar. Anyway, I can't believe I might meet the author of *The Handmaid's Tale*."

Siobhan gave her a sympathetic squeeze on the arm.

"Oh, Lena, I'm afraid there's only a very slim chance of Margaret Atwood appearing tonight."

Her friend sighed, resigned, and shrugged.

"Well, I hope at least the canapes are kosher."

"But Alex Shapiro's coming, right?" Paige said, studying her cuticles.

"I suppose so."

"And . . . ?"

There was no need for anyone to say his name. Siobhan shook her head dejectedly and touched her chest. Apparently, her heart had forgotten to beat.

"You know what I say, girls?" said Paige, after Lena shot her a warning look. "This isn't the moment to be sad, it's time for . . . a selfie! Look at the camera and say . . . Leo DiCaprio!"

Inside, the atmosphere oozed exclusivity. The golden lights seemed to make the beautiful people even more beautiful. The wooden ceilings, the velvet curtains, the baroque candelabra, and the polished bar that reflected the floor's zigzag pattern gave the place a cinematic glamour. The waitstaff moved about with aplomb, carrying trays of sparkling glasses that were quickly emptied. Paige devoted herself to photographing everything, while Lena speculated on other people's conversations. Siobhan, however, felt out of place, as though she didn't fit in with all those people who greeted her, whose smiles she had to mirror, even though she didn't know them.

She had just had a dull conversation with her agent about the importance of book clubs—"Do you know what made Lucinda Edmonds a success before she became Lucinda Riley? Book clubs"—when she heard someone call her name. Turning around, she saw Alex waving at her from across the room. He said something to the man he was talking to, drained his glass, and moved toward her. Siobhan excused herself from Bella Watson and went to meet him.

"I'm so happy to see you!" he said as they exchanged a warm embrace.

A sensation of well-being flooded through her right away. She loved Alex Shapiro.

"You too, Alex. It's nice to see a friendly face among all these strangers. Tell me. How are things? Busy?"

"Well, you know, same as usual. Is Paige here?" he asked, craning his neck to look over her head across the crowd.

Siobhan laughed. Yup, straight to the point.

"Of course she's here. She wouldn't have missed this for the world." She glanced around and lifted her chin toward the dance floor. "There she is, with Lena, my other best friend. And she can't wait to see you," she added, with a mischievous tone.

Alex seemed delighted to receive this information.

"Really? Wow, that's . . . great. I'll go over and say hi. But first, I want to tell you something: I loved the novel," he said, as though he had been keeping it a secret for a long time. "I liked it so much that I read it in one day. A hundred and four thousand words in one day! You know how much stuff I have to read for work? Well, I put it all aside. I just couldn't stop, and that's a good sign. I can see Marcel's hand in it, but your passion and your freshness are there too, in every line. The balance between the murder investigation and the love story is perfect, and the character development is very interesting, particularly Jeremiah's. It's going to be a huge hit, Siobhan, I'm certain of it."

"Thank you. Your opinion means a lot to me."

"Oh, you don't have to thank me for being honest," he said, flapping his hand to play it down. Then he leaned toward her with a confidential air and murmured: "Gunton is going around boasting about you like you were a trophy. You're the writer of the moment; I'm afraid you have a busy night ahead of you. The big fish at Baxter Books will be vying for your attention. But you leave them to me, okay? I'll get them off your back. Unless you object, of course."

Suddenly, a warm and brilliant glow lit up in the depths of her brain. Alex was trying to protect her, there was no doubt about it. And that could only mean . . .

"Did Marcel ask you? Did he ask you to look after me tonight?" she asked hopefully.

Compassion flickered across Alex's face.

"I'm sorry, Siobhan. He didn't ask me anything. It was my idea."

Her hopes sank in the mire of disappointment.

How could she have been so naive?

Marcel had erased her from the map.

"I understand," she muttered. Of course, deep down she didn't understand, nor did she want to.

Alex kept talking, but Siobhan had stopped listening. She could see his lips moving, but his voice was lost in the echoes of the party. She began to feel dizzy. The lights, the music, the people . . . It felt like her head might explode at any moment.

". . . and I know him well, so I can assure you he's a different man now from the one he was before writing this novel. Not to mention the business with the royalties."

This was when she zoned back in to the conversation. She furrowed her brow.

"What business with the royalties?"

"Well . . ." Alex's gaze roved around the room for a few seconds before returning to Siobhan. "I probably shouldn't tell you this, but Marcel wants to modify the contract for *Two Ways* so that you get 10 percent."

A sudden wave of anger, confusion, and sadness crashed over her as she absorbed his words. Because, despite everything it had meant for them to write this novel together, it seemed like Marcel wanted to cut all ties to it as quickly as possible. Then it struck her with the clarity of day: distancing himself from the novel meant distancing himself from Siobhan. With every day that passed, he moved further away. The conclusion reached her along with a mighty tide of tears that flooded her eyes before she could stop it.

"What's up, Siobhan? Why are you crying? Have I said something inappropriate?"

"No, I . . . Please, tell my friends I've left," she asked.

"What? But . . . where are you going? Do you want . . . ?"

The question was left hanging in the air. Siobhan turned on her heel and ran out.

Chapter 36

Marcel

Marcel was pacing around the living room, phone in hand, checking it compulsively. He was at a crossroads. Several times, he entered the passcode, went into his contacts, and searched for *Princess*. He knew Siobhan would be at the Baxter Books party; even so, the urge to call her prickled at his fingertips. Should he call her or not? No, that would be immensely stupid. Why on earth would he call her now? What would he say if he did?

Hi, Siobhan, I just wanted to tell you I'm dying to see you, but I'm terrified I'm not good enough for you. I only shut you out of my life so that you can be happy. That's all. Keep enjoying the party and let's pretend this call never happened.

What a bunch of horseshit.

Siobhan didn't deserve to have her feelings toyed with. She wanted the full fairy tale, and he only had crumbs to offer her. But he didn't believe in happy endings; the very idea of such a thing seemed fraudulent. Because people always ended up leaving, sooner or later. As a writer, Marcel had learned that the only way to keep it all under control was by planning each twist and turn of the plot, every detail, from beginning to end. But then, life wasn't a novel. He was writing blind when it came to real life. Unanticipated developments kept forcing him to rethink the original plan. He never—or almost never—knew what chapter he'd be writing tomorrow.

How many of those unplanned chapters had he written recently?

Unplanned chapter number one: In which Marcel meets his mother again after twenty-eight years.

Unplanned chapter number two: In which Marcel starts to wonder whether maybe, just maybe, in time, he could forgive her.

Unplanned chapter number three: In which Marcel discovers that one phrase holds the key. *Don't let life slip through your fingers just because your mother couldn't do any better. Keep going.*

Unplanned chapter number four: In which Marcel finally understands that perhaps not everyone leaves.

Unplanned chapter number five: In which Marcel decides to stop kidding himself.

He missed Siobhan. He missed her laughter, her freshness, the scent of her organic coconut shampoo, and every last inch of her body. He thought about her every minute of the day and imagined her by his side whatever he was doing: waking naked in his bed, sharing coffee at the kitchen island, working on a new novel together, or holding hands as they got lost in the streets of Manhattan.

Because it turned out his capacity to love wasn't limited. Quite the opposite in fact.

What if the possibility of a happy ending wasn't as remote as he had always thought?

He checked the time on his phone.

Eight on the dot.

"Shit," he muttered.

He sprinted up the stairs, feeling the adrenaline rush into his veins, entered the bedroom, and picked out his best suit. He took a quick shower, sprayed on some aftershave, and got dressed. Earlier, he had requested a car, which, luckily, picked him up right away. Marcel asked the driver to take him to 1 Oak as quickly as possible. It was time for him to be honest with her and with himself. *I want to mend my cracks. If the Japanese can do it, I can too.* He just hoped it wasn't too late. On the way, he considered sending her a message, but he decided he wanted to surprise her. After fifteen interminable minutes, the driver pulled up in the VIP zone in front of the club, where his passenger instructed him to wait. Marcel took a deep breath before leaving the vehicle. Never in his worst nightmares had he imagined going to the Baxter Books party, given how much he hated crowded social events. *The stupid things we do for love,* he thought. As soon as he entered, he felt overwhelmed. There were too many people, the music was loud, and the lights were blinding. He declined the glass of champagne offered by a young waiter and focused on finding Siobhan. He thought he saw Bob Gunton in the crowd and turned away to avoid an unwanted encounter. He scanned the room but couldn't see her anywhere. Desperate, he took his phone from his pocket and returned to the lobby to call her. There, he bumped into Alex and two girls. He recognized one right away and the other, though he had never met her, he felt sure he knew as well. They were Paige and Lena. And they didn't look happy.

"Marcel, what are you doing here?" Alex asked, with a note of doubt and surprise.

"I came to look for Siobhan. I need to talk to her," he said. Then he turned to Paige and said: "My name isn't actually Michael. I suppose you know that already. I'm Marcel." He extended his hand, though she seemed reticent about taking it. "I'm sorry about that night in Grimaldi's."

"You were a real jerk," said Paige. "But you know what they say: you can't judge a book by its cover."

Marcel smiled.

"Thanks, I think."

"And I'm Lena," the other girl said. "Why do you want to talk to Shiv, might I ask? Sorry to be so direct, but you've jerked my friend around quite a bit. You'll understand that I want to protect her from a diabolic character like you," she said candidly, scrutinizing him with a stern look over her glasses.

"That's fair. But I can assure you all I want to do is make her happy. You have my word." After a brief silence, Lena nodded. "Listen, I don't want to appear rude, but do you know where she is?"

"She left," Alex said. "About fifteen minutes ago."

Alex's reply made him frown.

"What do you mean, she left? Where to?"

"I have no idea. We were having a perfectly nice chat about the novel, and suddenly she burst into tears and ran out."

"She didn't even say goodbye to us," Paige added, in a melodramatic tone.

"She burst into tears?" Marcel said, slightly frantic. Then he rubbed his face. "Shit, it's my fault. I knew this would happen. I knew, damn it." He sighed. "Have you called her?"

"She won't answer," replied Paige. "Her phone might be on silent."

"Maybe she went home," suggested Alex.

"Of course. Do you have her address?"

"She isn't in her apartment," Lena declared, checking something on her phone. "According to Girlfriend Safe. It's an app we use when we go out at night. To feel a bit safer. If she was at home, this little dot"—she turned the screen to show the others—"would be green, not red."

Alex seemed puzzled.

"You use a geolocation app for women?"

"Sure," said Paige. "The world is full of depraved murderers and rapists. You know that better than anyone." She looked pointedly at Marcel, who was horrified. "Because you're a crime writer," she clarified. And Marcel's face relaxed.

"Where the hell can she have gone?"

"Maybe she's at your place," Alex offered.

"Doubt it. Gonzales would have told me. Let's see. Think, think, think," he said to himself out loud. A sudden thought occurred to him. "Has anyone checked her social networks?"

Lena snapped her fingers.

“Bingo! She posted something on Twitter. Just a minute ago.” She turned the phone around and showed him. “Look.”

Siobhan Harris @siobhan_harris 1m
Summertime. 

“Summertime? Like the song?” suggested Paige. “How strange, I didn’t know she liked Lana Del Rey.”

“She might mean the Nina Simone version,” said Lena.

“Or Billie Holiday,” said Alex.

“Whichever it is, what does she mean by this tweet?”

Marcel retreated into himself for a moment. Suddenly, a clear image floated to the surface of his memory.

Of course!

That was it!

Finally, these lousy social networks had served a purpose.

“I think I know where she is,” he told them. Then he looked at his watch. “And I’d better hurry.”

“I’m going with you,” announced Alex.

“Is there room for two more?”

◆ ◆ ◆

There was a traffic jam. At nine o’clock at night. The kind of thing that could only happen in New York. A car had broken down in the middle of the street by Anchorage Plaza, and everyone behind it was trapped in a commotion of blasting horns and flying insults. Marcel was getting desperate. He squirmed in the passenger seat and checked his phone in hopes that Siobhan had returned his calls.

“Calm down, man,” Alex said, patting him on the shoulder from the back seat. He was in between Paige and Lena, who hadn’t stopped asking indiscreet questions the entire journey. Particularly Paige.

“How can I calm down? My future is at stake!”

"I'm sure the tow truck will come soon and clear the street."

"I can't wait any longer," he said abruptly, unfastening his seat belt.

"My word, this is getting more and more interesting," murmured Paige.

"But, what . . . ? You aren't going to do what I think you're going to do, are you? We don't even know if she's there, Marcel. She isn't answering her phone."

Marcel turned to look his friend in the eye.

"If she's not there, I'll keep looking until I find her. You don't understand, Alex. The only thing I can do now is to go for it with all I've got. Wish me luck, will you? All three of you. And you too," he asked the driver, who smiled and gave him the thumbs-up.

And with that, he hopped out of the car and started running down Old Fulton Street. Alex, Paige, and Lena weren't far behind.

"Wait, Marcel! We're coming with you!"

"Yeah, we wouldn't miss this for the world!" exclaimed Paige. "Hey, would it be too much to ask you not to run so fast? I'm wearing four-inch heels!"

"Heels are the patriarchy!" shouted Lena, who had been smart enough to switch hers for flats.

But Marcel didn't slow his pace. The cars honked as he passed. One guy lowered his window and had the nerve to ask where he was going in such a hurry. "To make a declaration of love!" he yelled. To which the man answered: "Good luck with that, man!" He didn't even recognize himself. Was the guy running like a madman toward Brooklyn Bridge Park really him? Had he been abducted by the hero of a romantic comedy? He sped up and lengthened his stride until he reached the waterfront. Droplets of sweat ran from his neck down his back. His pulse was soaring, and his heart was pounding, as though shouting at him not to give up, begging some god, if there was one, for Siobhan to still be there.

Please, please, please.

Then he saw her.

She appeared before him like a dream.

She was right where he had guessed she would be. She was leaning on the railing, her gaze lost in the East River; as beautiful and vulnerable as on the night of his birthday, when she tripped and fell into his arms like a gift while a busker played "Summertime" on his saxophone.

I got you.

You got me.

How little he had known then about the true significance of those words, their hidden double meaning.

You got me, princess. You've always had me.

"Siobhan!" he shouted, sprinting toward her. "Siobhan!"

He was panting and grinning like a child. He was pumping with adrenaline and emotion.

She turned her head and regarded him incredulously.

"Marcel! What are you . . . ? How did you know . . . ?"

Marcel stopped before her, limp and dazed with relief, and doubled over, taking deep breaths to recover.

"Twitter," he managed to say, panting. "We . . . saw it . . . on Twitter."

"'We'?"

When Siobhan lifted her gaze, she saw Alex, Paige, and Lena bringing up the rear.

"For the love of god!" protested Paige, clutching her ribs. "I'm going to . . . puke up . . . every last canape."

"I don't get it," said Siobhan, her gaze slipping from one to the other quizzically. "What are you all doing here? And why were you running? From where?"

"From the Baxter Books party," explained Paige.

"You left so suddenly, we were worried about you," continued Lena.

"Then he showed up," added Alex, nodding at Marcel.

"And since you weren't answering our calls . . . ," continued Paige.

"And we knew from Girlfriend Safe you weren't at home . . . ," explained Lena.

"We decided to take a look at Twitter, in case you had posted anything. And Marcel said he knew where you were. And here you are," concluded Alex.

"Now can we clear something up?" asked Paige. "Which version of 'Summertime' did you mean?"

"George Gershwin." Siobhan swallowed and turned to Marcel. "You went to the Baxter Books party?" she asked, unable to hide the incredulity in her voice.

"Yes."

"But . . ."

"I came to find you, Siobhan," he replied as naturally as he could, although his heart was beating so hard he could feel it pulsing in his fingertips.

"What for? You and I have said everything we have to say, Marcel."

She sounded hurt.

Angry.

Sad.

And not without reason.

He deserved it.

"I think you should listen to Marcel, Shiv," Paige said. "This man almost ran the New York marathon to get to you. Strike me down right now if that's not romantic."

Marcel gave Paige a conspiratorial look.

"Thanks, Paige."

"Not at all. Would you sign a book for me?"

"And for me?"

"Girls, this isn't the moment," Alex said in a low voice. "Maybe we should give them a bit of privacy."

"You're right," agreed Paige. "Come on, let's go."

"But not too far. Just in case," added Lena, giving Marcel a pointed *I'm watching you* glare before turning away.

A few seconds later, they were alone. After a tense silence, Marcel decided to break the ice.

"You were crying."

"It was nothing." She gazed at the river for a few moments, rubbing her arms as though trying to get warm. "So that's why you came."

"That's not why I came," replied Marcel, taking off his jacket and draping it delicately around Siobhan's shoulders. "Well, not just because of that. I mean, I know the reason you were crying and ran out here is because of me. And my pathetic insecurity. So I owe you an apology. For making you cry, for being such a jerk, and for not having realized sooner that . . ."

"Marcel . . ."

"I'm in love with you."

"You don't need to . . . Wait. What? Did you say . . . Did you say you're in love with me, or is my mind playing tricks?"

An adoring smile lit up Marcel's face.

"Your mind is just fine, honey."

"Mm-hmm. Okay. Can . . . Can you say it again, please? Just to be sure."

Marcel studied her face. No one had ever looked at him like that before, with that wonderful blend of hope and fear. He took her hands, which burned feverishly and were slightly damp in his. He lowered his head and lost himself in her eyes, shining with the lively blue of youth.

"I'm totally, hopelessly, and madly in love with you, Miss Harris."

"But you don't . . . You don't believe in love," she replied.

And yet, it had happened.

"It's possible that I've changed my mind."

"Ah. Until when, Marcel? Until tomorrow morning when you remember you're scared of being happy? I know about the royalties. Alex told me. And I know why you made that decision."

He shook his head.

"It isn't what you think. I'm here, Siobhan. And I'm not planning to leave. I've taken too long, but I'm here now. For the first time in my life, I want to live a story more than I want to write it. You make me feel like I don't need to escape reality," he said, running his thumbs over her knuckles. "And yes, I'm scared. Of course I'm scared. I'm terrified of losing you. But do you know what would be worse? Not having tried." A tear rolled down Siobhan's rosy cheek, and Marcel caught it with his fingertip. "I don't want to reach the end of my life and say, 'Well, at least I was careful.' I don't want to live like that, not anymore. I want to leave the past behind and focus on the present, build a future, belong somewhere, to someone. To you. I love you, you know that? I've always loved you. Even when I didn't like you, princess." She laughed as another tear spilled. "And now that I've finally said it, I feel so liberated I feel like saying it again. I love you. Shit, I love you! Yes! I love you, I love you, I love you! My name is Marcel Dupont, and I love this woman!" he shouted to the four winds.

"Happy for you, dude," murmured a passerby.

They both laughed.

"God, what's happening to me?" he joked. "What's next? Eating rainbow popcorn and crying at a Meg Ryan and Billy Crystal movie about a commitment-phobe who finally sees the light?"

"Don't be embarrassed to admit it. I've done it plenty of times, and I'm still here. Of course, that guy's a bit of an idiot. He doesn't really know what he wants and takes an eternity to figure it out. But in the end, he goes looking for the girl, and she forgives him for being an asshole, which goes to show that happy endings are possible."

"Thankfully," said Marcel, tucking a lock of hair behind her ear, the way she liked. "I want to have a happy ending with you, Siobhan. Tell me we can be like Jeremiah and Felicity."

"We don't need to be like Jeremiah and Felicity, Marcel. Or like Harry and Sally. It's enough for us to be ourselves. That's enough for me. Because I love you too. I love every one of your imperfections and your cracks, your sarcasm, your bad moods, your social phobias, and even your incomprehensible aversion to sweets." Marcel laughed. "I love you because you're you, because you're real, not a fictional character."

Marcel nodded, too overwhelmed to speak. Then, he took her face in his hands and kissed her as the breeze from the river, the night, and the jazz playing in his memory enveloped them in a mist. Love tasted so good he wanted to lose himself in that feeling all night, all week, and—why not?—for the rest of his life.

The sound of cheering and applause caught them unawares. Alex, Paige, and Lena were celebrating their happiness nearby. Marcel rested his chin on Siobhan's forehead, and they both laughed again. The sound of their laughter blending together was the most beautiful thing he had heard in his life—and the most promising.

They were the present.

And they would be the future.

"You got me, princess."

"I got you, Mr. Black."

Epilogue

One Year Later

When he opened his eyes, he spent a minute looking at her. He loved watching her as she slept because there was something so intimate in the act, a feeling of belonging. Her rhythmic breath hit his cheek like a gentle ripple. She gave off such a serene aura that he felt lucky to wake by her side each day. He woke her the way he liked, with a trail of gentle kisses up her arm to her neck. That morning, however, he couldn't help taking a different route. He ran his hand over her collarbone and slid it inside her silk nightie. He found a breast and stroked it gently. He switched from fingers to lips, then lips to tongue. She moaned, rolled onto her back and opened her legs. And that was all it took for Marcel to know exactly what she wanted. He knew the slightest touch from him would turn her on. And it was the same for him.

"Good morning, princess," he whispered, positioning himself between her thighs.

"Very good, I would say," she replied, her eyelids heavy and her voice hijacked by a mixture of sleepiness and desire.

"You want chocolate for breakfast?"

"Mm-hmm . . . Yes . . . Give me all you've got."

"You're so greedy, girl," he said as he sank into her.

It was quick, but as satisfying as always. Afterward they remained tangled in the sheets for a while, lingering in that lazy postsex glow.

"What time did you say Chaz was arriving?" asked Siobhan, drawing swirls in his hair.

"Eleven. My plan is to leave for the airport in about an hour. It's quite a ways to Newark, and you know how she gets if you keep her waiting. Sure you don't want to come with me? Chaz will be disappointed not to see you there. It's her first time in New York."

"I know, and I'm really sorry, but I have a bunch of things to do before the launch. Tell her we'll see each other at the bookstore. Are you going to run?"

"I don't have time. Anyhow, I've done my exercise for today. It's a new discipline called the Extreme Pleasure Olympics. I'm training hard for the Games, you know?" he said with a wink.

"Ah, I see. Well, I'm no expert, but I feel like you're on track to win gold."

Marcel started laughing. He caught her hand and kissed it.

"You're something else. I'm going to take a shower."

"Okay. I'll make coffee."

But first she took a moment to enjoy watching his perfect naked body moving around the room: the broad back, the toned shoulders, the muscular arms, the sculpted ass, and the long, athletic legs. She sighed happily. Eight months earlier, when he had asked her to move into his apartment, she'd agreed without hesitation. Siobhan had spent around six weeks traveling for the promotional tour for *Two Ways to Solve a Murder in Manhattan*, and spending all that time apart had been harder on Marcel than he expected. While she was doing readings in Chicago, Boston, and San Francisco, he spent his time ranting about Baxter Books to Alex.

"When will this lousy tour end?" he complained one night over drinks in a jazz club in the Village. "I'm going to have to have serious words with Gunton. Eight states in a month. Eight. Don't you think that's bordering on exploitation? For the love of god, it's not exactly the caucuses."

His friend shot him a look and sniggered.

"So you're missing her, huh?"

"Of course I'm missing her."

Which was his way of saying: *I miss her so much I'm going crazy without her. And raunchy late-night video calls aren't enough to fill this devastating void I'm feeling.*

"It's about time. Anyway, don't forget this tour is good for her career. And for yours. See it as a transition to something better."

The novel had been both a critical and financial success. The reviews were mostly positive—except for the odd supposedly serious outlet that deemed it "not sufficiently literary." It had received the usual clichés of "fresh and original" and "daring and beautiful," and Book Riot even said that *Two Ways* was the most explosive combination of genres in the last decade. It was loved by crime readers and romance fans alike and had been given the seal of approval by Letitia Wright. Letitia herself had been present at the launch in New York. She was excited about the book, and about Siobhan.

"Oh, darling. You have no idea how happy I am that you and Marcel Black had that fight on Twitter," she said.

"I am, too, Letitia. Believe me."

The woman smiled in a way that Siobhan wasn't quite able to interpret.

"So, why hasn't your coauthor come?"

"I'm afraid Mr. Black is a tad antisocial."

"That's a pity. I would have liked to have seen with my own eyes whether he's as cute as the rumors say."

The same questions cropped up at every event:

"What was it like writing a novel with Marcel Black?" "What's he like in person?" and "What about the rumors on the internet about the two of you?"

To which she tended to reply with things like:

"It was the most stimulating of challenges, in many ways"; "To begin with, I thought he was arrogant; you know, the kind of writer who thinks writing a book is on par with discovering penicillin. Over time, I realized he was much better in person"; or "What rumors?"

She had learned to hide her nerves. Robin had once told her to pretend she was the one in the driver's seat, and that's what she did. She connected well with her audience. She was a born storyteller. Siobhan had discovered her natural charisma.

When Marcel went down to the kitchen and saw her making eggs Benedict, he felt every last fiber of his body soften. Cooking wasn't her strong suit. In fact, she was terrible at it; even so, she went to such lengths to please him that he would take a mouthful of her dreadful food over any dish from the finest restaurant in Manhattan. Breakfast at home was just one of the many things that had changed in his routine since they had been living together, but he didn't mind in the slightest.

He approached her from behind and grabbed her butt beneath her nightshirt.

"So, baby. Today's the big day. Nervous?"

"Shaking like jelly. I don't know if I'll ever get used to feeling these butterflies."

He took her by the waist and forced her to turn around.

"It will all be fine, you'll see," he said in a soothing tone.

"I don't know how you can be so calm. This novel belongs to both of us after all."

The success of *Two Ways* had led to another juicy contract to write a sequel; of course, this time, the advance and royalties were distributed more equitably. After Christmas—Marcel's first one at the Harris residence as their daughter's official boyfriend—they got to work. The new novel was called *Two Ways to Prevent a Murder in Manhattan.* In this installment, Jeremiah Silloway and Felicity Bloom traveled to the nineteenth century to prevent a crime from being committed, while navigating the obstacles destiny put in the way of their relationship.

"I'm calm because you were born for this. And everyone will be there to support you."

"Apart from the most important person," she complained, making a face.

"I'll be there with you one way or another, trust me."

Siobhan sighed. She knew that his reticence to show himself in public was a part of Marcel that she had to accept. He liked his anonymity. He preferred that she shine for the two of them.

While they ate breakfast, they chatted about the filming of *Knox*, the Netflix movie based on Marcel's work, which was about to start, although Marcel didn't like the actor they had chosen for the lead role.

"What's wrong with Chris Evans?" asked Siobhan, as she crunched her bacon. "The whole world loved him as Captain America."

"That's precisely the problem: everyone will see him as a goddamn superhero instead of my tormented detective. I'm worried the scriptwriters will screw it up the way they always do when they adapt a novel that requires a degree of historical accuracy."

"Then why don't you advise them on it? They've asked you dozens of times."

"If I didn't have my mind focused on other more important things, I might think about it."

"Like that apocalyptic thriller set in New Orleans?"

Marcel took a long slug of coffee before replying:

"Precisely."

"When are you planning to write it?"

"In a few months. I want to take you on vacation first."

Siobhan opened her eyes wide.

"Really? Where?"

"Well . . ." He frowned. "I haven't decided yet. Somewhere idyllic where we can spend all day in the hotel room drinking mimosas and doing it like animals in heat."

"You're quite the randy romantic."

"Randy romantic. I love it." He glanced at his watch. "Shit, it's late." He drained his coffee and stood up from the table. "I'd better go now, or I won't get to the airport in time. Oh, I didn't tell you: I've reserved a table at Le Coucou for tonight. For ten of us."

Siobhan's fair eyebrows arched quizzically.

"At Le Coucou? Table for ten? Wow, what are we celebrating?"

"Aside from the fact that my girlfriend, the brilliant writer with thousands of Twitter followers, is presenting her third novel at Barnes & Noble?" He shrugged. "No idea."

"We wrote it together," she reminded him again. "And since when has having thousands of Twitter followers been indicative of success to you?" He gave her an adoring smile and kissed her on the forehead. "Hey . . . you know she'll be at the reading too, right?"

Marcel sighed, his expression changing immediately.

She was referring to Claudette, of course. She and Siobhan had gotten close recently, but he wasn't ready to fully open the doors of his life to her. He was still struggling to turn the page. Forgiving his sister hadn't been easy, and he hadn't, not until their father died, shortly after entering the clinic. Marcel had returned to New Orleans for the funeral. In all honesty, he wouldn't have gone if it weren't for Siobhan. "Go. Say goodbye to your father like you should and make your peace with Chaz. It's time you two talked, Marcel," she had told him on the phone, promising to take a flight from Des Moines, where she was doing a reading, and meet him in NOLA as soon as possible.

"Say hi from me, will you?"

Siobhan nodded. Deep down, she understood. She knew his cracks weren't easy to mend. Were anyone's?

Hours later, while Marcel was taking his sister to see Times Square, she prepared for the big event. It was hard to explain how she felt. She couldn't believe she had written three books already—or part of them—when little more than a year ago she was taking her first steps in the publishing world. Paige had gone to her apartment to help her pick out her wardrobe; some things never changed.

"This sky-blue blouse brings out your eyes. Put it on," she ordered, tossing the garment at her. She kept rummaging in the huge walk-in closet that Siobhan now shared with Marcel. "Let's see, what else. No pants. Not today. Today you have to shine. This skirt. Or maybe this one," she corrected herself, taking out a fitted white number. "You'll be gorgeous. Oh, I'm so proud of you, Shiv! Do you realize you've got everything you ever wanted? You're a writer, you live in Manhattan, and your boyfriend is damn fine."

"Yours isn't so bad either."

"I won't deny he could do with a bit more hair, but he makes up for any lack every time he . . ." She stuck out her tongue and wiggled it between her fingers. "You know."

Siobhan swatted her on the arm.

"Paige! I don't need you to tell me these things about Alex! Might I remind you that he's my agent now!"

"Well, your agent knows how to make my vagina happy, honey. Which is excellent on a cosmic level. As Lena says, the more happy vaginas there are in the world, the better it is for humanity."

Ten minutes before the launch started, Alex was waiting for them outside 555 Fifth Avenue, where Barnes & Noble had one of the largest bookstores in New York. From the door, you could see the tip of the Empire State Building in the heart of Manhattan. Lena had arrived first and saved seats for everyone, so Paige wished her friend luck, kissed Alex, and went in.

Siobhan stayed behind with her agent.

"I don't want to make you nervous or anything, but there are a hell of a lot of people inside waiting to listen to you. So take a deep breath and have faith in yourself. This novel is just as good as the last one, okay?" Alex told her encouragingly.

One of Alex Shapiro's great virtues: understanding the inner workings of a writer's mind.

"I wouldn't be here today if it weren't for Marcel. There's nothing special about me at all. How could a story worth telling come from such an ordinary life, like the one I led before I met him?"

Alex shook his head.

"He doesn't like it when you talk that way, Siobhan. And nor do I."

"If only he'd come . . ."

Alex's thin lips instantly curved into a smile.

"It will feel like he's here, believe me."

She thought it strange that Marcel had said almost exactly the same thing.

The room where the reading was being held was on the top floor of the bookstore, and it was packed. Siobhan walked up onto the small stage, accompanied by Beatrix, the lovely public relations manager at Barnes & Noble. Copies of their book were stacked in piles on a nearby table. From her seat, she cast a glance over the crowd. In the front row, along with her agent, were Bob Gunton, various people from the Communications team at Baxter Books, and some well-known literary influencers. Behind them, Paige; Lena and her girlfriend, Noor; her parents and Robin—her parents waving at her, chests swelling with pride. She also spotted Jolene, her former landlady, whose thoughts she could almost read: *It was Jolene encouraged you to do this, girl. 'Cause Jolene has a nose for talent. And that's the truth. If Jolene hadn't told you to wise up, who knows where you'd be now. You'd probably still be in Brooklyn struggling to make your rent. Of course, Jolene ain't no NGO. Jolene is a businesswoman and* . . . blah, blah, blah. Then she spotted Chaz and her mother. Claudette gave her the timid smile with which she greeted her every time they saw one another. "Thanks for doing this, Siobhan. You're the closest I can get to my son," she always said. Siobhan nurtured the hope that, with time, Marcel would be able to spend more than ten minutes in her company without feeling he was betraying himself.

She cleared her throat, took a deep breath, and greeted the audience. First, she would read a selection of passages from the novel. Then, she would answer questions, and finally, she would sign copies. After Beatrix's very complimentary introduction, she read the four excerpts she and Marcel had carefully selected. She read slowly, adjusting her voice to the rhythm of the prose. Every now and then she lifted her gaze. At her own initiative, she added a rather torrid passage that made her blush as she remembered how excited she and Marcel had been after writing it and how they had ended up screwing with abandon on top of what they called the first-draft table. She still got the giggles recalling all those loose sheets of paper flying up and floating to the floor as her boyfriend did his best to satisfy her.

After a round of warm applause, the time came for questions.

"How did you come up with the idea?" "What was it based on?" "Will you write on your own again?" and "When will Marcel Black show his face?"

"I'm afraid I can't answer that one."

Beatrix was about to bring the Q&A to a close when someone suddenly spoke up:

"One moment. I have a question."

Siobhan's heart turned a somersault. Marcel stood up, handsome as ever in his elegant black suit. If he was nervous, he was hiding it extremely well. She had no idea what was going on.

What was he doing here?

Someone handed him the microphone.

"Thanks. Sorry for the interruption," he apologized to the audience. Then he looked at Siobhan and said: "I'd like to know whether you'd be willing to write . . . How should I put it? A different kind of story with Mr. Black."

She was disconcerted.

What was all this about?

"Well, I . . . um . . . ," she stammered. "Sorry, I don't understand the question. What do you mean by a different kind of story? Could you be more specific?"

Dozens of pairs of eyes lingered on him, waiting for an answer.

"One that's more . . . real," he explained.

"Like a true crime?"

Marcel gave a charming little laugh.

"More like a romantic comedy where the guy and the girl end up eating wedding cake. Mostly the girl, of course. Because the guy doesn't really like sweets. Something like that. But not fiction."

Siobhan swallowed.

She felt her pulse racing.

Suddenly, there was a commotion in the room. People began to murmur until the murmurs became clear and perfectly audible phrases like "It's him! It's Marcel Black!" People began to rise to their feet, cell phones in hand.

"But . . ."

She watched as Marcel pulled a velvet box from the inside pocket of his suit jacket, walked up to the stage, and kneeled in front of her. She lifted both her hands to her chest. A stunning engagement ring glittered inside the little box.

"Will you write that romantic comedy with me, Siobhan?"

"I . . . I . . ."

She couldn't speak. It was too much.

"Please, honey, don't make me beg. It's really uncomfortable down here. Just say yes so I can get up and put this ring on your finger like you deserve."

"Come on, say yes!" someone called out.

"And if you don't, Jolene sure as hell will!"

"Yes. Yes, of course!" she eventually managed to say, through a veil of tears and laughter.

Marcel stood up, slipped the ring on her finger, held her by the back of the neck with the swagger of a Hollywood star, and kissed her on the lips, to the great delight of the audience, who cheered and whistled from their seats.

"I'll be fresh meat for memes after this," he whispered in her ear.

She started laughing.

"But what were you thinking? Now everyone will know who you are."

"I don't care. I don't think I need to hide anymore. And you've been dreaming of this moment your whole life. I wanted it to be perfect."

"It is perfect. And no romantic comedy could ever live up to it."

Alex was the first to approach to congratulate them.

"You owe me a hundred bucks. Don't think I've forgotten," Marcel reminded him with a slight note of superiority.

"Bastard . . . Who would have thought you'd ever dare to commit a madness like this?"

"Wait. You knew?"

"Of course! We all knew! Paige, Lena, Robin, even Chaz." Siobhan turned her head, open-mouthed, to look at them all with an expression that said, *You'll pay for this.* "Did I or didn't I say that it would feel like Marcel was here?"

"You tricked me! Wait a sec. So, the reservation for Le Coucou . . ."

"It's to celebrate our engagement."

"And the idyllic vacation . . ."

"Our honeymoon."

"And how did you know I would say yes?"

"Because you're as predictable as one of those romance novels you adore, Miss Harris. And because you love my ass. You couldn't bear to be deprived of the sight of it for a single day for the rest of your life."

Siobhan rolled her eyes and huffed.

"It would appear you've dropped a little bit of ego on the floor, Mr. Black."

Her fiancé laughed loudly. Marcel grabbed her around the waist and trapped her in his arms.

"It's so easy to love you, baby."

"And you're so cute when you're not scared, baby."

They were about to sink into another kiss, but a teenage African American boy interrupted them. He addressed Marcel hesitantly and said:

"M-Mr. Black? Sorry to bother you at such an intimate moment, but since you're here . . . Would you sign a book for me? I'm a great admirer of yours. I . . . I want to be a crime writer too."

Marcel was rendered speechless. That had been totally unexpected. Becoming an accessible writer wasn't part of his plans. Although getting down on one knee in the largest bookstore in Manhattan hadn't been either. He studied the boy for a few seconds. He couldn't have been more than sixteen or seventeen, and, for a moment, he remembered himself at that age. He seemed nervous, his hands trembling. Then, in a gesture that might have been irrational or deliberate, he turned to the audience and met his mother's eye. She smiled, and he smiled back. It was a brief moment of connection.

Maybe it was time to reconsider some things.

"Sure, kid. You got a pen?"

Minutes later, he was sitting at a table next to Siobhan, signing copy after copy of their book. He wasn't sure what his next move would be. All he knew was that nothing would ever be the same again. Nor did it matter that much. He had just discovered that making a reader happy was almost as satisfying as doing the same for the woman he loved.

Or like making peace with the world.

Acknowledgments

While I was writing this novel, destiny dealt me an unexpected blow, from which I'm still reeling. I lost my older brother, suddenly. If I have anyone to thank for the person I am today, it's him. He always was and always will be one of the guiding lights in my life. Pablo, wherever you are, I'm sure you'll be proud of your sister. Thanks for having shown me, in your own inimitable way, that the most important thing is doing what you love. I promise I won't give up.

I also want to thank all the people who showed their concern for me and who helped me pick up my pieces from the floor at the worst moments, who wrapped me in words of encouragement, or who were simply there for me. Thanks to those who keep encouraging me now, when a simple memory can still take me right back to square one on this zigzagging path that is grief. There are so many of you I would need pages and pages to give you the thanks you deserve, but I can assure you that I carry each and every one of you in my heart.

Thanks to all my family, particularly my brother Dani, a tireless fighter (you know what I mean) from whom I've learned over the years that giving up isn't an option. And, of course, Salva, my husband and the compass that always leads me to the right place.

Once again, for the fifth time now, I would like to thank Principal de los Libros, for publishing another of my stories without doubting it. Thanks to both Elena (your master class was very useful) and to Cristina, for the care she always takes with the cover designs.

To Isabel Martí and Jordi Ribolleda, from IMC Literacy Agency, thank you for believing in me and encouraging me in this new bookish adventure. Without you, I wouldn't be here (or maybe I would have just taken much longer to get here).

Special thanks to Alexandra Torrealba and the entire team at Amazon Publishing, for giving Marcel and Siobhan's story such an incredible opportunity. Never in my wildest dreams did I imagine a novel of mine appearing in English. For that, my heartfelt thanks to Beth Fowler, for her wonderful translation and for capturing the essence of the story so well.

To Timothy White, for sparing me his time despite being a very busy man and for his invaluable gringo perspective. I just hope you think it breathes enough Americana (I'm not being ironic).

Special mention to Carlos Bassas, with whom I had a fascinating and revealing conversation about the human soul and its limits. Carlos, not only are you nicer than money in the bank, but you're also one of the best crime writers in this country.

Thanks to Juls Arandes, for saying the words I needed to hear at the precise moment I needed to hear them (although they might have been even more effective with a glass of wine).

To my darling Florita Vallcaneras, one of the most generous people I know, for taking such good care of me at my third *Feria del Libro* in Madrid and making it an unforgettable experience (although my credit card might disagree).

I mustn't forget the four Sassenachs (Diana, Eva, Pepa, and Bea), whom I thank from the bottom of my heart for the constant and unbiased support (virtual and in person) that you've given me since our paths crossed. I always say I have the best readers in the world, and you demonstrate that perfectly (but the Duke of Hastings is mine, and there's nothing more to be said about it).

To the fandom of Phoebe Dynevor and Regé-Jean Page (the wonderful muses for the novel you have just read), particularly to Mara and

Génesis, for having welcomed me into this precious community with such affection and commitment.

Of course, to my readers, old and new, because you are the ones who make all this make sense.

And finally, to Marcel and Siobhan themselves, because they started out as a couple of characters and ended up becoming my treehouse hideaway. It's true that writing is a refuge.

About the Author

Carmen Sereno was born in Barcelona in 1982, where she still lives. She studied journalism at the Universidad Autónoma de Barcelona and has worked as a writer for several media and corporate communication offices. In 2018, she won the first CHIC Romance Novel Prize with *Maldito síndrome de Estocolmo*, her literary debut and the first part of a duology completed with *Azul Estocolmo*. She is also the author of *Nadie muere en Wellington* and *Bajo el cielo de Berlín*. Today she is exclusively dedicated to her literary career. She reads all genres, but romance is the one she enjoys most.

About the Translator

Beth Fowler has been a translator since 2009, working from Spanish and Portuguese to English. She won the Harvill Secker Young Translators' Prize in 2010. Her published translations include *Open Door* (2011) and *Paradises* (2013), by Iosi Havilio; *Ten Women* (2014), by Marcela Serrano; and *We All Loved Cowboys* (2018), by Carol Bensimon. Fowler lives in the west of Scotland.